THE HU

Chris Kuzneski is the international bestselling author of numerous thrillers including *Sign of the Cross* and *The Death Relic*, featuring the series characters Payne & Jones. Chris's thrillers have been translated into more than twenty languages and are sold in more than forty countries. Chris grew up in Pennsylvania but currently lives on the Gulf Coast of Florida. To learn more, please visit his website: www.chriskuzneski.com

Praise for Chris Kuzneski:

'Kuzneski's writing has raw power'   James Patterson

'Excellent! High stakes, fast action, vibrant characters . . . not to be missed!'   Lee Child

'Kuzneski writes as forcefully as his tough characters act'   Clive Cussler

'Riveting and relentlessly paced'   James Rollins

'Kuzneski is a master in the making'   Vince Flynn

'If Indiana Jones joined the crew of *Mission: Impossible*, you'd get the action, history, and wicked sense of humor in *The Hunters*. With a thrill ride that pins you to your seat until the very last page, Chris Kuzneski sets a new standard for adventure'   Boyd Morrison

'*The Hunters* is taut and fierce . . . It could just be Kuzneski's breakthrough novel. It deserves to be'   *Daily Mail*

BY CHRIS KUZNESKI

Payne & Jones Series
The Plantation
Sign of the Cross
Sword of God
The Lost Throne
The Prophecy
The Secret Crown
The Death Relic

The Hunters Series
The Hunters

CHRIS KUZNESKI
THE HUNTERS

headline

Copyright © 2013 Chris Kuzneski, Inc.

The right of Chris Kuzneski to be identified as the Author of
the Work has been asserted by him in accordance with the
Copyright, Designs and Patents Act 1988.

First published in 2013
by HEADLINE PUBLISHING GROUP

First published in paperback in 2013
by HEADLINE PUBLISHING GROUP

3

Cataloguing in Publication Data is
available from the British Library

ISBN 978 0 7553 8649 9 (B-format)
ISBN 978 0 7553 9924 6 (A-format)
ISBN 978 1 4722 0433 2 (A-format)

Typeset in Monotype Garamond
by Palimpsest Book Production Limited, Falkirk, Stirlingshire

Printed and bound in Great Britain by
Clays Ltd, St Ives plc

Headline's policy is to use papers that are natural, renewable and
recyclable products and made from wood grown in sustainable
forests. The logging and manufacturing processes are expected
to conform to the environmental regulations of the country of origin.

HEADLINE PUBLISHING GROUP
An Hachette UK Company
338 Euston Road
London NW1 3BH

www.headline.co.uk
www.hachette.co.uk

Acknowledgements

As always, I'd like to start things off by thanking my family. They have given me so much over the years, both as a writer and as a person. Thanks for putting up with me for so long. I *know* I can be a giant pain-in-the-butt. Then again, so can you! (It must be genetic.)

Next, I want to thank my friend and agent, Scott Miller. Before we teamed up, I was a self-published author, selling books out of the trunk of my car. Now my books are available around the world. I owe a lot of my success to him. I also want to thank Claire Roberts – my foreign agent, who landed my British deal and many more across the globe. It's quite comforting to have Scott, Claire, and the rest of Trident Media in my corner.

Not only is *The Hunters* the first novel in a new series, but this is my first book with the Headline Publishing Group. They have gone out of their way to make me feel at home. In particular, I'd like to single out my editor, Vicki Mellor, for her suggestions and unwavering support. She helped this story come alive. I also want to thank Jane Morpeth, Martin Fletcher, Frankie Gray, Anna Bowen, Anna Hogarty, and everyone else at Headline/Hachette.

Next up is my longtime friend Ian Harper. I want to thank him for reading, rereading, and then re-rereading everything, and for answering my late-night phone calls and emails. His advice and expertise are truly invaluable. If anyone's looking for a freelance editor, please let me know. I'd be happy to put you in touch with him.

Lastly, I'd like to thank all the readers, librarians, book-sellers, and critics who have read my thrillers and have recommended them to others. At this stage of my career I still need all the help I can get, so I would appreciate your continued support.

Whew! I think that just about covers it.

It's *finally* time for the good stuff.

Without further ado, please sit back, relax, and let me tell you a story . . .

Railroads of Eastern Europe

Prologue

Friday, December 15, 1916
Iaşi, Romania
(246 miles north of Bucharest)

The biggest theft in modern history didn't occur at a bank. It happened in a train station in the dead of night, under the watchful gaze of armed soldiers.

Amazingly, no one knew it was a robbery until years later.

And by then, the treasure had been stolen again.

It was miserably cold as Béla Dobrev left the three-story building where he and his wife lived in a small, second-floor apartment. The streets were empty at this late hour, and the wind from the northeast carried the damp, dreadful smell of the Prut River. He pulled his new wool scarf higher on his face, over his full mustache to the bridge of his nose. He was grateful his wife had given him this Christmas gift early. The winter was unforgiving, the odors of sewage even worse. At least in the summer the winds tended to blow from the south.

From the moment he started out for his evening shift, he walked with his eyes downcast to protect them from the incessant wind. He did not have to look up to walk the three blocks to the sprawling station. He had worked there for over forty years, since the proud, palatial structure had opened in 1870. He knew the cobbled roadways stone by stone. He remembered when a carthorse had stumbled and broken this one, when an axe had fallen from a laborer's backpack and cracked that one. He remembered it all.

A block from the station, Dobrev smiled beneath the scarf, the bristles of his mustache prickling his upper lip. It was then that he always smelled the first, faint scent of the lubricants used to oil the trains. Crawling under the big locomotives to apply grease to the wheel hubs had been his first job here. That scent invariably took him back to a more innocent era. They were good times, when cities were being united by rail and each new arrival brought a sense of wonder, not dread. When the new year had brought hope and happy reflection, rather than fear of invading armies and the ghastly horrors of war.

Dobrev's gloved hands held the collar of his worn overcoat to his throat. His newly mended socks kept his heels warm, though his toes were starting to tingle from the cold. He quickened his pace, his eyes narrowing as he heard unfamiliar sounds coming from the tracks. He was accustomed to the clatter of unwieldy crates, to heavy machinery being loaded onto flatbeds by screeching mobile cranes, to the clomping of hooves as horses pulled baggage carts. But he had never heard so many sounds, so much activity, especially this late at night. His mind spun at the thought of the wages the stationmaster would have to pay – but for what?

He looked up and saw rows of canvas-backed military

trucks parked nose-in along the platform. That was not unusual: troops in their light-gray uniforms came and went from Iaşi, heading to the frontier. In the late summer they came from Bucharest, but the city was now in German hands. More and more they were returning to Iaşi from combat, along with crowds of refugees fleeing typhus outbreaks. These months since Romania had joined the war were the only time in Dobrev's married life that he and his wife were glad his only child had moved away. The sorrow in the homes of his neighbors was difficult enough to witness.

Cold as he was, Dobrev did not go straight to the cathedral doorways that fronted the towering facade. His curiosity wouldn't allow it.

This contingent was different from any he had seen. There were troops just beyond the parked convoy, but they were fresh and facing the street, holding rifles with fixed bayonets across their chests. Beyond them, illuminated by the hooded lamps that lined the platform, a train jutted far beyond both sides of the building. That was unprecedented. The tops of the cars were wrapped in steam from the locomotive. The train was 'active', ready to move at any moment. Given the cost of coal during winter – during *wartime* – this was most surprising.

Dobrev went to the west side of the terminal where, shielded from the wind, he lowered his scarf and wiped his tearing eyes with his sleeve. He saw boxcar after boxcar, twenty-one in all. On the platform beside them were dozens of crates, stacked in columns, with armed soldiers massed around each, but nowhere on the military train did he see the red, yellow, and blue flag of Romania.

The soldier nearest him took several steps toward him. He wore the insignia of a pigeon messenger. That was unusual too. In four months, Dobrev had never seen those troops as part of a guard detail. They were generally assigned to priority missions.

'What is your business?' the soldier asked curtly. His cheeks were red. They did not look old enough to support a beard.

'I am the assistant stationmaster,' Dobrev told him. 'I am beginning my shift.'

'Begin it inside,' the young man told him.

'I'm about to,' Dobrev said. 'But I'm wondering – there was nothing about a train this size on the sched—'

'Inside, Assistant Stationmaster,' the soldier ordered, shifting his rifle nervously so the bayonet was angled downward.

Dobrev's eyes lingered on the young man a moment longer. Then he raised a gloved hand in surrender, took a last look at the spectacle, and turned away. That exchange had told him more about the war than any of the reports in the newspapers. The situation was desperate when a young Romanian talked to an elder Romanian with no show of respect. Even youths from the capital had better manners.

This boy was tense, afraid.

Dobrev walked back to the front of the station. He noticed that the treads of the trucks were badly worn. This too was an indication that things were going poorly.

What an ill-advised venture, he thought as he neared the door.

Romania had joined the war on the side of Russia, France, and England in order to seize Transylvania from the Austro-Hungarian Empire. Most of the people Dobrev talked to thought that was a waste of men and resources. The population in Transylvania was already largely Romanian. Did it matter who actually owned the high, daunting mountain ranges?

Dobrev stopped abruptly. He saw something on the ground beside one of the bare truck tires, a flash of golden light. He shuffled over and picked it up.

It was a valuable, twenty lei gold coin issued in 1868. Dobrev's first thought was that it had probably been dropped by a harried passenger. The wealthy often departed by train for day trips to country estates. Mishaps like this occurred when they eagerly pulled gloves from their coats, searched with panic for misplaced tickets, or checked a pocket watch to see if they had time to visit the bar. As a youngster, Dobrev used to supplement his income handsomely with dropped coins. French francs, Turkish lire, and once a silver Russian ruble. Local coins were not as highly prized as foreign coins, which always seemed to be rising in value.

But he had never found a coin of gold.

Feeling a flush of warmth, as if he had just downed a nice plum brandy, he stood and tucked the coin in a pocket that he knew did not have a hole. Then, fueled by his good fortune, he decided to push his luck. Standing just out of view of the soldiers, Dobrev peeled back the corner of the canvas and peered inside the back of the truck. The space was empty, except for two benches along the sides, a few crowbars on the floor, and a pile of bent nails.

The cargo has been opened, but why?

For an official examination? Or something criminal?

As he walked into the station, Dobrev considered the possibilities. Glancing east, he stared at the powerful locomotive. He pondered the significance of the guarded cargo, the pigeon messengers to signal its progress, and the unscheduled departure in the dead of night.

None of this makes sense, unless—

Dobrev stopped and trembled at the thought.

His feeling of good fortune disappeared when he realized that the coin he found was probably a tiny fraction of the contents of the dozens of crates. Vast tons of coins and treasures, all being taken away. The wealth of a nation being removed from his homeland.

The chill he felt as he entered the cavernous waiting area was deeper than any he had felt during his short walk through the winter night.

It was the chill of despair.

I

Present Day
Tuesday, August 21
Brooklyn, New York

The surveillance van was parked down the street on the left. The same place it had been the day before and the day before that. Its location was the second-worst-kept secret in the Eastern Bloc neighborhood of Brighton Beach.

The *first* was the name of the man that the FBI was watching.

Vladimir Kozlov had built a criminal empire in Moscow. He dabbled in everything from drugs and weapons to prostitution and smuggling. In recent years, he had discovered the advantages of cybercrime, though he rarely used computers himself. Through it all, he had managed to avoid prosecution. Thanks to the liberal free-trade laws established after the fall of the Soviet Union and, more importantly, millions of dollars in bribes to key officials, Kozlov was viewed by most Russians – the same people that he secretly robbed, and threatened, and extorted – as a national hero.

But to the FBI, he was something else.

He was a person of interest.

Possibly the most interesting man in New York.

Because of his 'clean' criminal record, Kozlov was allowed to enter America in order to expand his legitimate businesses. He immediately bought the largest house in Brighton Beach, an area of Brooklyn known as 'Little Odessa' because of its huge population of Ukrainians. He then used his reputation and connections to unite the local *bratva*, a term that meant 'brotherhood' to Russians but meant 'mafia' to everyone else. In less than five years, the Brighton Beach Bratva had become the most notorious syndicate in New York. They weren't the largest operation in the city – that distinction still belonged to the Sicilian Cosa Nostra – but they were considered the deadliest.

In the media, they were known as the Killer Bees.

Inside the van, they were called something worse.

'I'm telling you,' Special Agent Jason Koontz said as he stuffed noodles into his mouth from a takeout carton, 'these guys are cold-hearted Russian motherfuckers. American criminals don't think like them. Neither do the Italians. These Commie bastards are a different breed. They're as nasty as the Triads, only a lot less Asian.'

His partner, Rudy Callahan, nearly spit out his luke-warm coffee. He quickly glanced at his computer screen and made sure that neither of their microphones was actively transmitting. If they had been, his partner's profane and racist rant would have been recorded on the Bureau's mainframe, and it undoubtedly would have been red-flagged by their superiors and cited in Koontz's ever-growing discipline file.

'Stop doing that!' Callahan demanded.

'Doing what?' Koontz asked, seemingly oblivious to the problem. He accented his ignorance by slurping up more lo mein. Soy sauce sprayed everywhere.

'Saying stuff like that in the van. Do you know what would happen if the director heard what you just said?'

Koontz shrugged. 'He'd probably agree with me.'

'No, he wouldn't,' Callahan assured him. 'He'd probably suspend you. You know damn well we can't make racist comments during an operation. Your comments could be used against us in court. It makes our observations seem biased.'

Koontz shook his head. His partner was such a boy scout. 'You think I'm bad? You should hear some of the stories I've heard from the Narco units that cover the streetwalkers downtown. They say this one Czech chick can fit a—'

'Jason!' Callahan interrupted. 'Do you ever listen to yourself? Just about everything you say is racist!'

'Racist? How can I be a racist? I'm eating *Chink* food with chopsticks. A real racist wouldn't do that.'

'Oh . . . my . . . God,' he mumbled in disbelief. 'I'm stuck in a van with a total idiot. Why do I even bother?'

'Because I'm your only friend.'

'Shut up.'

Koontz laughed to himself. He loved getting on his partner's nerves, especially on long stakeouts like this one where nothing major was expected to occur. The two agents were there to take pictures of Kozlov's minions, fresh-off-the-boat recruits who were smuggled to America with promises of power and money but were actually brought here to do the dirty work that Kozlov's top earners couldn't risk doing. These thugs were recycled so quickly that the Bureau had to maintain constant surveillance to keep track of them. Conveniently, most of them lived in the houses that bordered Kozlov's property. In many ways, they were like a community watch program in reverse.

They warned Kozlov when the cops were around.

Lately, that had been twenty-four hours a day.

As part of a cooperative arrangement with the NYPD's 60th Precinct, the FBI maintained an ongoing presence in Brighton Beach at the behest of community leaders who were trying to combat the notorious reputation of Little Odessa. This was particularly true in the summer months when tourists flocked to the local beaches with pockets full of cash and plenty of entertainment options. With Coney Island to the west and Manhattan Beach to the east, the businesses of Brighton Beach had to work extra hard to attract visitors. That meant convincing locals and tourists alike that foreign gangsters wouldn't rob them before they had a chance to spend their hard-earned money on beers, souvenirs, and cotton candy.

But unlike the 60th Precinct, which was tasked with patrolling the streets and walking the beat, the Bureau took advantage of this special opportunity by parking one of its state-of-the-art surveillance vans fifty feet from

Kozlov's house in an attempt to spook him. Initially, his high-powered attorney had tried to argue harassment – after all, Kozlov was a businessman to be 'respected', not a criminal to be 'persecuted' – but a federal judge dismissed the motion after the Bureau's attorneys argued that they were watching the house, not the man. It was a technicality that stood on weak legal legs, but the judge agreed with the distinction.

That was why the van never moved.

And why Koontz was bored silly.

Sensing a chance for some privacy, he did everything he could to agitate his partner. 'Seriously, what did I say that was so wrong?'

'Everything!' Callahan explained. 'First of all, half of his men *aren't* Russian. They're Ukrainian. And Chechen. And Georgian. Furthermore, how can they be less Asian than the Triads when most of Russia is in Asia?'

'Whatever.'

'Don't "whatever" me! I get enough of that from my kids and my ex-wives. I don't need it from you, too.'

Koontz rolled his eyes, agitating his partner even more. 'Fine, but you're like a broken record. I know Kozlov's men aren't all Russians, but calling them "multi-ethnic motherfuckers" doesn't have the same zing to it. Of course, you're probably quite familiar with ethnic insults. You're Irish.'

'That's it! The final straw!' Callahan took off his headset, which had been wrapped around his neck, and threw open the back door. 'I need some fresh air.'

11

Koontz smiled in victory. 'Fresh air, my ass! It won't be too fresh with a cigarette in your mouth!'

Callahan slammed the door in frustration. He knew damn well his partner was trying to piss him off, but it didn't make it any easier to deal with.

If anything, it made it worse.

If Koontz needed a few minutes to himself, why didn't he ask for it? Why did he have to resort to childish games to get what he wanted?

Irritated beyond belief, Callahan decided to take a walk. He hoped a long stroll would calm his nerves.

Instead, it put his life in danger.

2

The intruder floated effortlessly above the buildings, indistinguishable from the nighttime sky. Tethered by a line that had been anchored more than three hundred feet away, the kite-like contraption hovered over its target. The offshore breezes kept the slack taut while the intruder completed her graceful descent to the rooftop below.

She landed without making a sound.

With the flick of her wrist, she unhooked the kite from her harness and then tossed the assembly into the air, as if she were freeing a giant bird. No longer burdened by her bodyweight, it immediately took flight. She watched as the line and the device shot out of sight. It had served its purpose well: delivering its cargo undetected.

Unfortunately, this was only her first obstacle.

There would be many more to come.

She would have preferred to land on top of Kozlov's oceanside house, but the sharp peak of his roof had prevented it. Instead, she was forced to make do with the flat roof of a neighboring property – a three-story townhouse that served as a bunkhouse for his guards and his newest recruits. On a mission like this, the guardhouse was less than ideal, but what choice did she have? Had she approached the house on foot, she would have been spotted by Kozlov's men *and* by the Feds in the surveillance van.

She couldn't risk either.

For her to escape, she needed to avoid *both*.

Thanks to the crescent moon above, she was virtually invisible as she scampered across the guards' roof. Her matte-black bodysuit absorbed light, leaving no trace of reflection. To complete her outfit, she wore black shoes, black gloves, and a blank mask. Not just black, it was actually *blank*. No eyes, no nose, and no mouth. Not even ears. They were all tucked behind an elastic, cutting-edge hood that allowed her to breathe, hear, and see, but prevented her features from being detected.

The effect was beyond creepy.

Slowing to a stop near the edge of the roof, she studied the structure that she intended to breach. Styled like a Colonial home, its walls were made of the highest quality bricks, which had been expertly laid in both curved and straight swaths. She noticed the limestone accents and the two-tone stucco before she rested her gaze on the rear balcony. The place was handsome, but not ostentatious. It was cleverly designed to seem commonplace, but full of elegant architectural touches for anyone in the know.

And she was definitely in the know.

Her reconnaissance had been thorough.

Before crossing the gap between the homes, she reached into her pocket and pulled out several blobs. They looked like sticky toys – the kind that kids threw at walls. They had been colored the same shade as the house's bricks. When thrown, they stayed wherever they hit, like spitballs on a chalkboard.

Inside each was a powerful transmitter that would pick up sounds, even through a brick wall.

They were the latest gizmos in her bag of tricks.

Aided by the breeze, she tossed the rubbery splotches across the narrow stretch of grass between the homes. They splatted softly against the side of Kozlov's house. The sound of their impact was so quiet that it was drowned out by the pounding surf. Before long, the outside wall was lined with devices. They were nearly undetectable.

Within seconds, data streamed from the bugs to her earpiece. She listened to their chirps and interpreted their sounds as her eyes scanned the darkness below. She wouldn't begin until she was sure the coast was clear. Anything less would lead to certain death, and she enjoyed life too much to risk it.

A full minute passed. Then another.

Midway through a third, she had heard enough.

It was time to commence the breach.

She reached inside her cargo pocket and pulled out a small baton. It was painted matte black. She pulled on either side of the device to extend it. It grew longer than any layman would expect. Two feet, then five, and finally ten. She repositioned her hands in the middle of the baton while swinging it in tight little circles. Telescoping sections continued to grow from both ends. It lengthened while getting impossibly thin – as well as impossibly straight – until it was twenty feet long.

It was the exact length she needed.

Wasting no time, she extended the baton between the two homes. To her, it looked like a long, black sliver of air, as if a demon had sliced open the night. Even if someone from the house had been looking, they would have been hard pressed to see it.

Next, she angled the far end of the baton toward a balcony in the rear corner of Kozlov's house. She positioned the far tip between two banisters and made sure it wouldn't shift. Then she laid her end of the baton on the edge of the roof and quietly tapped a long, arched nail into the wood. Once it was secure, she slid her end of the baton into the hook – just enough to hold it in place, but shallow enough that she could pull the baton free once she had reached the other side.

Kozlov's balcony was lower than her position by about twenty degrees. That angle was nearly perfect. She took a deep breath, checked the chasm for eyewitnesses, and then climbed over the lip of the roof. Without pause, she grabbed the baton with both hands and slid across the narrow gap like water down a string.

In less than five seconds, she had glided from one house to the other like a cloud across the moon. She pulled herself over the railing and onto the scenic balcony. She stuffed the baton inside itself, then shoved the device into her pocket.

A moment later, her hands were on the curtained French doors that led to the rear of the house. Her gloved fingers moved quickly and quietly, as if assuring the door that everything would be fine. She kept at it until she heard a *click*.

A wide smile spread across her face.

Her blank mask revealed nothing.

With a twist of her wrist and a turn of her body, she stepped inside the most expensive and most heavily guarded house in Brooklyn.

3

She entered the house and immediately froze in place.

Her surprise had nothing to do with alarms or warnings. It had to do with the striking difference between the exterior of the house and its lavish interior. From the outside, the house appeared to be an extra-large Colonial on a nice street in Brooklyn. Inside, the place was more like the Taj Mahal, the Winter Palace, or Versailles.

It reeked of wealth and opulence.

The master bedroom yawned around her, like the treasure cave of the forty thieves. The sheer scope of the white walls and the wooden floor was incredible. Kozlov and his guards could have played basketball in there – it was that high and wide. The cathedral ceiling had sloping sides with multiple skylights. Each had a motorized shade. A king-size bed with a hand-carved mahogany frame sat along one wall. Magnificent bureaus and dressers lined another. Elaborate panel molding adorned them all.

As she was admiring it, a warning chirped in her ear.

Someone was approaching.

She went from still observation to quick, silent movement in the blink of an eye, racing across the floor to the master bath just as the bedroom door opened. With steady nerves, she crouched next to the elevated soaking tub and hid in the shadows. From there, she was able to use the large bathroom mirror to her advantage.

She watched the reflection of two muscled men in severe dark suits as they entered the bedroom. They flipped on the light and walked across the room toward the balcony window where she had been a moment before. Neither man had seen her.

'Is the art ready for auction?' one asked in Russian.

The other unlocked a writing desk near the window. '*Da.*'

'All of it?' the first responded.

He nodded as he grabbed a key from the drawer.

The two men hustled back toward the bedroom door, as if taking their time would have been unwise. They turned off the light, then closed the door behind them.

She breathed a sigh of relief as the muttering in the corridor diminished. She hoped they had ventured far enough away from the bedroom for her to use the hallway. Otherwise, she would be forced to exit the balcony and find another way to reenter the house. Moving carefully, she returned to the bedroom and listened intently at the door.

Nothing but silence.

She smiled and opened the door just a crack.

The view was remarkable.

It looked like the main gallery of an art museum. A circular mezzanine surrounded an indoor courtyard, framed by an ornate, jade-colored railing. It sat beneath a diamond-shaped skylight. Hanging from the center was an extravagant, hand-etched crystal chandelier. Thankfully, the upstairs hallway wasn't spotlighted. Instead, it was bathed in soft-white light that seemed to emerge from the walls themselves instead of the well-hidden, recessed fixtures.

She continued to listen closely but heard nothing once the guards had disappeared: no idle chatter or detectable noises like the blare of a radio or the squawk of a television. In some ways, the silence made her life easier. She could easily tell if someone was approaching. In other ways, it made her mission harder. Any noise she made would stand out in the silent house.

Moving like a shadow, she stepped into the hallway and closed the door behind her before she dashed the length of the corridor. She stopped in front of the locked door of the next room, but only long enough to pick it open. Ten seconds later, she was standing inside the library and admiring the hand-carved shelves and mahogany floors. It was so beautiful, so opulent, she almost felt guilty for what she was forced to do.

She silently and efficiently tore the room apart.

Every page of every book. Every shelf and every drawer. Every map, every picture, every chair, and every inch of every table. She checked the slats of the herringbone floor and checked every inch of the walls for secret panels and safes. She even climbed the shelves and furniture to check the ceiling and the recessed light fixtures.

But she found nothing. The library was clean.

Undeterred, she exited the room and headed toward the stairs. The walls were so white that her sheer black outfit stood out like a neon sign. Her trip wouldn't take long, but she knew she would be totally exposed until she reached the ground floor.

She moved with silent assurance.

Never pausing. Never doubting.

Never taking a moment to consider the risk.

She had spent years in the field in her former career where the stakes had been even higher. Back then, she had worked her magic for the stars and stripes. Now, she was working for herself. She liked this a whole lot more.

She reached the bottom of the stairs without incident. She looked left, then right, making sure she was alone. With no one in sight, she hustled straight ahead.

The entry was lined with marble floors. It was flanked by a huge living space on one side and an equally large dining area on the other. The spaces were separated by a barrel ceiling, supported by elegant columns and accented by traditional wainscoting. A crystal chandelier, matching the large one in the mezzanine, dangled in the center of each room. Neither was turned on, but they sparkled like diamonds in the faint light.

Who said crime didn't pay?

She scanned both areas for any signs of a recessed safe or a hidden door, but came up empty. Just as well. Anyone could have spotted her in there, whether they were hired to protect Kozlov or just waxed the floors on weekends.

She continued forward, finding the kitchen beyond. Not surprisingly, it was massive and had two of everything — stoves, sinks, dishwashers, and refrigerators — as if Noah had ordered the appliances. In reality, she knew the real reason for all the duplicates: Kozlov was feeding an army.

For some reason, Russian mobsters took care of their men like doting mothers. They housed them. They fed them. They gave them gifts. In return, they expected unwavering loyalty and utmost respect. All it took was a whiff of betrayal for heads to roll. The betrayer's head. His family's heads. His pet's head as well. In one memorable case, they even hunted down his 'friends' on Facebook and killed them, too.

The Russian *bratva* didn't mess around.

She forced those thoughts out of her mind as she opened the lone door in the kitchen. It led to a concrete staircase that disappeared in the darkness below. Weighing her options, she closed the door behind her and tested her sight.

She saw nothing. Absolutely nothing.

She cursed to herself.

Although her mask had built-in night vision, it only worked when there was ambient light. In the basement, there would be none. If she wanted to see, she knew she had to take a giant risk. Reluctantly, she pulled out a small flashlight from her pocket. She turned it on and followed its beam down the stairs.

The basement came as another surprise. Not only because Kozlov had built one so close to the water's edge, but because of its simplicity.

It was the opposite of everything she had seen above.

The red floor was nothing but painted cement. The walls and ceiling were lined with plastic and insulation, probably to absorb sound more than heat. It looked like the 'boiler room' of a telemarketing firm that went bust. Ironically, she got the sense that more business was done down here than anywhere else in the house. The kind of business that involved a pair of pliers, a baseball bat, and a screaming victim.

She focused her attention on the gray metal door in the center of the far wall. It sat next to an elaborate cooling system that clanked in the corner. Blueprints and work orders had led her to believe that there would be a room in the rear of the basement.

In a flash, she realized it wasn't a room at all.

It was a walk-in meat locker.

4

It wasn't the polished steel exterior of the giant door that had given the freezer away. It was the oversized, single-handle latch.

She had come prepared for every kind of door. Even the simplest, most well-concealed vaults were protected by a lock of some kind. Bank and casino vaults – the gold standard by which vaults are measured – employed everything from analog pin-and-tumbler combination locks to next-generation biometric triggers, such as palm and retina scanners. She had even seen systems that monitored perspiration and blood pressure. If someone showed any signs of distress while attempting to access the vault, the software would deny access – even if the correct codes had been entered.

Fortunately for her, this door was pretty basic.

All it required was a simple tug.

A rush of cold air pushed against her as she peeked inside the freezer. The walls were lined with steel racks that held bins of frozen vegetables, as well as store-bought items such as ready-made pasta entrees and desserts. In the center of the room stood a butcher's station – a heavy, stainless steel table and an assortment of saws, cleavers, and carving knives. Two sides of the steel island were surrounded by hanging slabs of meat. Sides of beef, as well as whole hogs, slabs of mutton, chicken, rabbits, and duck dangled from hoists like a wide curtain of flesh.

As she closed the door behind her, the unit's compressor hissed. The vents spewed freshly chilled air in an effort to compensate for her body heat.

She shivered as her breath crystallized.

For all its innovations, her suit did little to shield her from the cold. Then again, it wasn't the frigid temperature that bothered her the most. She was more interested in the size of the room. Large as it was, it was still much smaller than she had been led to believe. This room should have consumed nearly a third of the basement, but it wasn't close to that. Either the blueprints were wrong, or this freezer was more than it appeared to be.

Five minutes later, she had her answer.

Thanks to the icy walls, the second door was virtually invisible in the back of the freezer. What gave it away was the set of hinges that allowed the racks in front of the door to pivot forward and swing aside. Once she pushed the frozen vegetables out of the way, she spotted a tiny slot in the metal surface of the rear wall. She immediately recognized it as a card reader, like those used in fancy hotels.

Unfazed, she produced a slim device from one of her many pockets. She flipped open the cover and inserted the gadget into the card reader. It fit perfectly. A flurry of access codes streamed across its tiny screen. She raised an eyebrow when the microcomputer continued to process after matching a fourth number. ATMs only require four-digit pin numbers, so a fifth digit seemed slightly excessive. By the time her device had acquired the tenth and final digit, she was beyond intrigued.

What the hell is he keeping in here?

The Ark of the Covenant?

With a faint click, the door popped open. She wrapped her fingers around the edge of the door, then pulled it toward herself. She was expecting to see stacks of cash, mountains of cocaine, or something that would justify the security measures.

Instead, all she saw was a giant.

At nearly seven feet tall and roughly 400 pounds, the Russian guard literally filled the doorway. Standing face to face – make that *chest* to face – with a crafty ninja, he panicked and reached for his pistol instead of wrapping her in a massive bear hug that would have squeezed the life out of her in a matter of seconds.

It was a mistake he would later regret.

The moment he pulled his weapon, she thrust her right hand into his throat as if hurling a javelin. It was a knuckle punch – what mobsters called a 'bear claw' and martial artists called a 'panther fist.' Her thumb was pulled tight, her palm distended, and her four fingers were curled to provide a hard striking surface. It was intended to slip under the chin in a way that a normal punch couldn't.

It was the perfect choice for a taller target.

Her strike was so violent and so precise that it collapsed his trachea and damaged his vocal cords, temporarily rendering him mute. More importantly, the force of the blow and the pain of the impact caused him to lose his grip on the pistol. It flew from his hand and slid to the rear corner of the secret room, far from his immediate reach.

Unfortunately, all that did was piss him off.

Fueled by rage, the giant lowered his shoulder and charged at his opponent, driving her back toward the butcher's station. She glanced over her shoulder as she stumbled backwards. Given the force he exerted, she realized that the table's blunt edge would most likely crush her spine, so she dropped to the floor and allowed the brute to kick her underneath. She slid across the floor and quickly bounced to her feet. Staring across the table at the hulking guard, she waited for his next move.

She didn't have to wait long.

The Russian grabbed a large carving knife from the butcher's block. He grasped the edge of the table with his other hand. With little more than a swipe of his arm, the guard flung the heavy steel table across the room. It had taken four men to bring it into the freezer, yet he had tossed it aside with no more effort than swatting a fly.

He lumbered toward her, his eyes ablaze. He swung wildly, then caught his balance. Again he struck out at her, and again it took him a moment to regroup. Clumsy as he was, she knew that he only needed to connect once. With his fury and strength, one blow would take her head clean off.

After his third swing, she struck back. The moment the blade sliced past, she stepped forward and delivered a vicious jab to his lower abdomen. The bastard barely winced, so she changed her approach and went for his face. She aimed for the bridge of his nose, but connected with his orbital cavity. It felt like she had punched a cement wall. Almost instantly, his eye swelled shut. Blood trickled down his cheek from a wide gash under his brow, but he shrugged it off like a boxer in the ring.

He swung again, but this time she defended the strike. She knew she could never fully stop his arm's momentum, but by focusing her block on his wrist, she was able to disarm him. The impact sent the knife flying across the room. Unfortunately, the guard followed this blow with a punch to her ribs, which sent *her* flying across the room in the opposite direction.

The guard took the opportunity to retreat into the hidden room. After scanning the floor, he found what he had come for and grabbed the pistol.

Time to end this, he thought.

Standing in the doorway between the rooms, he grew confused. He had expected to find her crumpled in the corner of the freezer, coughing up blood from his vicious blow. But she wasn't there, or anywhere, that he could see. He moved forward to investigate.

Unbeknownst to him, she had scrambled across the floor and taken refuge behind the door. The instant he was fully inside the freezer, she slammed the door shut behind him. Darkness swallowed them both.

Without light, they were forced to rely on sound, and the only thing they could hear was each other's labored breathing. The giant pointed his gun in the direction of the door and fired. He held his breath, hoping to hear the squeal of his victim, but was greeted by silence.

He fired again . . . then again . . . then again.

Each time aiming in a different direction.

Each time coming up empty.

Her matte-black bodysuit helped her stay hidden in the maze of dangling carcasses. With every flash of the guard's pistol, she moved closer and closer to her target. Once she had narrowed the gap to three feet, she made her move.

She swept her foot violently behind his knee, knocking his leg from under him. As he crashed to the floor, she launched herself toward the ceiling. Clutching the hanging side of beef as if it were a rope swing, she cut the nylon line of the hoist with a cleaver. In an instant, the combined weight of herself and the steer crashed down upon the guard. His hip took the brunt of the impact, shattering like fine china.

She stood and illuminated the scene with her flashlight. The guard's face conveyed the intolerable pain of his broken hip. Tears streamed down his chubby cheeks.

Thankfully, she had the perfect item to ease his pain.

Wrapping her hands around the brass knuckles that she never left home without – she had yet to meet a man who could withstand more than one good punch – she reared back and knocked out the giant with a powerful hook to his chin.

The big baby went right to sleep.

It was time to see what he was protecting.

5

She opened the door slowly.

In stark contrast to the dark freezer, the secret room was bathed in soft, warm light. It had the look and feel of a large, windowless office, complete with a desk, computer, and a landline phone. A Russian calendar – featuring naked women in fur hats – hung behind the door, but her attention was focused on the crates of antiquities that lined the other three walls.

Seemingly every culture was represented. There were tribal masks, Oriental vases, and Roman weaponry. Everything from intricate baubles to uncut jewels. She even spotted a Gutenberg Bible, one of the most valuable books in the world. It was sitting inside a glass display case, which sat on top of a carton of Fabergé eggs.

Turning to her left, she spotted a crate of paintings in the far corner of the room. She hustled forward and pried open the crate.

Inside were several paintings.

All of which had been 'lost' years ago.

Portrait of a Young Man – painted by Raphael in 1513. It was looted by the Nazis during World War II. *The Battle of Anghiari* – painted by Leonardo da Vinci in 1505. Often referred to as 'the Lost Leonardo'. *Portrait of Alfonso I d'Este*

– painted by Titian in 1523. It disappeared from the Royal Alcazar of Madrid during the eighteenth century. *The Storm on the Sea of Galilee* – painted by Rembrandt in 1633 – stolen from the Isabella Stewart Gardner Museum in 1990, the biggest art theft in US history.

Masterpiece after masterpiece, just sitting on the floor.

All of them there for the taking.

And yet she was forced to ignore them.

Rummaging through the canvases, she quickly discovered the small, framed arrangement of stained glass she had been told to locate.

Arguably, Marc Chagall's most notable works of stained glass are the windows at the synagogue of Hebrew University's Hadassah Medical Center in Jerusalem. But long before he set about that large-scale project, he created each window in miniature. These 'rough drafts' and their finalized counterparts represent the twelve tribes of the Israelites – one picture for each tribe. Pulling a photo from her pack, she matched the image in the picture to the seventh piece in the series.

'Beautiful,' she said aloud.

Then she smashed the art into pieces.

Hidden inside the frame, sandwiched between two opaque plates of glass, was a single sheet of paper. She carefully removed the dried, cracked parchment, taking every precaution to prevent further damage. Without taking the time to read it, she inserted the document into a flexible, tear-resistant membrane and secured the package in a hidden pouch inside the back of her suit.

Then she checked her watch.

A minute or two more was worth the risk.

She darted over to the small desk and studied the system. Tapping on the mouse, the monitor flickered to life. She plugged a portable drive into the port on the side and copied the entire hard drive. Kozlov had art around the world, and she wanted to know who supplied it. Maybe she would come back for these treasures another time.

Satisfied with her haul, she made her way back into the freezer. Her contented smile quickly vanished when she realized that the wounded guard was no longer on the floor. Scanning the room, she saw that the other door was open. Bracing herself, she stepped out of the freezer and into the basement.

The moment she cleared the steel walls of the walk-in, the connection to her earpiece was restored. The voice on the other end of the mic was freaking out.

'Sarah, can you hear me!' the voice shouted. 'If you can hear this, you need to evac immediately. I repeat, get the hell out of there!'

'Calm down, Hector. What's going on?'

'I'm not sure, but it's major. Everyone mobilized about a minute ago. The guards are pouring out of the neighboring houses, and they're coming your way!'

* * *

Hector Garcia studied the array of computer screens that he had assembled for this particular job. Although he was two thousand miles from the action, he had been feeding Sarah information from the moment she had landed in Brooklyn.

His guidance had been invaluable.

In addition to the data from the FBI surveillance van – which he had hacked with relative ease – Garcia had been monitoring the transmissions from the sticky blobs. His software processed the collective data stream in ways that would stagger the imagination. By differentiating and triangulating sounds, Garcia could not only determine how many people were inside the mansion, he could also tell which floors they were on and whether or not they were moving.

* * *

Sarah followed a trail of blood and boot prints to the stairs that led to the kitchen door. There was no mistaking the giant's size-twenty shoes.

'Shit,' she mumbled under her breath. She sprinted up the steps and jammed the lock from the inside. It wouldn't hold long, but it would buy her some time. 'I think I know why the natives are restless. I should've killed Shrek when I had the chance.'

'Shrek?' Garcia said, confused. 'Are you feeling alright?'

'I'm feeling fine. I'll feel a lot better if you can get me out of this basement.'

'Do you have the package?'

'Of course I have the package! I wouldn't be looking for a ticket home without the goddamn package. What do I look like? An amateur?'

'How should I know? We've never met!'

'And we never will unless you find me a route out of here.'

'I'm trying. Trust me, I'm trying!'

Sarah could hear shouting in the kitchen. She tried to decipher what they were saying, but the walls were too thick. 'Can you make any of that out?'

'I can make *all* of it out,' Garcia said. 'Unfortunately, I can't speak Russian so I don't know what they're saying.'

'Don't you have software for that?'

'I can only do so much at once!'

'Fine,' she said stubbornly. 'Then I'll find a way out myself.'

'The kitchen is not an option,' he assured her. 'There's so much activity up there, I can't even get an accurate count. You'll have to find another way.'

'What about back through the vault? Maybe a ventilation shaft?'

'You know the schematics as well as I do,' Garcia said. 'It's an old house, but they refitted the basement with modern ventilation a few years back. There's no way you're fitting through a three-inch exhaust.'

'Maybe I won't have to,' she said as her mind whirred through a list of possibilities. She had studied enough floor plans and security systems in her life to recognize the details that most people would miss. 'I think I found another way.'

Sarah studied the column in the center of the room and slid open a wooden panel in the front. She had glanced at it earlier and had quickly dismissed it as part of the cooling system, but then she remembered that this house had been built decades earlier. In order to feed the occupants and their staff, several pounds of meat and vegetables were cooked daily. The intense, continuous heat of the cooking fires would have made the kitchen unbearable, so the ovens had been relegated to the basement. Rather than make the staff carry the food up several flights of stairs, the architect came up with an alternative.

'You aren't going to believe this,' she said as she shined her flashlight up the elevator shaft. 'This house has a dumb waiter.'

'To where?'

'I don't know,' she said as she climbed inside the shaft and closed the door behind her. 'I'll let you know when I get there.'

6

Agent Callahan was a block away from the surveillance van when he used his cell phone to call his partner. 'Are you seeing this?'

Koontz stayed focused on the monitor in front of him. 'Of course I'm seeing this. The Angels have the bases loaded in the bottom of the ninth. One hit and the Yankees can suck it!'

'You're watching the Yankees?'

'Of course I'm watching the Yankees. We get great reception with our satellite. Why do you think I wanted you out of the van?'

Callahan fumed. 'You're such an idiot! We finally see some action, and you're jerking off instead of taking pictures?'

'Action? What action?'

'Look out the damn window!'

Koontz did as he was told and was stunned by the sight. Guards poured from the surrounding homes like a flood, filling the streets with crew cuts and guns. 'Holy shit! What the hell happened? Did someone find the *Red October*?'

'I don't know what happened. I was hoping you could tell me!'

'Heck if I know,' Koontz admitted. Instead of monitoring

35

local chatter, he had been listening to the audio feed of the baseball game. 'Give me a minute, and I'll check the tape.'

'Screw the tape! Check the live feed from the house.'

Despite his lackadaisical demeanor, Koontz was actually a talented field agent, one who knew Russian, Ukrainian, and several other languages. It was that skill more than any other that had led to this particular assignment. He could eavesdrop on any conversation in Brighton Beach and figure out what was being said.

Koontz listened and translated for his partner. 'They found a body in the kitchen. A big fucker named Boris. He was just lying in the middle of the floor.'

'A body? As in, someone died?'

The news excited Callahan. A dead body, no matter who it was, would give them cause to knock down the door. Not only that, it would tie Kozlov to a murder.

His mind raced at the possibilities.

'No, not dead,' Koontz informed him. 'Just really messed up. There's a lot of commotion, but I think someone said he broke his hip.'

'Shit!' Callahan blurted. His vision of storming the mansion was replaced by thoughts of an old man slipping on an ice cube.

Koontz continued to listen. 'Now they're talking about killing someone.'

'Killing who?' Callahan demanded.

He paused for a moment. 'You.'

'*Me?* They're talking about killing *me?*'

Koontz laughed. 'Nah, I'm just messing with you. They're looking for some intruder. They think he's in the vault, and they're gathering the troops to find him.'

'What intruder? What vault?'

'How the hell should I know? I can only translate so many things at once – especially since I'm flying solo. It might be nice if I had some help.'

*   *   *

Compared to traditional elevators, the dumb waiter shaft was dark and cramped, but it felt downright spacious compared to the chimneys, crawlspaces, and ventilation ducts Sarah had shimmied through over the years. And since the dumb waiter car had been removed long ago, she had plenty of room to maneuver.

Splaying her legs to the sides, she climbed the chute with relative ease. All she had to do was maintain enough side-to-side pressure with her arms and legs to support her bodyweight while she crawled vertically toward the roof. She wasn't sure if the top of the shaft would offer an exit or if she would have to create one herself. For the time being, her only goal was to avoid a messy confrontation in the basement.

When she reached the pulleys that had once held the support ropes in place, Sarah realized she had come to the end of the line. The exit door to the third floor had long since been covered by plasterboard, but it wasn't all bad news in her mind since they hadn't reset the studs in the wall. She knew she could punch through drywall, but two-inch-thick boards would have been a different matter.

Before she did anything drastic, Sarah pressed her ear

against the shaft and listened for any signs of life on the other side of the wall. Guards scurried on the floors below, desperately searching for the evil ninja who had defeated the giant ogre they kept locked in the basement, but she heard nothing but silence outside the chute.

It was now or never.

She walked her feet around the perimeter of the shaft and planted her shoes firmly against the frame of the opening. Holding onto the pulley above, she curled her legs against her chest and swung out from the wall with all her might. As gravity reversed her course, she combined her momentum with a violent thrust of her legs.

The wall splintered on contact as she drove her feet through the drywall. Chunks of plaster flew into the hallway and clanked down the shaft to the basement below, but she knew the noise was worth the risk. She repeated the process again and again, widening the hole until she could slip through the narrow gap.

She looked like a gopher searching for hawks when she peeked her head through the hole. She turned left, then right, then left again, making sure the coast was clear before she fully emerged from the wall. Satisfied with her surroundings, she dove through the small fissure, launching all but her lower legs into the hallway beyond. She quickly pulled her calves, ankles, and feet through the wall and rose to one knee.

She listened, wondering if her breach had been detected.

'You're good,' Garcia said in her ear. 'The mass of guards hasn't moved from the lower floors. I think you're clear unless . . .'

'Unless what?' she whispered.

'Hold on! We have movement. One person, heading your—'

'Shit,' she blurted.

Not thirty feet in front of her, Kozlov himself emerged from a room at the end of the hallway. He stared at her, consumed with rage. Although he was unarmed, she half expected fireballs to burst forth from his eyes – that's how angry he was.

'Here!' he screamed in Russian. 'The intruder is standing right in front of me! Someone, grab him!'

Even with the language barrier, Sarah understood that she wouldn't be getting a holiday card from Kozlov anytime soon. Preparing for the worst, she slipped her brass knuckles on and took a step toward the crime boss.

'Shit!' Garcia yelled in her ear. 'Here comes another!'

Almost instantly, a single figure appeared on the stairwell nearest Kozlov's room. Dressed in a dark suit, he dashed up the steps two at a time while pulling a pistol from the holster inside his coat. His eyes locked on Sarah as he charged at her with his gun raised. Kozlov sneered and pointed at Sarah as she turned and sprinted down a hallway toward the back half of the house.

Thinking quickly, the gunman leaped over a railing in the open mezzanine and tried to catch her before she reached the back deck. He fired once, barely missing her right shoulder but hitting the French doors in front of her. The glass shattered on contact, which surprised everyone in the hallway because it was *supposed* to be bulletproof.

*   *   *

Despite the chaos, Kozlov made a mental note to kill the contractor who had installed the window. Then he returned his focus to the gunman.

He fired again. And again. And again.

Every time his bullet just missed.

Kozlov watched in amazement as the intruder reached the end of the hallway but didn't stop running until 'he' leaped off the third-story patio with reckless abandon. His national pride soared when he watched the gunman do the same. Kozlov thought it was suicide to go after the thief in that way, but he appreciated the dedication. As soon as he learned the new guard's name, he would reward him for his bravery.

Just to be safe, Kozlov waited for several guards to join him before he led them down the hallway to where the intruder had made 'his' escape. In Kozlov's mind, the intruder had to be a *man* because women were incapable of such feats of strength. Of course, it was assumptions like *that* that helped her get away.

Hoping to find the intruder's blood on his carpet, Kozlov saw nothing but broken glass. Disappointed, he raced to the balcony where he expected to see two crumpled bodies on the pool deck below. Instead, he saw something that sickened him to his very core: the gunman was helping the intruder out of the pool.

It took a moment for it to all sink in.

The two of them were working together.

Kozlov's face turned red as he roared, 'Kill them both!'

7

It took Callahan nearly ten minutes to reach the surveillance van through the mob of gunmen that filled the street outside of Kozlov's house. Not because the guards were hassling him – just about everyone in the neighborhood knew what the Feds looked like – but because Callahan was hassling *them*.

When it came to gun laws, New York City had some of the strictest in the nation. Callahan knew he could bust all of them on felony charges if he had wanted to. Instead, he tried to use the threat of arrest to obtain more information about that night's events while Koontz filmed the scene from afar.

Callahan realized the odds of getting information from one of Kozlov's men was pretty unlikely, especially with so many of them packed together. But he hoped this approach would spook someone into revealing something of value in the crowd.

As luck should have it, one of the lead guards spotted Callahan and spread the word through the ranks: if anyone told the Feds about the upcoming art auction or about the intruder who had tried to rob the basement vault, the offending party would be shot in the face and fed to the sharks. That message was repeated again and again in Russian and Ukrainian until everyone on the street had gotten the word.

Unfortunately for them, Koontz got it, too.

Inside the van, he laughed at the irony of the warning. By telling his underlings what they shouldn't say, the lead guard had actually revealed everything.

That was taking stupid to a whole new level.

Koontz was still laughing when his partner reached the van. He looked forward to briefing Callahan on everything he had heard – and how he had obtained it – but before they had a chance to speak, gunfire rang out from across the street.

Koontz threw open the van door and pulled Callahan inside.

'Who the hell is shooting?' Callahan demanded.

'I don't know,' Koontz said as he turned his attention to the van's computer system. He punched a few keys and tried to locate the source of the sound, using the parabolic microphones that a tech team had covertly planted around the neighborhood.

Callahan checked his weapon. Unlike the thugs outside, he was legally allowed to shoot people in Brighton Beach. 'Please be Kozlov. I want to be the one to arrest him.'

Koontz shook his head. 'Sorry. He's shouting, *not* shooting.'

'Figures. What's he shouting about?'

'He just yelled, *kill them both.*'

'There are two of them?'

Koontz nodded. 'That's what "both" means.'

Callahan sneered. 'And *both* of them are in the house?'

He shook his head. '*Were*. They *were* in the house. They just jumped off a balcony into Kozlov's pool.'

Callahan waited for more. 'And?'

'And nothing. The guards are looking for them.'

'Then so are we,' Callahan said as he opened the van door. 'If they've been inside Kozlov's house, we need to find them before the guards do.'

* * *

Jack Cobb was soaking wet, but at least he was alive.

And, thankfully, so was Sarah.

Water poured from his suit as he yanked her from the pool. He had millions of questions for his partner-in-crime, but they would have to wait for now. There was little time for chitchat with Kozlov's guards giving chase.

Despite the danger, Sarah scolded him as they hustled toward the fence in the back of the grounds. 'I could have done it myself, you know. I didn't need your help.'

'I could see that,' Cobb replied sarcastically. 'You had them right where you wanted.'

'It wasn't *them*,' she countered. 'It was one man. No, scratch that. It was *the* man. I could have ended everything right there.'

'Ended what, exactly? Our mission wasn't to kill him. It was to rob him. You need to put your Agency training behind you. The only way you'll survive as a criminal is to think like a criminal.'

'But I'm *not* a criminal!' she insisted.

'Not yet, you aren't. That's what I'm trying to tell you!'

Sarah realized there was no point in arguing. They could pick up this discussion later, once they had evaded the Russians and made it safely to their rendezvous.

That is, *if* they made it to their rendezvous.

'Okay, Mr Helper,' she said as they scaled the fence together. 'Now that you've decided to get involved, what exactly do you have in mind?'

Cobb scurried to his right and scanned the terrain. 'I say we run down the beach as fast as we can and hope the Russians don't catch us.'

'That's it? That's your big plan? I swoop down like a bat in the middle of the night and break into the most heavily guarded compound this side of the White House, and your big plan is to run as fast as we can?'

Cobb shrugged. 'Part of it.'

'Wonderful. What's the other part?'

He fought the urge to smile. 'Hey McNutt, can you hear me?'

A new voice entered the conversation. 'I can hear *you*, I can hear *her*, and I can hear gunfire. The only thing I can't hear is the nerd. Is he still on the line?'

'Still here,' Garcia assured them.

'Oh goody,' McNutt teased, 'if we have any questions about *Star Wars* or time travel, we'll be sure to let you know.'

Cobb cut them off. It was bad enough that Sarah was giving him lip. He couldn't afford antics from the other guys on the team, too. Not with hostiles in hot pursuit.

'Josh, what's your position?' Cobb asked.

'Two hundred yards west,' McNutt answered.

'Sarah and I are headed your way. We're going to need cover.'

'It's about time. Shoot to kill?'

Cobb shook his head. 'That's a negative.'

McNutt grumbled but followed his orders.

8

The man with the dirty beard and unkempt hair had been patrolling the sand with his metal detector for several hours. His ratty clothes and strange demeanor kept passersby at a safe distance, not that there were many at this time of night. Every so often he would dig in the sand and search for buried treasure, but he never came up with anything more substantial than an aluminum can or a foil wrapper.

To most observers, he fit in with half the scavengers who roamed the beaches at night. Over the years, Kozlov's guards had dealt with so many of these people that they had learned the best way to handle them was to simply ignore them. That might have been a wonderful policy for tourists, but it wasn't the best strategy when it came to guard duty. If Kozlov's men had been paying closer attention, they would have realized the crazy man in the Hawaiian shirt wasn't searching for treasure, he was actually planting devices in the sand. And the 'metal detector' that he had been using for half the night couldn't actually detect metal – but it sure as hell could deliver it.

As Josh McNutt climbed the steps of the lifeguard shack, he detached the circular 'sensor' from the end of the bar and examined its contents. He had loaded fifty high-powered rounds into the custom drum magazine. He checked the barrel and the stock that been disguised as the unit's shaft and stabilizer, then pulled himself on the roof of the stand. By the time he reached the edge, he had reassembled the metal detector into its preferred configuration: an Armalite AR-30 .308 Winchester sniper rifle.

'I'm in position,' McNutt informed the team.

'Beta plan is a go,' Cobb confirmed in his ear.

'Beta – as in Beach Bum.'

'No more jokes,' Cobb snapped. 'Watch our six.'

'Can't I do both?' McNutt asked rhetorically.

The alpha plan was simple, as most plans were on paper. Sarah would infiltrate the mansion from the sky, find the package, secure it, and make her way back to the rooftop. From there, she would travel across the tops of several neighboring buildings until she could safely descend to street level.

As for Cobb, he would blend in with the guards outside the house, ready to provide on-site support at a moment's notice. McNutt and his sniper rifle would remain at a distance, in position to cover their escape. Meanwhile, Garcia would monitor all electronic aspects of the operation and update them on the status of everyone involved: the guards, the Feds, and innocent bystanders.

Unfortunately, plans change.

Now that the Russians had been alerted to their activities, the team had to adapt to the situation. Using real-time satellite images, Garcia was able to direct Cobb and Sarah into the shadows of the nearby houses and through the first wave of guards. The duo were more than a block from Kozlov's mansion, but they were far from safe. They knew his henchmen were somewhere in the dark behind them, and stopping only closed the distance.

'They're hunting in packs like wild dogs,' Garcia informed them. 'The good news is they don't have your scent. The bad news is they're getting close.'

Cobb slipped off his soggy jacket. 'Civilians?'

'Plenty,' Garcia said. 'But it will be tough to blend in. Everyone knows everyone in this part of town. The only visitors are here for the beach.'

Cobb smiled. 'That's exactly what I had in mind.'

'What do you mean?' Sarah asked, confused.

He inspected her from head to toe. 'Take off your pants.'

'Excuse me?' she barked. 'What the hell do you mean, "take your pants off"? What exactly do you think—'

Cobb brought a finger to his lips, asking her to stop.

Normally, he would have reached out and clamped his hand over someone's mouth, ensuring his or her silence. But he had the feeling that with Sarah, such action might have resulted in the loss of a finger . . . or a testicle.

'Look at yourself,' he explained. 'You're *not* going to blend in like that. Right now you don't even have a face.'

'How does taking off my pants make things better?'

McNutt chimed in. 'In my experience, it never makes things *worse!*'

Cobb removed his shirt, exposing washboard abs. He wasn't as fit as he had been in his twenties, but he was still in better shape than most. 'Kozlov saw you in the catsuit. We have to assume he spread the word to all his guards. They'll be looking for someone dressed in black.'

'Fine!' Sarah conceded. She quickly unlaced her booties, kicked them off, and peeled off the lower half of her suit. Standing there in a black thong, she mockingly posed for Cobb. 'Happy?'

He turned his head from the athletic blonde, focusing his attention on his shoes and socks. She was stunning, he had to admit, but there was a time and place to acknowledge it. That sure as hell wasn't now. 'What about your bra?'

'Screw you!' she snapped. 'I'm not showing you my boobs!'

'Now we're talking!' McNutt said, trying to find her in his sniper's scope. 'Should I get undressed, too?'

Cobb tried to explain as he took off his own pants. Underneath, he was wearing a pair of boxer briefs that looked like swimming trunks. 'That's *not* what I meant. Does your bra look like a bikini, or does it actually look like underwear?'

'Oh,' she said, finally understanding his meaning. 'It's a sports bra.'

'Great. Hurry and take off your top.'

She rolled her eyes. 'My prom date said the exact same thing.'

Cobb smiled. 'You can tell me about that later. For now, let's worry about getting out of here.' He changed his focus to his earpiece. 'McNutt, how we looking?'

'Good enough for a threesome.'

'Focus!' Cobb demanded. 'Are we clear?'

'Not really,' McNutt answered, 'but the situation isn't going to get better anytime soon. You should move now before it's too late.'

Cobb nodded at Sarah, who looked like a swimsuit model in her bra and panties. She reluctantly stuffed her catsuit in a trash barrel as they made their way onto the beach. Cobb put his arm around her shoulder to complete the look of two lovers headed for a late-night swim, but the only thing bulging in his shorts was a concealed pistol.

*   *   *

Koontz called for backup from the van while Callahan started his search for the two intruders. He knew he was taking a big risk by putting himself in the line of fire while his partner stayed behind, but Callahan saw this was a special opportunity. If they could prove through eyewitness testimony that Kozlov's vault was filled with stolen art, then they could get the warrants they needed to search the mansion.

In Callahan's mind, *that* would be a career changer.

No more vans. No more stakeouts. No more bullshit.

He would *finally* get the respect he deserved.

Oh, and Koontz might benefit, too.

Callahan, who had several years of tactical experience and was an expert on Kozlov's local infrastructure, realized only the dumbest thieves in the world would try to escape through the streets of Little Odessa where thousands of interlopers would be willing to help Kozlov. On the other hand, a smart criminal would head toward the beach where they could use the darkened waters of the Atlantic to slip away unnoticed.

Running as fast as he could, Callahan dashed between Kozlov's mansion and his neighboring guardhouse, hoping to spot the intruders before they reached the water. He had no idea who he was looking for, but he hoped *someone* would stand out.

Unfortunately, that someone turned out to be him.

9

During combat situations, it is quite common for inexperienced personnel to make astoundingly stupid mistakes. Whether it's the rush of adrenalin, the fear of death, or a combination of the two, new recruits have been known to do the dumbest things – the kind of errors that lead to casualties and bloodshed.

It has been that way since the dawn of time.

When Kozlov first sounded the alarm, word quickly spread through the ranks that two intruders had been spotted: one dressed in black, the other dressed in a suit. Eventually, other details emerged. The second suspect was a middle-aged white guy. Average build. Average height. And armed with a semi-automatic. Caution should be used when taking him out because the Feds were snooping around.

Somehow that message was garbled along the way. Maybe it was lost in translation. Or maybe it was something else. Whatever the reason, the four guards on beach patrol heard the following: *Use caution when taking out the Fed.*

He is the middle-aged white guy dressed in a black suit.

Unfortunately for Callahan, that described him perfectly.

He hoped to find the intruders on the beach, but quickly found himself in the crosshairs of half the Russian Army, who chased him with guns blazing.

One moment he was the hunter.

The next he was the prey.

* * *

Cobb and Sarah flinched when they heard the gunshots. They quickly realized that they weren't the targets – but one of the FBI agents was.

'Shit,' they said in unison.

In their former lives, both had served their country with pride. Cobb was an ex-soldier, and Sarah had worked for the CIA. At one time or another, each of them had benefited from outside assistance, so neither was willing to leave the agent in his time of need, even if it meant hindering their own escape.

'McNutt,' Cobb said to his sniper.

'Already on it,' McNutt assured him.

Agent Callahan had no idea what he had stumbled into. Fortunately for him, McNutt had his back.

He fired four times in rapid succession. The first three ripped through his targets' knees, instantly dropping them to the ground. The fourth hit a guard in his ass cheek simply because McNutt was tired of shooting them in their knees. From this distance – with this rifle and this scope – he could have shot off a nipple if he had wanted to.

Callahan seized the opportunity to hide, diving behind a red canoe that was upside down in the sand. He didn't know who had shot the guards or why they were willing to rescue him, but he said a short prayer of thanks while keeping his head low.

* * *

The guards on the street heard the gunshots on the beach. A moment later, they heard the wails of men who had never taken a bullet.

The sound was unmistakable.

Like injured coyotes calling to their pack, the screams of the injured men were an announcement to the entire community. Their message was loud and clear: *Everyone, come quick! They're right here! Just follow the sound of my voice!*

The gunmen came in astonishing numbers.

Cobb drew his pistol and turned toward Kozlov's mansion. He couldn't see them yet, but he knew the Russians were coming. They weren't the most highly trained guards, but they were headstrong and dedicated to their cause. And there were dozens of them. He and Sarah crouched low, waiting for the inevitable firefight.

'Get moving!' McNutt demanded. 'Get to the water behind me! You'll be okay once your feet hit the surf.'

Cobb argued. 'We'll never make it if we don't slow them down. Without a show of force, they'll—'

'Just get to the water!' McNutt shouted. 'Let me worry about the show of force. You guys just turn and run.'

Neither Cobb nor Sarah moved.

McNutt kept shouting. 'Do it now, or I'll shoot you myself!'

With that, Cobb and Sarah sprinted toward the water.

As gunmen emerged on the beach, McNutt picked them off, one by one. Eventually they slowed down and hunkered behind garbage cans, sand dunes, and whatever else they could find to offer them protection from the hail of bullets.

But the break was only momentary.

They quickly realized they severely outnumbered the intruders, so they spread their troops out wide. McNutt tried to keep pace – sweeping his rifle from left to right and back again – but he couldn't compete with the sheer numbers. It seemed that every man he shot was instantly replaced by another, who was equally willing to take a bullet. McNutt was happy to oblige, but his single-shot rifle limited his effectiveness.

'Screw this,' McNutt said. 'I'm going to plan C.'

Cobb glanced at Sarah. 'Plan C? What's plan C?'

'No idea,' she admitted.

'Me, neither,' Garcia said in their ears.

McNutt pulled a flat controller from the pocket of his cargo shorts. It looked as if he had installed two rows of light switches in a small cigar box. 'Plan B stands for *beach bum*. That plan ain't working, so I'm moving to plan C.'

'I say again,' Cobb yelled as they ran past McNutt's position, 'what the hell is plan C?'

McNutt smiled. 'C stands for *cars*.'

The sniper put his forearm against the first row of switches and flipped them all at once. A split second later, ten cars exploded in the neighborhood. Some of them had been parked near Kozlov's mansion. Others had been parked on surrounding streets. All of them were now little more than twisted piles of burning fuel and melting metal.

McNutt grinned like a mischievous kid.

* * *

One of the targeted cars was parked less than a hundred feet from the surveillance van. The explosion was so powerful it shattered the van's bulletproof windows and knocked the surveillance feeds off the air.

Koontz, who was calling for backup at the time of the blast, was thrown violently to the floor. He quickly scrambled for cover in the corner of the van.

'They've got missiles!' he shouted into the phone. 'The Russians have missiles! Someone call the President! We're being invaded!'

* * *

Crouching in knee-deep water, Sarah could see flames shooting higher than the roofs that lined the beach. 'Holy shit! What the hell was *that*?'

'*That*,' McNutt laughed, 'was plan C.'

Kozlov's forces, once unified in their assault, were now thoroughly confused. Most of the gunmen retreated to the house. They knew protecting their boss was their first priority, and whatever this was — whether a diversionary tactic or the start of World War III — could be dealt with *after* they were sure that Kozlov was safe.

However, a few hard-core assailants held firm in their pursuit of McNutt. He watched in amazement as they fired aimlessly toward him.

'Persistent pricks,' McNutt said under his breath before turning his attention to Cobb and Sarah. 'You guys alright?'

Cobb answered. 'We're fine. What about you?'

'Don't worry about me. I have one more surprise for these bastards.'

'Do I want to know?'

'Probably not.'

Cobb glanced out into the water where two single-rider jet skis were anchored in the surf. He and Sarah would use them to flee the scene.

'You're sure you're okay?'

'I'm better than okay,' McNutt bragged. Then, as if to prove a point, he fired one more shot at the guards. In the distance, one of them squealed in pain.

Cobb nodded. 'Nice shooting. See you soon.'

'You got it, chief.'

Whistling to himself, McNutt dismantled his rifle while Cobb and Sarah swam toward their jet skis. Once they were out of range, McNutt flipped the second row of switches on his controller. In a flash, a wall of flames rose from the sand. It stretched the entire length of the beach – Cobb, Sarah, McNutt, and Callahan on one side, the fleeing mob on the other. It was as if the coast had been hit with a strafing run of napalm. In reality, it was all the devices he had planted while he was pretending to look for treasure.

McNutt cackled with glee as he jumped from the roof of the lifeguard shack. He jogged over to a nearby fence where he uncovered the motorcycle he had stored there hours before. He stowed his rifle in the saddlebags then climbed aboard his bike as if mounting a horse. He even patted its side while making horsy sounds.

To complete his charade, McNutt tipped an imaginary cowboy hat toward Callahan, who was still trying to figure out why the mysterious stranger had saved his life. Then, before the Fed could see his face or try to question him, McNutt revved his bike's accelerator and roared up the beach into the darkness.

IO

Friday, August 24
Fort Lauderdale, Florida

The early-morning sun streamed into Terminal 1 at the Fort Lauderdale-Hollywood International Airport. The over-worked air conditioner tried to compete, but it was fighting a losing battle. During the summer months, the local weather forecast rarely changed: temperature in the mid-nineties with a chance of afternoon thunderstorms. And when it did change, it was only because a hurricane was passing through.

Needless to say, Cobb wasn't thrilled about the locale.

He had spent enough time in Iraq to be an expert on stifling heat, but there was something about the shirt-drenching humidity of Florida that really pissed him off. He was dressed comfortably – black T-shirt, blue jeans, and sneakers – yet he could already feel his clothes sticking to him as he strolled up the walkway.

Of course, Cobb had no one to blame but himself. If he had used the first-class ticket that had been bought for him, his flight from LaGuardia wouldn't have landed until later that afternoon. But due to his careful nature, he decided to fly in several hours early under an assumed name. And he wouldn't be traveling from New York.

This was his first chance to meet the man who had assembled the team for the job in Brighton Beach. Having passed that test with flying colors, Cobb had been summoned for a meeting with his new employer. Perhaps to discuss another job.

Cobb planned to control the terms as much as possible.

In the military, this kind of advance jaunt was known as a 'rekky' or 'recce', short for reconnaissance. As time went on, a rekky came to mean any preceding trip to scope out the locals, but originally it meant surveying a region to obtain information specifically regarding enemy troops.

With that in mind, Cobb had used money from his personal stash to purchase the redeye ticket from Las Vegas, where he had been decompressing for the past few days. He spent the majority of the flight learning as much as he could about the airport and region from the mini-computer that was still laughably called a cell phone.

Within minutes of takeoff, Cobb knew he'd be landing in Broward County, three miles southwest of Fort Lauderdale's central business district and twenty-one miles north of Miami. Although his arrival in Florida would be well concealed – the airport was ranked the twenty-second busiest in the US and one of the fifty busiest airports in the world – he knew he had a full day of work ahead of him.

Why couldn't it have been Sarasota instead?

If it had been, he could have checked out the much

smaller airport in ten minutes and would have had plenty of time to grab a newspaper at Circle Books and an early lunch in Saint Armand's Circle before his original flight had even landed. But here in Fort Lauderdale, he'd have to cover four terminals, six concourses, and fifty-seven gates. He'd even have to 'look for a friend' in three private airline clubs. Not bad for a place that was originally built on an abandoned nine-hole golf course.

While deplaning, Cobb didn't race ahead with all of the others. Instead, he stepped out of the crush of passengers and took a moment to get his bearings.

'May I help you?' someone said.

Cobb wasn't surprised by the question, but he was pleasantly surprised by the woman asking it. He turned to see an attractive ground attendant standing beside him at the line where the gate becomes the concourse. In the earliest morning light, her red hair was lustrous, and her green eyes sparkled. She looked professional but sexy in the blue skirt-suit and starched white shirt of the airline uniform.

He read her nametag. It said TIFFANY.

'I'm okay. Just trying to get my land legs.'

'So,' she said, 'what brings you to Florida?'

'Work,' he answered. 'Were you on this flight?'

She nodded. 'I worked the first-class cabin. I saw you through the curtain. You were the only one not sleeping.'

'Who can sleep when he has three flight attendants all to himself?'

'Three? There were only two in the rear cabin.'

Cobb shrugged. 'Math was never my strong suit.'

In reality, his math skills were fine. He was simply testing her. He hadn't noticed her on the flight, and he wanted to make sure that she had actually been on it.

She laughed and handed him a business card with her cell phone number written on it. 'Well, I'm stuck in town until tonight. If you're bored or need some help with your land legs, just give me a call. Maybe I can show you a thing or two.'

He took the card with a suspicious smile. It could be the layover loneliness that he knew all too well. Or it could be that his new employer had anticipated Cobb's rekky and had sent Tiffany to meet him at the gate. Although it wasn't likely, it was possible.

Mercenaries survived by considering everything.

'Thanks, Tiffany. Maybe I'll give you a shout.'

'Great,' she said. 'I hope you do.'

Cobb moved away, cursing his luck. It would have been nice to get to know her better. On any other day, at any other time, he would have. But due to his circumstances, he had other things to worry about, including miles of reconnaissance before he circled back to the gate where he was 'supposed' to land that afternoon.

In the next six hours, he had to eyeball all of the escape routes and avenues of attack at that terminal. He wanted to watch the limos as they arrived out front. He wanted to look for men or women who might be watching his gate.

His phone was programmed with facial recognition software that was linked to a database of domestic and foreign reps who hired American talent. To improve his odds of survival, it would help to know who hired him before he actually met the man.

*   *   *

Cobb was a shade over six feet tall. His hair was short and a lighter shade of brown, almost reddish in color. His handsome face was somewhere between triangular and oval. For some reason, people always told him that he looked like a racecar driver. He didn't know what that meant, but he was assured it was a compliment.

Of his features, what stood out the most were his eyes. They were gun-gray and piercing.

They were so distinct that he was forced to wear colored contact lenses on missions for fear of recognition. In Brooklyn, they had been blue. Today, they were hazel. Just to be safe, he wore aviator sunglasses to hide his eyes completely.

Cobb did a full circuit and saw nothing suspicious. So he planted himself on the periphery of Terminal 3, Concourse E to scope out the disembarking American Airlines passengers. No one there looked familiar or set off any mental alarms. If he was supposed to be seated next to a particular first-class passenger, no one caught his attention.

Furthermore, he didn't see Tiffany anywhere. He had been watching for her legs – since her red hair could have been a wig and the uniform could have been discarded – and listening for her voice. But she was nowhere to be found.

Eventually, he trailed the passengers from 'his' plane to

the baggage claim area. He stayed against the back wall, his eyes constantly moving as he tried to watch everyone. When the luggage conveyer clanked to life, he shifted his gaze toward the approaching travelers and spotted one person of interest. Not because he recognized her – he didn't at first – but because she was staring at him.

'I'll be damned,' he mumbled to himself.

Thanks to her disguise – complete with ponytail, headphones, oversized sunglasses, and a local college back-pack – Sarah Ellis looked like a demure, eighteen-year-old student, not the half-naked operative he had parted ways with in New York.

On the beach, she had been a fearless woman.

Here, she resembled a lost teenager.

The difference was truly remarkable.

Sarah nodded subtly toward the parking garage, then strolled in that direction. At no point did she turn around to see if Cobb was coming.

She knew he would be close behind.

After all, she was the one carrying the merchandise.

There was a saying among covert ops: *Who watches the watchers?*

The idea was to always assume that while you were observing an activity, your own tactics and techniques were under observation. Cobb had arrived several hours early in order to learn more about his new employer. Unfortunately, since he had spotted no one in the field, Cobb had to assume that *he* had been the one under the microscope.

In some ways, it made him feel foolish.

In other ways, it made him feel at ease.

It was safer to work with professionals.

Cobb's suspicion grew when he reached the parking garage and ran squarely into a white stretch limo that was just pulling up to the curb. Sarah was standing ten feet away, pretending to wait for a taxi while bopping her head to an imaginary tune. He knew there was no way she was listening to music at a time like this. Her sense of hearing was far too important to sacrifice in an employer meet-and-greet.

Or whatever the hell this was.

A muscle-bound chauffeur hustled around the back of the limo, and then opened the rear door for his boss. A few seconds later, a man in an expensive, custom-tailored suit stepped out. Made of light gray silk, the suit was accompanied by a light-yellow, open-necked shirt and handsome loafers. An expensive watch glistened in the harsh fluorescent lights of the parking garage. So did his pinkie ring.

The man smiled while sauntering forward. He had exquisitely styled gray hair and a perfectly landscaped mustache. He smelled of expensive cologne. Not the kind that peasants buy in stores, but the kind the über-wealthy have personally designed.

Cobb sensed the man was friendly, but he wasn't about to let down his defenses. The last week had left him with a lot of questions and a city full of enemies. He also knew the mission in New York was only the beginning.

'Mr Cobb,' said the man with the mustache. His French-accented voice was almost as smooth as the suit. 'I am Jean-Marc Papineau. It is a pleasure to finally meet you. I hope you had a pleasant early-morning flight from Las Vegas.'

Cobb nodded, but said nothing.

Papineau continued. 'At this point of our relationship, I am quite confident that personal safety is still your number one concern. However, due to the private nature of our business and the smoldering temperatures in this garage, may I recommend the air-conditioned comfort of my limousine?'

Cobb shook his head. 'Not until I frisk the guy inside.'

'Go frisk yourself!' said a gruff voice from the limo.

Cobb could only see the guy's legs, but he recognized the voice at once. He crouched and peeked into the car, fully expecting to see the beach bum he had left in Brooklyn.

He was shocked to see a clean-cut McNutt. Although his shoulder-length hair could still use a trim, McNutt was actually a good-looking guy – with stubble, high cheekbones, narrow blue eyes, a longer than usual nose, cleft chin, and a curving mouth.

Cobb nodded his approval. 'Glad to see you took a shower.'

McNutt smiled. 'Glad to see you're wearing pants.'

Papineau nodded. 'Yes, thank goodness for both.'

'You guys are idiots,' Sarah grumbled as she pushed past Papineau and climbed into the limo. 'In case you didn't know, the goal was to *not* be seen together in public. So quit chatting and get in the damn car before they charge us for an extra day of parking.'

Cobb and Papineau quickly joined her inside.

The limousine was sumptuously appointed, stocked with the best food and liquor Cobb had never consumed – from Dom Perignon to Iranian Karaburun Ossetra caviar. The 'snack' table separated the group into two pairs. Sarah and Papineau faced forward, while Cobb and McNutt sat with their backs to the chauffeur. The sound-proof partition was currently raised, keeping the group's conversation private.

That is, if they decided to talk.

The passengers were silent as the limo joined the afternoon traffic. The quiet lasted for several minutes as Sarah checked her e-mail, McNutt took a short nap, and Papineau regarded Cobb, who was staring out the smoky glass window at the tropical landscape.

Papineau had heard wonderful things about Cobb and his ability to pull off miracles in the field. To find out if this was true, he had given Cobb a next-to-impossible mission, a ridiculously short timeframe, and a ragtag group of specialists brought together specifically for their unique skills. Then he watched in amazement as Cobb figured out a way to make it work with people he had never dealt with before.

'So,' Papineau said to break the ice, 'I'm sure you're wondering why I invited you to Florida instead of paying for the item in New York.'

'Not really,' Cobb said. 'I assume you brought us here to officially team us up and ship us out-of-country for something even bigger.'

The Frenchman smiled. 'The team-up was obvious. Why do you assume the rest?'

'Why? Because we're in Fort Lauderdale, the Venice of America, a city known for its extensive system of canals. The location gives you quick access to international waters, but keeps you away from the drug cartels in Miami. Based on your car and clothes, I know you have money to burn, which means you probably took advantage of the real estate collapse and bought yourself a nice estate – or three – near the beach. Not because you like playing in the sand, but because you need water access for, um, *business*.'

Papineau stared at him. 'And what *business* do you think that is?'

'I'd hate to be presumptuous. That would be rude.'

'Indeed.'

An uncomfortable silence filled the limo for the next several seconds as Sarah and McNutt waited to see Papineau's reaction to Cobb's analysis. Although they had spoken to him on the phone, this was the first time any of them had met Papineau, so they were anxious to see what kind of man had hired them. Was he a vicious tyrant like Vladimir Kozlov, or was he a tough-but-fair leader like Cobb himself?

Papineau continued to stare. 'I see you've given this a lot of thought.'

'More than a little, less than a lot.'

'And what conclusions have you reached?'

'No conclusions. Just observations.'

'Don't undervalue observations, Major. I learned quite a bit about you by observing you from afar. Not only did I tap into the FBI feed in New York, but I also watched you conduct countersurveillance in the airport. I didn't want to miss a thing.'

Cobb smiled. He had been right all along.

Whoever watches the watchers was the key to everything.

He reached for the crackers, which looked like saltines but were probably baked in tandoor ovens in India somewhere. He hadn't eaten all day. Hunger kept him alert, but he needed sustenance to keep up his strength. 'Do me a favor. Don't call me "Major". It's a bad habit to get into. You might slip up, do it around secret police in a foreign land, and earn us a set of eyes we don't want.'

Papineau nodded. 'Good to know.'

'That is, if I decide to work for you.'

'You're already on the payroll.'

'I am?'

'You *are*,' he assured him. 'Unless, of course, you're here to let me know that you don't wish to be paid for services rendered. Is that why you're here, Mr Cobb? To refuse my money?'

'No,' Cobb admitted, 'I'm here to learn more about your plans for us. Once I know the details, I'll let you know whether I intend to work for you ever again.'

Papineau smiled. He loved Cobb's experience, intelligence, and directness. He had everything he was looking for and more. 'Trust me, Mr Cobb. Once you hear my offer, I am quite certain that you and your team will sign on for more. Offers like these are rare indeed.'

Cobb studied his face. 'Then why wait? Why not tell us now?'

'Why?' the Frenchman teased with a devilish smile. 'Because you still have to meet the rest of your team.'

I 2

The limo slowed and turned off the scenic highway, leaving the paved road for a dirt path that had been cut through the overgrown marshes. McNutt saw WARNING and NO TRESPASSING signs as they drove toward a twenty-foot-tall gate in the middle of the jungle. It reminded him of the entrance to Jurassic Park.

'Hey, Papi!' McNutt said as he put his nose against the window. '*Please* tell me you have dinosaurs. I want to play with some.'

In this part of the country, 'Papi' (which sounds like *pa-pee*) is a slang term that literally means 'father', but can also mean 'boyfriend', 'big daddy', or many other things. McNutt intended no disrespect by using it. He liked it simply because it was easier for him to say than his other options.

Papineau shook his head in frustration. 'Joshua, in the future, please address me as Mr Papineau or Jean-Marc. *Not* Papi. *Never* Papi.'

'Sorry,' McNutt mumbled, 'I prefer Papi.'

Cobb tried not to smile. He prayed that McNutt's childishness was just an act. Otherwise, there was a decent chance that he was mentally challenged. Nevertheless, he did his best to protect McNutt by quickly changing the subject. 'Despite the size of your fence, I'm assuming you have other security measures in place. Or do you actually use raptors?'

Papineau shook his head. 'There is electrified mesh netting comprised of twenty-eight AWG, heavy poly nylon one-five-five magnet wire behind the fence, reaching to the base of the marsh. It encircles the entire six-acre property within the reeds.'

Then he added, 'It cannot be cut.'

'There is nothing that cannot be cut,' Sarah said.

'That may be true – if you're willing to accept several fatalities en route to that goal.'

'So, is the high voltage to keep people in or out?' Sarah asked.

'Objects in, people out,' he answered vaguely.

The chauffeur touched the right-side frame of his sunglasses. Then he pressed an eight-button combination on another remote control. The gate swung in slowly.

'The combination changes every hour,' Papineau bragged. 'It is beamed from security central to a heads-up display in his eyewear. Very high-tech.'

A cobblestone road greeted them on the other side of the fence. The car continued along an extended, stretched-out 'S' curve until the flat top of a single-story ranch house could be seen. It was surrounded, as far as they could see, by an artificial inlet.

'Damn,' McNutt said. 'Not what I was expecting.'

Cobb saw his point. The unassuming structure was made of concrete block stucco with a tile roof. He guessed it to be about four thousand square feet. On the surface, it

74

appeared no different from the other homes they'd passed on the highway – which was the point. There was a practical side, too. A low house would be better equipped to handle the ubiquitous Florida storms – and easier to armor, since impact-resistance diminished exponentially the higher from base a wall reached. If the grounds were electrified and the windows were bulletproof, he had a hunch the walls would be designed to withstand a rocket-propelled grenade, at the very least.

Cobb noticed a wellhead in a patch of land; that meant the place maintained its own water supply. He also saw an Echelon-class Signals Intelligence (or SIGINT) satellite dish. Except for a slight size differential – it was about twenty percent larger than a standard home dish – no one would know it was the same kind used by the military for highly secure SIGINT transmissions.

As they rounded the driveway in front of the house, Cobb saw that they not only had a moat but also their own canal and marina.

The chauffeur parked outside a four-car garage, then hustled around the limo and opened the door. Papineau, their host, took the lead in exiting the vehicle. He helped Sarah from the car, then turned his back on Cobb and McNutt. Cobb was impressed by his actions. The first was a show of chivalry; the second was a show of trust.

So was bringing them to his home.

'Welcome to La Trésorerie, my friends,' Papineau said as he opened the heavy, crystal-inlaid, carved wood door. The latch had popped open an instant before he grasped the handle thanks to facial recognition software in the surveillance camera.

It had happened so smoothly only Cobb had noticed.

'How much French do you know?' McNutt whispered to Sarah.

'It means "Treasure-House",' she said.

'Oh,' McNutt grunted – as his eyes drifted obliviously past a Van Gogh hanging just inside the doorway while searching for dinosaurs lurking within.

The small foyer door opened onto a magnificent living room of columns, elaborate chandeliers in recessed sections of high ceilings, semi-spiral staircases, hardwood and marble floors partially covered by obviously exotic rugs, built-in bookcases, and heavy, inviting furniture. It was too much for any of them to take in with a single glance.

'Feel free to explore,' Papineau said.

Cobb glanced at Sarah. 'But *only* to explore.'

'I'm an acquisitions expert, not a thief,' she protested.

'Interesting distinction,' McNutt said.

She wandered off, ignoring him.

The three newcomers each studied a different section of what Cobb now realized was actually three separate rooms: a living room, library, and parlor. That accounted for about three-quarters of the square footage. Except for a rectangular section housing a fireplace, the first floor of the home was mostly living space.

Sarah looked around the fireplace at an impressive dining area, but that's as far as she got. Her attention was drawn to a huge picture window that doubled as one full wall of the dining area. She gasped involuntarily at the sight of a magnificent terrace interspersed with interlocking swimming pools, sculptures, and palm trees.

The men joined her there. Their eyes were immediately drawn to the luxurious lounge chairs facing the pool. Cobb zeroed in on the one with the young man. He quickly deduced who he was. Meanwhile, McNutt studied the one with the young woman. She was wearing a one-piece, blue, clip-back bathing suit with white piping.

'Now this is a balcony to do Shakespeare from,' Sarah remarked.

McNutt grinned. 'I couldn't agree more – if *her* name is Shakespeare.'

Papineau swept by them and slid open a large section of the glass wall. It led directly to the deck. 'After you.'

The trio wandered out, dwarfed by the blue sky and the overpowering sight and sound of the ocean. Alerted by the whoosh of the door, the occupants of the terrace rose. The young man was the shorter of the two – probably five-six, with spiky, dark brown hair and medium brown skin. He wore sandals, cargo shorts, and a T-shirt that had a Wi-Fi symbol. Fifteen or twenty years ago Cobb might have labeled him a nerd, but he was the sleeker, more recent model, with a trim waist and well-exercised arms.

Still wet from a recent swim, the young woman was spectacular. By the sleek shade of her black hair and the deep brown of her almond-shaped eyes, Cobb knew she was Eastern. However, her height – she was at least five-foot-seven

– and her generous curves made him think that part of her genetic make-up was Western.

'My friends,' Papineau announced as he turned to the loungers, 'I'd like to formally introduce Hector Garcia – who helped you in New York – and Jasmine Park.' He glanced back at the trio. 'This is Sarah Ellis, Josh McNutt, and Jack Cobb.'

The six of them said hello for a few seconds. Then they just stood there, looking from one to the next. Eventually, everyone was staring expectantly at Papineau.

He smiled warmly. 'Would anyone care for refreshments?'

13

The group relocated to the home's expansive gourmet kitchen, which sprawled beyond the dining area by way of a wide counter. Once the newcomers discovered that Papineau had no kitchen staff, each made his and her own exploration.

Garcia went right to the old-fashioned cast-iron stove, grabbed a skillet, and declared his intention to make his famous breakfast burritos. Jasmine, who had tied a blue wrap dress around her, was at the sink cutting up melons. McNutt had his head in the gigantic, silver fridge, pulling out luncheon meats – freshly sliced, not packaged – while Sarah squeezed oranges for juice.

Coffee had already been made, and Cobb poured some, black. Then, standing by a butcher's block at the far end of the counter, he set out a variety of breads he cut from a selection of fresh-baked loaves. It was a perfect vantage point from which to watch the others, in particular the one he had never worked with.

For one reason or another, Jasmine puzzled him. She did not have the kind of muscle tone that suggested anything more than low-impact workouts: health and vanity workouts, he called them. Her knife skills, at least on a melon, seemed ordinary. She had been reading from an e-reader on the terrace, but she had turned it off before he could see what was on it. He knew he could just go over and ask her questions, but where was the fun in that?

He preferred to figure it out on his own.

Jasmine pulled some wicker trays from a cabinet beside the sink. She set them on the granite tabletop – not avoiding eye contact with anyone but not going out of her way to make it, either. She seemed oblivious to McNutt's wide-eyed admiration.

No doubt she got that a lot.

Their host, who had disappeared for about five minutes, returned. He stood at the edge of the kitchen and stated, 'If everyone will please take their refreshments into the dining room, I would like to make this a working lunch.'

* * *

Dark clouds had rolled in and the daily Florida summer rainstorm was in full swing by the time the group got to the long dining room. Papineau stood at the head of the large table, waiting for each to take a seat.

Garcia sat with his back to the sea, closest to their host. Jasmine put a plate of sliced fruit on the table, selected some, and sat opposite Garcia. That made it easier for McNutt, who sat next to her with a self-conscious laugh. Sarah sat opposite.

Cobb took a seat at the end of the table, opposite their host. He put the platter of sandwiches there, and checked his cell phone in his lap while he waited.

'You are aware by now that each of you has been recruited and tested,' Papineau said. 'This was done so that I might offer you the opportunity to become part of a unique mission – one that, if successfully completed, will shower you in riches.'

Papineau let that sink in, and the reaction was gratifying. McNutt smiled crookedly. Sarah grinned with anticipation. Garcia's eyes sparkled. Jasmine was reflective. Cobb just watched the others and could see all their minds racing.

Papineau continued. 'Jasmine Park is fluent in many languages, with an exhaustive knowledge of ancient cultures and world religions. She is our historian.'

'What did you test her with? A pop quiz?' McNutt asked.

'No,' Papineau said. 'Jasmine? Would you care to share?'

The young woman looked at the others. 'I work at the *Korean Daily News* in Orlando. Yesterday my editor asked me to investigate a document that had been sent to the FBI. He's got a friend in the Bureau who sometimes gives him leads, and in exchange we've held certain stories or disseminated information in ways that can help investigations. His friend explained that it was supposedly a ransom note associated with two young girls who had recently been kidnapped, but they couldn't make head or tail of the language used. He knew I had a knack for that sort of thing and thought I might be able to help.'

Garcia wrinkled his brow. 'He asked you to translate? Why didn't they use computers? Just scan it in and *presto!* The program spits out the translation.'

'No,' Jasmine assured him. 'A computer translation wouldn't have worked. The document was written in five distinctly different languages. Not colloquial slang or dialects, but languages that grew from entirely separate roots. What's more, their syntaxes were blended.'

'I don't follow,' McNutt said.

'The conjugations and grammatical structure were a combination of the various languages represented. Greek words were rearranged into Gaelic formations. Sometimes the sentences themselves were inconsistent. Phrases that began in Italian ended in Swedish. It even included defunct language concepts that have long since been lost to cultural evolution.'

'Like Middle English?' Sarah asked.

'No, like ancient *Andorran*,' Jasmine replied. 'Middle English is easy. Anyone who's ever studied Chaucer has dealt with that. But some of the words in the document were taken from languages that were only briefly spoken in their prime. Today, they have been absorbed into neighboring languages or discontinued altogether. No one studies them, because understanding them doesn't provide any more information than understanding the languages they became. The history of these places has been passed down in much more accessible documentation.'

Jasmine caught herself. She could go on with the explanation, but she doubted that the others shared her fervor.

'No one studies them, but you do?' Cobb asked. His tone stressed curiosity, not ridicule.

Jasmine shrugged. 'What can I say? I like history, and words, and the history of words.'

'Fair enough,' Cobb replied. 'So, what did the document say?'

Jasmine's eyes lit up. 'It revealed the supposed hiding

place of the girls. When I offered my translation to my editor, I insisted that he introduce me to his connection, in case there were follow-up questions that needed immediate answers. At the time, I thought two young lives hung in the balance, so he arranged a meeting.'

Every eye in the room turned toward Papineau.

He met their collective gaze with a guilty smirk.

Sarah glanced back at Jasmine. 'You played right into his hands.'

'My driver transported Ms Park to this location,' Papineau explained. Before Cobb could challenge his statement, Papineau anticipated his question. 'No, Jack, her editor has no idea concerning our whereabouts. His instructions were handed down from his superiors, namely, the newspaper's board of directors.'

'Namely, *you*,' Cobb surmised.

Papineau smiled.

'You control a newspaper?' McNutt asked.

'I control several newspapers,' Papineau answered. 'Among other things.' He turned to address Cobb. 'If her editor is questioned, he is simply to respond that Jasmine is "on assignment".'

'Must be nice to control the flow of information and have it reported to you before it's ever made public,' Cobb said.

'Quite,' Papineau replied.

Cobb and Papineau stared at one another, each trying to better understand the man across the table. The moment lingered a little too long.

To break the tension, McNutt pointed at Garcia's shirt. Outside in the sunlight, it had appeared to be a normal T-shirt with an ironed-on Wi-Fi symbol. But now that they were indoors, McNutt realized that the decal was actually animated.

'What's up with your shirt?' he demanded.

Garcia glanced down at the symbol. At that moment, it was glowing green. 'My shirt is actually a battery-powered Wi-Fi detector. Depending on the signal strength, the number of bars that are glowing on my chest will fluctuate between one and four. Obviously, the more bars, the better.'

'*Obviously!*' McNutt said with fake enthusiasm.

Too bad Garcia didn't have a sarcasm detector because it would have been beeping like crazy. Instead, he smiled with pride. 'I bet you've never seen anything like it.'

'Actually,' McNutt teased, 'I have something very similar in my shorts. Anytime I get horny, my sensor rises into position. Obviously, the longer, the better.'

Garcia quickly deflated. 'Not funny, dude.'

'And unlike your shirt, my sensor will actually help me get laid.'

14

Papineau sensed that Garcia might need an ego boost after the verbal thrashing he had received from McNutt, so he took a moment to praise him.

'Most of you know bits and pieces about each other's pasts, but in order to get Jasmine up to speed as quickly as possible, I thought it might be best if we spent a moment to discuss your backgrounds.' He pointed at the young Hispanic. 'Let's start with Hector.'

'Let's not,' McNutt grumbled.

'Hector Garcia,' Papineau announced, 'is a self-taught, top-level computer genius with a photographic memory. His IQ is off the charts. He had been employed by the FBI in Miami, but once he realized how little government employees make, he decided to forgo his pension for an opportunity to make some real money in the private sector.'

Papineau paused for acknowledgements of Garcia's abilities.

There were none.

That is, until Cobb felt sorry for him.

'Thanks to Hector,' Cobb said, 'we don't have to worry about any blowback from the Brooklyn job. Before he quit the Bureau, he created a backdoor in their computer systems, which means he can tap into their files anytime we need him to. Over the past few days, I've had him search their databases for any references to us. So far, all they have are vague descriptions from eyewitness testimonies.'

'They would have turned up more,' Hector assured them, 'but I intercepted all of the live feeds from their surveillance van and cleaned them before I sent them on.'

'Define *clean*,' Sarah said.

Hector smiled. 'I erased every file – audio and video – that featured you, Jack, or Josh. It's like you were never there.'

'Never where?' Jasmine asked.

'Our tryout,' Cobb answered as vaguely as possible. 'You had a pop quiz, and we had some homework.'

'And by homework,' McNutt bragged, 'he means we actually invaded a home. You should have seen it: there were bombs, and guns, and swimwear. It was great.'

'Wow,' Jasmine gasped as she took a deep breath to calm down. The tension in her face and the anxiety in her eyes told Cobb a lot about her state of mind. Until that moment, she didn't have a full understanding of the risks involved. Now she did.

'Sarah Ellis,' Papineau said, moving the conversation forward. 'She is former CIA – a prodigy in her field, I might add – who is an expert in security systems and border crossings. She is our worldwide ambassador.'

McNutt picked up from there. 'Her interests include hang-gliding, fighting giants, and skintight catsuits, but whatever you do, *don't* call her a thief.'

'Why not?' Jasmine wondered.

'Because she'll kick you in the nuts.'

'But I don't have nuts.'

'Then you can probably get away with it.'

Sarah stared at Jasmine from across the table. The intensity of her glare said it all. *If you* call me 'thief', *I'll come up with something even worse.*

'Moving on,' Papineau said. 'Josh McNutt was a decorated Marine sniper – at least until they threw him out. Where armaments are concerned, he is as experienced as they come. He is our weapons and security expert.'

Sarah shifted her gaze to him. 'Why'd they throw you out?'

McNutt grinned. 'I ran the table at a shooting gallery in a carnival. I wanted to win a stuffed bear for a little girl. When the proprietor objected, I objected back with the gun.'

'You shot at the guy?' Jasmine asked.

McNutt shrugged. 'Don't worry: it wasn't a *real* guy. It was a carnie. Bullets can't kill carnies. Nothing can. They're like cockroaches.'

Papineau rolled his eyes and continued. 'And finally, allow me to formally introduce you to Jackson Cobb, Junior – son of Brigadier General Jackson Cobb, Senior. Our Jack began his career as a member of the Army's one hundred and sixtieth Special Operations Aviation Regiment—'

'The Night Stalkers,' McNutt elaborated.

'– much to the reported displeasure of his father, who wanted him to join the Marines. In fact, once the Marines finalized their Special Operations Regiment in 2007, General Cobb used his far-reaching influence, both personally and professionally, to see that his son took a commanding post in the unit.'

'You name it, they can do it,' McNutt said with admiration.

Papineau elaborated. 'According to my sources, Major Cobb had an exemplary career in many bases of operation. He is one of the finest leaders the US military has produced in the last few decades. Exceptional at empty-handed combat, extremely well regarded amongst international authorities, he is our . . . hmmm? What would you call yourself, Jack?'

Papineau already knew the answer to his question. He meant to put Cobb – the obvious leader of the group – on the spot.

Cobb shrugged. 'I would call myself the fifth member of this team.'

McNutt laughed. 'Don't let his modesty fool you. The SEALs begged the Marines to loan him out for a couple of missions. So did the MANIACs. And if *they* wanted to work with him, you know he's the best of the best.'

Sarah eyed Cobb with a new level of respect – and curiosity. *Why was someone like him sitting in a room with them?*

She pulled no punches. 'Sorry to be nosy, Major Cobb, but what did you do to fuck up such a perfect life? Did you shoot a carnie, too?'

'Something like that,' Cobb said as he turned his attention to the tropical landscape outside of the dining room window.

Sarah smelled weakness and pounced. 'That's it? That's

all you're going to give us? You teased me all week about my checkered past, now you're unwilling to tell us what you did to end up here? What kind of bullshit is that?'

Cobb remained silent.

He knew Papineau would fill in the blanks for her.

'Jack was court-martialed,' Papineau explained. 'For "offenses against the uniform code of military justice". Articles eighty-seven, eighty-eight, and ninety-nine, I believe.'

Sarah frowned. 'Sorry, I don't speak military. What did he actually do?'

'I really wish you'd shut up,' Cobb said quietly.

Papineau ignored him. 'The thing about Jack Cobb, according to the court-martial transcript, is that when he was assigned a mission, he finished the mission, even when the senior brass changed their minds. In this case, they wanted to spare a terrorist to use as a political pawn. A knife, concealed in Cobb's palm, disagreed.'

'What kind of blade?' McNutt asked.

'Enough,' Cobb said louder.

Papineau continued. 'Suffice it to say, Monsieur Cobb got off fairly lucky considering what they could have charged him with. He received a dishonorable discharge with no prison time. I'm guessing his father had something to say about that as well.'

'I said, *enough*!' Cobb glared at Papineau. He had no idea what the Frenchman was trying to achieve, but the bastard had gone too far. It was one thing to highlight his résumé for the team; it was quite another to reveal classified details of his court-martial.

Sarah patted his shoulder, trying to calm him. 'Relax, Jack. You did what you thought was right. I see nothing wrong with that.'

'Me neither,' McNutt agreed.

'Nor do I,' Papineau said in a tone that was tough to read. 'I apologize if I brought up an incident that you would rather not talk about, but as I said early on, I think it's important to clear the air before we proceed any further.'

Cobb continued to glare. 'I couldn't agree more, Papi. With that in mind, why don't you tell us about your past? Specifically, how did you acquire your money?'

Papineau forced a smile. He didn't like being on this side of the spotlight. 'I made my fortune in a variety of businesses too numerous to recount.'

'Name one,' Cobb demanded.

'Pardon?'

'One business in which you invested. Something Hector can check.'

Garcia glanced at Papineau. 'Yeah. That would be nice. Your name doesn't show up anywhere I've looked.'

'I noticed,' Cobb said, holding up his phone and wiggling it.

The Frenchman explained. 'My background is very private, and my investments are deep and diverse. Energy, banking, entertainment – anything that is profitable and challenging.'

'Enron? Pyramid schemes? Porn?' Sarah pressed.

'I have money managers who handle that. I do not become directly involved.'

Cobb leaned forward. 'Except here.'

Papineau nodded. 'Except here.'

Cobb was willing to bet the man wouldn't know an annual report from a yearbook, and he was confident that 'Papineau' wasn't his real name, either.

But that was a mystery for a later day.

15

Papineau sensed the troops were getting restless. He knew he needed to grab their attention before they turned against him completely. He raised his finger to his lips, asking for silence.

'Thank you,' he said politely. 'Now that we know a little more about each other's accomplishments, I think it's time that we get to the purpose of this gathering.'

'It's about time,' McNutt grumbled.

Papineau chose to ignore him. 'As I entered the dawn of my twilight years, I became intent on finding a way to leave my mark in history. Initially, I had no intention of focusing on the subject of history itself, but after giving it some thought, I decided to use the mysteries of the past as a starting point. To achieve what I had in mind, I understood the error of simply hiring the top experts in a variety of historical fields. Rather, I wanted to assemble the best team possible: a group that would combine to form the ultimate squad of hunters, whose talents were specifically tailored to meet my goals. I spent months searching for each of you, and several weeks more finding the proper way to test you all.'

Sarah frowned. 'What was your criterion?'

'I used a test called SAR, which stands for Stress-Action

Ratio. It was developed by NASA when they first began recruiting men to fly into space. The examiner took something that people claimed to be an expert in and tested that skill under pressure. Either the pilots succeeded in overriding a malfunctioning space capsule system – or they perished. Even with that initial test, at least one of the original seven astronauts appears to have cracked under pressure on a mission. So NASA instituted double-jeopardy examinations unimaginatively called SAR-B. The systems fail *and* the lights go out, or some combination of troubles.'

Cobb wasn't buying it, not entirely. NASA's half-century-old winnowing process was not part of any modern curriculum he had heard of, but Cobb was willing to play along for now. 'Which explains our homework assignment in New York. You wanted to see how we would handle ourselves in a life-or-death situation.'

'Something like that,' he admitted.

Sarah's cheeks flushed with anger. 'You mean I risked my life for nothing? You were simply testing me?'

'No, my dear, it was more than a test. The document that I asked you to retrieve is actually an important part of your main mission. Furthermore, I am prepared to pay you significant amounts of money for your time. Naturally, my entire estate is at your disposal in terms of equipment and materials. Anything you need, ask. Here, you answer only to me. When you're in the field, to your team leader.'

All of the eyes in the room shifted toward Cobb.

'Excuse me,' Jasmine said, 'but will we be asked to do anything illegal?'

'Yes,' Papineau said. 'In fact, almost everything. Is that a problem?'

'It might be,' she said.

'You send half of your weekly take-home pay to your parents in Seoul,' he said. 'It would take you decades to send them what you can earn here in a few months. Is it still a problem?'

'Some of us have been in prison,' McNutt said. 'It's not fun – unless, of course, you enjoy rape.'

'Fortunately we function under the Marine praxis that no member is left behind. That includes being kept in a prison, anywhere. Illegality is only a moral limitation for us, not a physical one.'

'What about killing?' McNutt asked.

'Hopefully that will not be necessary,' Papineau said.

'But you wouldn't have hired him otherwise,' Sarah said.

Papineau's silence was confirmation enough.

'How much is this "significant amount" you referred to?' McNutt asked.

'Five million dollars to each of you,' he replied. 'Cash, wire transfer, bank check, gold – however you want it.'

He had them. Cobb knew it and so did the Frenchman.

'Anyway, that's all I have to say,' Papineau said. 'Are there any questions?'

McNutt raised his hand. 'What's a praxis?'

'A practice,' Jasmine said.

'Ah. Thanks.'

Papineau took some of the breakfast burrito Garcia had

made, some of the fruit Jasmine had cut, a half of a sandwich Cobb and McNutt had made, and a little of the juice Sarah had squeezed. The man was nothing if not diplomatic.

'Do any of you need time to think over your involvement?' the Frenchman asked. 'We're on somewhat of a tight schedule.'

Jasmine surprised everyone by being the first to speak. 'I'm in.'

She looked at Hector, who said, 'Yeah. Yeah, I'm in, too.' He looked at McNutt diagonally across from him.

'Are you kidding? I wouldn't miss this for all the tits at Hooters,' McNutt exclaimed.

The momentum stopped there. Papineau stared at Sarah.

'Ms Ellis?'

She looked to where her forefinger was making a little circle on the table next to her drink. 'Well, since you went to so much trouble to bring me here . . . why the hell not?'

Papineau smiled and turned his attention to Cobb. 'And what about you?'

Cobb glanced around the table. 'Before I make a decision, I'd like to mention the one thing that Papi has not yet shared. This is not his home, it's a training facility.'

'For what?' McNutt asked. 'Being rich?'

Papineau returned Cobb's stare. 'You're referring to the air vents?'

'Among other things.'

'Someone want to catch us up?' Sarah asked.

'Mr Cobb looked for and spotted the air duct that—'

'Two air ducts,' Cobb interrupted. 'There's one at basement level in the front, hidden by the landscaping, another about ten feet lower on the beach.'

Papineau made a face. 'That's a big assumption. A vent down there would be flooded during high tide.'

'Hence the out-of-place sea wall,' Cobb said. 'There's nothing else it could be shielding.'

Papineau nodded appreciatively. 'Yes, there are two air ducts.'

Cobb smiled. 'Care to show us the rest of the facility?'

'Now that we have gotten to know each other a little, let us have a look at what Mr Cobb alluded to. I'm sure you'll be impressed by what I have below.'

Papineau led the team downstairs past an indoor swimming pool. Through double doors they glimpsed a pier angling out into the sea and a motor yacht, four levels high and roughly sixty-five feet. Lights were on fore and aft, revealing a white hull and the inscription TRÉSOR DE LA MER painted on its stern.

'Treasure in the Sea?' McNutt attempted.

'Treasure of the Sea,' Jasmine corrected.

'Damn. I was close. If I stick by you, I may get an education.'

'You need one,' Sarah teased.

The group followed Papineau down another flight of stairs to a sub-basement, toward a door heavy enough for a bunker.

'This is modeled after the design of the White House situation room,' Papineau said.

'How do you know?' McNutt asked.

Papineau grinned. 'I stole the plans.'

16

On the other side of the door was a luxurious conference room, climate-controlled to museum-level perfection and decorated with fine art, gold and silver trappings, and expensive carpets. To Cobb, the décor looked out of place – even for a man like Papineau. Cobb immediately looked beyond the distractions, searching for the telltale edges of a vault or signs of whatever else Papineau was trying to conceal. After almost a minute, he still hadn't found what he was looking for; it was hidden even to his trained glance.

Cobb intentionally caught the Frenchman's eye so Papineau would know exactly what he'd been doing. He wanted to make it clear to Papineau that he understood the situation. Papineau, in turn, seemed pleased that his secret had stumped Cobb . . . at least for the time being.

The focus of the room was a large video screen – a nautical chart – that completely covered the far wall, facing long couches and amply padded easy chairs. The room had the same showroom quality Cobb had found strange in the upper rooms: a 'just removed the plastic' feeling – even, somehow, the gourmet food they had found in the kitchen.

Everyone took up positions in front of the nautical map. Papineau pressed a button on a remote control. The lights dimmed, and the sea map vanished, revealing a land map of Eastern Europe, circa 1914. The map slowly zoomed on a shape that was colored yellow.

Papineau stared at the group. 'Romania is located at the crossroads of Central and Southwestern Europe, on the lower Danube River.' He turned and aimed a laser pointer at the map wall, and a red dot appeared. 'Ukraine to the northeast, Austria–Hungary to the west, Serbia to the southwest, and Bulgaria to the south. Its capital city is Bucharest, currently the sixth largest city in the EU.'

'Population?' Cobb asked.

'Romania or Bucharest?'

Cobb smiled. 'Go for broke. Both.'

'Now or in 1914?'

'Your choice.'

Staring at his phone, Garcia answered for him. 'Modern-day Romania has approximately twenty-two million people. Bucharest, around two million.'

'Thanks,' Cobb said, with a sidelong glance at Garcia. His curiosity was satisfied. Papineau was not immersed in whatever they were about to do. He knew only what he needed to know.

'Ms Park, perhaps you can fill in the blanks before World War One,' Papineau said.

That suggestion straightened her posture and brightened her eyes. 'Confederated in 1859, it adopted one of the most advanced constitutions of its time in 1866,' she said in a clear, concise voice. 'This allowed for the modernization of the country outside the previous dependence on the Ottoman

Empire. The Ottoman Empire, of course, was one of the largest and longest empires in history, lasting from 1299 until 1923, and at its height stretched from southeast Europe to North Africa to western Asia—'

'Stay in country,' Papineau suggested.

She adjusted without hesitation. 'Romania declared its independence from the Ottoman Empire in 1877. It was internationally recognized in 1878 and proclaimed the Kingdom of Romania in 1881. Under the reign of King Carol the First – who was named ruling prince in 1866 – the country enjoyed an era of relative stability and prosperity—'

'With the king, of course, being the most prosperous,' Papineau interjected.

'– he ruled for forty-eight years, the longest rule by an individual that Romania has ever known.'

'Then came the First World War,' Papineau prompted.

'Yes,' Jasmine said. 'King Carol the First was German-born, so he wanted to side with his homeland, which was in league with Austria–Hungary and Italy. The Romanian people, however, wanted to ally with England, France, and Russia. Unbeknownst to anyone, the king had already signed a pact with the German-led Triple Alliance in 1883.'

She paused to make sure everyone was keeping up with her. They were.

'There was an emergency meeting with his court and cabinet,' she said without inflection. 'There was a strong disagreement between the king and his people. His death on September twenty-seventh, 1914, at the age of seventy-five, was blamed on the stress of this break with his subjects.'

'Very good, thank you,' Papineau said. 'I'll take it from there.'

He turned from Jasmine to address the entire group. 'Romania delayed its decision to enter the war until 1916. They had other, more pressing concerns.'

The Frenchman turned back to the map and pressed the remote control. Images of gold coins, bars, bricks, armor, decorations, accessories, jewelry, dishes, tableware, and even furniture danced before their eyes. 'The new leaders quickly grasped that whether the Germans invaded or were invited in, the nation's treasures were in danger of being seized. Thus, the ad hoc administration made the difficult decision to send it out of their country for safekeeping in a series of rail shipments.'

The image changed to a map of Eastern Europe. An animated arrow grew out of Romania's top right corner, passing through the countries to the northeast and ending some fifteen hundred miles away.

McNutt groaned at the sight.

'We are interested in one of those treasure trains,' Papineau continued. 'One in which almost a hundred tons of gold and jewels were sent away.'

Sarah's eyes lit up in thought. 'In modern terms, how much loot?'

Papineau smiled. 'Billions.'

17

Cobb stared at the map. According to the animation, the treasure had been taken from Romania to Russia. Amongst the vast quantity of details he had learned about the Soviets during his years in the service, three things about Mother Russia had always stuck with him: *it had eight time zones, widespread poverty, and a pervasive black market.*

Cobb was excited, but he was not pleased.

Jasmine continued her history lesson. 'Germany controlled Central Europe, so the Romanians saw no safe way of getting the gold to where they wanted to send it – the United States or the United Kingdom. They considered Denmark and Sweden next, but German submarines ruled the North Sea.'

'Those Germans really knew how to wage war, huh?' McNutt interjected.

'Only to a point,' Papineau said, with a flourish of French pride.

'So the Romanians felt that there was no other choice,' Jasmine said. 'They made a treaty with tsarist Russia. The White Army would safeguard the treasure until after the war.'

'And then – oops! – they lost it,' Sarah said.

'You're getting ahead of us,' Papineau said. 'Jasmine, tell them more about the players involved.'

'On December the eleventh, 1916, General Mossoloff extended a written guarantee promising the safety of the Romanian National Treasure. He had this authority as the Chargé d'Affaires of Russia in Romania – basically, he gave the final opinion on all Russian matters in Romania. Three days later Mossoloff and Ion Antonescu, the Finance Minister of Romania, signed what is known as the Romanian–Russian Protocol. That guaranteed, in great detail, the transport, safekeeping, and return of the treasure. Before the ink of their signatures was dry, Russia took possession – temporarily, the Romanians believed – of seventeen rail cars of Romanian gold. There were over fifteen hundred crates containing over one hundred tons. Worth roughly three hundred million dollars at the time, or upwards of five billion dollars in today's market.'

The recitation was met by silence. It wasn't the silence of the dumbstruck, but rather the mute inability of anyone in the room to fully process the amount in question.

'That wasn't all,' Jasmine continued. 'Also onboard the seventeen rail cars were crates containing Queen Maria's jewelry.'

'And that was just the first shipment?' Cobb asked.

Papineau nodded. 'Twenty-four additional train cars were sent in 1917. These transported more gold and money from vaults of the state's financial institutions, as well as cherished jewelry and other historical artifacts from state and private collections.'

'Jewelry?' Sarah asked.

Papineau nodded. 'Bronze Age jewelry from approximately

1500 BC; Dacian jewels, precious stones and gold mined from their lands before the formation of Romania; jewelry belonging to the Wallachian and Moldavian ruling class; and the Romanian royal jewels. Even at that time, it was worth one and a half billion dollars, give or take.'

'Take,' McNutt said. He winked at Sarah, who didn't respond.

'Excuse me, Mr Papineau,' Garcia said, his fingers flying on his phone. 'Could you be more specific? Specific sums are easier to trace backward than round figures.'

Papineau straightened. 'Various documents record the value as one billion, five hundred and ninety-four million, eight hundred and thirty-six thousand, seven hundred twenty-one.' The Frenchman waited until Garcia caught up. 'And nine cents.'

McNutt could only laugh, unable to fully comprehend that much wealth, even as thoughts of strippers and private jets danced in his head.

'Some consider this estimate to be on the low end,' Papineau continued. 'The *very* low end, as the value of much of the artwork and other personal items simply cannot be ascertained.'

'The very definition of "priceless",' Sarah offered.

'Indeed,' Papineau replied.

Garcia added, 'By the way, the newly created US Federal Reserve was given intelligence of the relocation on January twentieth of the following year.'

'Well done,' Papineau said.

Garcia glanced at him to see if he was being sincere. Confident that he was, Garcia looked down and tapped his phone screen again. 'The Fed references other intelligence reports. Get this. One of them was from a guy named William Friedman – a geneticist who studied cryptology at the Riverbank Laboratories Cipher Department.'

Cobb was familiar with the name. 'That's where it all started. The military's Signals Intelligence Service – the code-breaking division.'

'Correct,' Papineau said. 'Mr Garcia, do you have the Friedman report?'

'Yeah, and wow. Every dime – excuse me, every leu – and all the stocks and securities of the National Bank of Romania, as well as all deposits from the Romanian Savings and Loan, were sent on the later trains. That's all the wealth of the royal family, the government, and the people. It included documents from the Romanian National Archives, papers from the Historical Archives of Brasov, art belonging to museums and private collections, manuscripts and rare books from libraries and universities, and even the entire inventory of every Romanian pawn shop.'

'Did any sane human being think that treasure was ever coming back?' McNutt said.

Papineau held up his hand. 'In Moscow on August fifth, 1917, representatives of the Romanian and Russian governments signed a codicil to their agreement, authorizing the creation of a depository in the Kremlin to protect the Romanian treasure. There were two sets of keys needed to open the gigantic depository. One was held by the Romanian National Bank, the other by the Russian tsarist government.'

'Two-key systems are like marriages,' Jasmine explained. 'They only work if both parties remain civil. And in this case, they didn't. The Soviet government declared war on Romania less than a year later, January 1918, and announced that the Romanian treasure was no longer accessible to Romania. The decree was signed by Lenin himself.'

Sarah laughed. 'The Soviets were a real pain in the ass, weren't they?'

Papineau nodded. 'The French – who had fought valiantly alongside the Russians and the Romanians during World War One – tried to intercede on the Romanians' behalf. The Consul General of France took possession of the Romanian key in an effort to broker a deal. He went to Moscow to negotiate and was promptly arrested by Soviet authorities. They seized the Romanian key and didn't return it until 1926.'

Sarah smiled. 'In the meantime, let the looting begin.'

'Indeed,' Papineau said. 'The Soviet government immediately confiscated eight crates filled with more than a million dollars' worth of bank notes, claiming it was owed to them as compensation for their "good work". When peace between Moscow and Bucharest was fully restored in 1934, the USSR returned almost fifteen hundred crates—'

'Exact numbers please!' Garcia snapped.

'One thousand, four hundred and thirty-six crates,' the Frenchman informed him. 'Although they were replete with valuable documents, the crates contained nothing of monetary value.'

'The art?' Sarah asked.

'Returned in 1956,' Jasmine said.

'And the rest of it?' she asked. 'Surely the Romanians protested.'

'Vigorously and often,' Papineau said. 'Although nearly forty thousand—' he stopped, bowed slightly to Garcia, – 'thirty-nine thousand, three hundred and twenty artifacts were returned, actual monies received by Romania consisted of only thirty-three kilograms of gold and six hundred and ninety kilograms of silver.'

McNutt whistled. 'The Russian bear just stomped through that campsite, didn't it?'

Jasmine nodded. 'The Romanians have repeatedly tried to reopen negotiations for the return of the bulk of the treasure. Unfortunately, Brezhnev, Kosygin, and Andropov all refused to negotiate. They have even said because of Romania's debt that they owe Russia money.'

Papineau took over from there. 'No one outside an elite few in the Kremlin has had access to the vault or its treasure for decades. The best of the Romanian treasure – the parts that would be easiest to pawn or "fence", if you will – has already been looted, I am sure. I am aware that some of the items have been on the market over the years – though not publicly, of course. They are still stolen goods—'

'You mean jewels, paintings, rare books – most of the "priceless" things,' Sarah lamented.

'Exactly.'

'But not the gold,' Garcia stated, looking at his screen. 'Gold prices went up and up and up until 1931, and they only fell because the Brits abandoned the gold standard and speculators pounced on the outflow. There was no other influx of gold into the world market.'

Sarah nodded. 'Thieves wouldn't have bothered holding it for the best price. They would have melted it down and sold it right away.'

'Exactly,' Papineau said. 'The gold apparently has not, as of yet, been circulated.'

'Wait, wait, wait,' McNutt chimed in. 'Just wait a minute. Let me get this straight. You're not one hundred percent sure the gold's even there, but you want us to break in anyway? Into the goddamn Kremlin? The one in goddamn Russia?'

18

Cobb smiled, realizing that McNutt and the others had gotten ahead of Papineau's explanation. Had they let him finish, they would know what Cobb had already figured out.

'It's not in the Kremlin anymore,' Cobb announced.

'Just because you say it isn't?' Garcia challenged.

'No,' Cobb replied. 'Not because of what *I* say.' He nodded toward Jasmine. 'Because of what *she* said.'

Jasmine didn't know how to respond, but her look said it all: *Who, me?*

'Yes, you,' Cobb assured her. 'You said it just a moment ago. *They refused to negotiate.*'

'I don't follow,' McNutt admitted.

Papineau beamed across the table, pleased that Cobb had put the pieces together.

'They won't negotiate,' Cobb explained, 'because if they did, someone might find out that they don't have the treasure anymore.'

'How can you be so sure?' Sarah asked.

'Simple,' Cobb continued. 'They haven't told anyone where it is.'

'Chief,' McNutt said, 'I still don't—'

'It's the twenty-first century,' Cobb exclaimed. 'Simply locking the gold away in a depository doesn't mean anything in this era. There's no pleasure in just looking at it. The treasure does them no good stashed in a vault, *unless they declare it and use it as collateral*. If they can't draw against it, what good is it? And if they had taken out a loan against it, the whole world would have known by now. Ergo, they don't have it.'

Jasmine wasn't satisfied quite yet. 'Couldn't they simply be hoarding it in secret?'

'To what end?' Cobb replied. 'The only reason to keep it secret would be to privately negotiate its return with the Romanian government. But you already told us that they refuse to negotiate. So unless you can look me in the eye and honestly tell me that you think every Russian prime minister of the last century chose to perpetuate a ruse against Romania rather than bolster his crumbling economy, they simply don't have the gold.'

The room was silent again as everyone considered Cobb's statement. Papineau was contemplative too, but mostly about Cobb. He wondered how he had figured it out so quickly.

'So – we're not going to Russia?' McNutt said. 'I'm confused.'

Cobb ignored McNutt and turned toward Jasmine. 'Things were far from stable in Russia during World War One, right?'

'Yes. By any standard, it was basically chaos,' she replied. 'During the time when the Romanian treasure shipments were sent and secured, Tsar Nicholas the Second and his family were murdered, the Romanov dynasty ended, and the revolutionary Bolsheviks took power. Furthermore, the

Red Army and the White Army factions were tearing each other apart, and there were military disasters plaguing the Russian Army at the German front. Between the violent uprising of the new regime and the soldiers everywhere dying and deserting, it was a complete disaster.'

'Anything else?' Cobb asked.

'Let's see . . .' Jasmine thought. 'In October 1916, with the Germans a mere two hundred miles from Moscow, the rail workers went on strike. Soldiers from the front were sent to force them back to work. Instead, the soldiers joined the railway workers.'

'So the lines of defense are disintegrating, the enemy is at the gate, and the capital is in ruins. Time that out with the shipment.'

'Two months after the second Romanian shipment arrived "safely" in Moscow' – she emphasized the irony of the word *safely* with air quotes – 'Nicholas the Second abdicated. The provisional government which preceded Lenin and the Communists was ineffective, to say the least.'

'What was the mood in Moscow?' Cobb asked.

'Confused. Unhappy. Desperate. They had to burn furniture to keep from freezing. They were starving. Finally, in December 1917, there was an armistice with Germany.'

'Who did or did not know about the Romanian treasure?'

'I'm sure the Germans knew there were treasures,' Jasmine surmised. 'If not from their extensive spy network, then from the Romanovs or the Communists who were pawing at power and infiltrating government offices one after the other. Even after the armistice, the Germans kept coming in a classic nineteenth-century-style land grab. They marched into the Ukraine unopposed. The Russians ceded that territory and other contested or coveted regions to protect themselves, to give themselves a geographical buffer.'

'Where?' Cobb wanted to know.

'The Baltic Provinces. Finland, parts of Poland—'

'Which the Russians could never have held,' Papineau reminded her. 'Even absent the Germans, the war had not left them with the necessary manpower.'

'Very true,' Jasmine said. 'That's when the Allies invaded Russia, just to stop Germany from getting their hands on Russian resources.'

'Okay,' Cobb concluded. 'So let's say you're Russia. You've got Germany in your face and France, Britain, and America breathing down your neck. What would you do with – let's round it off to a nice, round number – a hundred tons of gold?'

He watched the group ponder the question.

Even Garcia was still. His fingers had nothing to check.

'I'll make it simple,' Cobb said. 'Would you keep the gold where it was?'

'No,' Sarah decided.

'Neither would I. So the question is: where did they move it?'

Papineau smiled. That was the billion-dollar question.

'Indeed, Mr Cobb,' Papineau said. 'That is exactly what I would like you to determine.' He paused, letting it sink in. 'I want you to find it, secure it, and transport it to a safe location of my choosing. The gold and any other valuables you find along the way.'

'Ohhhhh,' McNutt drawled. 'Is *that* all?'

Sarah leaned forward in her seat. 'And what if we fail?'

'If you fail, I'll pay you for your time, but you won't get the five-million-dollar bonus,' Papineau said flatly. 'Your bonus comes from the treasure, not my pockets.'

Sarah nodded her acceptance. That seemed fair to her.

Intrigued by the mission, Cobb turned to face the group. 'All right, everyone, listen to me. If I'm going to lead this team, here is what I require. First, what I say goes. I'll accept short discussions on anything and everything except in times of danger. Agreed?'

He looked to each team member for an answer. McNutt and Jasmine nodded. Sarah didn't object. Garcia shrugged in submission. Cobb turned to the Frenchman. 'You're responsible for all of our expenses. You'll pay for everything we need.'

'That is a given,' Papineau said.

'I don't think you understand,' Cobb replied. 'Your bank account is now *my* bank account. You're going to trust me not to take anything more than we require. If I say we need something, we need something. You can ask me why, and if I have time, I'll tell you. But if you decide against it, even once, I'm out.' He let that sink in for a second. 'Are we in agreement?'

Papineau nodded.

'Okay, Sarah,' Cobb said, 'let's start with you. Jean-Marc, will you bring up the map of the area?' With a click of the remote control, the wall became a modern map of Eastern Europe. 'I want you to study the transportation routes and modes throughout the areas we've discussed – then blow it out, mile by mile, until you find a viable location for the cache.'

'Sure, but do you have any suggestion on where I should start?'

'I do,' Cobb said, 'but I want you to tell me what you think. That will vet my own findings. If we reach different conclusions, we'll have to talk. Just put yourself in the position of a Russian politician when the tsar was the rock and Lenin was the hard place. Where would you put a hundred tons of gold?'

'Damn good question,' she said.

'A gold filling for every Russian peasant!' McNutt suggested. 'Then have them spit 'em out after the war.'

'That's just stupid,' Garcia said.

'Welcome to me,' McNutt replied.

'Where can she work?' Cobb asked Papineau, ignoring the exchange.

'Right here, if she likes,' he said. 'Mr Garcia can set her up with a laptop.'

'Fine,' Cobb said. He turned to McNutt. 'While Sarah does that, and assuming you're through joking—'

'For the moment,' McNutt said.

'– make a list of the transport and armory requirements you think we'll need once we're on the ground in that region. We should be okay in the cities. It's the rocky or watery countryside that we need to worry about.'

'Artillery? Heavy as well as light?'

'Whatever you think, as long as you remember that we'll need to transport it once we're there. Give me a wish list.'

'I'll do that on the terrace,' McNutt said. 'I think better in the open.'

'That's good to know,' Cobb remarked.

McNutt shrugged. 'It's where I've done most of my heavy mental lifting, though usually with people looking to kill me.'

'I'm sure that can be arranged,' Cobb said with an accusing glance at Papineau. He turned next to Garcia. 'Hector, I want to know a couple of things. When Sarah and I have our target, you'll have to become familiar with the police and military of every force in every village we might find ourselves up against. In the meantime, I want the specifications of all the communication systems we might require in terms of both hardware in-country and satellite access above. Finally, you'll need to make all the security systems of all the companies in that region an open book for Sarah.'

'Is that all?' Garcia joked.

'For now,' Cobb said.

'You can do that before dessert,' Papineau remarked.

'We should make him do it *for* dessert,' McNutt suggested.

Cobb looked at Jasmine. She was the team member he knew the least about. 'Quick question: if I were to punch you in the face, what would you do?'

She shrugged. 'Probably cry.'

He laughed. 'That's what I figured. There's no doubting your skills as a historian – you've just demonstrated them. But I need to be sure that you can take care of yourself in the field. Starting early tomorrow morning, I want you to learn the rudiments of self-defense. Preferably judo or jiu-jitsu.'

'Why Japanese?' she asked.

Cobb smiled. 'Good question. Those styles are directed outward, designed to use an opponent's attack against him. The Chinese forms use inner strength and four-point movement from center. They take longer to master.'

'I understand,' she said. 'I'll find a good school.'

'No, find a good sensei for private lessons,' Cobb said. 'Eight hours a day. You won't have a lot of time. Don't worry: once you start, it'll become addictive. And Hector?' He turned back toward Garcia. 'When you have the information I asked for, join her. That would make it after breakfast tomorrow, I'm guessing.'

'I'm kind of a klutz,' Garcia said.

Cobb glared at him. 'Hector, that was our short discussion. You're taking lessons.'

Garcia's mouth didn't move, but his eyes said, *Yes sir!*

'Hey, chief!' McNutt called as he headed upstairs. 'We've got our marching orders. What are you going to be doing?'

'Me?' Cobb said. 'I'm going on a rekky of Eastern Europe.'

19

Three weeks later
Friday, September 14
Moscow, Russia

Andrei Dobrev roamed the reception, looking for someone to talk to, but his presence was mostly ignored by the well-dressed guests. There was a fake smile or two, and a few polite nods, but other than that, a lot of blank stares – especially when they learned that he was a semi-retired member of the working class, and not a dignitary or a well-connected politician.

But Dobrev didn't take it personally.

At his advanced age, he was used to being ignored.

The only reason Dobrev had been invited to the Leningradsky Rail Terminal for the announcement of the new American–European train survey was because of his long career as a railway worker. He was nothing more than a token laborer to put a blue-collar spin on the proceedings. Having worked on thousands of miles of track and at various stations throughout Russia, Dobrev knew more about the railways than most of its executive officers.

When it came to trains, he was a walking encyclopedia.

His was a proud railroad family, dating back more than a hundred years. His grandfather, Béla, worked all the way through the mobilization and nationalizing of the system through World War I and the Revolution. His father, Cristian – who married a Russian woman and moved to Moscow from Romania – worked the lines at the height of the railroad industry's golden age. And he, Andrei, had survived the screeching, convulsive collapse of the Soviet Union and the rise of the new Russian railway. Foreign investors had made financial and engineering contributions, but it was still a Russian line, sprawling through some of the most hostile rail territories on earth. It was the lifeline of towns and villages that could not be reached by any other means.

Two months earlier, after forty years of honorable service, Dobrev had lightened his load by becoming an advisor. He had surrendered his day-to-day activities with regret. Those first few days when he did not put on his coarse, bull-hide work gloves, he had felt worse than naked; he felt useless. But it was good not to be hurrying from one station or another, to one crisis or another, to one bar or another to find a local railway authority. His reassignment had been mandated by the implementation of Government Order #384:

When a member of the track workforce shall reach a certain age, that age being sixty-five . . .

But Dobrev was occasionally invited to major railway

events, a proud example of Russian industry and dedication. And he never failed to feel an overwhelming rush of pride whenever he stepped into any station in Russia – particularly in Moscow, the shining city which the last three generations of Dobrevs had helped to connect to the rest of the continent.

The Leningradsky terminal was a particular favorite. It was the creation of the great Konstantin Andreyevich Thon, Imperial Russia's official architect, who also designed the Grand Kremlin. This square, spired, palatial place was created in the great architect's later years, but it still served as something of a revolution. Completed in 1851, it combined the best of old and new by rejecting Roman neoclassicism in favor of what became known as the Russian Revival style, identified by cunning and clever steel work, which was then one of the newest construction techniques.

Dobrev drank in the rail terminal's handsome exterior as he looked around at the small crowd. This party – announcing and celebrating a new rail survey that would improve track conditions in rural regions – was suitably austere and ostentatious. They had cordoned off a corner just inside the main entrance so passengers could flow by with a minimum of inconvenience to them. Dobrev noticed that the rush and bustle of commuters, crowded but never congested, would be visible to the foreign guests.

The organizers had set up a cocktail bar and several tables of caviar, buckwheat blinis, pelmenis, and pierogis in a cordoned section off to the right of the main entrance, with enough security guards to discourage the gypsies and mafia wannabes who always hovered nearby anything of significance in Moscow. Dobrev studied the crowd: minor dignitaries, lesser committee members, petty trade representatives, and unimportant railway officials.

Obviously they wanted to put on a low-level, dog-and-pony show for the 'Amerikos'. That was how Russians termed ugly Americans, men and women who came with money and opinions but very little experience. Sometimes, no experience at all. Therefore, the total absence of Russian, state-run media wasn't much of a surprise. The only other guest who stood out was the thin, bald man in a black tunic, pants, boots, and coat. Dobrev felt a chill, remembering the black, ripstop uniforms of the Russian OMON – a special-purpose mobile unit deployed during violent situations, including some Dobrev wished he could forget.

But it was more than his outfit that set this man apart. The bald figure in black had beady, attentive eyes, giving the impression that he was half security officer, half vulture. Just as Dobrev was heir to a great railroad tradition, this man was a throwback to Okhrana, the secret police of the Romanov dynasty. Not only did he observe, he judged with his gaze.

A minute later, Dobrev's attention was drawn to the team of surveyors who entered the side door to polite applause. They were led by the study sponsor, Jean-Marc Papineau, who waved to the crowd like a visiting king. While most of the male guests gawked at the blue-eyed blonde in the form-hugging black dress and heels who was standing beside Papineau, Dobrev focused on the Asian woman in the pencil-skirt suit and bone-colored, high-necked blouse. He knew she would be treated poorly because she was *different* than him and his comrades.

Sadly, that mattered to Russians who were Russian to the core.

But Dobrev wasn't like that. He didn't care about race, or age, or anything superficial. He only cared about the person inside. Intrigued by her presence, he took it upon himself to watch over her at the reception, like a parent keeping an eye on his child at the playground. He gave her plenty of distance, but was ready to spring into action if he deemed it necessary.

The rest of Papineau's team seemed to hover near English speakers. The man with short, light hair was joking with the politicians. The man with longer hair hung out at the bar with the serious drinkers. The small, Latin-looking man only had eyes for the tablet screen he carried. And the blonde was busy turning all the men who approached her to stone.

As expected, virtually no one was speaking to the Asian girl, so he decided to strike up a conversation. She stood with a closed leather notebook clutched to her chest and drank white wine almost wistfully as he approached.

'It is very odd, yes?' Dobrev said in Russian.

She turned toward him. 'What is?'

'Of your delegation, you are the only one I have heard speaking Russian. Yet no one is talking to you.'

She laughed quietly, which brought a wide smile to Dobrev's face. Most women – Russian or foreign – dismissed him quickly. He was clearly of the old guard: squat, stocky, square-headed, and partial to ill-fitting tan suits that allowed his big arms to move. His white shirts were always stained with grease or oil because he couldn't help touching things on trains, and he wore dark ties no matter what the weather or occasion. Although he'd had a son, Ivan, out of wedlock, he rarely felt comfortable with the opposite sex. He spoke easily to locomotives and stubborn rail spikes, less so to human beings, and rarely at all with women.

But this women was different. She was open, responsive, almost excited to talk to him. Like a granddaughter meeting her grandfather for the very first time.

'Have you seen the train selected for your survey?' Dobrev asked.

'I have,' Jasmine answered. 'It seems very nice.'

'She *is* very nice,' Dobrev insisted. 'She is the pride of the fleet. Perhaps the most efficient engine ever run in our system. You will have no issues with her.'

'That is certainly good news,' Jasmine replied. 'Although I highly doubt that I would be the one having problems. I think driving a locomotive is a bit out of my league.'

'It has never been easier, my dear,' Dobrev countered. 'Operating an engine used to be an art, requiring both skill and instinct. The best engineers were those who understood the nature of the beast, who listened to the engine's every creak and groan and felt her most subtle wobbles and shimmies. Knowing when to lay off or when to throttle up meant the difference between delivering the cars safely and tumbling down the side of the mountain.' Dobrev stared in the direction of the tracks. 'Today's engines have more bells and whistles than a luxury automobile. Even a child could set the autopilot. What was then is now gone.' Dobrev hung his head, mournful of the days gone by. 'The best engineers are no longer needed.'

Jasmine nodded. 'You mean, experts like you?'

Dobrev lifted his head and smiled. 'Perhaps in my heyday, yes. But that time has passed. These days I am never called upon to participate in the day-to-day activities of our great railway, only to regale the current regime with stories of our history. Young, bored dignitaries who always seem to have better things to do than listen to the ramblings of an old man.'

Jasmine understood the implication of his words: if she wanted to end this conversation, he would understand. But she had no intention of cutting him off.

'What makes you such an authority?' she asked.

'More than a century of first-hand knowledge,' he answered. 'Information passed down from grandfather to father to son. Three generations of Dobrevs, all in love with the same mistress: the railway.'

Jasmine laughed at the comment. She found his commitment to his work to be honest and oddly gratifying. Here was a man who made no illusions about who he really was. Even if his knowledge hadn't been directly connected to their task, she still would have enjoyed listening to his stories about the past. As it was, she was beginning to think that he could be a valuable asset – even more valuable than they had originally thought when they added his name to the guest list.

'Well, I'm not sure if I still qualify as "young" or as a "dignitary", but I know for certain that I am not bored,' Jasmine assured him. 'If you don't mind, please, regale me.'

Dobrev smiled. It would be his pleasure.

20

Sunday, September 16

Two days later, Jasmine and Dobrev met again to continue their discussion. This time, under the watchful eye of the rest of the team.

Jasmine laughed at Dobrev's choice of meeting spot – the Soviet retro-chic restaurant on the fourth level above the check-in area of the Sheremetyevo Airport's Terminal F. But she also appreciated its functional, 1960s 'charm'.

'This is like the restaurant version of you,' she pointed out with a smile.

He was not offended in the slightest. As she took in the dark, plain decorations, heavy curtains, and faded carpet – all in shades of dark red – he explained why he had selected it.

'I wished to find someplace you could get to easily, one with a minimum of danger from lecherous drunks or racist skinheads.'

'It was very easy, thank you,' she said.

'There is none easier, in fact,' he said proudly. 'The Aero express train from the station runs every half-hour, and you were here in thirty-five minutes with a minimum of fuss, muss, or whistles. Whistles from men,' he teased, 'not—' He finished the statement by pulling on an imaginary train whistle and blowing two short bursts of sound from his pursed lips.

She laughed, which made him laugh as well.

As they watched the tarmac through the restaurant's window and enjoyed a bowl of borscht, they talked about all things Russian. After dinner, he walked her back to the Aero express entrance. Since she seemed amenable to another get-together before setting off on their survey, he cautiously suggested that they meet at the true repository of his family's legacy: his apartment.

'Please understand,' he assured her, 'I mean nothing untoward. It is just that, with your interest in our rail history and my unique collection, I thought you'd be interested.'

'I definitely am.'

'You are?' he said, half surprised.

She laughed at his reaction. 'I'm free now if you have the time.'

'Yes! That would be wonderful!'

In a blur of trains and stations and people and sights, they arrived at his apartment. She was quickly impressed by what she saw. His collection of Russian railroad memorabilia covered the walls, lined the shelves, and filled the cabinets of his longtime residence. It took up roughly one-third of the floor of a nondescript apartment building in Kartmazovo, twenty-nine miles outside of Moscow. The building was constructed in the industrial egg-crate style of the 1950s on an unremarkable street just off the M3 highway. The apartment had originally been intended to house a family of five but when his parents died and his younger brother Vlad joined the army, there was only Dobrev. It was strange to see the place through the first fresh set of eyes that had been there in years. He looked with approval at the floors covered in dark, Russian rugs, the smallish room decorated with ornate if time-worn furniture, the light fixtures of heavy, antique iron and pelican-shaped glass lamps which bathed the towers of well-maintained memorabilia in soft, yellow light.

He offered her a drink, but she declined.

She said, 'And risk missing a single detail of these glorious maps?'

That had made him smile even wider as they plunged into his collection. Instead of the customary response of tolerant boredom from young workers, the woman absolutely sparkled at his stories about the heroes of Russian rail: Yefim Cherepanova, and his son, Miron, who built Russia's first steam-powered locomotive; Pavel Melnikov, creator of the first Russian railway; Fyodor Protsky, inventor of the first electric tram, and more.

Finally he got to his own family's contribution, starting with his grandfather, Béla. He showed her his most prized treasure, which he kept tucked behind a vintage railway lantern.

'It is the history of my grandfather's homeland in a single small disc,' he said as he reverently picked up an old velvet-lined wooden box that Jasmine had originally mistaken for a magnifying glass container. His thick, stubby fingers showed remarkable gentleness as he removed the object within. The murky, butter-colored light gleamed off the coin.

'Wow,' she breathed, slowly raising her hands to her cheeks.

Using the cover story that Papineau had organized for them, Cobb had assigned each member of his team a different group to investigate. McNutt was rooting out black marketeers who may have trafficked the gold or knew of someone who did. Garcia was hanging out with railroad software designers. Sarah kept her ears open around officials' wives, girlfriends, and mistresses, who learned more from pillow talk than most intelligence services discovered through wiretaps.

But Jasmine had hit the jackpot with Andrei Dobrev.

He knew more about the railroads than their other sources combined.

* * *

'Whoa,' Hector Garcia said in their tiny office at the Moscow train station, approximately nineteen miles to the northeast of Dobrev's apartment. He looked up from the image on his screen, an image that was being transmitted from a button camera on Jasmine's blouse.

'What is it?' Papineau asked, coming around his desk in the unadorned guest offices the train station had supplied them.

'You tell me,' Garcia replied from his table, which was covered in computers, cell phones, modems, routers, and wires.

Papineau leaned over his shoulder and whistled softly at the sight that bounced on the tablet screen. 'My word!' he marveled. 'That's a gold leu!'

'A gold what?' Garcia asked.

'Did you not do the reading that Cobb and I assigned to the team?' Papineau scolded.

'I read it all. I just don't remember it.'

'Tragic,' Papineau said, only half paying attention to the younger man.

'It's called the Internet Era,' Garcia said in a defensive tone. 'It's knowing where to find information instantly that matters, not memorizing it.'

'And if, let's say, you were on river rapids or in a cave with no reception?'

'Then I wouldn't be worried about a leu. I'd be worried about drowning or starving,' Garcia assured him. 'So, what is it again? The coin, I mean.'

'It's a first-series leu,' Papineau said, leaning in to get a better look. 'The gold twenty-lei coin was issued in 1868. Less than five hundred were minted, so this is a rarity.'

Garcia glanced at him, confused. 'Is it a leu or a lei?'

'Leu is singular; lei is plural.' Papineau practically put his nose against the screen. 'Zoom closer. I want to see it better.'

Garcia tapped the screen to freeze the image, then slipped the live feed to the side so he could study the coin without losing Jasmine's progress.

Papineau studied the image just to make sure. As expected, the left profile of Carol I appeared on the front. The inscription read: CAROL I DOMNULU ROMANILORU. In

English, it meant: Carol the First, Prince of the Romanians. 'What a beautiful coin. I wonder, where did the likes of Andrei Dobrev get something like that?'

'He said from his grandfather.'

'I meant his family in general. How did they get a coin of such value?'

'Guys,' McNutt whispered from his perch across the street from Dobrev's apartment.

Papineau ignored the voice in his earpiece. He still wasn't used to the tiny, flesh-colored communication device that Garcia had inserted near the bottom of their auditory canals. It served as both mic and speaker, and it was so precise that it could detect the faintest whisper.

For privacy purposes, team members selected codewords – one for the mic and one for the speaker – that would temporarily deactivate their personal unit. Say the 'mic' word, and the microphone toggled off. Say it again, and it came back on. The same applied for the 'speaker' word. To prevent accidental muting, team members selected codewords that wouldn't come up in everyday conversation. Words like *pumpernickel* and *Travolta*.

Papineau continued to speak. 'Perhaps it was a bribe of some kind.'

'Or a very generous tip,' Garcia suggested.

'I wonder, is there any way you could check his bank records from that time?'

'Guys!' McNutt shouted. 'Quit your blabbing and listen to me!'

His voice was so loud it caused their earpieces to squeal.

Papineau winced from the sound. 'Why are you yelling?'

'*Why?* Because you're ignoring me!'

'That's because we're working.'

'Well, *I'm* working, too,' McNutt growled. 'And I wanted you to know that someone is coming!'

21

McNutt had been watching Dobrev's apartment – and everything that happened inside – from his vantage point on a rooftop directly across the street. From there, he could also keep an eye on the hallway outside Dobrev's door. His line of sight gave him the opportunity to warn Jasmine and the others of any unexpected visitors. His Soviet-made *Snaiperskaya Vintovka Dragunova* sniper rifle, or SVD, gave him a way to make those unexpected visitors go away forever.

McNutt peered through the Barska tactical scope and explained the situation. 'You've got a white male standing outside Dobrev's door.' He was a short, wiry, young man with a crew cut and a sour expression. He was wearing sneakers that had no shoelaces, black pants, a black leather jacket, and a faded T-shirt. 'He must've come from one of the apartments.'

'How do you know that?' Papineau questioned.

'Well,' McNutt explained, 'he wasn't at the door five seconds ago when I scanned the hall, so unless he came down through the ceiling or materialized out of thin air, I'd say he just stepped out from one of the neighboring units.'

'Understood,' Papineau agreed.

'*Thor Steinar* mean anything to anyone? It's written across his shirt.'

Garcia's fingers pounded his keyboard as he searched the Web. He skimmed the results before he informed the team. 'Thor Steinar is a clothing designer. It seems he's especially popular among skinheads and neo-Nazis. He has a lot of fans in Russia.'

'Hold up! Thor is a skinhead?' McNutt said, confused. 'That doesn't make any sense. He has long hair in the comic books. It's even longer than mine.'

'Different Thor,' Garcia assured him.

'Thank God! Because *that* Thor is tough to kill.'

'Of course he's tough to kill. He's the God of Thunder.'

'No shit, Hector! I *know* he's the God of Thunder. I'm not an idiot.'

*   *   *

Sitting outside in an SUV, Cobb rolled his eyes at the discussion that was clogging the intercom. The more he listened, the less confident he felt. It was the type of conversation one would expect at a comic book convention, not in the middle of an important mission.

Cobb growled, 'Knock it off! Tell me what's happening!'

McNutt quickly snapped to attention. 'Thor is trying to pick the lock on Dobrev's door. Just say the word, and I'll take him out before he can.'

'That's a negative – not until we ID the target.'

*   *   *

Dobrev heard somebody in the hallway outside of his apartment. More curious than alarmed, he walked toward his door to investigate. He glanced through his peephole and saw his neighbor, a troubled youth named Marko Kadurik, trying to pick the lock.

Dobrev opened the door. 'What are you doing?'

'Me?' the skinhead screamed. 'What are *you* doing with that foreigner – besides disrespecting the memory of your grandson? You know how he felt about Chinks.'

'You're drunk, Marko. Go home before I call the police.'

Kadurik looked past Dobrev. 'I'll go home when *she* goes home – back to China!'

'I won't have this,' Dobrev shouted.

'Have what? The truth? Yury loved you, and you piss on his ideals with this filth!'

Filled with anger and embarrassment, Dobrev slapped the young man across the face with a meaty hand. In the narrow hallway, the sound of his palm hitting the young man's cheek was like a pistol shot. The young man staggered, more from shock than pain.

Kadurik stared at Dobrev, who stared right back.

'You may think you knew my grandson,' Dobrev said slowly, 'but you only knew the monster he became, not the promising young man that he once was. You, and your kind, and your unspeakable behavior – there is no excuse for you.' Dobrev's eyes burned with rage. 'Leave. *Now*. While the only injury is to the respect of my guest.'

'Your whore, you mean.'

Dobrev went to slap him again. This time the young man was ready. He pushed the old man back so the blow fell short. Then he shouldered past him.

'We don't want your kind in our country!' the punk yelled as he approached Jasmine. He put his right hand in his jacket pocket as he circled around her. He used profanity so offensive that she wasn't familiar with the terms. But Dobrev was.

'Enough!' the old man boomed.

Dobrev started toward him again, but the young man turned, revealing a fist that was now fitted with hard, black plastic knuckles.

'Don't even think about touching me again!' Kadurik yelled.

'Take those off, and never come here again,' Dobrev said coolly. 'Your kind is unwelcome in my home.'

'*My kind?*' He sneered toward Jasmine. 'You welcome this trash but you insult *me*? Our language itself is profaned coming from her filthy mouth!'

Jasmine maintained a neutral expression. Her hands rested at her sides as the angry young man stared at her with blazing eyes. Loathing crushed whatever lust a normal young man would have felt. That was a new feeling for Jasmine – to be hated for her race rather than wanted for her beauty. Fear expanded like a balloon inside her chest and stomach. Her sensei had told her not to run from that feeling but to accept it. To ride it. To use it to her advantage.

Don't let it distract you from what must be done to survive.

Mentally she knew she had command of the skill set that he had given her. But she had never had to test herself in the field. It was very different to be in a strange, dark room instead of in a bright gym with cushioned mats.

The anger was different, too.

This punk looked as if he wanted to tear her head off.

He is looking down, she told herself. *He is a coward – a brute. That's why he put that thing on his hand to fight an older man and a woman. He is afraid.*

She straightened to her full height. Not swiftly but slowly, in total control. She did not take her eyes from him. She did not assume a stance. She just – stood.

Their eyes were level now, but they were not equal. She was confident and poised. He was angry and unsure. She knew exactly what she would do if she had to. She knew, from his action, which hand would come at her and that it would be with a hooked swing. She had already scoped out her immediate surroundings using peripheral vision. The first lesson she had learned from her sensei: get out of the way. Let your attacker move past you with wild momentum. Then attack from behind.

Her resolve was apparent. His uncertainty was equally obvious . . . even to him. After a moment or two more of alpha-dog huffing, he clamped his mouth shut, spun away, and left the apartment – slamming the door behind him.

22

The rage hung in the room for a few moments, then it evaporated. As it did, Jasmine saw Dobrev racked with shame.

'I am so sorry,' he said miserably.

'There's no need.'

'I'm ashamed,' he repeated, turning away slightly. 'So ashamed.'

She let him have a moment. Jasmine did not know if Dobrev knew it, but those were reportedly the very words Nicholas II said to Alexandra after he was forced to abdicate.

When he looked at her again, his face was regretful. 'My grandson, Yury . . . he held so much promise. He was named for Yury Lomonosov, the designer of the first diesel locomotive. His father thought that he would take after him. But it was not to be.'

Jasmine was cautious, but she couldn't help herself. She took a few steps toward the man and placed a hand on his shoulder, letting him know that she, and the situation, were all right.

She knew from what Garcia had researched and whispered in her ear that the young man's father, Andrei's son, was Ivan Dobrev. Newspaper accounts and police reports said that Ivan had been a proud railroad man during the industry's most trying time in the 1990s. Yury had been just a baby when the Russian mob, competing with the dying Soviet government for control of the railway workers, had opened fire on a picnic in the Lyubertsy neighborhood just outside Moscow city limits. Yury had survived the slaughter. His father did not.

'My son was a good man,' Dobrev said sadly, succinctly. 'He was killed in an unfortunate incident. His mother, Dominika, lingered – but as you can imagine, she was never the same. She drank to bury her pain. She couldn't control Yury, even when he was a child. I tried, but I was around infrequently. I found her dead one morning when Yury was eleven. We never did discover whether she simply gave up or committed suicide with the bottle. Yury was sitting by her side, reading a book about the Revolution. I can still see the cover, *February and October*—'

Jasmine nodded. 'The abdication of the tsar, and then the rise of the Bolsheviks.'

'That's right,' Dobrev said admiringly. 'After the ambulance came, and the police, I asked the boy to join me at the rail yards. He didn't answer. I referenced the book. I told him that in spite of everything that had happened, he was lucky not to have to live through the time of hunger and change. I told him how we had to work with military tanks in the streets, gunfire in our ears, and the smell of acrid smoke in our nostrils. He listened, looked at me for a moment . . . then he spit at me.'

Jasmine made a sympathetic sound in spite of herself. 'He was just eleven?'

Dobrev nodded. 'I didn't strike him. I grasped him tightly by the arms and asked him why he had done that. He said that my trains had caused the trouble. Ease of travel from foreign countries. The influence of foreign culture and values. He blamed that on men like me.'

'Where did that come from?' Jasmine asked.

'The RNU.'

Cobb whispered in her ear. 'The Russian National Unity Group. Russian Nazis. Mainly young punks who embrace the label because they think it's cool . . . By the way, we're outside. Cough if you need us.'

'Russian Nazis,' Jasmine said.

Dobrev nodded. 'They recruit young boys to program with their mindless fervor. Yury kept getting angrier and angrier. When I saw him, which wasn't often, his talk was increasingly spiteful and sadistic. It was this behavior that took him from me.'

'What happened?' Jasmine asked. She was speaking to both her immediate company and those listening on their closed frequency.

Garcia pounded his keyboard, frantically searching the Web for anything related to Yury Dobrev. 'I've got nothing,' he answered.

Andrei Dobrev took a deep breath, steadying himself before he continued. 'Even among those united by hate, there are grave differences.'

Jasmine sensed he wasn't finished and didn't interject.

'Not quite a year ago, Yury and his new "friends" traveled to Zvenigorod, about sixty kilometers to the west.

Zvenigorod draws numerous foreign tourists, all seeking their destinies.'

'Legend holds that the dreams one experiences in Zvenigorod foretell the future. It dates back to a story about Napoleon's stepson, who saw his own fate while staying in a monastery there.' Garcia and Dobrev spoke almost in unison, with virtually the exact same words, as if the former was quoting from a book that the latter had written.

'The legend attracts foreigners,' Dobrev continued, 'and the foreigners attract nationalists. Or at least those who spit venom from behind the cloak of nationalist pride. Nazis, white supremacists, Aryans. Once a year, they all turn out en masse to show their strength. An event that quickly collapses into chaos.'

Dobrev paused, and his eyes glazed over.

Jasmine could see the pain in his memories.

'That's a lot of collected anger,' Jasmine offered. She didn't mean to salt the wound, but she knew she needed to hear the rest of the story.

Dobrev nodded. 'It would seem that the only thing these groups hate more than foreigners are those who don't know how to properly hate foreigners. The Nazis feel that the supremacists and Aryans impede their cause with unprovoked violence. The supremacists and Aryans feel that the Nazis are too concerned with politics, particularly international affairs. Perhaps the only thing they agree on is that the RNU has yet to earn their respect. Insults were exchanged, and punches soon led to weapons.'

Tears welled in Dobrev's eyes. 'Yury was stabbed. He did

not survive. His so-called friends buried him somewhere in the forests between here and there. To this day, I do not know exactly where. I'm not even sure they know where.'

Jasmine pointed toward the door. 'That was one of Yury's friends?'

Dobrev nodded. 'His name is Marko Kadurik.'

He took a bottle of vodka from atop a desk in his small living room, poured himself three fingers' worth, and downed it with one quick swig. His eyes never focused on the task. He was still consumed by the memory of his grandson.

Jasmine took a deep breath. 'I should probably go.'

'All right,' Dobrev agreed.

Jasmine felt the pangs of remorse, and she wondered if she had taken her questions too far. She had assumed that Dobrev would object to her departure and beg her to stay longer. Instead, he seemed to welcome the impending solitude.

'I will make sure you get safely to—'

'There's really no need,' she said. 'It's early, and I saw a taxi station just down the block. I will be perfectly safe.'

'Please, I—'

Jasmine smiled and took his hand, holding it gently in a show of affection. 'Thank you for sharing your treasures and keepsakes. You'll never know how much it meant to me.'

* * *

Marko Kadurik heard the conversation through the thin wall that his apartment shared with Dobrev's. He hadn't lived there long – less than a year – only in the months since Yury's death. Yury had often bragged of his grandfather's old-country regalia, and he had mentioned their value on more than one occasion. One item in particular had caught Kadurik's interest: a gold coin. He had already broken into Dobrev's apartment several times in search of the treasure, but he had yet to locate it.

It is only a matter of time, he thought.

When the woman left, he stared into the darkness of his apartment. His walls and windows were covered with RNU flags. They were emblazoned with swastikas and modified swastikas – symbols that looked like four deadly, interlocking tonfa batons.

Yes, he thought. *Go to the taxi stand. Go where you think you'll be safe.*

The only illumination in the room came from the cell phone he held at his waist, his thumb dancing across the tiny keyboard. The dim backlighting of the device gave his tortured face an even more satanic glow.

A few seconds passed. The cell phone vibrated in his hand. He glanced down and saw the message clearly. His comrades-in-arms were on their way. And they were coming fast.

Kadurik smiled like a wolf when he heard the outside door of the apartment building slam shut. He peeked from behind one of the banners and looked at the street.

There she was. Walking proudly. Not knowing the fate that was about to overtake her.

His group's leader had made it clear: Russia was for the Slavic – not the Jews, not the Muslims, not the Gypsies, and certainly not the hated Asians. He had been vehement about that. The Russian national identity must be protected from dilution by other races, liberal sympathizers, cross-breeders, mixed progeny, and temptresses – especially the exotic ones. The ones that made normally sane men, like Yury's grandfather, dribble like senile old men.

Kadurik opened his door and grinned in anticipation.

This was going to be fun.

23

Cobb was waiting at the curb for Jasmine when she emerged from the squat apartment building on the suburban street. He was leaning against the gray UAZ Simbir that their railway partners had loaned to him – a plain but fairly powerful four-by-four that looked like a western SUV but with a more prominent snout and an overall look of Communist reserve.

Cobb had left the vehicle when things looked like they might go south. He held back as Jasmine regained control of the situation with Kadurik. Now he smiled as she approached.

He was glad to see her safe.

Jasmine looked both ways down the bleak, harshly lit, cement-enclosed street. She was relieved to see that the area was all but empty. Little wonder. The entrance to the Dobrev apartment was tucked into an unnatural pyramid with a curving wall beneath a roadway forming one side, the apartment building forming another, and the maw of a dark alley comprising the third.

In Manhattan, this would have been the butt end of the building.

In Kartmazovo, it was the grand entrance.

'Hope I didn't make you wait too long,' Jasmine said with

a mixture of sarcasm, relief, and pride – the pride that came from successfully pulling off a first assignment.

'You did great in there,' Cobb assured her. 'I was thinking, though, we missed a golden opportunity. We should have brought one of those gold foil chocolate coins and done a switcheroo. He probably wouldn't have noticed for years, if ever.'

She laughed at the suggestion. 'Honestly? I was trying to think of some way to palm it. I would have felt bad, but not—'

'Извините!' came a loud, rough voice.

'Shit,' Cobb whispered under his breath. He saw two uniformed patrolmen out of the corner of his eye. 'What'd he yell?'

'Excuse me,' she translated.

Cognizant of the button camera on his shirt, Cobb turned toward the cops, giving Garcia a clear view of what they were dealing with: two veteran Russian patrolmen, both with square-brimmed gray caps and gray pants, one with a matching gray shirt, the other with a light blue shirt with epaulettes on his shoulders. Both had heavy, brown belts complete with handcuff holders and large, worn, leather holsters.

One was taller than the other, but both were overweight. They had buzz-cut hair, double chins, bobbed noses, and suspicious eyes. The expressions on their flushed faces were smug.

'What can we do for you, officers?' Jasmine asked in Russian.

Both men were taken aback by the fluent Russian coming from the mouth of the statuesque Asian. They stopped a few feet away, their surprise fading as they became bossy.

'Записки хотеть,' said the taller, heavier one.

'Papers, please,' Jasmine translated.

Cobb was already pulling his passport and visa out of his jacket pocket. She did the same from her coat. They calmly handed them over to the officers and waited, apparently unconcerned, while the two conferred.

'Они не то, чтобы,' said the shorter one, looking up.

'These are not in order,' Jasmine translated, looking hopefully at Cobb. Thankfully his manner was as comforting as it was confident.

'Ah,' he said, nodding. 'Give them my apologies, tell them that it's all my fault, and if they'd be so kind as to hand our documents back for a moment, I'm sure I can correct my mistake.'

Jasmine did so, while the cops used it as an excuse to stare at her as if she was a particularly clever animal in a zoo. They handed the passports and visas back. Cobb returned them with a one-hundred-ruble bill tucked between each set. The cops' eyes brightened at the sight, but they still put on a show of study.

'What's going on?' Jasmine whispered to Cobb.

'It's the Russian game, been going on for centuries,' Cobb assured her casually. 'They lie, we know they're lying, they know we know they're lying, they keep lying anyway, and we pretend to believe them.'

'How about if I just believe you?'

'That works.'

The heavier officer looked up and held out the passports and visas – minus the money, of course – with a smile on his face. He opened his mouth, probably to say that their papers were in order this time, but he never had a chance to speak.

Instead, a jagged rock smashed into the side of the cop's head.

He fell to the ground like a shot duck.

Jasmine screamed as Cobb moved her behind him and twisted to get a clear view of the entire area. The other cop stumbled back and started clawing for his gun.

Unfortunately, he wasn't fast enough. A lead pipe struck the side of his head. He hit the ground with a heavy thud. Blood poured from the wound, staining the street.

Three skinheads in camouflage pants and mock leather jackets had rushed out of the alley. Two had lead pipes, and one held a stained AK-47 bayonet – a straight, single-edged, five-inch blade with a dark wooden handle and a black ring under the hilt for attaching it to the automatic rifle's barrel. They came at Cobb and Jasmine like the pack of animals they were. The knife-wielding one in the middle, the pipe-swingers on either side.

Jasmine shrieked again when Cobb ran from her without a word, but the cry was cut short when she saw what he was doing. He wasn't running from the three men. He was running straight at them, launching off the balls of his feet, and moving so fast they started to falter even though they were much better armed than Cobb.

In a flash, Cobb was on the man in the lead. He blocked the knife hand by slapping his left hand hard on the man's wrist. That bought him the time he needed to bring his right hand to bear. Jasmine saw Cobb strike him in the face with the bony heel of his open hand. The man shuddered and staggered backward on legs that reminded her of cooked noodles.

Jasmine couldn't follow Cobb, he was moving so fast. Even before the knife-wielder was finished wobbling, Cobb was already shifting to grab the man to the left by his pipe arm. He grabbed the back of the man's wrist with his left hand and swung his right hand into the back of the man's elbow. One deft move from Cobb, and he had immobilized his opponent with a classic arm-bar. The skinhead went down on his knees. Cobb planted a foot on his back between his shoulder blades and pushed the rest of him to the pavement, face first.

She could hear the crunching of broken teeth.

The one to the right tried to redirect his attack, but the knife-wielder was in his way. He had to step around him, which cost him valuable time. With the pipe of the man he had just taken down, Cobb stepped forward, the pipe extended before him. It connected with the third man's chest, cracking something inside. Cobb quickly regripped the pipe and swung it upward, smashing the hard iron into the soft cartilage of the attacker's nose.

Blood sprayed in all directions.

Cobb's counterattack had taken about five seconds. That's how long it took Jasmine to suppress her fear, remember her training, and join the fray. The man Cobb had knocked to his face was trying to rise. Jasmine pounced, straddling his neck like a horse, grabbing his hair from above, and dropping. She allowed her entire weight to fall upon his upper back. That drove his face back into the street, knocking him out – along with more teeth.

She rose just as a fourth man darted from the shadows of the apartment building behind her. Jasmine chirped with surprise as she turned to face Marko Kadurik. There was a snarl on his face as his hand grabbed her by the throat. She remembered her training and tried to break the grip by laying her forearm on the groove of his elbow, pushing down, and twisting away, but he surprised her by punching her in the belly with his free hand.

She doubled over in pain.

He grabbed her by her hair, spun her around so she was facing Cobb, and pushed her left arm high up her back while clutching her throat in a death grip.

She tried to breathe, but Kadurik wouldn't allow it.

24

Kadurik wasn't just choking her, he was wrenching her forward and back, cutting off her air entirely each time he pulled back and strengthened his hold. Then he stopped moving. He stood erect, hugging Jasmine tight against him, lifting her onto her toes.

She tried to remember what she had been taught: focus on one finger. If she could pry one digit from her throat, his grip would loosen significantly. At the same time, she thought about her stance, and how she might be able to knock him off balance.

But training is not instinct. Thought is not muscle memory. And the seconds Jasmine squandered remembering the techniques cost her air and consciousness.

Now she was helpless.

Jasmine's face turned red. Her tongue stabbed out of her frighteningly twisted mouth. Then her body jerked forward limply as if she were trying to throw up. The sounds of her gagging made Garcia and Papineau sick with helplessness all those miles away.

'Sarah!' Papineau screamed in the Moscow railroad office. 'Where the hell are you?'

But Sarah wasn't answering.

'There must be something wrong with her unit,' Garcia said.

'Quiet!' Cobb whispered, low enough so that Kadurik wouldn't hear.

'You!' Kadurik snarled in heavily accented English. 'Kick . . . pipe . . . here!'

He clutched Jasmine to him, huddling behind her, shaking her head with his hand at Cobb like a mad puppeteer.

Cobb motioned to lower his elbow first, relax the choke.

'Do it!' Kadurik threatened.

Cobb shook his head. 'She dies, you die.'

Kadurik relaxed slightly – but it was enough. Jasmine was in no condition to fight, but at least she could breathe, albeit raspingly.

Cobb agreed to his end of the bargain. He slowly placed the pipe on the ground and kicked it forward – all the while deciding when to make his move. But before he had a chance to do anything, there was a blur of motion behind Kadurik, who made a whining, wailing sound, which was drowned out by the stomach-turning noise of ripping skin and smashing bone.

Kadurik crumpled to the sidewalk like a rag doll. Jasmine fell, too, but before she hit the ground, Andrei Dobrev caught her in his blood-splattered hands. To do so, he was forced to drop his nineteen-inch-long saddle-bolt spanner – an open-ended wrench used to tighten bolts in locomotives. Covered in strands of hair and bits of flesh, it clattered to the cement in the suddenly quiet night.

Cobb blinked a few times, surprised by the turn of events. Although Jasmine was his main concern, Cobb rushed to Kadurik first. Not to treat his wounds, but to make sure he was no longer a threat.

He wasn't. The skinhead was dead.

Cobb patted him down and searched his pockets. Then he placed the weapons back in the hands of the men who had been carrying them – including the rock, so the police would know who had attacked their colleagues.

All in all, it wasn't a bad result.

Six men down, but his historian/interpreter was still alive.

Cobb knelt beside her and pressed two fingers behind Jasmine's inner left ankle. It was an acupressure technique he had learned in the service, intended to help her recover. A few seconds later, her eyes fluttered open. Her pupils were clear and her flesh was pale in the streetlight, but she appeared okay, at least physically. And she would benefit from this experience: the next time she felt that fear, she would know it, confront it, and hopefully get past it.

That was how combat worked.

Jasmine looked up at Cobb in wounded wonder.

'What happened?' she croaked.

Cobb put his hand on Dobrev's shoulder. 'You survived – thanks to your friend.'

'Really?'

Cobb nodded. 'Really.'

She smiled at Dobrev and thanked him in Russian.

* * *

McNutt had heard the confrontation through his earpiece, but he never had a clear view from his vantage point across the street. And he felt sick about it.

'Chief,' he said sincerely, 'I didn't have a shot. I'm sorry.'

Cobb waved off the apology. 'It's all right.'

'I'm coming now. Two minutes out.'

'Don't. We don't need you . . . Sarah?'

'Ready,' was all she said.

McNutt slowed to a halt. 'Instructions?'

'B to A,' Cobb said quietly. 'We'll pick you up as soon as we can.'

'Outstanding,' McNutt replied.

Over the intercom, Papineau pleaded with the team, hoping that someone – *anyone* – would recognize his authority. 'See if you can get back upstairs. Tell Andrei that Jasmine needs a drink. If you do that, see if you can get the coin. We—'

'Shut up,' Cobb said.

'Boss man,' Garcia said fearlessly, 'it would be a big help if I was able to laser-scan it.'

'A painful process, if I shove that coin up your ass,' Cobb growled.

He practically heard Garcia's mouth snap shut.

Cobb helped Jasmine and Dobrev. He was angry with himself for having assumed Kadurik was among the initial gang of three. That was a mistake that could have cost them dearly.

'Now what?' Jasmine wondered.

'You hear that?' Cobb asked.

'Hear what? My ears are ringing.'

'Sirens,' he said calmly. 'Someone must have seen the fight and called the police. We need to go before they arrive.' He pointed at Dobrev. 'Tell him that.'

Jasmine did, and Dobrev replied sadly.

'He understands,' she told Cobb. 'He said he'll keep our names out of it if anyone asks.'

Cobb smiled. 'He doesn't get. I mean we *all* have to go. Now.'

Papineau objected from afar. 'Jack, what are you thinking? We don't know this man. His presence puts everyone in jeopardy if—'

Anger flared in Cobb's eyes. 'Another word and I terminate. Got that?'

Papineau's response was heavy breathing. The only reason Cobb was still listening at all was because he needed to stay in touch with the other team members. On most missions, this was the point when he pretty much stopped giving a damn about what the bottled-water-drinking bastards back in their ops tents thought, said, or did.

But Papineau wasn't the only one objecting to Dobrev's inclusion in their escape. Dobrev himself was arguing with Jasmine, shaking his head and pointing to his apartment.

It was obvious that he intended to stay.

Jasmine translated for Cobb. 'He says he's not leaving without the coin. He left it in the open, and he's afraid he might never see it again if he doesn't go get it right now. I think he'll come with us if we just let him run upstairs and—'

'There's no time for that,' Cobb replied.

The sounds of the sirens were growing louder.

'Sarah, you copy?' Cobb asked.

'Heard it all,' Sarah answered.

'Good. Smash and grab,' Cobb instructed. 'Two minutes. Then get down here.'

'Two minutes?' Sarah repeated. 'In two minutes we'll be two blocks from here.'

'Prove it,' Cobb challenged.

25

Sarah jumped backwards over the edge of the rooftop directly above Dobrev's apartment. Her rappelling gear held fast, preventing a quick plummet to her death. In a mere fifteen seconds, she had dropped several stories to Dobrev's locked window. A quarter-minute more, and she had popped the latch that anchored the window to its sill. She climbed inside the apartment then unfastened her harness, leaving the rope dangling down the side of the building.

She would need it again in less than a minute.

Darting through the apartment with the grace of a ballet dancer, she deftly avoided the floor lamp that cast a dim light on the apartment's only chair. The scene struck her as sad, and she couldn't help but wonder how many nights the old man had sat alone in the dark, staring at his treasure. But it was a thought she quickly dismissed when she spotted the coin on a small wooden table near the door, right next to the closet where Dobrev had grabbed the saddle-bolt spanner from his toolbox. With gloved hands, Sarah tucked the coin into a zippered pocket, then scampered back to the open window. She reattached her harness to the rope, closed the window behind her, and began her descent.

Anyone who happened to be looking up at the side of the building as Sarah made her way down would have been forced to choose between two, equally unlikely scenarios: Catwoman exists, or the laws of gravity had changed. Dressed from hood to booties in another black catsuit, Sarah literally *ran* down the edifice. The muscles in her arms burned as she pulsed her grips to keep her pace. It was not a beginner's move; it required practiced balance and unbelievable strength. But once Sarah had gotten the hang of it, she preferred it over the standard, backwards dismount. Today it actually served a purpose, as it was the fastest way to reach the ground . . . other than a freefall.

True to her word, it had been little more than a minute since Sarah had entered the apartment. As she hit the ground, she reached inside her suit and withdrew a credit-card-sized remote control. Sliding back the cover to reveal the buttons beneath, she entered the combination. On the roof, the electromagnet that held the loop of rope in place around the fire escape ladder decoupled instantly. Sarah could feel the slack, moments before the full length of the rope hit the pavement. It was the latest in climbing technology, a gift from McNutt.

This is too easy, Sarah thought as she spooled the rope around her arm.

* * *

'How we doing?' Cobb asked as he slammed the door of the SUV behind Jasmine and Dobrev. She was doing her best to keep the old man calm.

'Satellite says you're clear for about forty seconds,' Garcia said in everyone's ears. 'Cops are converging from the north and east.'

'Look to your left,' McNutt said.

Cobb glanced and saw a glimmer of light where the roadway curved. It could have been a small mirror, a pair of glasses, or a watch face, but he knew it was McNutt.

'On my way,' Cobb said as he climbed behind the wheel.

Cobb pulled the SUV into the street and started his U-turn. As he did, Sarah appeared from the shadows and ran to join them. She jumped into the passenger seat as Cobb pressed the accelerator to the floor.

'We're golden,' Sarah said. 'Literally.'

Cobb smiled. 'Jasmine, tell Andrei we got his coin.'

They drove forward as the faint red glow of police lights illuminated the horizon. Nearly a block away, Cobb slowed just enough to allow McNutt to climb into the rear of the truck.

'About time,' McNutt joked. 'I almost caught a cab.'

He slammed the tailgate shut as Cobb floored it.

Jasmine stared at the lights ahead. 'Where are we going?'

'B to A,' Cobb answered as he turned off the main road to avoid the flashing lights. It was the second time he had used that expression in the last five minutes.

McNutt, who was familiar with the term from the military, leaned back and smiled. 'B to A – music to my ears!'

'B to A?' Sarah asked. 'What does that mean? You keep saying it.'

'It's an exit strategy,' Cobb explained as he looked for lights in his rearview mirror. 'You've gotten to where you wanted to go, now you gotta get back to where you started.'

McNutt laughed as he closed his eyes for a quick nap. 'B to the fuckin' A.'

* * *

Their destination was the Moskva-Kazanskaya train station, the depot furthest southeast from Moscow's center and the one with the biggest train yard.

Andrei Dobrev watched in amazement as Cobb drove past the security booth and into the private parking lot. The wonderment did not subside as Cobb led him and Jasmine through the Venetian-style, green-tinted glass entrance beneath the four-tiered spire. The structure had been modeled on the glorious seventeenth-century Soyembika Tower in Kazan, supposedly built by Ivan the Terrible's artisans.

Cobb walked beneath it as if he had built it himself, and he led the two through the chandelier-lined, arched-ceiling lobby, along the tile-stoned floor, past the arched train platforms and granite columns, and around the advertising kiosks. He sauntered as if he owned the place; much to Dobrev's surprise, no one stopped or questioned him. Cobb walked them past the waiting areas and up to the door that separated the passengers from the workers.

He looked back at Dobrev with a knowing smile, then pushed open the door.

Stretching out before the veteran railroad man was a scene out of his dreams. It was the rail yard, lit up like it was a Spartak-CSKA match in the Russian Premier League. The lights illuminated four linked train carriages.

The first one was from a Grand Express, which was essentially a hotel on wheels. But Dobrev knew that this was one of the conference cars, designed for moving meetings of top-level businessmen, politicians, and dignitaries. It came complete with Wi-Fi, LCD TV screens, toilets, showers, and air conditioning. It was taken from the country's first private train company.

The second was a flatbed car, with a staging surface dotted with bolted-down handles and hooks. The third was a modified freight car with a new, dull gray, armored exterior and what looked like movable window slats at every level. Its ceiling also looked as if it were outfitted with tracking and surveillance devices.

The last was a classic first-class compartment car from the train *Lev Tolstoy*, which made the first direct trip between Moscow and Helsinki in 1975. It had sleeping quarters for six as well as a galley and restaurant area. As Dobrev watched, a four-man team was painting over the artful blue, white, and red exteriors of the once famous cars with a uniform dark gray.

He only managed to look away when Jasmine touched his arm.

Cobb stood behind her with an encouraging smile on his face. 'Please ask Mr Dobrev, what engine would he want if he had to drive this train through any condition?'

26

Colonel Viktor Borovsky, a member of the senior supervising staff of the Investigations Special Branch, leaned against the doorway of Anatoli Vargunin's tiny office in the Moskovskaya police station. The warrant officer became aware of Borovsky's presence before he saw his face.

'Who's there, and what is it now?' Vargunin asked irritably, pecking with stubby, inexperienced fingers on the keyboard of his relatively new computer.

Borovsky smiled at Vargunin's tone. The Moskovskaya station was in much better shape than most in the Moscow suburbs. Although the plain exterior of the station was ominous, the interior had been freshly painted in a cheerful sunflower yellow, and freshly redecorated with wide, white tile floors that were geometrically divided by glass and steel cubicles.

Borovsky remained silent as he studied Vargunin's office. He noted that the cramped space bridged the old and the new: the new being his computer, the old being everything else, most prominently the building's walls that seemed to loom more than stand.

'I asked you a question,' Vargunin said. 'Who's there, and what is it now?'

'What is it now?' Borovsky growled. 'That's what I was about to ask you, comrade.'

At the sound of the unfamiliar voice, Vargunin's large head snapped up. His eyes rose slowly, widening, but the annoyance fled like a rat when he saw the polished military bearing of his visitor. His blood-stained eyes, stinging from the new computer monitor and reddened by increasing amounts of drink the past few years, took in the visitor's proud, polished belt buckle, his gray jacket, the three-starred epaulettes, and the decorations over his upper left jacket pocket.

Vargunin had not yet reached the visitor's face when he jerked up to attention, sending his old wooden office chair banging into the wall behind him.

'Excuse me, comrade Colonel,' Vargunin said crisply. He kept his eyes straight ahead, focused on the wall, as he had been trained to do. 'No one told me of your visit!'

'Ana, Ana, Ana,' Borovsky laughed, fully entering the office now. 'Do I have to make appointments to see an old friend?'

Finally, Vargunin's tired eyes made it to his visitor's face. At that precise moment, his own face relaxed and broke into a welcoming smile.

'Viktor!' he exclaimed. 'Viktor, is it really you?'

'I hope it's really me. Who else would I be then?'

The two met at the front of the desk and gripped each other's forearms.

Borovsky looked his old militia friend up and down. 'Still in the blue-shirted, black tie and slacks uniform, just as I remember,' he said. 'Maybe a bit thicker around the middle and a bit thinner in the hair – but, yes, still the same old Anatoli.'

'No,' Vargunin said. 'I am a crabbier version, out of alignment with the modern world.' He dipped his head toward the computer. 'I hate that thing.'

Borovsky laughed. 'There was a time when *everything* was new. People adjusted.'

'They had time to adjust,' Vargunin countered. 'You had time to adjust to an electric light before there was an automobile. Today, it's one thing after another after another.'

'You're right,' Borovsky said, smiling. 'You are crabbier.'

Both men were silent for a moment, then they laughed.

'How long has it been?' Vargunin wondered, mentally counting backwards.

'Close to three years,' Borovsky informed him. 'Well before "the Bill" was introduced.'

Vargunin sneered. 'The Bill. I hate that thing, too.'

'I know,' Borovsky said. 'A plague on it.'

'It ruined enough people to qualify as one.'

'It was necessary.'

Vargunin shook his head. 'So is a tooth extraction. One doesn't hate the dentist, but don't ask me to cheer the decay.'

Borovsky laughed at the comment. It was the same debate that they'd had three years ago, mercifully reduced to this shorthand.

'The Bill' was the Bill on Police, one of the first major reforms of the department since 1917. It had previously been the People's Militia, but after almost a hundred years of growing corruption, President Dmitry Medvedev had introduced sweeping reforms in 2010. They were ratified by the State Duma in early 2011 and put into effect on March 1st of that year.

Borovsky had been one in the group of officers whose responsibility it had been to reduce the one million, twenty-eight thousand police officers to one million, one thousand. Most of his peers found it either an odious or vengeful task, but Borovsky approached it with the same professional pride he had brought to every aspect of his life.

In fact, he found it relatively easy. One recent study had maintained that twenty percent of the force routinely took bribes as well as extorting money from tourists and locals alike. Borovsky understood that the police department's poor pay contributed to that, but he felt more sympathy for the reported sixty percent who sought more work rather than affiliations with local mobs. The police officers that he and his confederates found worthy got salary increases of up to thirty percent. Those that they found unworthy were now, more than likely, part of the criminal organizations they had taken money from. The ranks of the criminals were swelled by the reforms.

Then there were the men like Vargunin. Men who were better suited to life in an office. Men who were not corrupt but who believed that confessions beaten from suspects were just as valid as those obtained by detective work.

Vargunin changed the conversation with a dismissive wave of his hand. 'Just two old war horses, eh?'

'War horses, yes,' Borovsky agreed. 'But not so old.'

'My spirit feels as if it fought the Mongols in the thirteenth century.'

'Maybe it did,' he teased. 'I think this office was here, too.'

Both men laughed, and Vargunin took a step back, finally taking the time to look his old friend up and down. If Anatoli were a workhorse, it was clear that Borovsky was still a thoroughbred. No thickening of his middle. And while his slicked-back hair may have had a little more gray on the temples, it was still enviably substantial.

The healthier life of the optimist, Vargunin thought.

In fact, age seemed to make Borovsky look even more impressive, from his angular face, probing light brown eyes, and sharp chin, all the way down to his long flat feet. Encased in specially made boots, they were one of Borovsky's only concessions to personal comfort.

'The changes to the uniform become you,' Vargunin decided, releasing his friend's forearms and turning back to the desk. 'Apparently, so do the changes to the force.'

'It's not that,' Borovsky said. 'I have just never been a pessimist like you.'

'That's anti-Russian,' his old coworker said. 'So. What brings you down here?'

'Couldn't it be a friendly visit?' Borovsky asked innocently, pulling forward a seat.

'Couldn't Lenin rise from his tomb and take a stroll

around Red Square?' Vargunin shrugged. 'I suppose it is possible.'

'I was wrong,' Borovsky said. 'You're not a pessimist. You're a cynic.'

Vargunin barked out a laugh. 'Years after "the Bill", you come to say "hi" to one of the officers who notoriously escaped your net and then slipped through another at the Forensic Expertise Center? I am not so old a detective as to consider your arrival merely a coincidence.'

'We were friends, despite the task that was given to me.'

'We were, yes,' Vargunin said. He hoped he hadn't emphasized the 'were' when he spoke it. 'Would you like a drink?'

'Why not?' Borovsky decided. 'For old times' sake.'

27

Andrei Dobrev didn't ask for a single train engine; he requested *two* – back to back, like a Siamese twin attached at the spine. 'The better to power it,' he explained.

Less than a day later, Dobrev watched with pride as the massive, red-and-black engine that he recommended lumbered up the sidetrack at the Moskva-Kazanskaya station. 'The Lugansk 2TE116,' he said to Jasmine. 'The true beast of the RZD.'

'RZD?' Cobb inquired.

Jasmine waited until Dobrev had finished explaining.

'It's what they call the Russian railways,' she simplified.

Cobb nodded and continued to watch the behemoth approach. He couldn't help feeling that this must be what a tyrannosaurus looked like when it tried to sneak up on its prey. He glanced over at Jasmine while Dobrev continued to speak. But for some reason, she didn't translate.

'Well?'

'Technical specs,' she said. 'I don't quite understand.'

'All Greek to you, eh?' McNutt teased.

'No,' she clarified. 'If it were Greek, I'd actually understand.'

'Let's have it anyway,' Cobb told her.

'All right. Let's see. Diesel engine, fifteen-twenty

millimeter gauge, three thousand horsepower at one thousand rpm—'

Cobb let out a low whistle of appreciation. That would be a very powerful dinosaur.

'Thirty-six meters long, twenty feet high, twelve feet wide, axle weight of twenty-three tons, full weight of two hundred and seventy-six metric tons—'

'My head hurts,' McNutt complained.

'Wait,' Jasmine said. 'He's off the details, talking about something else now.'

Cobb waited for Jasmine to catch up. Dobrev didn't seem to care, or even notice her translation. He seemed to be lost in his own railroad world.

'He's telling us what else we'll need,' she said, reciting the list to Cobb, who did not take notes but remembered every word she said.

Finding Dobrev a standard railroad worker's green shirt, green pants, green cap, black belt, black boots, and orange vest was not difficult – what with all the locker rooms within the station. In fact, the whole team except Papineau was dressed that way, so as not to draw unwanted attention. The Frenchman was in one of his suits as always. Jasmine had minimized her conspicuousness by pinning her hair into a bun, wearing sunglasses, and raising her shirt collar to cover the bruises that Kadurik had given her.

The team was gathered beside the massive vintage locomotive – all except Sarah and Garcia, who had disappeared into the first train car.

'According to Andrei,' Jasmine said, 'this engine was easy to obtain. The modernization of the Russian railways started around 2008, and they've been rolling out a thousand new locomotives a year. This vintage one was in a storage facility about an hour out of the city.'

Dobrev took a second to spit onto the track.

Cobb smiled. 'Apparently our friend doesn't think much of the new engines.'

'He does not,' Jasmine agreed. '"Give me this old beauty anytime," he says. With all the new trains running around, there were plenty of these vintage engines to pick and choose from.' Jasmine looked up at Cobb. 'He actually knows this one in particular. He says he could take it apart and put it back together blindfolded.'

'Good to know if we break down at night,' McNutt said.

Cobb stared at the monstrosity. It was an ambitious claim to make, but he wouldn't put it past Dobrev. The beast was a big, thundering mobile home on large metal wheels. Essentially rectangular with a slightly curving arched roof, it had two big rectangular windshield 'eyes' and a round spotlight 'nose'. Its 'mouth' was a low, broad cowcatcher – a plow-like attachment that pushed rocks, debris, and occasionally an animal from the track before it could cause damage to the wheels. This was framed by two more square headlights that looked like shining dimples.

As Cobb watched, two workers approached with the special license plate Papineau had secured; a license plate, he assured them, which would allow them to go anywhere the RZD ran.

Cobb was always impressed by the red tape the Frenchman seemed able to cut.

Or maybe it's just foreign money, he thought.

Papineau signed for the plate and slipped the workers a gratuity. From their grateful expressions, the Frenchman clearly owned them for life.

Cobb stepped to the side to take in the rest of the engine's architecture. Ten high-set, square windows, sixteen air vents, and two doors on each side. No ladders or narrow walkways along the outside. Cobb nodded with appreciation. *Easy to defend, tough to attack*. He was certain Dobrev had not taken that into consideration, but Cobb was pleased to see it nonetheless.

Dobrev moved forward to personally supervise the linking up with the rest of the train.

Cobb noted Jasmine's gaze. 'You're watching him closely.'

She nodded with concern. 'He's immersed himself in the work. I'm not a psychologist, but I suspect from the tone of his voice that he's trying to avoid thinking about what he did last night – and why he had to do it.'

'There's another thing, too.'

'Oh?'

'I bet he feels like this is his last adventure,' Cobb guessed. 'He, and his metal friend there, had been put out to pasture. This is his chance to prove that they still have some worth.' Cobb watched as Dobrev instructed the younger workers on the best way to treat the locomotive. 'I wouldn't be surprised if he had named this old girl.'

Jasmine grinned at the comment. 'Ludmilla. He named it Ludmilla.'

Cobb smiled at the humanity of it.

That was rare in his business.

28

Vargunin took an unlabeled bottle of clear liquid, two small glasses, and a small jar of raw peppercorns from his desk's lower drawer. Then he poured the liquid in the glasses, dropped two large peppercorns in each, and handed one over. He held up his glass.

'To new times' sake,' Vargunin said pointedly.

Borovsky grinned. It was said that only problem drinkers don't toast – and both men had seen ample proof of that among their comrades over the years – so he raised his glass, too. Both threw the vodka deep into their throats, but only Borovsky choked, coughed, and slapped the desktop.

Vargunin simply laughed.

'At least distilling has been improved,' Borovsky managed to choke out. 'Why do you still insist on drinking "two balls"?'

The balls were the peppercorns, used for millennia to soak up the poisons from regional vodka. The good stuff had always been exported, leaving the rotgut like this to the residents.

'To me,' Vargunin answered, 'it always reminds me of my lost youth.'

Borovsky smiled wistfully. 'Good times.'

'Good times, indeed.' Vargunin began to put away the

drinking paraphernalia. 'You have to admit that this battery acid is, at least, an improvement.'

Borovsky nodded. It was time to get down to business. 'All right, my friend. Now that you've tried, unsuccessfully, to kill me, bring me up to date on things.'

'Gelb and Klopov,' Vargunin said as he reached for a file. 'Cops on the take, but they only seemed to be out for themselves. Petty stuff, mostly. Links to the underworld were never fully established, nor had they ever received administrative penalties.'

'Yes, and somehow they managed to pass the new qualification tests.'

'You'd be surprised, my friend,' he told Borovsky. 'They might not have been great officers, but they were cunning and resourceful in their own ways. They had learned a lot about how to protect themselves on the street.'

Borovsky nodded. 'Which is why I was a bit surprised to hear that one was in the hospital and one was in the morgue. What has Klopov told you?'

'Nothing. He's still in a coma.'

'Expected to recover?'

Vargunin shrugged. 'Circumstantial evidence suggests a clash between the two officers and a local sect of the RNU led by Pavel Okecka.'

'What has he told you?'

'Also nothing.'

'Coma?'

'Close. Severe shock. He was found with his face collapsed and his memory gone.'

'So there are no clues.'

'Not quite,' Vargunin said.

'Oh?'

'Back in the day, what was it that I always said?'

'You said many things, most of them complaints,' Borovsky noted.

'True, but I also said: *The absence of evidence is sometimes a clue.*' Vargunin leaned back in his chair. 'The crime scene did not look like a normal brawl. In fact, the lack of evidence tells me it was more than that. It tells me someone messed with the crime scene.'

Borovsky grimaced in surprise. 'Someone messed with the crime scene?'

Vargunin nodded. 'The clash was violent. No one falls down holding their weapons, other than clowns who collide in the center ring.'

'How violent was it?'

Vargunin checked the paperwork. 'Two men dead – Officer Gelb and a local member of the RNU – both from blunt force trauma.'

'I know about Officer Gelb,' Borovsky stated. 'Tell me about the other one.'

'Marko Kadurik, a local troublemaker. Nothing major of note, but he was questioned in connection with a disappearance. A man named Dobrev.'

Borovsky arched his brow. 'Dobrev? As in *Andrei* Dobrev?'

Vargunin looked over with interest. 'No. His grandson, Yury. He disappeared about a year ago.' He paused for a moment, waiting for an explanation from his old friend.

When none was offered, he asked the obvious. 'How do you know Andrei?'

'Our paths have crossed at a function or two. Is he involved?'

Vargunin referenced his paperwork. 'It seems that this incident took place in front of his apartment building. Coincidence?'

'If it is, it's unfortunate for Andrei,' Borovsky answered. 'What did he have to say about the matter?'

Vargunin glanced at his notes. 'He has yet to be located.'

'I see. Go on.'

Vargunin studied his friend's face for any clues, then returned his eyes to the report. 'Little more to say. Officer Klopov is in a coma, and the surviving neo-Nazis all have broken skulls and severe concussions. They are all, for the want of a better word, uncommunicative.' He snapped the report closed, then looked back up at Borovsky. 'The doctors say that the odds are even that the survivors won't remember the attack.'

'If they wake at all.'

Vargunin nodded. 'If they wake at all.'

'Who's the supervising officer on the case?'

Vargunin checked the paperwork. 'Sergeant Rusinko. Anna Rusinko.'

Borovsky's reaction was immediate. 'May I see her?'

'Now?'

'Right now.'

Vargunin was a bit taken aback by Borovsky's urgency, but he immediately responded. 'Of course.'

The colonel may have been an old friend, but he was still Vargunin's superior – by quite a few steps up the ladder of command. The warrant officer leaned over to activate the intercom.

Borovsky interrupted. 'I wish to see her in person.'

Vargunin stopped in mid-click. 'Of course.'

The two men left Vargunin's office and headed past the road safety office, the organized crime unit, the white-collar crime desk, and several other units. Workers moved briskly through the hallway because they knew a superior officer was coming; word spread ahead like a shockwave, informed by whispers, gestures, and veteran instincts that detected a change in the atmosphere in the building. Of course, some of the police officers were actually working hard and fast. Mostly the younger recruits, the ones who had their eyes on the jobs of the sluggish veterans, like great apes sensing frailty in the alpha male.

The two men stopped at the morning briefing. It took place in the station's central booking area, in front of a white wall. The officers were lined up in their multi-pocketed, olive-colored uniforms: black, military-style boots; black berets with new Russian Police insignia; and side arms. They were taking notes on pads as the duty officer read off the day's assignments.

'Once again we have been alerted to a possible caravan of black market materials traveling through our region,' said the buzz-cut duty officer in his red-and-blue-billed hat, light blue shirt, and gray pants. 'This caravan could include anything from passports to electronics to plutonium, so be on special watch for any vehicles that seem suspicious.'

'Plutonium?' Borovsky murmured to his companion.

'Unlikely,' Vargunin replied in hushed tones before shrugging. 'But you never know. The one day we don't say that will be the day some Chechen decides to irradiate the Kremlin.'

'Has there been a drill paper on that?'

'We haven't done any preparedness checklists on things we probably can't prevent,' he admitted. 'We just send our people out with Geiger counters and hope for the best.'

29

On the outside, the train cars looked plain, even a little drab.

Inside, however, was a different matter.

They entered the first car, which had been cannibalized from an old Grand Express train. The eleven square windows on each side were individually curtained in red and gold. Two lighting fixtures ran parallel to each other across the length of the ceiling, divided by a burnished wood panel that was dotted with TV screens that could swing down.

The seats had been gutted, and an elaborate, L-shaped desk and workstation had been installed on the deep red, wall-to-wall carpet. The farthest section of the carriage had tables and couches for anything the team might require.

Papineau was at the desk, staring at a computer screen while a sleek earpiece glowed in his ear. The telltale blue light let everyone know that he was on the phone, performing his latest miracle in foreign bureaucracy. Meanwhile, Garcia sat at the workstation, with McNutt leaning over his shoulder. They were staring at what appeared to be a videogame cutscene – a computer animation that bridges two game segments with backstory. But once Cobb approached, he saw that it was an eye-tearing series of fast-action chases along hyper-realistic railroad tracks.

'What's that?' Cobb asked.

Without turning his face from the screen, Garcia explained. 'It's a program I just finished. It tracks every possible route a gold train could take from Moscow in 1917. I interfaced maps of that period with satellite images from today. My program converts that information to point-of-view graphics. If all goes well, we will figure out the treasure train's original route and, topographically speaking, know exactly what is ahead of us at all times.'

'Very impressive,' Cobb said.

'I call it . . . *Goldfinder*.' Garcia laughed at the name. He was the only one who did. 'You know, like the James Bond movie. Except it's *finder*, not *finger*.'

'Gotcha,' Cobb said.

'I've been working on a theme song, too. Want to hear it?'

'Not really.'

'Goldfinder!' Garcia crooned. 'I'm the man, the man with the—'

'Missing teeth,' Sarah shouted from across the car. Cobb turned to see her studying a map on one of the sofas. 'He's been trying out verses for the past thirty minutes. He's driving me crazy.'

McNutt laughed off her threat, anxious to rile her up. He patted Garcia on the shoulder and said, 'Sing all you want, José. I've got your back.'

Garcia glanced up at him. 'Thanks. But my name's Hector, not José.'

McNutt growled playfully. 'Don't correct me again. And *never* look me in the eyes.'

Cobb shook his head and walked toward Sarah. He could sense something was wrong. 'What's bothering you?'

She sighed. 'I'm trying to figure out every possible way someone could move that much treasure out of the country. The possibilities are endless.'

Cobb smiled. 'You're thinking like a thief, not a royal strategist.' He pointed toward the screen where Goldfinder was calculating the best route for an engine of that era while factoring in weather conditions and the topography of the region. 'Consider any person who wanted to steal the bulk of the treasure. He would take a very different approach from anyone who just wanted to lighten the load by a gold coin or two.'

'Like what?' she asked.

'Disinformation,' Cobb said. 'About the train, the treasure, and several other things. Whoever stole it would have taken the easiest, fastest route, the one ensuring the most success. Then they would have started rumors about how or why the treasure never made it. Avalanche, Bolsheviks, Romanian loyalists – there are any number of reasons. That being said, I tend to accept the simplest theory about the missing treasure: that the people transporting the gold were the same ones who took it. What do you think, Jasmine?'

Standing off to the side, Jasmine was lost in thought while staring out one of the windows. She flinched at the mention of her name. 'What's that?'

Cobb smiled. 'What do you think about my theory?'

'I agree,' she said, recovering quickly. 'Near the end of

the war, the Germans were getting perilously close to Moscow. There were many rumors that the Bolsheviks and the tsarists dispersed several treasures to the provinces, where they may have been lost or already stolen.'

Even Papineau looked up at that. 'And if those rumors are true?'

Sarah threw up her hands. 'Then we'll never find it! It's almost certain that those treasures have already been lost or stolen. What are we going to do, a house-to-house search in every village along every route, looking for clues as to where the gold went from there?'

Cobb sighed. 'Come on, Sarah. You're still thinking like a thief. Sure, maybe like a thief from a century ago, but still a *thief*. You should be reverse-engineering this: thinking like someone who wants to protect it from thieves.' He pointed at Jasmine. 'She might be able to figure this out, because she's the only one of you that doesn't want the treasure for personal gain.'

Sarah exploded. 'Cut the mind games, Jack! Just tell us!'

Cobb suddenly became serious – dead serious. 'Is that what you think these are? Mind games?'

'Yeah,' she said, challenging his methods. 'If one of us had information, you'd want it immediately, not dangled like catnip.'

'The lesson in tactics and logistics *is* the information!' he snarled back. 'I don't know where the damn treasure is. And I won't know unless I get some good minds thinking along the same track. That's the only way this is going to work!'

'The same track,' McNutt laughed. 'That's funny.'

Cobb glared at McNutt, then he glanced around at the team, ending on Sarah. 'Stop thinking about how to steal the gold and start thinking about how you'd protect it if you already had it.'

There was a thick, unhappy silence for several seconds.

Eventually, McNutt broke the tension with a laugh. 'Are you kidding, Jack? I wouldn't protect that treasure for more than a minute. That gold would be like honey to a bear. Only in this case, the bears it attracted would be heavily armed and ready to attack. In all seriousness, I'd take what I could grab and leave the rest. I'd grab some gold and roll.'

'Shit,' Jasmine said. 'We got it all wrong.'

'We got *what* wrong?' McNutt demanded. 'You mean the thing about the bears? Trust me, I know that bears can't shoot a gun. I'm *not* an idiot. Their paws are way too big to pull a trigger.' Sadly, he didn't stop there. 'Then again, under the right circumstances, I bet they could train a circus bear to fire a cannon. Believe it or not, I've seen one ride a bike, so I don't see why they couldn't teach one to light a fuse.' He laughed at the picture in his head. It looked like a cartoon. 'Imagine that: a *bear* firing a *cannon*. That's priceless.'

At that point, the whole group tuned him out.

Cobb looked to Jasmine for clarification. 'What were you saying?'

She looked at Cobb. 'You were right: we got it all wrong!'

Before she could explain, the entire train compartment lurched when the diesel engine coupled with the other cars. Jasmine nearly fell to the floor, but she hardly noticed. She was too overjoyed by her insight.

30

Vargunin stepped away as the roll call officer dismissed the constables. 'Sergeant Rusinko,' he called. 'A moment please.'

A tall woman with short, brown hair looked over to see who was calling. She quickly gathered herself, then approached in a brisk, business-like manner.

'Sergeant Rusinko,' Vargunin said. 'This is Colonel Viktor Borovsky.'

Anna gasped softly. For an instant her eyes widened, brightened, and her mouth dropped open. 'Of Special Branch?' she blurted. Then her face changed again, a flash of mortification battling with competence for control.

'At ease, Sergeant,' Borovsky chuckled, once he had gotten over his own surprise. 'An elder god has not descended from the firmament.'

Vargunin looked at Anna with a we're-never-going-to-let-you-forget-this expression before turning to the colonel. 'It would appear your reputation has preceded you, sir.'

'Apparently,' Borovsky said drily. 'You know me then, Sergeant?'

She looked nervously at the warrant officer.

'Not personally, sir, no,' she said. 'We've never met.' Her own face attempted a twitching smile, but failing that, her stare shifted to one of open respect. 'But everyone knows about your achievements, sir.'

'I am a great man,' he teased.

'Sir, the explorations and discoveries you undertook in your youth, your heroism and patriotism, your exemplary military career—'

Borovsky held up a hand, shaking his head with amusement. 'All right, Sergeant. I remember them well. I was just doing my job, which is all I ask of anyone.'

Anna obviously disagreed but was respectful enough to say nothing more – at least, with words. Her eyes still reflected admiration bordering on awe.

Her warrant officer got the conversation moving again. 'Tell Colonel Borovsky your impressions of the incident between our officers and the local RNU chapter, Sergeant.'

'Yes, sir.' She looked up at Borovsky from her full five feet, nine inches. 'An unusually violent confrontation, sir. We've been having increasing conflict with the members of the RNU here. They seem to be growing more aggressive and flagrant.'

'Seem to be?' Borovsky interrupted. 'Or are?'

Anna stopped as if she had been pinched. 'They are.'

'Go on. Omit nothing, including your impressions.'

'Sir, they are stepping up their black market activity. In addition to selling stolen electronic goods, accessories, jewelry, and bootlegs, they are now dealing in information. Identity theft, illegal databases, passport numbers, internet passwords, bank account numbers, credit card security information, arrest records, even tax returns – all stolen from government agencies.'

'Stolen how?' Borovsky echoed.

'Hacked,' Anna said. 'Or leaked.'

'Leaked,' Borovsky repeated. 'For money.'

Vargunin wasn't certain whether his superior was being critical of the profit motive or of the mentality that allowed a person to put personal gain before the sacred duty with which they'd been entrusted: preserving the security and honor of the nation. For his part, Vargunin wished he had the courage to do that. Then, at least, he could afford the kinds of comforts that would make his private life less stark.

'Money,' Vargunin said grimly. 'Selling such information to the highest bidder is a lucrative business. We estimate that the black market for such information is around fifty million dollars a year.'

'And that is just for the exchange of the raw data,' Anna added. 'Breaking into bank and insurance accounts, into private e-mail accounts for purposes of blackmail, into arrest records of officials who want to keep their prostitution arrests secret, these all generate hundreds of millions in revenue above that.'

Vargunin glanced at his old friend. 'That is why I'm having to learn new skills – to stay two steps behind the con men instead of a dozen.'

Anna continued. 'Perhaps Officers Gelb and Klopov insisted on a better cut of the action, and the emboldened RNU members confronted them.'

Borovsky stared at her, displeased by the accusation.

'You asked for her impressions,' Vargunin reminded him.

The senior officer relaxed. 'Do you think that is what happened?'

For the first time, Anna's eyes wavered, looking at her fellow officers in her peripheral vision as they slowly dispersed for their rounds. 'That was the consensus of the investigators.'

'Based on any evidence?' Borovsky asked.

'Cash folded in the hands of the officers,' she said.

Vargunin snorted.

Borovsky looked at him. 'Do you doubt this?'

'I don't dismiss it,' he said in measured words. 'But I stand by my earlier remark. The crime scene was still too neat.'

Borovsky considered that while he regarded the young woman's face. She was in her early thirties. Olive eyes, small, straight nose, and a flat mouth with lines at either bottom edge from too much frowning. Strong jawline and high cheekbones. Good, Slavic stock. Impressive mental attitude: deductive, alert to the thoughts of veterans and colleagues, but not necessarily seduced by the collective weight of their opinions. Borovsky was curious to know whether she joined the police because of the reform bill or in spite of it.

He turned toward his old friend. 'Is Sergeant Rusinko still assigned to this case?'

Vargunin was taken slightly aback. 'Well, the case hasn't been *officially* closed as of yet.' His emphasis on the word 'officially' told both of them that he wanted it to be. 'So, yes. Technically, she is still assigned to it.'

'Good,' Borovsky said with a nod. Then he looked at Anna as if his old friend no longer existed. 'Show me Marko Kadurik's body, please.'

Once everyone had steadied themselves, Cobb motioned for Jasmine to take the floor. He stepped to the side, leaned against the workstation, and crossed his arms in anticipation. He was pleased to note that even Garcia was looking at Jasmine, not his computer screen.

'We got *what* wrong?' Garcia demanded.

'Everything,' she said as she started to pace back and forth in the center of the train compartment. 'I don't know why I didn't think of this sooner. I mean, it's so *obvious*. Who knows? Maybe I was distracted by the violence, or maybe I've been worried about Andrei, I'm really not sure now, but this is something I should have focused on *much* earlier—'

'Jasmine!' Cobb blurted to stop her rambling.

She glanced at him, frazzled.

He flashed a warm smile to calm her down. 'Relax. Just relax. Don't worry about the past. Just take a deep breath, and tell us what you figured out.'

She did as she was told and took a deep breath.

He gave her a moment. 'Better?'

She nodded. 'Better.'

He smiled again. 'Good. The floor's still yours.'

She paused for a second to gather her thoughts. 'As I was saying, we've been looking at things all wrong. Instead of focusing on who protected the treasure, we should have been trying to figure out who moved the treasure to begin with. And if you think about it, history tells us that there's only one person who could have moved that much gold out of Moscow at that time.'

'*Mon Dieu!*' Papineau gasped. With his knowledge of European history, he got her reference before the rest of the team.

'Think about it!' Jasmine commanded in her excited, sincere way. 'The war was at its most oppressive point, the enemy was at the gates, everyone was starving and freezing. Who was the one person who could lead a train out of Moscow at that time? Who was the one person who could get through every station and every checkpoint with unquestioned authority?'

Garcia, McNutt, and Sarah had no clue. They looked like the Breakfast Club – a geek, a jock, and a prom queen – caught in the headlights of a pop quiz.

Shaking his head, Papineau muttered in French, 'Stupid Americans.'

* * *

The team huddled around Garcia as he brought up historical information about Tsar Nicholas II and the Romanovs on his computer screen.

'How'd you get this to work? Doesn't Russia restrict access to the Web?' Sarah asked.

Garcia chuckled. 'It's not like I'm *wardriving* – connecting to the Web through someone's Wi-Fi signal. I've got a direct link through Papi's satellites. He's got two, by the way.' He shifted his focus to the Frenchman. 'But you should have three. When they switch over in their orbit, there's a gap.'

'We're working on it,' Papineau said, scanning the screen.

Jasmine could have described what they needed to know, but Cobb wanted them to discover it on their own. He sensed that they would learn more that way.

'How long a gap?' Cobb asked quietly.

Garcia blinked up at him. 'Two to eight minutes. Why?'

Cobb grimaced. 'Blackouts are risky.'

'I know.'

Papineau interrupted them. 'Here we are.'

They all faced the computer. On the screen was a picture of a Romanov prince with an extremely long title: Prince Felix Felixovich Yusupov, Count Sumarokov-Elston.

Jasmine wasn't going to wait until they finished reading. She might not be able to shoot a pebble resting on the top of a mountain or steal a coin from a beggar's cup, but there was one thing she could do. She could narrate.

'After the prince was accused of being the brains behind Rasputin's murder, Tsarina Alexandra Fyodorovna – who was the aunt of Felix's wife – essentially placed the prince under house arrest in his estate outside St Petersburg.'

'Hold up,' McNutt said. 'I've heard the name before, but who is Rasputin?'

Jasmine answered. 'Gregori Rasputin was a Russian mystic and faith healer who greatly influenced the tsar and tsarina in the final years of the Romanov dynasty. Although many viewed him as a charlatan, the tsarina was under his charismatic spell.'

Sarah smiled. 'You'd have liked him, McNutt. His nickname was the Mad Monk.'

McNutt nodded. 'You're right. I like him already.'

'Well,' Jasmine said, trying to get them back on track, 'Prince Felix didn't, which is why he had Rasputin killed. The tsarina, who viewed herself as Rasputin's protector, was furious. So much so that she exiled the prince – even though he was a war hero.'

'And that's when he took the train,' McNutt guessed.

'No,' Sarah assured him as she continued to read ahead. 'Three months later, things went from bad to incredibly bad.'

Jasmine stared daggers at the back of Sarah's head, angry that her turf was being encroached upon. 'They were worse than "incredibly bad",' Jasmine corrected. 'The tsar's abdication and the February Revolution were events that shaped the course of our world.'

'Shh,' Sarah said, rebuking the rebuke. 'I'm reading.'

Jasmine ignored her. 'The prince couldn't have possibly known he was going to be exiled—'

Sarah interrupted her. 'But he absolutely knew which way the wind was blowing. After all, he had the stones and foresight to take out Rasputin. He had to realize things were precarious.'

Jasmine didn't reply. She was far too irritated.

Cobb was curious to see how this would work out, but he didn't get the chance. McNutt sliced through the tension.

'How many times did they try to kill him again?' McNutt asked.

Jasmine was back onstage. 'About a half-dozen,' she said. 'Poison, shooting, beating – supposedly he was nearly disemboweled by a woman three years before, but obviously that didn't kill him either.' She looked around at the others, intentionally skipping Sarah. 'And when they finally tried to burn his body after they found it in the Neva River, witnesses reported that he sat up in the flames.'

'I'm officially creeped out,' Garcia said.

'Most likely his tendons weren't cut before the funeral pyre,' Sarah said without inflection, her eyes still intent on the screen. 'The heat of the fire would make them shrink. Hence the incineration sit-up.'

Cobb smiled, impressed.

Jasmine noted his reaction and took a deep breath. 'That is what some biographers have said as well, but others have put forth the idea that he was a saint who cheated death.'

'A whoring, alcoholic, game-playing saint?'

Jasmine, who felt physically inferior to Sarah, hated where this was going. History was her area of expertise and she knew if she didn't stand her ground and protect her role on the team, then these interruptions would continue for the rest of the mission. To shut Sarah down, Jasmine went for her weak spot. 'Many theologians believe that sainthood is achieved through trial. It is not necessarily inborn. It is something that is *earned* over time, not stolen by a thief in the night. That's the easy way to get through life.'

Sarah winced. 'Excuse me?'

Jasmine didn't back down. 'Sorry. No offense intended.'

Sarah stood back from the computer, even more insulted

by the insincere tone of the apology. 'I would think not since we're *both* trying to steal this treasure.'

'Actually,' Jasmine stressed, 'I'm trying to *find* it, not *steal* it.'

Cobb sensed they weren't going to work this out on their own. He could see the aggressive tension in both of their bodies, particularly Sarah's. 'Take a breather,' he said to her.

'Glad to,' Sarah muttered as she left the train car.

'Man,' McNutt said, as if the confrontation hadn't occurred, 'I get the feeling that Rasputin was a guy who really didn't want to die.'

Cobb smiled. Sometimes McNutt's bubble was a useful place.

'Prince Felix wanted to live, too,' Jasmine reminded them. 'After the abdication three months later, he immediately decamped to Crimea.'

'How "immediately"?' Cobb wanted to know.

'No way of knowing for sure, but within weeks, possibly a fortnight, possibly less.'

'Surprising how much you can get done under house arrest,' Cobb said. 'Three months could be enough time to have made plans, written letters.'

'Undoubtedly,' Jasmine said. 'From Crimea, the family – including the prince – was able to secure passage to Malta on a British warship. From Malta, they went to Italy and London before eventually settling in Paris.'

'When?' Garcia asked.

'That was in 1920.'

'Two, three years after attacking Raspy,' McNutt noted.

'Wow,' Garcia teased. 'You didn't even have to use your fingers or toes.'

'Cut it out,' Cobb said before McNutt could respond. He didn't need another pissing contest. Or a dead computer guy, which is what Garcia would be if McNutt got a hold of him.

'How do you think the prince paid for all that?' Papineau asked Jasmine.

She thought about it for a while. 'There was some talk that he took jewelry and rare art from their palace before they left.'

Cobb glanced at Papineau. 'Does that theory sound right to you?'

'Yes,' Papineau mused, leaning back in his chair. 'Prince Felix was both an honorable man and a man of action. He must have known that securing the Romanov riches from invaders as well as his own enraged family would be impossible under those circumstances.'

'But maybe not the Romanian treasure,' Cobb said.

'How long have you known this, about the prince?' the Frenchman demanded.

'I still don't *know* it,' Cobb replied. 'But once I stopped thinking about how to find the treasure and started to think about how it could've been lost . . .'

'No one but a member of the royal family could've gotten it out of town,' Jasmine said. 'There are always royal loyalists in any revolution. Not even the highest-ranking general would have had that much pull.'

'And the prince was going to be on an exile train regardless,' Papineau marveled.

'Yep,' Cobb said. 'So I wouldn't worry about grave robbers. I bet they stopped looking for crumbs a long time ago. What was it that Sherlock Holmes used to say?'

'"When you eliminate the impossible,"' Garcia immediately quoted, '"whatever's left, no matter how improbable, has got to be the—"'

He never got to finish. At that moment a small red light on his workstation began to flash, a strident buzzer began to bleat, and the ceiling screens began to swing down.

'What is it?' Papineau snapped.

'Someone's done something to the train,' Garcia snapped back, his hands dancing across his keyboard as his computer screen filled with different images from outside. 'The security cams I installed have been on-line for hours.'

Cobb and McNutt flanked him instantly, their eyes intent on the screen.

'Do you see all the workers who were there before?' McNutt asked.

'The four that Dobrev was breaking in, yeah,' Cobb replied. 'The two that delivered the license left right afterwards. Where's Dobrev?'

'There,' Jasmine said from just behind them. She pointed at the corner of an image in the upper left of the screen. Dobrev was checking Ludmilla's undercarriage, carrying the spanner he had used to save Jasmine.

'Okay,' Cobb said. 'So what's the prob—'

They all snapped to attention when Sarah screeched like a wounded cat.

She was outside, and she was in trouble.

32

A morgue is a morgue. It has no personality. It isn't a cathedral where the deceased are remembered with tears and prayer. It is a collection of drawers and tables where the dead are all the same. They haven't 'passed' or 'gone to their reward'. There is nothing romantic, nothing hopeful at all. There is no modesty. Public faces and private parts are all equal here.

They are dead.

No matter where it is – in the oldest village or a brand new building – and no matter how much technology is employed, a morgue is a place where lifeless bodies are stored and dissected to see what the dead have to say to the living.

Today, Marko Kadurik was talking to Colonel Borovsky.

Situated in the cellar of the police station, this morgue was neither ancient nor cutting-edge. The fresh paint and new furniture that brightened the floors above had yet to trickle down into this dark, stone space. There were fluorescent lights in the ceiling, metal tables on the floor, and autopsy equipment in a long tray on the right. Several corpse cabinets lined the left wall. It was not like the morgues that Borovsky had seen on television or in the other countries he had visited overseas. Those places were always clean and antiseptic. None of them communicated the smell, look, feel, and choking weight of death like this place did.

He glanced at Anna Rusinko, looking for signs of distress. She had led him down the stairs and into the morgue and was now watching his every move like a wide-eyed rookie.

Remarkably, she appeared unfazed by her surroundings.

As per his orders, the dead body of Marko Kadurik had been placed on the center table, a single sheet discreetly draping his body from the neck down. The first thing Borovsky did was pull back the thin covering with a flourish. Then he tossed it against the wall.

The civilian morgue attendant, a pale-skinned youth dressed in a stained lab coat, swallowed hard. He was surprised by the behavior. 'The mortal wound is on his head, comrade.'

Borovsky looked at him dismissively. 'The autopsy is complete?'

'No, sir,' the young man replied. 'Not yet begun—'

'But you are certain the head wound is what killed this man.'

The youth stood there with an expression that said, *Do you not see the exposed section of brain?* But he wisely said nothing.

'Truth cannot enter a closed mind,' Borovsky said. 'Old Russian proverb.'

Anna looked at the attendant and motioned with her head for him to leave the morgue immediately. He did so without pause. When she looked back at her superior, he was examining every inch of the corpse.

'Upstairs,' Borovsky said flatly, 'you stated that the theory of this case was a consensus of your fellow investigators. Is that true?'

When no answer came, Borovsky glanced at Anna, who was trying to figure out the best way to respond. 'It's a simple question,' he said.

'True, sir,' she replied with obvious reluctance.

Borovsky nodded. 'We were taught as young children that religion is the opiate of the masses. However, I put it to you that lies are the true opiate. Repetition makes them seem real – just like religion. In this instance, the obvious solution takes on the mantle of truth and ruins an objective investigation. True?'

'True,' she said immediately.

He made his way to the ruined skull. 'Who do you think was the last man standing?'

'We are still canvassing residents, sir, gathering infor—'

'*Who do you think was the last man standing?*' he repeated without looking up. 'You had two officers and four skin-heads at the scene. Who do you think fell last: Gelb, Klopov, or one of the neo-Nazis?'

Anna exhaled, drew herself up, and tried to toe the station line. 'My investigators suspect that the officers were attacked when they asked the skinheads to depart the area.'

'Couldn't the officers have demanded money? I understand there was cash in their hands.'

Somewhat embarrassed, she said, 'We believe it came from a meeting, perhaps a chance meeting, with a motorist moments before.'

'A bribe,' Borovsky clarified. 'Money for them to look the other way.'

'Yes, sir.'

'Could the motorist not have been there still when the skinheads arrived?'

'It's possible,' she agreed, 'but we cannot track a hypothetical car since the officers did not report a traffic offense.'

'Fair enough,' Borovsky agreed. 'But if a bribe did occur, perhaps the skinheads witnessed the transaction. If so, perhaps the officers attacked them to keep them quiet.'

'It is possible,' she admitted.

'What else have your investigators suggested?'

She continued with reluctance. 'They believe the attackers succeeded in downing our officers before succumbing to their own wounds – wounds inflicted by Privates Gelb and Klopov in a vigorous attempt to defend themselves.'

Borovsky frowned at their conclusion. 'The skinheads had broken skulls and, in one case, a broken arm. What do you think our comrades used to accomplish that? Their fists?'

She opened her mouth to paraphrase the investigators, then closed it again. 'I couldn't say for sure, comrade Colonel. I honestly don't know.'

Borovsky looked at her with satisfaction. Then with the hint of a smile, he quoted another proverb. 'There is no shame in not knowing. The shame lies in not finding out.'

'Yes, sir.'

'Tell me,' he said as he returned his focus to the victim. 'What sorts of weapons were used in this attack?'

Anna straightened, relieved to report facts rather than theories. 'We found metal pipes, an AK-47 bayonet, and a large, jagged piece of masonry. All with blood residue.'

Borovsky motioned for her to come over. She did so without hesitation.

'What do you think made this head wound?' he asked, pointing at the jagged hole in Kadurik's skull. 'The rock, the knife, or the pipes?'

Anna examined the wound carefully. 'It is too wide for the pipes or the knife.' She paused to think, looking at it from every angle. 'Yet the depression is too uniform for the masonry.'

'Good,' he said. 'Knowledge is of no value unless you put it into practice.'

'Russian proverb?' she asked with a weary smile.

'Anton Chekhov,' he replied. 'Continue.'

'Now that I see it, I don't think this wound was made by any of the weapons we found at the crime scene,' she said.

'Then we have a missing weapon,' he said.

'Yes, comrade Colonel, I believe we do.'

'And when there's a missing weapon, there's a missing suspect.' Borovsky straightened to his full height. 'Perhaps the last man standing – is *still* standing.'

She nodded, impressed. Multiple investigators had examined the body, yet Borovsky had proven their theories incorrect in a matter of seconds.

'Comrade Rusinko, please take me to the crime scene.'

* * *

Anna drove Colonel Borovsky to the crime scene in an unmarked sedan. They conducted an exhaustive search outside before they asked the building manager to let them into Andrei Dobrev's apartment. At first, there was a fleeting moment of dread when they grasped the extent of his massive collection of railway memorabilia and equipment, but then Borovsky grinned with anticipation and snapped on the plastic gloves he had pulled from his jacket pocket.

It was obvious he loved a challenge, and so did she. She always had rubber gloves as well, and she joined him as they started going through every box, file, shelf, book, album, picture frame, and nook. What they were looking for was unspoken, but obvious. It was the weapon, or anything that might lead them to comprehend what had happened on the street outside.

For that, no words were needed.

After nearly an hour in which they rarely spoke, Anna broke the silence. 'Comrade Colonel, I think I may have found something.'

He withdrew his head from a low, dusty bookcase, happy for the break. He approached the policewoman, who was holding a velvet-lined rectangular box.

'Or,' she said, 'to be more accurate, I have found *nothing*.'

She opened the box to reveal that it was empty. But he understood. The box had clearly held something precious, and it was just about the only thing they could not find amongst the piles of maps, charts, books, plans, and paraphernalia.

Anna obviously didn't think that this small box had

housed a weapon large enough to inflict the wound that had killed Marko Kadurik, but from Borovsky's reaction, she knew she had hit on something potentially significant. He stood, fascinated, his finger slowly and carefully following the small, circular indentation in the red padding.

'A medal?' she suggested.

'Medals typically use cheap, lightweight metal. This was heavier. A coin, perhaps.' He leaned closer, angling the box toward the light. 'A coin that Dobrev felt was special.'

'Do you think Gelb or Klopov might have taken it?'

'You interviewed the occupants of this building. Did anyone mention the police searching any apartments?'

She shook her head. 'Perhaps they were afraid.'

'No,' he said. 'In any group there is always one who destroys the silence of the others, one who has integrity. If the officers had entered, someone would have mentioned that.'

'Some people on this floor reported footsteps and loud words in the hallway. We thought it might be the skinheads, calling on Kadurik.'

'Our men searched the clothes and bodies of the victims?'

'Thoroughly,' she assured him. 'There was no coin or medal or small memento of this kind. I read the itemized list.'

They stood silently for a few moments. Anna watched him think, but she couldn't read the parade of emotions that marched across his face like a procession in Red Square.

Back at the station, Vargunin had seemed none too pleased when she had left with Borovsky. With a grimace on his face, Vargunin had stared at her while tapping on his watch as a warning. Her warrant officer knew that she had many reports to read, annotate, and file.

'What shall we do, comrade Colonel?' Anna finally asked.

Borovsky thought for a moment, then snapped the box closed. 'I think you should accept the new post I will offer you, Sergeant Rusinko. I think I will need your assistance in finding Andrei Dobrev, at any cost and with all speed.'

33

Cobb and McNutt were out the doors instantly, one on each side of the car. Garcia stayed glued to his screen, while Papineau charged back through the train. But Jasmine hesitated. She wanted to warn Dobrev about the threat but felt like she had been a liability to the team at his apartment, so she decided to stay put, leaning over Garcia to watch the security camera feeds on his screen.

Cobb and McNutt dropped to the ground, both kneeling all the way down to get a better view beneath the train. They couldn't get a completely clear look because of the truck frames that held the big, metal disc wheels, as well as the fuel tanks and air reservoirs that hung beneath the train, but it was a start.

The only living thing that Cobb saw was McNutt, who was holding a Ruger Mark III pistol low in his hand. Complete with custom suppressor, the .22 caliber weapon looked bizarre – like a cross between the German Luger and the Japanese Nambu – but there was a reason it was nicknamed 'Assassin'. It was virtually silent and, in the right pair of hands, deadly.

McNutt had the 'right' pair of hands.

'No killing,' Papineau shouted on the move. Cobb and McNutt continued the sweep while Papineau raced above them, running across the semi-contained flatbed car. 'We can't afford to hide or dispose of a corpse this early in the game.'

'And I can't afford to be dead,' McNutt snapped.

Cobb saw McNutt – and his Ruger – from the corner of his eye.

'You heard him,' Cobb said. 'We are running ABM.'

The acronym stood for Anti-Ballistic Maneuvers: no fire-arms.

McNutt wasn't happy. 'Whoever we're looking for won't be playing fair.'

Cobb shrugged. 'Maybe so, but you have your orders.'

McNutt nodded and reluctantly stowed his weapon. The two men moved quickly in opposite directions, starting their complete search of the train.

Papineau made a quick visual check of the flat car as he crossed it. The five-foot-tall, slatted fencing created a lip around the surface. Sections or entire sides could be folded, flattened, or removed. Nothing seemed to be out of place. 'Anyone, is Sarah in view?'

Cobb and McNutt didn't answer since they had nothing to report.

'No,' Garcia said. 'No visual or sound since the screech.'

Not good, Cobb thought. That meant she was either down or in very serious trouble. Sarah was the type who'd find a way to make a noise, any noise, if she could.

Papineau disappeared into the freight car as Jasmine appeared on the train roof. To get there, she had climbed the ladder at the far end of the conference car. Cobb felt a flash of pride. It had taken a while, but Jasmine had decided to stop thinking of herself as a liability.

That was a major step in her growth.

Jasmine surveyed the area from her vantage point. 'No sign of Sarah or anyone else. She has to be under the train.'

The men had already come to the same conclusion. By then, they were on opposite ends and opposite sides of the four-car length.

'McNutt, under on three,' Cobb said quietly. 'One . . . two . . .'

As he said 'three', both men rolled and came up crouching low beneath the train. The underside of the train was like an iron enclosure, with openings between the wheels. The ground, like the turf of so many train stations, consisted of small rocks over earth that supported the wooden ties and steel tracks. Cobb and McNutt had unstable footing on loose, uneven stones, their backs bent by the unforgiving underside of the train.

Since Cobb was nearest the fourth car – the sleeping quarters – he spotted her first. Framed in the circle of one of the train's wheels was Sarah. Her back was to the wheel, which she was seemingly using as a cover or shield. But something about it didn't seem right. As Cobb peered closer, he saw that her eyes were closed and her head was lolling. She was unconscious.

'Fourth car,' he whispered. 'Back my play.'

Cobb knew what she had done in Brighton Beach. Whoever had taken her down so easily was more than likely not a Russian cop or a neo-Nazi. He was a professional.

'Wait for me,' McNutt whispered.

'No,' Cobb ordered, 'just back my play.'

McNutt growled softly but kept his mouth shut.

Wasting no time, Cobb crept closer and closer to Sarah. He quickly realized that her body was in an impossible position. If she was truly unconscious, she should have slumped over to the ground. Instead, she was sitting upright with an arched back.

Instantly, Cobb became still. It was different from freezing in place. When people froze they stiffened like ice, ready to crack or shatter. When Cobb stilled, he settled like calm water, ready to flow in any direction. He stilled because he realized that the backs of the train wheels were not black. They were shades of dark blue and darker gray. But behind Sarah's blond hair, white skin, and green clothing was a black shape.

Someone was holding her upright.

Approaching from the front of the train, McNutt saw the action before he could comprehend it. Cobb rushed forward in a controlled sprint as a lifeless Sarah – who'd been flung by her nearly invisible assailant – flew through the air toward Cobb. McNutt blinked a few times before he saw a black figure scurry through the shadows. Only then did McNutt realize that Sarah had been thrown by a man, not launched by a wizard.

Thank God, he thought. *We aren't prepared to fight magic.*

For Cobb, it wasn't about thinking; it was about reacting. He reached out with both hands as Sarah's body hurtled toward him. He caught her head in the crook of his left arm, cushioning and cradling it, while he stopped her forward momentum with the palm of his right hand. At the same time he lowered himself into a wide stance so they would be closer to the hard ground. It wouldn't have worked on anyone bigger, but this way he could open his arm and slide her head down to the gravel. The back of his left hand took the pain of settling her head down on the stones. The rest of her body might be a little bruised, but her head was safe.

At no time did Cobb lose his balance, but his maneuver meant a nanosecond of blindness when his focus was on Sarah instead of on his adversary. Had the shadow been attacking, that moment of inattention might have been a deadly mistake. Without coming up from his stance, he looked for the black shadow's position and listened for breathing. He quickly felt a presence.

The shadow hadn't fled. He had merely gathered himself.

He was preparing to launch an attack.

Cobb sensed a shift in air pressure in the blackness to his left. He responded by adjusting the back foot in his stance, then unleashing his right leg in a sidekick at his opponent's sternum. With his gloved hands, the shadow stopped Cobb's foot with a classic V-shaped block, driving down hard on Cobb's lower leg and pushing it to the gravel.

But Cobb did not panic. In fact, he became calmer.

Now he knew what he was facing.

The man was using a Russian martial art called Samooborona Bez Oruzhiya, which was often shortened to the better-known term 'Sambo'. Created in the 1920s by the Russian military, it literally translated as 'self-defense without weapons', but its combat style combined the most devastatingly effective means of killing from every other martial art in the world. Karate striking, jiu-jitsu choking, judo locking, muay thai crushing, and so on. Nothing was off limits in most martial arts around the world, but everything was encouraged in Sambo.

Cobb almost smiled. He still couldn't see his adversary, but that didn't matter. He slid his right leg forward, along the gravel, toward his opponent. That's all it took to break the figure's pincer-like grip on his leg. Cobb knew that to execute the move, the figure would have ended up bent slightly forward, presenting his head for whatever Cobb decided to do next. That would have been to grab the back of the individual's head and send his face into Cobb's knee, which was there and waiting. But the figure had anticipated his vulnerability and inverted the V of his arms so it was facing up, to catch Cobb's hand as he reached. That delayed Cobb's attack long enough for the figure to back deeper into the shadows – back to the left, from the crunch of the rock. Cobb thrust his already extended hand after him, grabbed cloth, but his opponent had enough momentum to spin out of his grip and run away.

Cobb hoped that McNutt knew what to do next. They'd saved Sarah; now it was time to get the attacker. A second later, Cobb was thrilled to see McNutt in hot pursuit.

Wasting no time, Cobb scurried back to Sarah. Even from a distance, he could see that she was breathing evenly, so he had no worries about her long-term health. But just to be safe, he checked her carefully and spotted no obvious damage. In Cobb's mind, her condition was both good and bad news. It was *good* because Sarah would recover and his team could move on as planned. It was *bad* because it reaffirmed his earlier theory: the assailant wasn't a thug; he was a trained professional. A corrupt cop, black marketeer, or psycho skinhead would have used a weapon to take Sarah out, but this guy took her down with ease.

Someone like that could ruin a mission like theirs.

'Gone,' McNutt whispered from the other side of the station. A minute later, he was crouching down next to Cobb, explaining how the assailant had escaped. 'I've never seen anybody move that fast without a jet pack. Who the hell was it?'

Cobb shrugged, his focus still on Sarah. 'I don't know, but I've got a bad feeling that we'll find out soon enough.'

34

Garcia accessed the video feed from a security camera outside the train yard and transferred it to his computer screen. Papineau and Cobb leaned over the seated tech expert and studied the digitally recorded image of the man in black, racing from the yard.

Meanwhile McNutt was in the freight car, doing an inventory to make sure nothing was taken, added, or sabotaged. Sarah was in her compartment, recovering, while Jasmine tended to her. Team members can bicker all they want – that's to be expected given the danger and their close proximity – but they're there for each other when it counts. As they went about their various tasks, they were all continuously linked via their earpieces, eliminating the need for repetitious explanations later.

'Any insight, Papi?' Cobb asked.

Papineau glared at Cobb. 'About what, specifically?'

Cobb was unfazed. 'The intruder.'

Papineau let Cobb's veiled accusation hang in the air for several seconds. He was ready to lash back when Garcia broke the silence.

'Well, I've seen him before.'

'Where?' Papineau demanded.

'Well, maybe not *him*,' Garcia corrected. 'But someone

who dressed like him. I figured he was some kind of priest. Russian Orthodox, or some religion like that.'

'We've all seen his kind,' Cobb said.

Papineau looked at him with surprise.

'Don't play innocent,' Cobb said. 'It doesn't suit you. There's been one of his kind virtually everywhere we've gone. Walking close, passing through, talking to others. Nothing secretive like today, but they've been around. The first time they showed up was at the reception. You looked at him longer than the rest of us – like you'd seen him before.'

Papineau pulsed with anger. He opened his mouth to ridicule Cobb, but he managed not to. He stood firm against the wave of emotion, realizing that it was anger rising to cover guilt.

'I have seen him before,' Papineau admitted carefully, staring into Cobb's eyes. 'Or at least, like Hector said, someone in similar attire.'

Garcia found that he was holding his breath, as the two seemed to be deciding just how far they were willing to bend before one of them snapped.

'Like you said,' Papineau continued, 'they've been hovering around the edges.'

Cobb seemed to drop some of his military posture. He sighed and scratched his head. 'Okay, if that's the way you want to play this . . .'

'What is "this"?' Papineau asked irritably.

Cobb folded his arms. 'I said from the beginning that I'd bail if you ever countermanded my orders. Stupidly, I never said I required full disclosure, so I suppose we're stuck with each other for a while. That said, I want to know what you know. All of it.'

The Frenchman stared in amazement, then he honestly and wholeheartedly laughed, clapping Cobb on the shoulder. '*Mon ami*, you are truly something.'

'Don't try to flatter me,' Cobb warned with a smile. He could play insincere as well as Papineau. 'We could've lost someone today based on what you didn't share. I'm giving you a chance to do that now. One time only.'

Papineau grinned. 'Do you really think you can threaten me?'

Cobb rolled the man's hand from his shoulder. 'If putting your head under the wheels of a slow-moving train is a threat, then yeah, I do.'

'черные робы,' blurted Garcia suddenly, defusing the confrontation in pitch-perfect Russian. He was smiling up at them as if expecting a reward. 'Jasmine has been teaching me correct pronunciation, or is it enunciation? Anyway, she figured I'd need it.'

They stared at him, waiting for his translation.

'Anyway,' he said as he filled the silence, 'I've been sitting here trying to remember their name. They're called the Black Robes.'

'Black Robes?' Cobb echoed.

'Yeah,' Garcia said, returning his attention to the computer screen. 'As I was about to say before you guys started antler-banging, I saw one enter an Internet café that I was checking out. I was trying to find some like-minded hackers in Moscow, just in case. Guys, I'm telling you: if you combined Sarah and me, you'd get someone like those Russian hack kids. They really are incredible. Money-crazy, but totally smart.'

'Back on topic?'

'Yeah, sorry. Uh, which one?'

Cobb shook his head. 'One of those Black Robes looked into the café? He didn't try to hide himself?'

'Nope,' Garcia said, getting back on track. 'But it was weird. When the hackers saw him, they recoiled in obvious fear. Someone mentioned that phrase: черные робы. When I asked Jasmine about it, she translated it as "Black Robes".' He looked back at his team leader. 'Apparently, they're a sect of some kind.'

'What kind?' Papineau asked.

Garcia shrugged. 'Damned if I know.'

Cobb looked at the Frenchman. 'You really don't know?'

'I really do not.'

'Where did you see them, then?'

'The same places you've seen them,' Papineau replied.

Cobb turned his eyes on Garcia. 'What about on the Web?'

'*Nyet. Nada.*'

'That's disquieting in and of itself. The only things not on the Web are things that don't exist,' Cobb remarked.

'Or things that cover their tracks faster than I can follow them,' Garcia suggested. The concept didn't sit well with him. He prided himself on his knowledge of technology. 'What about you? Did you learn anything from the guy? Anything at all?'

Cobb thought about it, and his expression did nothing to settle Garcia. 'All I know is that they're tough to kill. So when we step on them, we'd better step hard.' He held Garcia's gaze. 'Check the entire train, inside and out, for anything he might have left behind. And get some security cams on the undercarriages. We're vulnerable there.'

Cobb started toward the door, then stopped. He hadn't forgotten his confrontation with Papineau. He had merely benched it for the moment.

'And Papi,' he said, 'you're with me.'

* * *

As Cobb and Papineau made their exit, Garcia ran another search on the Black Robes. His results were varied and irrelevant – with no mention of covert ops.

Digging deeper, Garcia accessed a handful of 'off-the-grid' bulletin boards – websites on hidden networks that weren't accessible to most. These sites allowed hackers to carry on discussion under the cloak of anonymity. It took several refinements to narrow his search and translation software to decipher the answers, but Garcia found what he was looking for.

After scanning the information, he realized that Sarah was lucky to be alive.

'What's up?' Jasmine asked as he entered the command center.

'I was just doing a little research on the Black Robes,' Garcia answered. 'We think they're responsible for Sarah's attack.'

'I know,' Jasmine said, pointing to her earpiece. 'I meant, did you find anything interesting?'

'More like terrifying.'

'How so?'

Garcia summed up everything he had read. 'If you believe the rumors, the Black Robes have been around for over a hundred years. And during that time, they've been growing in prominence throughout Eastern Europe. No one knows exactly when the cult took shape, but—'

'They're a cult?' she interrupted.

'Well, they certainly fit the description. Not that they're overly religious – 'cause they're not. It's more of a spiritual bent. Revelation through suffering, that sort of thing. The punishment for one's sins serves to heighten one's understanding of the world.'

'What kind of sins?'

'Judging from the accounts of rape and violence, I'd say they're particularly fond of lust and wrath.' He paused, but Jasmine said nothing in reply. 'I know what you're thinking: why couldn't it have been sloth and gluttony? We could handle a bunch of lazy, fat guys.'

Jasmine was suddenly thankful for their lethal supplies.

'No,' Garcia continued. 'We get stuck with the guys who think the path to enlightenment is found through murder.'

35

Cobb entered the freight car with Papineau close behind. McNutt was in the far corner, going over the last of the equipment.

The freight car's walls, floor, and ceiling were armored, but with several sliding and slatted windows and doors so the gear could be moved, used, or launched in a thousand different ways. Along the west wall was an array of firearms of every shape and size, from handguns and sniper's rifles to automatic weapons. Cobb noticed the Mark III back in its place between a Kel-Tec P32 and a Springfield Armory XD9 Sub-Compact.

At Cobb's insistence, McNutt had supplied everyone on the team with a sidearm that best fit their size, weight, and temperament, along with intensive training during their weeks together in Fort Lauderdale.

Garcia got a Walther PPK or, as he called it, the James Bond gun. It was the one 007 used in most books and movies. McNutt chose it for him because it had good firepower in a nerd-friendly, twenty-ounce, six-inch package.

Jasmine had grudgingly accepted a Ruger LCR .38 Special revolver. Light, sleek, hammerless, and practically unjammable, it was a perfect point-and-pull weapon for their pacifist-leaning, but obviously eminently attackable, historian.

McNutt had wanted to give the similar Charter Arms .38 Special Undercover Model 13820 revolver to Sarah, but he knew she would balk at what she considered its traditional clunkiness. It was clear to him that she was ready to reject anything he offered, lest it weigh her down or hold her back. So he presented her with the Kimber Micro Custom Defense Package .380 automatic. At thirteen ounces and hardly bigger than her hand, she had almost grabbed it from his grasp before he could hand it to her.

'Find anything?' Papineau asked.

McNutt looked up from the polymer crates and canvas containers that lined the east wall, then shook his head. 'I checked every inch of this place for holes or punctures, even pinpricks. The only thing missing is some backup gear that would have been way too big to steal. My guess is it never made the original shipment.'

'Anything essential?'

'Nope. Just redundancies.'

Cobb didn't ask if the Black Robe could've slipped something through the slatted windows or rolling doors. They were created to both men's specifications. Nothing would get in or out without their say-so. 'Out of curiosity, how'd you get all this stuff in here?'

'What do you mean?' McNutt asked.

'Not you, McNutt.' Cobb turned toward the Frenchman. 'Getting us supplies in Florida is one thing, but smuggling an armory into Russia is quite another.'

McNutt furrowed his brow, perplexed, but Papineau just waved it aside. 'Don't worry, Joshua. This is just part two of something we started in the command center.'

'You got that right,' Cobb said. He began to walk around the compartment, taking in all the cutting-edge weapon technology that filled the car. 'I can't help feeling that we're moving faster and faster toward a collision with something that only *you* know about. Seriously, look at all of this artillery. Yet you smuggled it here – into the capital of Russia – so easily.'

'Hold up!' McNutt said, as if a light bulb had just popped on above his head. 'I think I know how the Black Robe got in here.'

'Me, too,' Cobb assured him.

'Yeah, right,' McNutt scoffed. 'You're just trying to steal my thunder.'

Cobb pointed to the empty crate where the missing gear would have been stored – if it had made the shipment. 'The Black Robe hid in the crate. One of our workers carried him in.'

McNutt nodded his approval. 'Shit, chief. That's *much* more realistic than what I was gonna say. My plan involved giant birds.'

Cobb ignored him and focused on Papineau. 'Finding and refitting these train cars is one thing, since all of them came from Russia. But this?' He pointed at everything around them. 'By all rights, Russian customs should have been on this like beef on stroganoff. Alarms should have sounded if they even caught a whiff of this stuff!' He marched up to Papineau and placed his face a few inches away. 'How did you do it?'

'Why do you assume that someone at Russian customs *hasn't* already seen these crates?' Papineau replied. The implication was clear: the Frenchman's connections ran a lot deeper than Cobb had anticipated.

'You might have friends in high places,' Cobb shot back, 'but every outsider that knows anything about what we're doing here puts the whole mission in jeopardy. And not just the objective. You're risking our lives.'

'Um, I hate to interrupt . . .' said a voice behind them.

They turned to see Jasmine in the doorway between the armory car and the private quarters.

Cobb glanced at her. 'What's up, Jasmine?'

'Could I see you for a second?' she asked.

'I'll be right with you,' he assured her, before turning back to Papineau. 'I'm kind of in the middle of something.'

'I see that,' she said, retreating. 'I'll be in Sarah's quarters.'

'Fine. See you soon.'

Cobb breathed slowly and deeply, but the Frenchman could tell the difference between a man who was doing that instinctively and a man who was trying to keep himself calm.

Of course, Papineau could see what was troubling Cobb. Despite their best efforts, two members of the team had already been attacked, and they hadn't even left the station yet. What would happen once the train started picking up speed?

Cobb leaned closer and whispered with menace, 'Tell me, Papi, what makes you so damn confident that we can pull this off? What are you hiding up your sleeve?'

Papineau stared directly into Cobb's eyes. When he replied, he answered with total honesty and complete conviction. 'You.'

36

Cobb made his way to their sleeping quarters where Jasmine was tending to their injured colleague. Since the car had been cannibalized from the first-class compartments of the *Lev Tolstoy*, it required very little improvement. There were six spacious cabins and two baths with multiple sinks and shower stalls.

Cobb was amused by the dichotomy between this luxurious train car, which was known for first-class travel between Moscow and Finland, and the frugal man it was named for. Lev 'Leo' Tolstoy was one of Russia's greatest writers, having written the monumental classic *War and Peace*. By the end of his life, Tolstoy was a fervent believer in nonviolent resistance and famed for his ascetic lifestyle. Cobb wondered if Tolstoy would be amused or outraged by the extravagant carriage that bore his name – especially since the other cars of the train were loaded with weapons. He also wondered which was louder: the rumble of the engine or the sound of Tolstoy spinning in his grave?

In either case, each cabin had one large, square window that could be covered with a set of blue and white curtains for privacy or sealed shut with a bulletproof grate that slid from the top. Every compartment had a sitting section, which looked like a restaurant booth, and a sleeping section with a comfortable bed beside a small chair and table.

Cobb knocked on the door of Sarah's compartment. He was about to walk in when Jasmine opened the door. 'How's she doing?' he asked.

'She's okay,' Jasmine said in the doorway. 'Embarrassed, but okay.'

'Why is she embarrassed?'

'Because someone got the best of her. She's used to delivering blows, not receiving them.'

Cobb smiled. 'How's her head?'

'Her head is fine. It's her neck that's killing her. The guy didn't knock her out. He choked her unconscious with some kind of death grip.'

He glanced at the bruises on Jasmine's neck. 'There's a lot of that going around.'

She nodded. 'I finally convinced her to get some rest. She wanted to go out and slaughter the first person she saw in a black coat.'

Cobb shook his head, his mouth stretched into something that denoted both a grin and a grimace. 'We have to assume they are all trained in Sambo. It's the Russian equivalent of the Israeli Krav Maga.'

'Rough-and-tumble, result-oriented?' Jasmine said.

Cobb nodded. 'Both were created by the military to be the most brutally effective self-defence systems they could think of. By the way he acted getting in and out, I'd guess he was ex-secret police. The KGB was big on organic infiltration like this, not break-ins. Let the inhabitants bring you inside with them.'

Cobb studied Jasmine's face. She was upset about something. He could see it in her eyes and the way she clenched her jaw. 'So, what did you want to talk about?'

Jasmine glanced away. 'Jack, I'm worried.'

'I can see that. What about, specifically?'

'I remember all the drilling, all the lessons I was taught back in Florida, but . . . you saw me in the field. When that punk attacked me, it all . . .' She tried to pinpoint the feeling the memory elicited. 'It all went away. Just vanished.'

Cobb smiled kindly. 'Let me ask you a question.'

She took a deep breath and met his gaze. It was clear from her expression that she didn't want to back away or back out. She was looking for something to get her back on track.

'Do you want to get attacked again?' Cobb asked.

'No!' she blurted, her voice filled with anger.

That was exactly what he wanted to hear.

'There you go,' Cobb said. 'You said it yourself: you know how to prevent it. What you didn't know was how it was going to feel. How *you* were going to feel. But now you do.'

She nodded slowly, trying to absorb his message.

'Pro athletes often talk about the speed of the game. It's something you can't fully grasp in a practice session. You have to experience it to understand it.'

'Are you talking about adrenalin?'

'Partly. But it's more than that. It's about making correct decisions under fire. A fist coming at you demands that you move or block. You don't have time to remember complex moves, and there's no need to. You just have to reply to whatever move is put on you. You're being choked from behind? You know where your opponent's eyes are for gouging, where the groin is for grabbing, where fingers are for bending back. Simply do what you've been taught.'

'You make it sound pretty easy, when you think about it,' Jasmine said.

'Actually,' Cobb laughed, 'I'm saying it's pretty easy when you *don't* think about it.'

Just then, they heard a noise inside the cabin. They both looked at Sarah, who was now sitting up on her bed.

'I'll tell you what I'm thinking about,' Sarah complained. 'That if you really wanted me to get some rest, you wouldn't be talking in my doorway.'

Cobb smiled. 'So, you're saying you're better?'

'I'm good enough.'

'Glad to hear it.'

She looked at Jasmine. 'Thanks for looking after me.'

Before Jasmine could answer, Garcia interrupted in their ears. 'I got it!'

'What's that?' Cobb asked.

'What the Black Robe wanted,' he said.

Cobb looked at the two women with encouragement. He was glad they were back on speaking terms. 'One drama finished, another ready to begin . . .'

* * *

Garcia was at his workstation, focused on a device that resembled a small spider that had died on its back with its legs up.

Papineau stood behind him, peering over his shoulder. 'Very apt. It even looks like a bug.'

Both of them looked up when the foursome entered. Cobb led the way, followed by Sarah, Jasmine, and McNutt, who joined the others when they came through the freight car.

'Where'd you find it?' Cobb asked, noting the six sticky antennae legs and the tiny central hub, no bigger than a Tylenol.

'In McNutt's car, inside an outlet plate,' Garcia said. 'At first I thought it actually was a daddy long legs, but a daddy long legs doesn't lie flat like this did.'

Cobb nodded. 'It's KGB all right. Or at least ex-KGB.'

'The KGB was that sophisticated?' Jasmine asked.

McNutt laughed. 'Oh, they've got a long history with bugs. Once they planted a listening device inside a Great Seal of the United States, which they gave as a gift to the US Ambassador in Moscow. It worked for six years. When we finally discovered it, the KGB had the entire construction crew essentially make the newly built US Embassy in Moscow one gigantic listening device. That lasted for ten years. And when it was finally discovered, there were so many bugs in the place we actually had to tear the whole thing down!'

'See?' Garcia interjected, holding up the device. 'The legs are a mixture of transmitters and microphones. It really is a clever design.'

'Are they listening now?' McNutt asked pointedly.

'Nope. I clipped all the wires and crushed the processors.'

Cobb shook his head sadly. 'Stupid of me. I should have told you to just find it. We could've used it to throw the Black Robes off track.'

McNutt clapped him on the shoulder. 'The good news is there's no telling how many others he installed before skulking away.'

'Good point,' Cobb said. 'Hector, take Jasmine and go tell the train workers to look for any more, just to be on the safe side. While you're out there, check with Dobrev to see if there's anything more he wants or needs. The sooner we get this show on the road, the better it'll be.'

'Don't worry,' Garcia said. 'If they're out there, I'll find them.'

'Not worried at all,' Cobb smiled.

'On the road?' Sarah asked. 'On the road to where?'

'We follow the prince's most likely trail,' he told her. 'Anything is better than waiting here for the next Black Robe.' Cobb turned to the Frenchman. 'You better get ready, Papi.'

'Get ready?' Sarah repeated. 'What does he have to get ready for?'

'His speech,' Cobb said.

Papineau straightened his tie. 'I am attending the official launch of the Eastern Euro Trans Energy Study at the Leningradsky rail terminal across town.'

McNutt, Sarah, and Jasmine looked at their employer in surprise.

'What do you mean?' Sarah demanded.

'I mean that I will be suffering through many hours of

238

boring speeches from a variety of low-level Russian dignitaries while toasting many glasses of middling vodka. Then I will board a non-luxury train and lead the study toward the Bering Strait – in the opposite direction of you.'

The trio continued to stare at Papineau.

Cobb let them stare for a while. 'You didn't think he was coming with us, did you?'

McNutt looked from Cobb to the Frenchman, realized the beauty of the plan, and then grunted in realization. 'Oh, I get it! You're the decoy.'

'Exactly,' Papineau said. 'If it hadn't been for our black-robed friend, you might have gone completely unnoticed. But now I have to do my best to lead the hounds away.'

'Don't you need me there as translator?' Jasmine asked.

Papineau looked at her with mock disdain. 'Now, you don't think a man as important as I am has just one interpreter, do you? Besides, I need you to stay here and take care of Andrei.'

Jasmine nodded. 'It will be my pleasure.'

Cobb glanced at Papineau. 'Any final words?'

He smiled at Cobb. 'Hit the road, Jack – but stay in touch.'

37

The public launch of the new American–European survey was going exactly as Papineau expected. Talk, talk, more talk, and then even more talk about nothing that had yet been done. But as he sat on the upraised dais at track number one of the Leningradsky rail terminal, listening to the fifth speech declaring collaboration, dedication, and international cooperation, it gave him time to consider his confrontation with Cobb.

Everything Cobb had questioned about the delivery of the train and the weapons resonated with the Frenchman. Cobb had said nothing wrong or unfair. The main reason Papineau couldn't reply honestly was because he didn't know all the answers. He understood that it was the recovery of the letter from the Brighton Beach estate and its delivery that had set things in motion, but he wasn't aware of the specifics. He knew his colleague had numerous connections in Russia and throughout Eastern Europe, but the speed and ease with which Papineau's most recent requests had been fulfilled was truly impressive.

Getting one train across the continent's rail system was remarkable enough, but two? Not to mention the small armory of weapons and other equipment that passed through customs without incident. Getting them out of America was one thing, but getting them into Russia was quite another. And all in exchange for a single letter?

After thinking things through, Papineau came to a disturbing conclusion: what if his associate had cut a side deal with the Black Robes? These men did not seem to be interested in material things. At least, not the kinds of things people traditionally coveted.

What had he promised them to get them involved?

And why hadn't he told Papineau of their involvement?

On his way to the reception, he had spotted another cloaked figure as he entered the station from Komsomolskaya Square. These men – for he had yet to see a woman in the telltale black outfit – had to be very well connected if they were able to exert their influence while wearing such recognizable vestments.

The Frenchman turned to his right, then glanced back as if he were simply surveying the crowd of low-ranking rail and local dignitaries. In the dark red and yellow light of the terminal, the Black Robe looked like a cockroach on a wedding cake. These men seemed to revel in an attitude that screamed, *Here I am, what are you going to do about it?*

They had the kind of pervasive access and freedom of movement that no single Russian group possessed – not even the black market. Black marketeers were not monolithic. They were like the old Bolsheviks and Mensheviks of the Revolution, warring factions within the rebellious movement. And they would want a very, very large percentage of any take.

With growing concern that these confederates were in

fact his adversaries, Papineau took stock of their actions. So far, it seemed that the Black Robes were pretty intent on keeping track of his team and every member thereof. The attempt to plant a listening device was unexpectedly clumsy. Papineau did not expect their next attempts, if there were any, to be as haphazard or ineffectual. Papineau still hoped that the attack on Sarah had been little more than misguided, overzealous, or panicked thinking on the part of the bug planter. But it raised more uncomfortable questions.

Was that their first-and-only attempt to piggyback on the mission?

Were the Black Robes looking to eliminate his team if they were successful?

Am I sending my team into an inevitable and inescapable trap?

Papineau's meditation was ended by a gentle poke in the side from a neighboring elbow. The Frenchman jumped slightly and looked over to his new interpreter, a six-foot-four-inch Russian with a dark, bushy beard named Mikhail Ivanov. The translator nodded gently at the podium.

Papineau turned to see the Under Deputy Minister of Transportation smiling, applauding, and looking at him. Everyone on the dais, and everyone in the small throng of onlookers, was watching and clapping.

'He has asked for you to say a few words,' Ivanov whispered.

'Apparently,' Papineau responded, raising himself from the thoughts that had transported him far from this event. Thankfully he had assumed this was coming and had a general idea of the kind of boilerplate remarks the moment required. He rose, bowed slightly, motioned for Ivanov to accompany him, and stepped up to the microphone.

'My friends,' Papineau said as if he had been waiting to say it all his life, 'this is a moment to remember, when people across continents and oceans meet with the understanding that to improve any one life is to improve all lives.' He waited for Ivanov to translate, then he delivered his pièce de résistance, in Russian: 'To quote the great Chinese philosopher Confucius, "Every journey begins with a single step." So let us take our first.'

Papineau smiled, waved, and stepped back to thunderous applause. He accepted the warm congratulations, handshakes, back and shoulder pats, even a hug or two as he made his way to what only he knew was the decoy train. It was three comfortable carriages with a classic green and red ChME3 locomotive.

Rail workers had decked out the engine's railed walkways with banners and drapes to honor the occasion. The plan was to have Papineau and the dignitaries wave from the train as it left the station. Once away from the crowd, the dignitaries would return to their offices while Papineau and Ivanov would make their way into the carriages.

Although not luxurious by any means – a clear indication of this survey's true place in the mind of the Russian government, despite the fanfare – the train included comfortable sleeping quarters, dining facilities, and a fully equipped video station so the survey team could keep a careful eye on the tracks – among other things.

'I am very grateful you chose me to accompany you on this trip, Monsieur Papineau,' Ivanov said as they made their way toward the train. 'I have always wanted to make this journey to Uelen at the Bering Strait. The mountains and wilderness are said to be magnificent.'

'Indeed,' Papineau murmured, his mind not on the video team he had hastily hired, but on his other team. He got into an automatic rhythm of shaking the hands of the boisterous crowd with both of his: gripping their palms and shaking them up and down without stopping his passage. Therefore, he was slightly taken aback when he reached out toward a striking older man and an assured young woman.

Unlike the rest of the crowd, they offered no hands to shake.

The woman held up her police identification, and the man kept his hands folded in front of him. They wore full dress uniforms, befitting the occasion – the man in dark green with a peaked hat, and the woman in blue with a knee-length skirt, low high heels, and garrison cap.

Ivanov too was slightly surprised by their seemingly sudden appearance, but he responded by leaning down to study the proffered ID.

'Sergeant Anna Rusinko,' the translator said.

The older policeman looked up at him with a calming smile. 'No need to translate, my friend,' he said in Russian. Then he looked at Papineau. 'I will be pleased to do it,' he said in French. 'My name is Viktor Borovsky, Colonel Viktor Borovsky. And this is Sergeant Anna Rusinko. We are with Special Branch, Main Office of the Interior for Transport and Special Transportation.'

'Part of the Federal Migration Services Office,' Papineau said.

Borovsky's smile remained placid. 'You have done your homework.'

'No,' Papineau replied. 'I am educated.' He resented the implication that he had boned up just to be here, like a politician on the stump.

'My apologies,' Borovsky said, apparently in earnest.

'What can I do for you, Colonel? As you can see, I don't have much time.'

'You do not,' he agreed with a touch of vagueness. 'I'm sorry for this distraction, but we only learned of your impending departure a short while ago.'

They had, in fact, broken several traffic laws getting here after extensively questioning several very frightened veteran railway employees. Memories of the KGB had become part of the collective DNA here.

'If it's about permissions, they were cleared quite some time ago,' Papineau said, beginning to shuffle toward the train. 'You may check with the Minister of Transport as well as the Minister of Natural Resources and Environmental Protection.'

'Of course, of course,' Borovsky repeated soothingly. 'It is not that at all. Here, allow us to walk you to the train. We can talk on the way.'

Papineau looked dubiously at the pair. In his mind, a colonel and sergeant suggested something other than 'routine', but he went along with it.

What else could he do?

38

Papineau and Borovsky set off side by side, with Anna just behind them. Ivanov trailed behind her, ready to translate anything if it became necessary.

The effect of their casual, new 'police escort' was immediate. The rest of the well-wishers parted for them like the Red Sea for Moses.

'Be assured that we are not looking to delay your departure in any way,' Borovsky said, giving the impression of two old friends on a leisurely stroll. 'We are simply trying to locate a man named Andrei Dobrev.'

Borovsky let that statement hang in the air, carefully gauging the Frenchman's reaction. Papineau didn't display one . . . physically. But mentally, he was doing gymnastics.

'Dobrev?' he echoed, deciding that the more truth he could include, the better. 'I seem to remember someone by that name at the inaugural reception.'

'Do you? Did you take note of every name?' Borovsky asked.

'In fact, I did,' Papineau said, buying time. 'It is a habit.'

'What other names do you recall?'

Papineau rattled off several, effortlessly. In his brain he was thanking Garcia: the IT man had been eavesdropping on the entire conversation, and with the time Papineau had bought, he had brought up the guest list and was reciting it into Papineau's ear.

'Impressive,' Borovsky said. 'Very, very impressive. Do you also remember what he looks like, then?'

Papineau smiled softly. 'There, I'm not sure I could help you.'

Borovsky held his hand up to about Dobrev's height. 'Stocky, with a square-ish head, short gray hair standing straight up, probably wearing a tan suit?'

Papineau laughed quietly. 'Colonel, that describes about a million Muscovites.'

Borovsky's mild smile widened as if it was their inside joke. 'Only a million? I'd say more than that. So, you didn't talk to him then.'

Papineau stopped a few feet from the smoking locomotive as the other minor dignitaries made their way onto the walkways behind him. 'Colonel, to be honest, I'm just not sure.'

'Let me put it another way,' Borovsky said. 'He would have been the only one you may have spoken to who possessed an encyclopedic knowledge of the train system. I believe he is involved as a consultant.'

Papineau was stuck. It would seem odd if he had not been introduced to someone who was, in fact, a key member of the survey planning team.

'The man who knew about the trains,' Papineau said generally. 'Yes, yes – I believe we exchanged a few words.'

'A few cocktail party platitudes?'

'Something like that,' Papineau smiled. 'You know how

it is.' He gestured at the crowd behind them. 'You've seen how it is.'

'Indeed,' Borovsky assured him. 'Well, that was all I wished to know.'

Papineau looked at the woman. He knew she would probably say nothing, having deferred to her superior, but he wanted to give the appearance of cooperating.

'You, Sergeant? Is there anything you'd like to ask?'

She seemed surprised by the attention. 'Not at present.'

'When, then?' Papineau joked. 'At the Bering Strait?'

Borovsky stared at him. 'If need be, yes. We will be there.'

The laughter stopped, and Papineau no longer felt like joking.

This man was not only a veteran; he was hard-core.

Borovsky clicked his heels together – actually clicked his heels, his own salute to an apparently worthy opponent in something that clearly was not finished – and put his arm out, giving his grateful permission for Papineau to join the others on the front of the engine. The Frenchman noted that Sergeant Rusinko did not look at all happy about her own performance.

Papineau took two steps up the platform before he turned and looked back. 'Colonel?'

The officer was still standing there, watching. 'Sir?'

'We'll have real-time video journals posted on our survey website,' he shouted over the growing noise of the train engine. 'You can text me anytime.'

'I am not comfortable with that technology,' he replied.

Papineau smiled. The colonel had let down his guard for

249

an instant and allowed the Frenchman to know he was strictly old school. It wasn't much, but it was something.

Borovsky nodded his head, surrendering that point. He waved expansively and stepped back to where Anna was waiting for him.

'Sir, is that it?' she said, confused. 'Let me go aboard. I can get off at—'

'No, Sergeant,' he said. 'There is no need.'

He waved and smiled until the train began to leave the station amid the cheering crowd. Borovsky remained in place long after the last of the well-wishers ran past him, cheering.

'Colonel,' she said, 'forgive me, but I am mystified. They were never introduced at the reception. We have seen the video.'

'Exactly.'

She stood straight up, gaining at least two inches. 'Sir?'

'The Frenchman does not speak Russian. Dobrev does not speak English. They could not have chatted about anything. He lied – but why?'

Anna considered this and failed to reach any conclusions.

'Mr Papineau had a translator at the reception,' Borovsky said. 'She spoke at length to Dobrev. She had to have told Mr Papineau about him.'

'Yes,' Anna said, still trying to get ahead of her superior.

'She and Mr Papineau were on somewhat familiar terms, laughing, talking, conferring,' Borovsky went on.

'Again, true—'

Borovsky shrugged. 'She has not left the country. Why, then, was someone so trusted and apparently close to him not here, translating? And what about the other members of his staff – those with whom his interpreter occasionally interacted at the party? Where are they? Not one of them was here for the start of the survey.'

Understanding came quickly. 'They are somewhere else.'

'Exactly,' he said with a smile. 'Come. We must find them.'

39

Anna Rusinko was angry.

Some of that anger was because of Borovsky, who had run this operation by not sharing key tactics and information with his partner. Yes, she was a subordinate, but she was here to support a goal that was larger than themselves: finding a killer. He could have told her what he was planning to do, that he apparently suspected – or simply sensed – a larger plot.

But she was angrier at herself.

No, not angry, she decided as they weaved through traffic. She was frustrated that she had not been thinking the way he had been thinking. She had always done police work by starting small and working out. This man obviously worked the other way, throwing out a big net and seeing what he dragged ashore. Then he sifted through the fish and debris.

'Do you play chess, sir?' she asked.

'No,' he said. 'I already sit too much. I prefer darts, among other hobbies.'

'Darts?' she said, surprised. 'To relax, or is there some kind of competition?'

'Purely to relax,' he said as he stared out the passenger window. 'The brain gets a much-needed rest when you perform a task that is purely a hand–eye challenge.'

'It *is* a tiny bull's-eye, Colonel,' she laughed.

'Oh, I rarely aim for that. If you go for the same spot all the time you fall into a rhythm. You never want to do that in anything. No, I select different bands, different colors, different numbers so I have to keep adjusting.' He nodded with satisfaction. 'It's a good life lesson.'

Anna felt a little foolish for having offered a statement about the bull's-eye instead of asking questions.

It's okay, she told herself. *That's a good life lesson, too.*

They rode in silence until they reached their destination. The Pushkin State Museum of Fine Arts was across the street from the Cathedral of Christ the Saviour. Its golden dome towered over the Moskva River.

'A nice balance,' she commented.

'What do you mean?' Borovsky said.

'Well, sir, one building is full of human outpouring, the other a house of solace.'

He laughed. 'Sergeant, those descriptions could apply to either one equally.'

'I know that, sir.' She grinned as she pulled to the curb.

He looked at her with admiration. 'Well done.'

Now it was his turn to play catch-up.

They stepped out in unison, but Borovsky waited before moving toward the museum. Anna followed his eyes and sensed a bit of the patriotic pride he must have been feeling when taking in its exterior. It looked like a temple to culture on a high podium.

Borovsky glanced over to see her staring, and tapped her upper arm with the back of his hand. When she looked over, he pointed and said, 'Copied from the Erechtheion on the Acropolis. Ionic colonnade. Finished in 1912. Just in time for World War One, and everything that followed. Originally called the Alexander the Third Museum, then the State Museum of Fine Art. Our great poet Alexander Pushkin died five years later, and they added his name.'

The colonel pointed left and then right. 'Three buildings. Two atrium courtyards. Glass roof lets the sunlight in.'

'It's impressive. I'm ashamed I haven't visited before now.'

He shrugged, and they started walking toward the steps. 'Who has time in this modern age, what with gangs, the black market, the mafia, and a four-year-old daughter?'

Anna stopped in place, but she caught up to Borovsky, who kept on walking, near the museum's magnificent entrance.

He glanced at her. 'Do you really think I would ask you to assist me without checking your records?'

'No, sir,' she fibbed. That meant he knew about her marriage and divorce as well. She felt both naked and protected at the same time, exposed to his scrutiny but allowed into his circle.

'Alma was one of the reasons I asked for you,' he explained. 'You were eminently qualified, of course, but so are many persons of your rank and station. The younger generation is the main hope of Russia's future. I want someone who has a reason to preserve that future and work to make it better.'

Anna was once again surprised by this man. Her heart swelled. Here was a real patriot, not one who used platitudes to control others.

He looked at her. 'You did not put your daughter in a child care center. You had your mother move in. I like that. I like it very much.'

Then they were inside.

Anna put her personal thoughts aside and focused on the building. The clean opulence impressed her. It was large, light, and airy, with a mix of clean colors and expertly designed moods.

Borovsky pointed left. 'Art of Ancient Egypt.' He pointed right. 'Art of Germany and the Netherlands in the fifteenth and sixteenth centuries.' He pointed ahead of them. 'Italian art from the thirteenth century, flanked by the Greek court-yard and Italian courtyard.'

'Come here often?' Anna asked with a smile. She felt as if a level of trust and familiarity had been achieved.

Borovsky gave her an amused look. 'You could say that.'

The sentries and staff didn't ask for any pass, ticket, or donation. Their uniforms alone would have ensured that, but Anna got the more-than-distinct impression that his face was familiar to them.

'The core of the museum is Moscow University's collection of antiquities,' he said. They had circumvented the galleries and reached a hall of clean, crisp, new offices. He pointed at a teak and glass door.

COINS AND MEDALS DEPARTMENT, she read to herself as Borovsky twisted the doorknob.

'Viktor!' was the first thing she heard as he entered before her. And the first thing she saw was a young, straight-haired woman in a simple sweater and skirt erupt from her desk and practically leap into an embrace with the colonel.

He smiled back at Anna and made a 'what can I do?' face.

The young woman gripped his shoulders, pulled back to arm's length, and took a long, lingering look at him. 'Viktor Stanislav Borovsky! Why didn't you warn us you were going to visit?'

'*Warn?* Am I a threat?'

'You are!' the woman continued, speaking to Anna, not the colonel. 'He is a storm, a veritable cyclone.'

'She is referring to one of those hobbies I alluded to,' he said, half turning to Anna with mild embarrassment. 'There is nothing – *nothing*—'

'Romantic? Lord Jesus across the street!' the curator laughed. 'No, Viktor comes in with questions, more questions, then questions inspired by the answers to those questions. Mostly it's about the gold of Troy. We have it here,' the woman boasted. 'Do you know its discoverer, Heinrich Schliemann? He was quite the character!'

Borovsky changed the subject. 'Natalia, this is Sergeant Anna Rusinko.'

'How rude of me!' The young woman collected herself and offered her hand to Anna. 'It's just that we don't see him as much as we used to. You understand.'

'Much more now than I did before,' Anna answered with a smile.

'Where's Olga?' he asked.

'Where she always is,' she answered, sweeping her arm

toward a door at the end of a row of light brown coin drawers.

Borovsky smiled broadly and hurried by. Anna followed, trying to interpret Natalia's quiet smile as she went back to work. *A young subordinate worker here who wasn't romantically involved with Borovsky?* Anna guessed he had helped her with something personal. She wasn't wearing a wedding band. *Perhaps her brother needed help getting into the police force? Or he got into trouble and needed help getting out?*

She still didn't understand Borovsky.

But this was a start.

40

Borovsky and Anna entered the room beyond the row of drawers. It was dark, but it wasn't a menacing dark. It was welcoming. The only illumination came from a bright light attached to a large magnifying glass on a flexible pole. Behind it was what appeared to be a classic crone from a folk tale. She was lanky, gray-haired, and dressed in a bulky dark brown sweater and wool skirt that looked like they were spun from the fibers of tree bark.

'Close that door!' she commanded, eyes intent on the glass and what it was magnifying. Borovsky hastily ushered Anna in and closed the door behind them. 'What do you want?'

'What do I ever want?' Borovsky answered. 'Your help.'

Anna expected the response that he got.

'Viktor?' the woman said. 'Viktor, is that you? Viktor!'

The crone was not much taller standing than she had been sitting. She came forward quickly and then there were more hugs.

Anna got her bearings after a second round of introductions. Olga Uritski turned on the bright overhead lights, drew up three stools, and gave them each a small glass cup of *sbiten* — the popular Russian drink of blackberry jam, honey, water, and spices.

After the urgency Borovsky had expressed to get in here, she was surprised to see him take his time now. Or rather, be forced to take his time. Then she understood the politics: unlike Natalia, this woman required nurturing. It was the difference between the gatekeeper and the one who possessed what you really needed.

There was general chatter as they sat around a large, square table covered in felt, in the center of a large, square room. All four walls were lined with long wooden drawers designed to safeguard coins. The table had several examining devices attached to it, as well as many drawers of its own. Anna did her best to soak it all up.

'The department was created after World War Two,' Borovsky told Anna, 'to house the coins and medals from the Imperial Moscow University.'

'But it soon became much more than that,' Olga said. She appeared to be older than the colonel, but it was hard for Anna to be sure. She had the flat face and granite-like head of an aged Latvian, as well as a shock of Brillo-like white hair. An incongruous but beautiful pearl necklace was around her sagging throat. 'Presently we have more than two hundred thousand pieces from all over the world.'

'Olga is the curator of the Russian and Soviet portion,' Borovsky informed Anna. 'They have one of the best and oldest numismatic collections in Russia.'

'The world,' she corrected proudly. 'And Viktor was quite a friend of the department . . . the entire museum, in fact.'

'Was?' Anna wondered between sips.

Olga smiled at him. 'Well, you can't be running off on

archeological digs all the time with the Soviet Union disintegrating around you.'

Anna blinked a few times. It was amazing how wrong she had been about the colonel. The more she learned, the more impressed she became. 'So you went on digs?'

Borovsky made a dismissive gesture, but Olga wasn't having it.

'Viktor often joined us in Tuva, the Crimea, even in the Ukraine and Romania.' She looked at him with affection. 'And he never failed to help – at least when he wasn't wandering off on his own.'

'Enough, enough,' he grunted. 'As I said to Natalia, this is official business, Olga.'

'I suspected as much, which is why I made you slow down. I know how you get on cases.' Olga smiled at him and sighed. 'So tell me, what kind of official business?'

Borovsky unbuttoned his uniform coat and reached inside. 'This kind,' he said, showing the thin box Anna had found in Andrei Dobrev's apartment.

The old woman took the box, pulled it under the adjustable arm's illuminating magnifying glass, and clicked off the lights from a switch under the table lip.

'Inside,' Borovsky suggested.

Olga opened the box and peered at the indentation inside the padding.

'Well?' he asked.

She glanced at him from over the edge of the glass. 'I'm guessing you know as well as I do.'

'I thought so,' he said.

Anna was dying to know. She did not ask.

Olga looked at Anna, but her question was for Borovsky. 'May I?'

'Of course,' he said.

The curator motioned Anna forward, pointing through the magnifier. 'See the outlines within the indentation?' Through the glass Anna saw what seemed to be an etching in the felt of the hollow box. 'It's unique, like a fingerprint,' Olga said. 'Romanian, gold, first-series leu, twenty lei, 1868.' There was a moment of appreciative silence before she looked up through the magnifying glass at Borovsky's wide eyes. 'Where did you get this?'

Borovsky took the box back and spoke before Anna could answer. 'I'm sorry, that's privileged information.'

'Ah!' Olga exclaimed. 'That means we are done.' She added sadly, 'I should have taken more time. When will we see you again?'

'Sooner than you think,' he said cryptically. 'Come, Sergeant. We have work to do.'

Anna was about to follow when she felt a hand on her arm. She turned to see Olga looking at her with a concerned expression. 'Look after him, will you? He likes to think he's younger than he is.'

Anna placed her hand on Olga's and nodded more reassuringly than she felt. When she went through the outer office, she noted that Natalia also looked concerned at the speed of Borovsky's departure and the brevity of his farewell.

Anna caught up with him in the middle of the Black Sea

exhibit. It showcased ancient sculptures, vases, urns, and other artifacts — some dating back as far as the fourth century BC — that had been recovered by the museum's staff. But Anna remained silent despite the questions that had started to pile up like the coins on Olga's desk.

As they neared the front door, he said suddenly, 'I want to thank you for your assistance, Sergeant. I will no longer require your services on this matter. You may take the car and report back to your station, discussing it with no one.'

Anna felt as if she had been punched in the gut. During their walk she had noticed the change in him, but she attributed it to contemplation. Something had set Borovsky off. His gentle humor and paternal guidance had evaporated — *all because a suspicion had been confirmed?*

As his subordinate, she knew she should do as ordered. For one reason or another, he didn't want her help any more. In the past, she would have nodded and gone back to the station. But the new Anna wasn't going to do that. She was going to risk a big toss of the net.

'No, sir,' she said.

'Thank you—'

'I mean, "no sir" as in, "I'm not going."'

He stopped. 'You forget yourself.'

She stopped. 'Quite intentionally, yes. I believe you still require my services.'

Now surrounded by stone and wooden sarcophaguses, statues, papyri, vessels, amulets, and stone hieroglyphic friezes, Borovsky's stern face softened. 'Go back to your daughter, Anna. Keep her safe. Make her happy. Raise her well.'

He walked away.

She caught up to him again outside. He was looking across the street at the church and the Moscow River beyond. 'How can I do that, sir, if I can't say to her, "I did what was right, not what was ordered"?'

She saw regret, then admiration and appreciation fill his features, before he once again settled into the Viktor Borovsky she had come to know.

He nodded his approval. 'You are right. A philosophy that is irrefutable.'

That made her smile.

'Come then,' he said, 'we must hurry.'

'Where to?' she asked as they hustled to the car.

His answer caught her by surprise.

41

Pavel Dvorkin knew this city well, almost as well as his native Moscow. Since joining the Black Robes a decade ago, he had made hundreds of trips to the capital city of Kazan – trips he *usually* looked forward to. But that wasn't the case today.

Not after his failed mission at the rail yard.

Dressed in the high-collared black tunic, black pants, black boots, and specially tailored jacket of his sect, Dvorkin noted the eyes of those pedestrians passing him on the bright, sunny street. By now his presence on the streets of Kazan was a familiar sight to many. In them he sensed respect and envy, but also concern. That was only right. That was only fair. They had a reason to be scared. He had served his masters for many years, and he had served them well. That was obvious in his bearing and expression, as well as his clothing.

The design of their uniform was truly inspired. Had they donned the long, skirted garment that had served as their wardrobe's inspiration, they would have been seen as pale imitations of the original. But in this modern version of the traditional garb, they were able to declare their allegiance without words, as well as mark themselves as a group to be reckoned with.

Dvorkin was proud to be a member of the Black Robes. Gone was the stench of the *Komitet Gosudarstvennoy Bezopasnosti*, the Committee of State Security, which he had fought so hard to become part of as a young man. That organization, known everywhere as the dreaded KGB, had been magnificent when Dvorkin had struggled to impress them.

He had just turned eighteen and had spent his young life preparing for his eventual acceptance into its ranks. He had joined the Communist Party as soon as they had allowed him to and had joined the Party's security agency shortly thereafter. With the mighty Vladimir Kryuchkov at the helm of the KGB, there was the promise of an even more powerful agency, one in which Dvorkin would've had an important role. But somehow that dream never happened.

By the end of the 1980s, head of state Mikhail Gorbachev launched radical reforms that led to national instability. Naturally Kryuchkov wanted to hold the country together. He gathered all his newest, strongest agents, Dvorkin included, for a coup in 1991. But Gorbachev turned Kryuchkov's solid ground to sand – and he did it brilliantly. Instead of cracking down on Kryuchkov and his followers, he left them alone. Because Kryuchkov did not have a reason to complain to the Communist Party, the Party would not give him the authority to retaliate, and that led to the smoldering destruction of the KGB.

In 1991, the Union of Soviet Socialist Republics formally dissolved. The KGB was quickly divided into several weaker organizations, all under the direct control of the new Russia – and make no mistake about it: the new Russia was *not* the Communist Party.

Pavel Dvorkin, like so many others, was set adrift.

For a time, he took jobs that suited his temperament and training. A shakedown here, a robbery there – until one day in 2002 when he was asked to obtain incriminating evidence against a high-ranking member of the Politburo. Dvorkin did more than find it; he *supplied* it in the form of a male prostitute. The scandal that followed was when and how he came to the attention of an exciting new group: the Black Robes. Now, more than a decade later, he was deeply ensconced in their midst and well trusted by his colleagues.

Some of his fellow congregants were perplexed by their presence in Kazan. Why not work out of Tiumen Oblast, Siberia – once known as Pokrovskoe – where their master had been born? Or what about St Petersburg, where their master had healed Prince Alexi of hemophilia and brought royal-lady-in-waiting Anya Vyrubova out of a coma after a train wreck?

Instead, their leader had chosen Kazan as their head-quarters, a place where their master had lived in 1902 and had begun gathering his first disciples. Known as the 'third capital of Russia', Kazan was a splendid, sprawling city at the juncture of the Kazanka and Volga Rivers.

Thanks to the diverse, ever-growing population, the town was full of mosques, cathedrals, churches, and temples. Here, amongst pilgrims of many religions, the Black Robes could hide in plain sight.

Dvorkin walked over the bridge spanning the Bolaq channel – just one of many waterways that reflected, literally and figuratively, the sparkling architecture consisting of white stone buildings with red clay roofs, interspersed with soaring communication towers, stadiums, academies, palaces, and even circuses, complete with elevated 'big tops'. In the distance, he could see the Millennium Bridge, named for the city's thousandth anniversary and marked by a giant yellow 'M' pylon. In another direction was the Kazan Kremlin, an historic citadel built at the behest of Ivan the Terrible on the ruins of a fallen castle.

Dvorkin took a final look at the city he knew so well, then directed his attention to their headquarters. It was a relatively small, innocuous building – just three stories tall – that blended into its surroundings. Although it was dwarfed by many of Kazan's edifices, it remained the biggest building on this block. Its architecture was similar to the others, except it had a slightly sloping brown roof, while the others had slightly pointed reddish ones.

With eight tall, narrow windows on each side of every floor, plus corner windows allowing for views in all directions, it seemed sedate, civilized, and unassuming. But as Dvorkin approached the nondescript entrance, he knew at least three cameras and a half-dozen people, both inside and outside the structure, were watching him. He pressed the thumb piece of the door's handle set and waited. No key, code, or identity card was needed. His entry was allowed from the guards within. There was a buzz and click, and then he went inside the plain antechamber. It was a solid steel box, covered with dark wood paneling.

Dvorkin waited in the eight-foot cube until the door closed behind him, sealing out all light. He stood in total darkness and waited until the infrared sensors had scanned his entire body. Then there was another buzz and another click, and a sliding panel opened in front of him. He stepped through and entered another world.

It was as if he had been transported to 1916 and was standing in the macabre quiet of the Crimson Drawing Room of the Alexander Palace – the preferred home of Nicholas II and his family. A gilded chandelier hung from the ceiling. Marble columns braced heavily draped walls. The chairs were richly upholstered in crimson cloth. The carpet was deep and crimson. The walls were covered with the same sort of emerald wallpaper that had adorned the royal home.

At first glance, there were only two major differences between the original room in St Petersburg and this facsimile in Kazan. One, there were no windows looking out on the royal grounds, and two, the building was filled with gorgeous women dressed in white.

Like angels in a twisted dream.

Following their leader's directive, the women adhered to the precepts of the *Khlysty* sect. It preached salvation through sin, with spirits and sensuality being the devices to divine grace. As such, heavy crystal decanters of brandy were on virtually every other table, and languid women rested here and there, all in attire that sexualized royal refinement. The two women in the crimson room wore tight, white lace shirts over white, whale-boned corsets; long, clinging silk gowns with slits up the leg; white lace, thigh-high stockings; and white, high-heeled, button-up ankle boots. The women were both tall and slim, with long, glossy, light brown hair.

That was another benefit of headquartering in Kazan. The streets were full of hopeful actresses, models, athletes, and students – many of whom were so frustrated at their lack of success that they were willing to receive a relatively substantial salary to serve the greater good.

Neither woman looked at him. In fact, their eyes were hooded with heavy lids over unfocused pupils. Dvorkin knew they were most likely sedated, hungover, or both. He hadn't spoken to the staff members who were responsible for these women, but he did not have to. Their behavior reflected alcohol, leisure medications, and the 'additives' thereof.

Dvorkin had once heard their leader say, 'If our suppli- cants require external encouragement to reach internal enlightenment, then they shall have it.'

Whether they knew about it or not.

Dvorkin glanced to his left when a short man in a black tunic walked through the far door. He had a severe expression on his face and slicked-back hair. The man said, 'We've been expecting you. He will see you now.'

'Which room?' Dvorkin asked.

'The sitting room.'

Dvorkin breathed a sigh of relief. The sitting room was the re-creation of Alexandra's formal reception area, up on the third floor. That was where their leader customarily had his minor meetings, so that gave credence to Dvorkin's hope that their leader only wanted to assure himself that all was proceeding on schedule.

Dvorkin left the other man in the Crimson Study and went up the wide stairs to the third floor. The second floor, as he well knew, was filled with offices and planning rooms where the organization members carried out their leader's bidding.

He went left at the landing to walk a wide, well-decorated hall. He passed the re-creation of Alexandra's Maple Room, her Mauve Room, and the Pallisander Room, before approaching the door of the Formal Reception Room. He stood outside and prepared to knock, when he noticed something out of the corner of his eye.

He turned to see a pair of the white, high-heeled ankle boots lying, unbuttoned, outside the cracked-open door of Alexandra's Imperial Bedroom re-creation. He tried to peer into the bedroom but only glimpsed dark hints of the overstuffed interior. He thought he might have heard muffled human sounds, but he wasn't sure. It appeared as if whoever had stood in those shoes had been pulled right out of them.

Dvorkin knocked and pushed open the door. The room was like it had been in Alexander Palace. The walls were

271

covered in artificial marble topped with an ornately molded entablature. Heavy, cranberry-colored curtains covered the windows. The floor was of dark gold parquet topped with a French Savonierre-style rug. Scattered around the room's edges were various chairs, tables, bookcases, and writing desks, all in the style of eighteenth-century France.

In the middle of the room was a small table, flanked by chairs.

In one sat Grigori Yefimovich Sidorov.

The leader of the Black Robes.

42

The sight of their leader never failed to affect Dvorkin. There was a palpable thrill, knowing how clever and commanding he was, the power he wielded over the Black Robes and beyond. But that same knowledge also conjured a feeling of unease. Even today, it stopped him in his tracks.

The hawk-faced man didn't seem to notice. He motioned for Dvorkin to sit opposite him. Dvorkin nodded gratefully, then paused in mid-step as he noticed another high-heeled boot out of the corner of his left eye. This one, however, was filled with a dainty female foot. It led to a long, shapely leg attached to the torso of another seemingly comatose young woman in white, draped across a sofa along the wall. She, like the others, seemed unconcerned or unaware of his presence.

Dvorkin looked back to his leader with a silent question. Sidorov stared back, expressionless, then looked over as if seeing the woman for the first time. He seemed to think for a moment, then rolled his eyes, stood, stepped over to the sofa, and perched beside her. He pulled a napkin off a nearby table, folded it carefully, and used it to blindfold the girl. Dvorkin was not overly surprised that she did not react.

Sidorov was about to get up, but he thought better of it. He leaned over her to open the drawer of a table, removed an iPod and headphones, inserted the earbuds deep into the woman's ears, turned up the machine, and placed it in the crook of her corseted waist. Then he returned to his seat at the table. 'There,' he said. 'Better?'

'Yes, *strannik*. Thank you,' Dvorkin said with appreciation. The term '*strannik*' meant 'religious pilgrim'. It was a nickname their master was often called in his early years.

Sidorov waved the gratitude away as if it were a pesky fly. 'You have served me well and our cause even better. You deserve every possible consideration.'

'Thank you, *strannik*. Thank you.'

Although Dvorkin was still aware of the young woman in the room, she was only a dim presence now – especially in the shadow of an important man like Sidorov. Even when he was being complimentary, it was probably wise to pay strict attention.

'Would you like a drink?' Sidorov asked.

Dvorkin shook his head no.

'Would you mind if I had one?'

'Of course not, *strannik*.' For Dvorkin, it was much more comfortable to call him '*strannik*' rather than 'sir', or 'leader', or 'Grigori'. One was too formal, the next too venerated, and the last too familiar.

Sidorov rose from his chair and walked over to a rolling cart at the foot of the sofa where the woman lay. Dvorkin was once again hyper-aware of her shapely leg and the swath of soft naked flesh between the top of her stocking and the top of the long skirt's slit, as his superior poured some amber liquid into a cut-glass snifter.

'That is why I have brought you here,' Sidorov said. His icy tone sent a disproportionately large chill through Dvorkin.

'I don't understand,' he replied.

'Even though your dedication to our cause cannot be faulted, even by your critics, some have said that your understanding of it has left something to be desired.'

'Critics?' Dvorkin was taken aback. 'Who has said this, *strannik*?'

Sidorov waved that away as well. 'I am here to heal, not accuse.' He took a sip of brandy. 'Just tell me what you feel. Tell me what you know, so I can put your mind at rest.'

'About what, *strannik*?'

The man shrugged lightly. 'Anything. Anything at all that pertains to us.'

Dvorkin leaned back, blinking. 'Where to start? There is so much.'

Sidorov dismissed that statement. 'Not really. Start here, in this very room.' Then he looked slowly at the lounging female and smiled.

'Ah,' Dvorkin exclaimed. 'Our master traveled to the Verkhoturye Monastery at the age of eighteen or so. There he learned of the *Khlysty*, or "Christ-believers".'

Sidorov made a look of distaste. 'I prefer, "They that purge".'

'Of course, of course. I was getting to that,' Dvorkin hastily added. 'The *Khlysty* did away with saints, and priests, and books. They – I mean *we* – practiced divine attainment through the repentance of sin.'

'And to repent sin . . .?'

'We have to experience it.'

'Go on,' Sidorov said as he took another sip of his drink.

'The greater the sin, the greater the repentance.'

'Yes?'

'Our master found great power within himself with this practice. He was able to heal the sick and see the future.'

'And?'

Dvorkin was confused. He was unsure as to what his leader wanted, so he was only able to parrot back the same question. 'And?'

Sidorov lowered his glass and pointed it at Dvorkin. 'There, you see? This is what I'm sure your accusers are talking about. You know the story, yes, but you do not appear to understand it. Do you bring insight to it?'

Dvorkin desperately wanted to respond in the affirmative, but Sidorov's next words were already rolling over him.

'The more the master sinned and repented, the greater the power he had. He healed the tsar's son of his bleeding ailment. He brought the tsar's lady-in-waiting back from the dead. He cried for them, he worked for them, he loved for them, and he lived for them – no matter how great the jealousy, hatred, and misunderstanding that he faced.'

'I understand his greatness,' Dvorkin said feebly.

But Sidorov's words were more than an education. He used his oratory to stir himself to an emotional frenzy. This was how Sidorov had become the leader of the Black Robes, by stoking flames within himself, flames he passed on to others.

'The priests sought to banish him,' Sidorov preached,

'and they were banished themselves for their sins. Their agents tried to kill him with a knife, but they were humbled by his survival. And the tsarina loved him in return, as did all the princesses. Why else was he allowed in their bed-chambers? The ladies of court loved him, and that was truly why he was most hated by men of power. They all wished they were loved as greatly. Yes?'

'Yes,' Dvorkin replied.

'Yes?'

'Yes!' Dvorkin exclaimed, catching fire. 'That's why Prince Yusupov, the Grand Duke Pavlovich, and Duma representative Purishkevich plotted to kill him.'

Sidorov put the snifter down so hard Dvorkin thought it might break. His leader's smile was wide but his eyes were cold. 'Yet they could not kill him, could they?'

'No, *strannik*.'

'What else did they call him?'

'I – I must think—'

'What else did they call our master besides *strannik*?'

Dvorkin's mind raced. They had called him the mad monk, but he dared not say that.

'Later in life, Pavel! What did they call him?'

'*Starets!*' he suddenly remembered. 'Venerated teacher. Elder monk confessor.'

Sidorov calmed. 'Yes,' he breathed. '*Starets*.' He looked at the ceiling as if searching for a sign or message, then looked upon his associate with pitying intensity. 'And our master *starets* sinned so much, and repented so much, that he could heal the sick and see the future, yes?'

'Yes . . . Yes, *starets* . . .'

Now that a different title had been indicated, he had better use it.

Sidorov stared at him. 'But there's *more*. You know there's more.'

'. . . I do, yes,' Dvorkin said while he racked his brain for answers. *What more does he mean? What other feats in the palace? What other liaisons did he have?*

Sidorov was standing over Dvorkin now, looking down at him as if from a great height. 'Our master could transcend death.'

Dvorkin felt his face flush with humiliation. 'Of course! How stupid of me! How utterly shameful!'

Much to Dvorkin's amazement, Sidorov laughed in delight. 'Good, good,' he approved. 'Remember, part of the *Khlysty* sect is self-flagellation. "I whip myself, I seek Christ" is what they chanted, yes?'

'Yes, *starets*,' Dvorkin said with relief. 'If you have a whip, I will gladly use it.'

Sidorov smiled at the offer. 'Oh no, there will be no whips for us. We don't have time for self-flagellation any more. Our task is too great.'

'Yes, *starets*,' Dvorkin agreed, suitably humbled.

'Tell me, Pavel, what is our task?'

'Our task?' he echoed.

Sidorov furrowed his brow. 'Surely you remember our master's story. Surely you remember the task of his followers.'

'It is . . . it is to find him.'

'Yes,' Sidorov breathed. 'They slit his stomach open. He did not die. They poisoned him. He did not die. They shot him three times. He did not die. They beat him. He did not die. They drowned him. He did not die. They burned him. He . . . did . . . not . . . die. Our master still lives!'

Sidorov turned from his associate. 'I have spent my life following his example. I have sinned. I have repented. I have gained influence.' He started to move around the room, as if gaining power from the trappings of royalty. 'I have followed every lead, I have explored every clue. And finally – *finally* – I discovered a way to locate him.'

He was back by Dvorkin, just behind his chair. He put his left hand on Dvorkin's right shoulder and sneered. 'All you had to do was wait, and watch, and let the Americans find him for us, but you were too weak to do your part!'

Fueled by rage and disgust, Sidorov plunged a silver fruit knife into the left side of Dvorkin's stomach, then dragged it across to the right. The part of Dvorkin's brain that wasn't in paralyzed shock, that wasn't shrieking in high, inaudible agony, was impressed at the strength it took to pierce flesh, cut across organs, and slit muscle with a fruit knife, even one from Imperial Russia.

Dvorkin opened his mouth to scream, but only a small 'uh' emerged. His hands came up, but they stopped when his mind couldn't decide whether to claw at the knife, the hand that held it, or Sidorov's face. Ultimately, his reflexes decided for him, and he reached down to try to keep his intestines from spilling onto his knees.

Sidorov cut as far as he wanted, then shoved Dvorkin to

the floor. The man fell mostly on his side, his hands clutching at the jagged, blood-wet wound. He looked up at his leader, his eyes bulging and his mouth opening and closing like a beached fish.

Sidorov stood there, the bloodied fruit knife now in his left hand. 'Our master is waiting for my arrival – waiting to give me his power. All you had to do was wait. But no, you wanted to cut corners. You wanted to follow the Americans from inside a nice warm room. So you tried to plant a bug on their train. And one of them saw you. She came to investigate. You panicked and seized her. And now they know we are tracking them.'

Sidorov grabbed him roughly by the shoulder and turned him onto his back. 'But don't worry: you will get the same chance that the prince, the duke, and the Duma delegate gave our master.'

Sidorov wrapped his hands around Dvorkin's throat and squeezed.

A soft gurgle escaped his mouth as the life was choked out of him.

Satisfied with the punishment, Sidorov rose and walked over to the sofa. With a bemused smile, he sat next to the still, young woman, and tenderly removed the heavy blind-fold – heavy because he had soaked the cloth in a trans-dermal anesthetic that had seeped through her skin and into her bloodstream within moments of its application.

He watched her sleeping for a few moments.

She had never looked better, he thought.

Like an innocent angel.

He realized this is what she must have looked like before family abuse, self-loathing, and desperation had brought her here.

Sidorov lay beside her and took the unconscious beauty in his arms. She would help him repent, he decided. Long into the night.

43

Garcia followed their progress on his Goldfinder program. They had traveled nearly nine hundred miles since they had left the station, and thus far everything had gone smoothly. 'Good news: we have left the Ukraine and entered Romania. Next stop: Gold City.'

McNutt groaned at the comment. He was an optimistic fellow, one who lived in a dream world where bears could fire cannons, but he knew this mission was still a long shot unless all of the team's theories proved to be accurate.

First, they assumed that Prince Felix had taken the treasure train from Moscow. Second, they believed that every soldier capable of walking had been massed for an aborted attempt to slash through Poland and attack East Prussia. This meant that the treasure could not have been offloaded from the train because there was no one on board to do the heavy lifting. Third, they guessed that the train would head to at least one major spur where they could

283

change directions to confuse would-be followers. However, this change needed to be done without witnesses. That meant a well-hidden spur in a thinly populated region.

After punching all that information into the Goldfinder program, it spit out a logical choice: the Transylvanian Plateau in Romania. Despite its name, the Transylvanian Plateau was a land of steep hills and valleys. The higher peaks of the Romanian Carpathian Mountains rose in nearly every direction, but here in the middle the rocky terrain gave way to vast forests and scenic cliffs. Given the difficulty of locating anything among its seemingly endless woodlands, they figured it was a great place to hide treasure.

Now all they had to do was find it.

McNutt, who had openly wondered if they were on the wrong train heading in the wrong direction, glanced at the screen. 'There's the calm before the storm, but this is nuts. Nearly twenty hours, and there isn't even a breeze out there.'

He was right. There was nothing ominous on the overhead satellite feed, nothing in the 360-degree video sweep, no radio chatter, no complaints from the pressure-sensitive tabs in the couplings, and nothing but Russian folk tunes from Andrei Dobrev in the engine. Dobrev had shown Jasmine the rudiments of how to run the engine so that she could spot him for rest periods. She was up there with him now.

Cobb, via his earpiece, told McNutt not to worry. 'Sometimes a day with nothing but sunshine is just that: a sunny day. Don't read into it.'

'Actually, I'm pissed because it's sunny.'

Garcia turned around. 'You're pissed at the sun?'

McNutt nodded. 'I was hoping to do some sightseeing before we left Moscow, and today would've been a perfect day to stand in line at Red Square. I could've worked on my tan.'

Cobb ignored the 'tan' part and focused on 'Red Square'. He was stunned that McNutt wanted to visit a historical site. 'I didn't know you were a history buff.'

'I'm not,' McNutt assured everyone, 'but I'm a *huge* Beatles fan. Before we left town, I was hoping to visit Lennon's tomb.'

Laughter erupted all over the train, so much so that Garcia had to temporarily excuse himself from his workstation to avoid laughing in front of McNutt. Even Jasmine, who could barely hear the chatter over the roar of the engine, laughed so hard she started to cry. Confused by her outburst, Dobrev demanded to know what had happened on his train. While giggling uncontrollably, it took her nearly five minutes to translate the story into Russian, but once she did, Dobrev laughed harder than anyone – so much so, he had to run to the bathroom because he was afraid he was going to wet his pants.

Meanwhile, McNutt had no idea what had set them off.

'I don't get it,' he mumbled to no one in particular. 'Is it because I like the Beatles? I know they're old, but I *love* their songs. Lennon was a musical genius.'

* * *

It took a while for the laughter to subside. Once it did, things returned to normal.

With Papineau elsewhere, Cobb had commandeered the desk, which was covered with paper maps and charts. Garcia returned to his workstation where the extra monitors he had initially ordered as back-up were now arrayed to accommodate the new security cams he had installed on, over, and under the train. The screens now stretched around him like blinders.

Between fits of pacing, watching over Garcia's back, and doing squat-thrusts and deep knee bends to stay limber, Sarah was lying on the sofa, studying maps on her tablet. Except for a few bruises on her neck, she was outwardly recovered from the Black Robe attack.

'This is so boring,' McNutt announced from a chair beside the couch, where he was enjoying a pungent sandwich he had just made in the galley – black bread, chopped sweet gherkins, crushed garlic cloves mixed with olive oil, black forest ham, Küsendorf Swiss cheese, and cucumber slices. 'Come on, Jack. I want to shoot somebody. When is that going to happen?'

'Hopefully, not on this trip,' Cobb said.

'Bite your tongue,' McNutt snapped.

Sarah rolled her eyes. McNutt was still having trouble with the big picture. 'Let me ask you a question: why would anyone try to stop us when we have no real idea where we're going?'

'Because Russians are ornery that way.'

'You make it sound like we should be watching out for Cossacks on horseback.'

'Hey, watch what you say,' Jasmine cautioned from the

engine. 'There are still large pockets of Cossacks, and they are intensely xenophobic.'

'See?' McNutt said.

Sarah and McNutt both happened to glance over at Cobb. He seemed to have tuned them out. His focus was a pin that let the air out of the conversation. The car was quiet, save for the endless clack of the heavy cars passing over old rails set in a slightly uneven track bed.

They were all wearing what had rapidly become their uniforms. Black, ultra lightweight, long-sleeve T-shirts made of the latest sports fabric. It kept them cool in heat and warm in cold. Their Eisenhower-style jackets and cargo pants were dark olive and featured stealth material that made the soft, strong cloth virtually silent. They were equipped with cunningly placed pockets for a variety of each person's needs – mostly extra ammo, since the jackets were long enough to cover their dark brown holster belts. Their shoes were also black and looked like a cross between hi-top slippers and combat boots. They were waterproof, slip-proof, and insulated, much like their shirts. In addition, every team member wore a watch that was synchronized and had a reflection-free face. The crystals were polarized along a vertical axis, meaning no one could read the watch except the owner, and ambient light bounced up, not out.

After a few minutes of silence, Cobb told Sarah to bring up a specific map on her iPad. He pointed to a variety of lines he had made on his own map with different colored pencils.

'I think the prince was trying to both find a place to hide

the treasure and make sure his family's path to Yalta was still clear,' he said. 'So we're looking for a road less traveled.'

'To Yalta?' she said.

'Toward Yalta,' he corrected.

'Aren't we a bit far afield, then?' Sarah asked, pointing east. 'We're headed southwest. Isn't Yalta a few hundred miles that way?'

'I don't think the prince wanted to hide the treasure in the Ukraine – or, as it was known then, Little Russia.' He shook his head. 'Too close to anti-Romanov armies. I'm betting that somewhere along this path he split the two groups – family one way, the way which led out, and the treasure another way.'

'Was it Malta or Yalta that his family left from?' McNutt wondered, chewing on a crunchy bite of sandwich. 'I can never keep those straight.'

'Malta,' Jasmine said. 'British warship – remember?'

'No,' he said as he wiped his mouth with a cloth napkin.

Changing the subject, Cobb drew his thumb across his throat, signaling that everyone should deactivate his or her microphone. He wanted a private conversation.

Everyone nodded in understanding. Around the room, team members whispered their personal codewords, the ones they had personally chosen to mute their individual microphones. One after another, their vocal feeds shut down. Cobb scanned the room, watching his team as they gave him the sign they were all clear.

He finished with Garcia, who gave him a thumbs-up.

'We're good, Hector?' Cobb asked.

'Good as gold,' Garcia replied.

'You're sure?'

'Of course, I'm sure. Why wouldn't I be?'

Cobb held up his hand, signaling Garcia to be quiet.

'Panther,' Cobb stated. It was the code word for his microphone, which was now reactivated. 'Jasmine, do me a favor.'

Garcia scanned the room nervously, suddenly realizing that not everyone was present and accounted for in the command center.

Cobb continued. 'Please confirm that Garcia's microphone is still active. Did you hear his chatter from a moment ago?'

'I sure did,' Jasmine said. 'He said we're as good as gold, then you challenged it.'

Cobb grimaced. 'That's what I figured.'

McNutt instantly raised his MP7 and aimed it at Garcia's chest. Garcia looked down and saw the bright red dot that was projected by the laser sight attached to the rifle's barrel.

One false move, and he was dead.

44

As part of his operational checklist, Cobb had insisted that Garcia divulge the location of every camera on the train. That way, Cobb knew every angle he could call upon if there was an emergency.

Shortly after the train had left the station, Cobb asked McNutt to check the control center for renegade cameras. The weapons man had found one, and only one. It was set in a screw at the base of a window. It was also a camera that Garcia had not mentioned in his discussion with Cobb. At the time, they weren't sure who had planted it: the Black Robes, the Russian government, or someone on their team.

So Cobb and McNutt had run an internal op to find out.

While glancing at Garcia's wall of monitors, Cobb had found the diagnostic screen that tracked the status of every video and audio signal being fed into the system. To the untrained eye, the feeds appeared as little more than solid green lines that continually scrolled across the screen. Only the time stamps that periodically marked their progress gave any indication as to what these lines represented. Fortunately, Cobb was familiar with the software. A green line meant that the feed was streaming normally. If the line turned red, it meant that an error had occurred. Clicking on any point in the timeline would open the data stream and allow the user to view or listen to anything recorded by the device.

In his gut, Cobb sensed that Garcia was involved.

To test his theory, Cobb monitored the communication feeds on Garcia's computer screen while McNutt placed a mug of coffee in front of the camera. A few minutes later, the coffee had spilled, as planned, when the train took an especially hard turn. The liquid caused a short circuit in the camera. Cobb knew if Garcia had been aware of the hidden camera, its feed would be among those listed on his screen. As Cobb watched, the corrupted feed had changed from green to red on Garcia's system. Just like that, they knew that Garcia had planted the rogue camera in the control center. They weren't sure why, but they knew he had done it.

Of course, they didn't challenge him right away.

That would have been a wasted opportunity.

Instead, Cobb called the team together, minus Garcia, for a private meeting. He warned them to watch what they did and said in front of Garcia until they could use the hidden camera to their advantage. Cobb guessed it would take twenty-four hours – tops – for the circuits to dry, and that time was almost up.

That meant it was time to confront Garcia.

* * *

Garcia went from relatively calm to totally panicked in a flash. His face, which was normally a medium brown, turned shockingly pale – as if he was about to pass out.

'I had to!' Garcia pleaded. 'Papi's got enough on my hacking to put me in jail for years!'

Cobb dismissed that with a grimace. 'I'm sure he's got something on all of us, Hector. That's irrelevant.'

'To you, maybe. But not to me! I'd never survive in pris—'

Cobb cut him off. 'Not interested. Just shut up and listen.'

Garcia forced himself to sit still. At least as still as a terrified man with sudden facial tics could manage.

'I figured you were Papi's inside man from the start. I knew he had one, and I assumed it was you.' Cobb shook his head with disappointment. 'That's fine. Part of your job description, I guess. But it has to end now. You can't – I repeat, *can't* – feed him our plans or let him deprive us of information. That could have tragic consequences.'

'You – you know everything,' Garcia protested.

McNutt stormed toward Garcia but was stopped by Cobb's extended arm. One word from Cobb, and McNutt would finally get to kill somebody.

'Couldn't find dirt on Papi or the Black Robes?' McNutt shouted as spray flew from his mouth like a junkyard dog. 'Give me a fucking break!'

Garcia's eyes went from one member of the team to the next, but he found no sanctuary. 'No, really. There wasn't anything of significance. I swear, I would have told you! My life is on the line, too!'

'More than you realize,' Cobb said menacingly. He lowered his arm a few inches. McNutt leaned forward as though he were on an invisible leash. 'So how about this, then? We need you, and you need me. As far as I'm concerned, the past is the past. No hard feelings. But here's the deal: get me that information. *Now.*'

Garcia opened his mouth again to plead, then he saw the look of disappointment on Jasmine's face. He lowered his head in shame. 'Okay.'

'Good,' Cobb said, speaking for the group. 'You get our trust back when you get us that information. Do we have a deal?'

'Of course,' Garcia said, sniffing. 'I'm—'

McNutt cut him off. 'Don't say you're sorry! The only reason you're apologizing is because you're afraid I'm going to throw your ass off a moving train.'

'No,' he protested. 'The guilt's been killing me.'

'Cry me a river! I knew you were a weasel from the start. *Your kind* always is!'

'That's enough,' Cobb ordered.

'My kind?' Garcia blurted. Despite his guilt, he knew he needed to stand up for his family and its proud Mexican heritage. 'Take that back!'

'No way!' McNutt shouted. Suddenly, he felt the harsh glare of his teammates focused on him. He glanced around the train car, trying to figure out why. 'What'd I say?'

Jasmine spoke up. 'There's no place for racism on this team.'

'Racism?' McNutt shrieked, even more confused than normal. 'I wasn't talking about Puerto Ricans. I was talking about *nerds*. I can't stand you fuckers – always reading books and shit. How can you trust someone like that? Turn on a TV like a normal person.'

'First of all,' Garcia argued, 'I'm *not* Puerto Rican. Secondly—'

'Enough!' Cobb shouted, growing more impatient by the second. 'We need to move on starting *now*. Garcia, get that information you promised me.'

Garcia nodded. 'Yes, sir.'

Cobb turned toward Jasmine. 'What's the latest from Dobrev?'

She answered, 'He said we'll never get anywhere if we stick to the main lines.'

'These are main lines?' McNutt exclaimed, happy for the change of subject. 'Those dirt roads, old villages, and mountain passes would put a Dracula movie to shame.'

Jasmine smiled. 'Actually, we're pretty close to Transylvania.'

'Did Dobrev have any suggestions?' Cobb asked.

'Of course,' Jasmine said. 'He wanted me to tell you there's an unused track that will bring us into the plateau region. He said—'

'If someone were going to split a shipment, this is where,' Sarah interrupted.

Cobb nodded. This was one of those fortuitous moments on any mission when theory and reality reached the same conclusion.

'Where is this track?' Garcia inquired, preparing to program it into Goldfinder.

His eagerness to get back in the mission caused both McNutt and Sarah to turn away in disgust.

Jasmine smiled thinly at him. 'You won't find it,' she said. 'Andrei says it's not on any map or chart.'

'I'll find it,' he insisted.

'Shouldn't you concentrate on getting the information Jack asked for?' she said.

'I'm already running that search,' he said. 'Just tell me what you know.'

'I don't know anything,' Jasmine said. 'Apparently not even who to trust.'

'All right, that's enough, kids,' Cobb stated.

'He wants to see you, boss,' Jasmine said to Cobb.

'All right. McNutt, Sarah – play nice here. Let Garcia do his job.'

'For once,' McNutt said bitterly, walking away.

'Garcia, I'll expect some good news when I get back.'

'You'll have it,' Garcia promised. 'I swear.'

Cobb glanced at Sarah, who held up her hands in mock surrender and went back to her sofa and the maps. McNutt collapsed onto the chair where he'd eaten his sandwich.

Cobb nodded at them, then joined Jasmine. 'Let's go.'

The two walked through the command center toward the engine. As he took a step across the linkage, Cobb got his first real-world glimpse of the surroundings.

Views from train windows must be similar throughout the world, he thought. *Rail-side cities whose population is rattled and shaken yet largely oblivious to the noise from passing trains, giving way to hillsides, grassland, and waterways.*

He tried to see it through the prince's eyes, but the world of the Romanovs was not the world of today. He knew that Felix, in order to safeguard the Romanian treasure, would have wanted to get as far from civilization as possible.

Cobb's thoughts on the outside world were cut off by the reality of the locomotive. The brief exposure to the wind and nature between the cars was slammed out of his mind by the dragon-roar of the engine. He and Jasmine had to twist and duck to avoid the head-end power unit on the floor and the cooling fans on the ceiling.

'Do you think Mr Papineau is really plotting against us?' Jasmine shouted back as they navigated the machinery. Her tone, even muffled by the noise, was fretful.

Cobb shook his head. 'No, but there's definitely something he's not telling us, and that makes me uneasy.'

They marched by air compressors and filters, then turned sideways to shuffle along the big main generator, while crouching slightly to avoid the dynamic brake grid and the dynamic brake fan that hung from the ceiling.

'Why?' Jasmine wanted to know.

'Exactly,' Cobb said. 'Why would he? I can think of a few reasons, and none of them fill me with confidence.'

'Anything we should be looking out for?' she asked.

'Everything.'

They stopped talking when they had to turn the other way to slide by the main generator and engine turbocharger to finally reach the cab. Thankfully, the fuel tanks, batteries, and compressed air tank were beneath their feet, attached to the underside.

Andrei Dobrev turned his head when the rear door of the cab opened, letting in the roar until Cobb closed it behind him. He smiled, happy to see the leader again. The man who had given him the opportunity to leave his detested semi-retirement. The man who had put this aged but still regal queen back into operation. Dobrev was proud and eager to show off what he called his 'old dancing partner'.

That is exactly what they were, Cobb thought as they entered the cab. The machine did not, could not, fail to impress. He understood how a boy could fall in love with it and never love anything else equally, ever.

Jasmine took her place on the second of two seats in the small, half-octagonal space that she and Dobrev occupied. It was adjoined by the slightly larger half-rectangular part Cobb stood in. Looking dead ahead out the smallish windshield, he saw more track, more grass, more trees, more hills, and more horizon. From the window to the side, he saw it all speed by.

Dobrev sat in a tall seat with its own suspension system to Cobb's right: the engineer's station. Spread before him were the brake, throttle, speedometers, and more than two dozen buttons dealing with systems spread throughout the train.

Jasmine sat in the same sort of seat to Cobb's left: the fireman's station. Here there were more controls and indicators, as well as the radio to make sure they didn't collide with anything and nothing collided with them. There was also a narrow door behind her that led to a toilet.

A minute later, Cobb noticed the terrain outside start to slow noticeably. He glanced at the controls. 'The throttle is at notch two. That's pretty slow.'

'Almost the slowest,' she replied. 'The cut-off that we're looking for is somewhere up ahead. We'll actually have to leave the train in order to find the switch. You might want to let everyone know that we'll be stopping frequently. Everyone except Garcia.'

45

The train squealed loudly – she had a right to, at her age – then hissed steam as she came to a slow stop. Cobb hopped from the engine, then helped Dobrev and Jasmine out.

As she translated, Dobrev said they were at a spot that he had known about for several decades: 'the dead end', he had called it.

'The junction switch was disabled long ago by whoever was leaving,' Jasmine said.

'Not the track?' Cobb asked.

Jasmine asked Dobrev. 'Not the track, he says.'

Dobrev continued as Jasmine translated.

'According to lore, the Russian White Army stranded a large faction of the Russian Red Army on the other side, then laid siege. No one has gone back there since. There are rumors of dead lying in the open, deadly munitions hidden by grass.'

Cobb smiled. 'In other words, disinformation to keep people out. Stronger motive than just having to repair a junction switch.'

'Exactly,' she said before she took a moment to explain the theory to Dobrev. 'He says he likes our explanation better than the traditional one.'

The engine was sitting on the somewhat steep side track

that had taken them away from the main line about twenty kilometers back. It was, as Dobrev had promised, a less traveled route. Gone were the villages, waterways, and protective walls. They had left the cow pastures and hay meadows far behind. Now it was just dirt, grass, forests, and hills. At times they couldn't even see the sky through all the oak and beech trees.

It had taken an engineer of Dobrev's skill just to get them this far. There were times when even Cobb doubted the wisdom of the move, as Dobrev navigated sharp turns on steep inclines and seemingly impossible declines. Cobb found it only mildly amusing as he heard the others react in his ear as if they were on a roller coaster climbing for a drop – or just coming out of one.

Nearly the entire time Cobb was in the cabin, Dobrev was talking to himself. Even now, outside the train, the old man continued.

'Anything we need to know?' Cobb asked.

'No,' Jasmine told him quietly, so as not to disturb or embarrass the engineer. 'Most of it is about trains, about the old days. Some is about his son and the life they all thought they'd have. And some of it is about the coin and the lost glory that was old Romania. He sounds sorry that his father's bloodline was mingled with his mother's Russian blood.'

'Ethnic conflict in your own head,' Cobb said. 'Not pretty.'

'I've got that with North and South Korea. I'm a second-generation schizophrenic.'

Cobb smiled. 'Let me know which side wins.'

She grinned. 'You know, I get the impression that Andrei

is doing more than babbling. He is taking stock of his life at what he knows is a significant juncture.'

'His life and our train, both diverging. It's fitting, somehow.'

Back in the command center, Garcia sat amongst his video screens, checking the surrounding woods by satellite. He also used his 'roof-cam' to look for any sign of life that wasn't bird, animal, or insect. Meanwhile, McNutt was crouched on the rear lip of the engine roof, covering Cobb, Dobrev, and Jasmine with a Heckler & Koch MP7 submachine gun, complete with sound suppressor and reflex sight.

'Is there a reason for the firepower?' Cobb asked him.

McNutt nodded. 'I'm still worried about Cossacks. Hordes of 'em.'

Cobb grinned. It wasn't a big leap of the imagination. This kind of rocky, scrubby terrain – miles from any signs of the modern world – did things to a person's mind.

Feeling well protected, Cobb turned back to the matter at hand.

Finding the junction switch.

At all the previous junctions, either Dobrev or Jasmine had used the radio to call ahead with instructions for the station controller to throw an electronic switch that would move them onto the various tracks they required. Most of those transfers had been on the main line, to let faster trains pass. Two had been on a parallel track they had used to avoid a bridge. Cobb did not want them on a sixty-meter-high trestle or inside a mountain tunnel if they could avoid it.

Those positions would have been tough to defend.

Since leaving the main line, Dobrev had jumped to the track to pull the old, heavy metal switches himself. As they got deeper into the wild, Dobrev thought it would be best if he had reinforcements, just in case.

Cobb was actually pleased to leave the hot engine for the cool, dry, Romanian autumn weather. They were lucky to be here during the moderate season between the sweltering summer of August and the numbing snows of November. He was also happy to be on solid ground. It was subtle, but the vibration of the train made him feel he was being shaken like a cocktail.

'So this is Transylvania,' McNutt said. 'If I see any fucking bats, I'm blasting them out of the sky. I'm not taking any chances with my blood.'

Jasmine laughed, not sure if he was serious or not.

Just to be safe, she filled him in on some history.

'Transylvania was once the Kingdom of Dacia,' she told everyone. 'The Roman Empire gutted it a couple of hundred years after Christ's death. After that, all bets were off. The country has been overrun by Avars, Bulgarians, Carpi, Gepids, Huns, Slavs, and Visigoths, just to name a few. Then the Hungarian Kingdom took over in 1003. After that, the Ottoman Empire. Then the Habsburgs got it in 1683. In 1867, it became part of the Austro-Hungarian Empire.'

'Fascinating,' Sarah deadpanned. 'The games of impotent men.'

'Listen or don't,' Cobb said, 'but don't interrupt.'

'There's not much more,' Jasmine promised them. 'After World War One, Austria–Hungary dissolved. The ethnic Romanian population, which was in the majority here, proclaimed union with Romania on December 1st, 1918.'

McNutt cleared his throat. 'What about Dracula?'

Jasmine tried to explain that even though Vlad Tepes – the notorious impaler of the fifteenth century – was real, Dracula was not. He was merely the protagonist of a novel written in 1897 by an Irishman who wanted to decry the foreign influence on the English Rose.

Of course, McNutt tuned her out early on.

'Vlad the Impaler?' he said, having heard nothing after that.

'He was a patriot who fought Ottoman rule,' Jasmine explained. 'He lined the roadways with impaled soldiers. The higher the rank, the higher the stake.'

'Talk about scarecrows,' McNutt said.

Jasmine continued. 'Unfortunately, the bodies drew vermin, which attracted disease, which killed Romanians. Not a brilliant tactic.'

Cobb let them babble for a while. It was a good way to let off tension. But he ordered them to stop when he heard Dobrev calling his name. Cobb hustled over to where Dobrev was pointing. It was a spot just in front of him.

'He says to check there,' Jasmine said.

All Cobb saw was what appeared to be heavy foliage, dwarfed by fang-like trees. He took a step further and peered closer to see that there was a heavy batch of coralroot, but it was coralroot wrapped around a skeleton of metal bones.

It was a long-forgotten switch – or at least part of one.

'We're going to have to rig something to move it,' Dobrev said through his translator. Then the two of them disappeared into the train. A minute later, Dobrev emerged with a pick and heavy rope while Jasmine took her spot in the engine.

From the roof, McNutt stared at her through the engine window. 'What in the hell are you doing in there?'

'I'm going to drive us back if he needs me to.'

Sarah chimed in. 'You never know when we might be attacked by vampires.'

McNutt held his weapon a little tighter. He wasn't sure what scared him more: hordes of Cossacks, flocks of vampire bats, or Jasmine driving the train.

With Dobrev's help, Cobb cleared away the foliage near the base of the switch. It had been sawed, he could see, close to the bracket that fixed it to the base. Holding the head of the pickaxe, Cobb dug the sharper of the two ends into the remaining wood to scoop it out. Then he stuck the iron point into the empty socket.

'Is this what you had in mind?' Cobb asked.

'*Da, da*,' Dobrev said approvingly.

They tied the rope around the pick handle to form a loop. Slipping it over his chest, Cobb faced away from the switch.

'You want a yoke-mate?' McNutt asked.

'I'll let you know,' Cobb said.

Gathering his energy, Cobb gripped the side lever and pulled, expecting quite a struggle. To his surprise, the switch moved easily, as if it had been oiled earlier in the day. Puffs of rust rose like pollen as he pulled. He saw what looked like tree roots shift over and the telltale glint of dull metal amongst them. It was track that hadn't been exposed to the elements for decades.

Then there was a solid-sounding click.

He heard Dobrev cheer quietly as the old man turned and hurried back into the cab. Cobb slipped off the noose, grabbed the pickaxe, and followed him.

The train began to rumble as Cobb swung onboard then trotted back toward the command center, waving at McNutt to do the same. The two met at Cobb's desk.

'Impressive,' Sarah said. 'Brains and brawn.'

Cobb flashed her a smile as he took his seat. 'Get ready, everybody. We're entering terra incognita.'

'I'll say,' Garcia added.

'What do you mean?' McNutt asked, slinging the MP7 across his back.

'This route goes into the woods and up the mountain. It's dressed to look like an old mine track.' Garcia switched to a spectroscopic analysis of the satellite image. It was the kind of technology that the Department of Defense used to search for lead containers in ordinary rail and seagoing cargo, capable of distinguishing variations in density and creating what looked like a negative image of the surrounding area. 'There are mining tools, hats, abandoned carts, and lanterns amidst the rocks and shrubs.'

'How do you know it wasn't a mine, once?' Sarah asked.

'The rails are the wrong gauge for those carts,' he said, pointing to a mine cart site on the Internet. He looked to the group for praise, but none was forthcoming.

The air was thick with expectation as the train poked ahead for a half-hour. It did not move steadily but in stops and starts, as Dobrev studied the condition of the tracks.

'Speaks well for Russkie construction,' McNutt said as they gathered behind Garcia, watching the nose-cam.

'We're in Romania,' Sarah reminded him.

'You know what I mean. All those old-timers. They did things right.'

'Except for revolution,' Sarah said, repeating her mantra about impotent men.

'Actually, women had a hand in this one,' Jasmine explained. 'They marched against the tsar, and it was Alexandra who invited Rasputin into—'

The train lurched, then stopped. Dobrev mumbled something.

'He says we're close,' Jasmine told the others.

'How does he know?'

Jasmine said, 'The slopes ahead are too steep for most trains, especially fast ones.'

Cobb studied the charts on his desk. 'I'm not surprised. Since we left the junction, the line hasn't been on any map.' He looked over at Garcia. 'Find us, Hector.'

The hacker's fingers flew across his keyboard, then he looked up at a screen with a glowing blue dot on it. 'There we are.'

Sarah leaned over him, looking closer. The dot glowed

and moved as they moved, but the background was blank. 'Okay, so where's "there"?'

Garcia stared at the screen intently, trying to bring some geographical grid into play. 'Tough to say.'

'Explain,' Cobb barked.

'GPS says we are in Chioar,' Garcia said slowly, enunciating carefully, eyes darting. 'But the maps say we could be in Lăpuş . . . or Cavnic . . . or even Campia Transilvaniei. Truth be told, we're actually in some sort of border null-space between those places.'

'Hold on,' McNutt said. 'How can the GPS be wrong?'

'It isn't,' Garcia said. 'But the regions have been redrawn over the last century, sometimes officially, sometimes unofficially by people with ethnic interests. Depending on what maps we use, all of those regions apply.'

He screen-grabbed an image and sent it over to Cobb.

Cobb looked closer himself and compared it to his charts. Sure enough, the Romanian ethnographic regions were denoted with different colored blobs. But there were relatively wide white borders between them with no name or denomination. The glowing, pulsing blue dot representing their train was smack dab in the middle of one of the largest white spaces, between four colored splotches.

'Taking every map into consideration,' Garcia said, 'only one thing is certain.'

'And that is?' Sarah asked.

'We're *literally* in the middle of nowhere.'

46

Cobb stood and marched to the end of the car. He hit a recessed button on the wall, waited for the door to slide up, then stepped through to the flatbed.

The view was spectacular. The train was slowly rising up the last of the track, climbing a steady incline as if they were in a scenic tram. McNutt appeared behind him and looked over the side of the five-foot lip that encircled the flatbed. The track seemed part of the earth.

'Holy mackerel,' he said.

'Yeah,' Cobb agreed.

Though it was chipped and faded by whatever sunlight had blazed through, the track had been painted brown to appear as if it were roots or the ground itself.

Sarah went to look over the opposite side, and was nearly knocked down by a tree branch as they entered an even thicker part of the pine and poplar forest. Cobb looked beyond them to the rolling green mountains, white clouds, and blue sky.

'I wish I knew where the hell we were,' Sarah said. 'I don't mean on a map – I mean, what's lurking under all that brush? There could be crevasses that cut us off if we have to travel by foot. Dry riverbeds with sinkholes.'

'Quicksand?' McNutt asked. 'I hate that. It always scared me in movies.'

'I doubt it,' Garcia said. 'The spectro isn't showing a lot of moisture in any form. No creeks, no bogs, no wells.'

'No wells?' Cobb said. 'Interesting. That means this area was completely deserted, even to farmers and shepherds.'

As he spoke, the train emerged into a more open space where the trio could finally get an unobstructed view. Now it was only the train itself that looked wildly out of place amid layers of green, spread amongst leafy dots of red, yellow, and orange fall foliage. The only thing missing was any hint of other humans.

'Too bad,' Sarah said.

'About what?' McNutt asked.

'That there weren't any sheep or cow herders,' she said. 'This is great pastureland.'

'Or battleground,' Cobb said from the rear of the car.

They turned to see their commander standing on the top rung of the ladder attached to the outside of the freight car. Sarah and McNutt ran back to join him. McNutt put both hands on the top of the flat car's fencing and vaulted up to the top of the lip. He put one hand on the side of the compartment car, twisted his body, and looked to where Cobb was staring.

The train was halfway up the open section of green grass and white flowers, heading toward another long, thick line of trees. The trees were so tall and narrowly spaced that they looked, to Sarah, like the tarnished, bared teeth of a giant bear.

Something was emerging from those teeth.

'Josh,' Cobb said, 'do you have your binoc—'

He looked over to complete the question, but McNutt was gone. The sniper reappeared a few seconds later with a pair of Steiner 1600 Yard Laser Range Finder Military Binoculars. He handed them to his commander.

'Thanks,' Cobb said as he put the fog-proof lenses up to his eyes.

'Do you see this?' Garcia asked in his ear.

'Yes,' was all Cobb needed to say.

Coming from between the trees were a herd of horses: white Lipizzaners, praised for their riding; mottled Hungarian Warmbloods, noted for their stamina; and brown Shagyas, depended upon for their endurance.

'Riders!' Cobb and Garcia shouted, almost at the same time.

'I knew it! Cossacks!' McNutt raised his own binoculars – a slimmer Apache 10x25 compact model – as he retook his position on the lip top of the car.

'We don't know that!' Jasmine said, maintaining her cool in the face of what could be her first firefight.

McNutt saw the horses – now at least three dozen, with more joining them from the tree cover – and their riders: men of every age group, holding reins in one hand and waving something above their heads with the other.

'Are those Mosin-Nagants?' McNutt asked incredulously. 'Those were the standard issue rifle of Soviet troops in World War One!'

When no one answered, he lowered his binoculars and understood why.

McNutt was alone on the flatbed.

He jumped to the floor of the car and charged into his armory.

* * *

The next thirty seconds felt like thirty minutes.

'Two hundred yards, Jack,' Garcia announced anxiously. The IT wizard was intent on the video screens, trying to get a good look at the riders despite the train's constant up-and-down motion and side-to-side sway, not to mention the bounce of a man on horseback. Even his seasoned fingers couldn't digitally stabilize the images with that many variables.

'Who are they, Garcia?' Cobb asked. He was visually sweeping the terrain, settling on nothing but seeing everything.

'I'm trying to get an image I can profile,' Garcia said.

'Is profiling illegal here?' McNutt joked.

Cobb didn't have to tell the sharpshooter to focus. His fall into silence said that, and more.

McNutt was in the freight car, breaking out the Mossberg 590 and Benelli M4 shotguns. He considered both weapons, one in each hand, remembering that the 590 weighs about half a kilogram less but doesn't have the range of the Italian shotgun. He put down the Mossberg in favor of the one preferred by the Marine Corps. He turned toward the slats on the west side of the car and prepared to open one as he spoke to everyone on their earpieces.

'Could use a little help manning the barricades,' McNutt called.

'Hold your fire,' Cobb snapped from the command car.

'Your wish is my command,' McNutt retorted. 'But just so you know: they may have vintage rifles, but their carbine rounds could still pop your head like a balloon.'

Cobb ignored the chatter in his ear and contemplated their next move. Once again, he reminded himself: *this is why McNutt was with them and not still with Special Forces.* Any regular unit on the globe would have followed Cobb's orders without backtalk.

'One hundred fifty yards,' Garcia called out.

'McNutt,' Cobb said sharply, 'get to the engine and protect Dobrev and Jasmine. Ward the riders off if they try to stop us or board. No killing, if at all possible.'

'What?!' McNutt and Sarah shouted as one.

'Um . . . Jack?' Garcia begged.

Cobb ignored him. 'Use your brains, people! They're waving the guns, not aiming them!'

'That's because they're on horseback on uneven terrain,' McNutt argued. 'From this distance, they'd be wasting ammo.'

'You heard my orders, McNutt. Now follow them!' Cobb barked.

'Jack!' Garcia shouted.

'What?' Cobb shouted back.

'They're aiming at us now,' Garcia said, watching in fear and admiration as the lead riders used their thighs to control their horses while raising their guns with two hands. 'Not just random potshots. They're lining up their sights with both arms!'

'That's what the Cossacks did,' Jasmine contributed.

'See?' McNutt said. 'Didn't I warn you?'

Garcia couldn't help but wonder how they did that. He had been on a horse exactly once, and even though he never went faster than a trot, he had bounced up and down like a dribbled basketball. 'One hundred twenty-five yards,' he said.

'Now? Can I shoot them now?' McNutt demanded.

'Get to the engine!' Cobb barked.

'I'm already on my way!' he yelled back, throwing the door open wide to accommodate his duffel bag as he moved between the cars.

Cobb was no longer watching the riders. He was in seemingly manic motion.

Sarah gasped when Cobb suddenly lifted sofa cushions and opened or overturned everything that could move. As if waiting for that moment, the glass beyond the curtain cracked, and they heard a distant rifle report a quarter-second later.

'A hundred yards,' Garcia gulped audibly.

Cobb dropped the curtain and continued his frantic search. 'Nice shot,' he muttered.

'Jack!' Sarah started.

'Just a glancing hit,' he said quickly. 'Maybe even a rico-chet.'

'What are you looking for?' Sarah exploded.

Cobb stood in the middle of the command center and calmly said, 'Does anybody know where I can get a tablecloth?'

47

McNutt charged into the engine cab, swinging his bag in ahead of him. Dobrev was crouched, his eyes just over the ledge of the controls, while Jasmine had her back against the lavatory door, her revolver up by her head. She was breathing heavily through her nose, her chest was heaving. But she was alert, steady.

McNutt threw the duffel down and thrust the Benelli shotgun into Jasmine's other hand. 'Take this, would you?'

She looked incredulously at him. 'I've never fired one of—'

'Good time to start,' McNutt said.

'Seventy-five yards,' Garcia said in their ears.

Jasmine examined the weapon.

'Use it as a club if you have to,' McNutt said. 'Though if it was up to me, they wouldn't get that close.'

'It isn't, so shut up,' Sarah said in his ear.

McNutt was now too busy to argue. He was on one knee, intent on getting the duffel open.

Dobrev said something.

'What does he need?' Cobb asked over the earpiece.

Jasmine answered. 'He just wants us to know he can't put on more speed and plow through them. He doesn't want to go off these old tracks.'

'Thank him for the alert,' Cobb said. 'But that's not my plan.'

'Yeah, we'd run out of track, and then they'd be on us, really pissed,' Sarah said.

Jasmine translated for Dobrev as she flattened herself back against the lavatory door. They all heard more snapping and cracking sounds from the riders' rifles.

'Fifty yards,' they heard Garcia say.

'Jack said "no killing", Jack gets "no killing",' McNutt said. He straightened, holding the weapon up proudly and looking at Jasmine with a big grin. 'But I still get to shoot.'

To her eyes, the weapon looked like the back of a big, gray flare pistol, with a muzzle or barrel or whatever you called it that seemed like a cross between the end of a fireman's water hose and a big flashlight. As she watched, McNutt added a shoulder stock for better control, then a sniper's scope for better aiming. She looked down. In the duffel bag were five more devices.

'Twenty-five yards,' Garcia croaked.

'Net gun,' McNutt proudly announced while pushing open the cab's small side windows.

'What?' Jasmine said. 'It fires—'

'Nets. Yes. I figured we might need something, or someone, caught and—'

'Josh!' Jasmine screeched, pointing behind him.

McNutt whirled to see a rider coming up the engineer's side, pointing his rifle at Dobrev.

McNutt only got a glimpse of the ruddy, mustachioed rider in his baggy, beige pants, brown boots, belt, and vest before there was a *bang* and a *whoosh* – and what looked like a baseball shot from the end of McNutt's big-mouthed weapon. Once it was outside the window, the casing of the projectile opened and fell off to the sides, then a big, flying spider's web spread out and slammed into the rider from his head to his waist.

Jasmine watched, mesmerized, as the rider was thrown from his horse as if he'd been swatted off by the hand of God. She instinctively leaned forward and checked that the man landed okay before Dobrev pushed her back. She saw, in fact, that the man hit the ground as if he were used to falling off a horse. The net didn't let him get right up, but the way he was kicking and clawing, it didn't cause any permanent damage either.

McNutt was already screwing in another net ball when Cobb came barging in with a tablecloth tied to a curtain rod. Pulling Jasmine out of the way – but protecting her with his own body – he shoved the makeshift white flag out the window and began waving furiously.

'What the fuck, chief?' McNutt exclaimed, almost with resentment.

'Shut up!' Cobb snapped. 'They're peasant villagers!'

'So? They can still kill us.'

'Dammit, will you think with your brain instead of your trigger finger?' Cobb yelled. He continued to wave the flag, making sure it was seen as far as the most distant rider. 'Why would they attack us? You think they've never seen a train before?'

Dobrev said something. He sounded reflective.

'He says we're trespassing,' Jasmine said. 'But the word he used . . . it's not exactly trespassing . . .'

'He means we're not welcome here, not just uninvited.'

'Yes,' Jasmine said, impressed. 'That's exactly what he means.'

Cobb said, 'That's because they're protecting something – something that makes them risk their lives to attack a train while on horseback!'

'The treasure,' Sarah gasped in their ears.

McNutt and Jasmine looked at Cobb with newfound appreciation.

'They might know about the treasure,' Sarah said accusingly, 'and you wanted to gun them down, McNutt.'

'Sorry if I didn't want any of my teammates to take a musket ball in the brain!'

'They didn't want to kill,' Cobb said. 'They just wanted to let us know they can.'

'How considerate,' McNutt said.

'Jack, do you know the story of the Golden Fleece?' Jasmine said.

'Oh goody,' Sarah said. 'A story.'

'A relevant one,' the historian said. 'Jason and the Argonauts sailed from Thessaly to Colchis to steal the Fleece. King Aeëtes allowed them to make landfall – then attacked them. Though Jason got what he came for, it came at loss of life on both sides.'

'I won't cut them down,' Cobb said.

'Humanitarian gesture – or because they know where the treasure is?' Sarah asked.

Cobb didn't reply. Which was a reply. The answer was both. Plus, it occurred to him that this generation might be happy to be rid of their stewardship after a century. For the right price, they might even help them load up the train.

McNutt clearly didn't agree, but he said nothing as he watched and waited for his next target to ride by.

'Слушайте!' Dobrev said suddenly.

'He wants us to be quiet and listen,' Jasmine said.

Cobb did, still waving. The engineer's trained ears had listened through the noise of the train and heard what they had all missed.

'No more shooting,' Jasmine said, smiling.

'He's right,' Sarah said.

The horsemen were whooping, whistling, and waving their rifles, but they weren't aiming and shooting any more. They rode around, beside, in front of, and behind the train with remarkable displays of horsemanship, but it was now obvious they weren't intending to attack.

'I'm thinking they just don't want to get netted,' McNutt said.

Cobb lowered his arms and tightened his grip on the flagstaff out of frustration. He turned on the sharpshooter. 'If you'd been paying attention, you would have noticed they didn't go for the tracks. All it would have taken was a mallet or axe head to bend a single rail enough to force us to stop. They didn't have to put themselves at risk. But they didn't do that.'

'Not if it was some macho Cossack thing,' McNutt grumbled.

'Why don't you just admit you were wrong?' they heard Sarah say.

McNutt looked away, annoyed that they weren't even allowing that he could be right – which he still believed he was, having put on reckless, bravado-induced displays like that himself. But he brightened when he saw the man he had net-gunned reappear outside of the side window. The man was back on his horse with a gap-toothed smile that went from ear to ear, holding his rifle up proudly, angled slightly outward.

'Wow,' McNutt breathed.

'What?' Jasmine asked.

'He just saluted me with a Mosin-Nagant M91–30,' McNutt marveled, seeing three R's surrounded by crossed stalks stamped on the rifle's breech. 'Those were specially modified for Romania and reserved in case of invasion.'

Suddenly, the team was distracted by a voice from outside the window where the white flag flew. It was a commanding, male voice, rough from years of sharp mountain air and tobacco.

'Who are you?' he demanded in a Slavonic language.

Everyone in the cab looked to Jasmine.

'He's the leader, asking who we are,' she informed them.

'In Romanian?' Cobb wanted to know.

'No, Russian,' Jasmine told him.

'Maybe he recognizes the markings on the train,' Sarah suggested.

'Only one way to find out,' Cobb said. 'Tell him we are explorers who come in peace.'

'Tell him we have every intention of upholding the Prime Directive,' McNutt added.

Jasmine looked at him as she maneuvered past Cobb, back to the window.

'*Star Trek*,' McNutt said. 'Don't interfere with indigenous life forms.'

'Oh great,' Sarah sighed. 'Our gunman's off in fantasyland again. I wish we could beam his ass back to Florida.'

48

Cobb ignored his team's bickering and focused on the handsome older man in a dark, zip-up jacket, pants, boots, and wool cap.

He rode his horse as if he were born on it.

The man trotted alongside the still slowly moving train in perfect rhythm. Yet as much as he looked the part of an old-guard horseman, Cobb sensed there was something off about him – something modern. *The straight teeth he flashed? The hands that didn't look like they spent much time moving rocks or swinging an axe? His posture in the saddle seemed formal: more trained and drilled than native-born.*

Jasmine told the rider what Cobb had asked her to say. The old man listened to the young woman's fluent Russian words then spoke again.

'What do you want?' the man asked in Russian.

Jasmine translated it for the group.

Sarah spoke in their ears. 'What are you going to tell him, Jack? No truth, half-truth, or whole truth?'

Cobb had been thinking about it. For the first time in awhile he was unsure how to attain the best result.

'Jack?' Jasmine urged quietly.

The Russian looked at Cobb expectantly.

'I'm talking because I want him to hear words,' Cobb

said. 'Otherwise he'll think I'm standing here formulating a lie.'

'Are you?' Jasmine asked.

'Considering it,' Cobb admitted.

Suddenly, a hand fell on Cobb's shoulder. Dobrev was beside him, the train slowing to a crawl. He said something that Jasmine translated.

'Andrei wants to tell the man something,' she said.

Dobrev didn't wait for Cobb's approval. Technically, that was his prerogative since rules of the rail put him in charge of the train. Cobb had the manpower to disagree but not the right. So Cobb deferred. Dobrev stuck his head out the window and immediately started talking to the leader of the horsemen. His tone was affable, familiar, even jocular, but still somehow sincere.

Cobb and McNutt both looked at Jasmine.

'Andrei is telling the man about his life and travels,' she said. 'About how he and his family have dreamed of these hills since he was a boy. He says he finally decided to bring his old self and his old train here. The horseman laughed at that, wants to know whether we are vacationers. Dobrev says not exactly and that your description of "explorers" is more accurate. He says that the man's accent tells him that he, too, is a proud Russian, and that our visit carries a purpose that is important to all loyal Russians as well as our hosts, the Romanians.'

'Does he say what the purpose is?' Cobb wanted to know. *That was really the crux of it.*

'Andrei just – what is the football word? Punted?'

'That's the word,' McNutt said.

'What did Dobrev tell them?' Cobb asked.

'That you would explain the purpose, man-to-man, over a glass.'

'In other words, he bought you time, boss,' Sarah said.

'Time and an equal standing,' Jasmine said. 'Chief to chief. That's a big concession to someone who was "not welcome" just a few minutes ago.'

'Oh,' said McNutt quietly. 'This guy's good.'

Jasmine looked straight at Cobb. 'Andrei asked the man to come onboard. He declined. He wants us, all of us, to come out. The horseman is telling him to stop the train and we can share a glass of *tuica* in their village.' Before anyone could ask, Jasmine explained. 'It's a Romanian peasant drink; a brandy made from apples or plums.'

'I am *so* in favor of that,' McNutt blurted.

As the gunman was speaking, Dobrev moved back and started to brake the locomotive without awaiting instructions. Meanwhile, the lead horseman started speaking again.

'He wants to talk to you,' Jasmine told Cobb.

Cobb shrugged a silent 'okay' and stuck his head back out the train window. While the man spoke, Cobb took a moment to savor the beautiful countryside and the remarkable sight of the surrounding horsemen. It was as if they had now fully been transported to the dawn of the twentieth century.

'He says, "You are their leader, yes?"' Jasmine translated.

'*Da*,' Cobb replied.

'*Americanski?*' the man asked.

'*Da.*'

'Is that really how they refer to us?' McNutt asked.

Jasmine nodded.

'Wow. I thought that was a joke,' he said.

The horseman paused. He was studying Cobb's face with the wisdom of many years more than Cobb had under his own belt.

The man spoke again. 'He says, "This is going to be a very interesting talk, is it not?"' Jasmine translated.

Cobb smiled philosophically, and nodded. '*Da.*'

The Russian leader of the Romanian villagers shrugged in return, spoke once more, and started to turn his horse back to where they came.

'"A bad peace is better than a good quarrel",' Jasmine translated. 'Old Russian proverb.'

'They're all full of them, aren't they?' McNutt asked.

'This man more than others,' said Jean-Marc Papineau, very unexpectedly, in the ears of the team. 'He is Colonel Viktor Borovsky of the Russian police. He questioned me in—'

Cobb didn't hear the rest of Papineau's statement. Not because the feed was cut, but because a shot rang out from the nearby trees. A split-second later, the horse ridden by Colonel Borovsky lost its head in an eruption of bloody shreds as bone, brain, and hair filled the air.

49

To reach the isolated village, Colonel Borovsky and Anna Rusinko had boarded a helicopter that he had commandeered from the *Gosudarstvennaya Avtomobilnaya Inspektsiya* – better known as the GAI, or the Moscow highway patrol. The chopper had ferried them unobtrusively to Kursk where, during a refueling stop, Borovsky called an associate in the Romanian Ministry of Internal Affairs to clear their passage to Vascauti. After surrendering their sidearms to local authorities, Borovsky had told the deputy minister that they were just going to meet some old friends – friends he had met long ago on an archeological dig.

From there, it was smooth sailing.

At least until the train arrived.

Anna had tried to discourage Borovsky from his plan to stop the train, on horseback, with old rifles. But ever since they had left Russia, he had become increasingly less communicative. Anna had a stronger and stronger sense that he had a private mission apart from finding Andrei Dobrev and solving a murder. The colonel belonged to some century other than his own. He certainly didn't belong in this era with its layers of bureaucrats and desk-police and regulations.

In that regard, he was more cowboy than cop.

An old-school hero in a new world.

Standing on a rise while glancing through seventy-year-old binoculars – with superb optics, she had to confess – Anna had seen Borovsky ride toward the train, fire at the ground, then trot alongside the engine. The entire time he was smiling, like he was having a total blast.

From her vantage point, it had looked like a nest of insects swarming around a toy train. She had looked helplessly at the villagers around her. They were not fearful of the sharp reports of weapons or the danger faced by loved ones. They were completely silent while they watched, intently, as events unfolded.

A few had even seemed proud.

But that only made sense. It wasn't every day that the local peace officers received a call from a colleague in Moscow – one who wanted them to join him and do what they were trained to do. And on a matter of international importance. Most of these people had never been more than twenty-five miles from their village.

To do something that affected the world was an honor.

But after ten minutes, the action was over.

That part of it, anyway.

She was about to get in a waiting hay cart – a hay cart! – for a ride back to the village when a crack had rolled ominously from somewhere behind her. In a panic, she quickly raised the binoculars and studied the scene before her.

Only one man had appeared to be hit.

Colonel Viktor Borovsky.

*   *   *

Cobb slammed onto the floor of the train cab, temporarily dazed by the blood and horse brains that had splattered the side of his face.

Jasmine ducked as she yanked up the shotgun like she was about to blow the roof off the train, riding the fear as she'd been taught. Her survival depended upon treating her emotion like an unwelcome friend, not the enemy itself.

'Can I kill someone now?' McNutt spat sarcastically as he spun in the direction of the shot. He saw the attackers a second after Garcia did.

'ATVs, AK-47s – Black Robes!' they all heard in their ears.

A dust cloud filled the horizon. Tearing up from the southern woods with the ear-slicing roar of a hundred dragons were dozens of dark, four-wheel, all-terrain vehicles, ridden by men cloaked in black robes and carrying AK assault rifles. They tore up the grass and shredded the flowers as their bulky, industrialized, heavy-tired machines buzz-sawed furiously up the slope, while the horsemen raced for the far side of the train where their leader still was.

Cobb's head came up as McNutt dragged Jasmine and Dobrev down.

'Full metal jackets!' the sniper hissed as he grabbed the Benelli shotgun from Jasmine, twisted toward the southern side of the cab, then cursed.

'What?' Cobb said.

'Too far, damn it!' McNutt said. 'Out of range!'

Then McNutt was gone, out the back of the cab, so fast that he practically left a puff of cartoon smoke.

Jasmine stared after him then spun her head back toward Cobb, who was still on the floor, his head raised. Half his face looked like it was slapped with red warpaint. He was trying to look out the window without losing the top of his head.

'Jasmine, you stay back,' Cobb said. 'I can't afford to lose my translator.'

The remark stung a little. His concern wasn't for *her*, it was for what he had often referred to as the 'mission assets'. Whenever she thought she might be starting to like him or one of the others, that reality always intruded.

As Jasmine stepped back, Sarah appeared in the cab door. She was fully dressed in her Type IV Modular Tactical Vest and Ops Core Ballistic helmet – the best bullet-resistant gear money could buy. The former looked like a tailor-made down vest, and the latter looked like a particularly aggressive bike-riding helmet. Even so, they were made to withstand everything up to, and including, thirty-zero-six armor-piercing bullets.

Sarah's arms were full of additional gear for the rest of the team. She tossed vests and helmets to Cobb and Jasmine, along with a spare for Dobrev, then she swung a SIG 553 Commando assault rifle around from where it was strapped on her back. The seven-pound, twenty-eight-inch, five-point-six-millimeter, thirty-round weapon was also considered one of the best in the world.

'Thanks,' Cobb said as he pulled Jasmine lower and helped her suit up before putting his own equipment on.

'No problem,' Sarah said. 'I gotta get back to McNutt.

He's setting up the armory for war.' She smirked at the thought. 'He said we have permission to kill them. True?'

In the pause that followed, they heard the slapping metallic noise of lead hail hitting the southern side of the train.

'Yes,' Cobb said.

'Wait!' Papineau shouted in their ears.

'Sarah, go,' Cobb said, ignoring the Frenchman. He looked at Sarah, pointed toward the armory, then pulled his finger across his throat.

Sarah gave a thumbs-up and disappeared. Better protected now, Cobb went to the door for a clearer view of the Black Robes. From this vantage point, he heard a scratching just beyond the lavatory door on the other side. He twisted around to see a stunned, winded Borovsky, his face covered in his horse's brains, feebly trying to pull himself up the cab ladder.

'Jack, are you there?' Papineau said.

'Shut him down, Garcia,' Cobb shouted, clearly referring to the Frenchman, while reaching out to the Russian.

'Just his broadcasts or—' Garcia started.

'Everything!' Cobb bellowed as Jasmine and Dobrev, who had put on his own, slightly ill-fitting protective gear, rushed to help Borovsky. It didn't matter that he was a Russian police officer or the leader of the villagers. Cobb sensed that Borovsky would be more of an asset than a threat, particularly after saving his life.

Garcia cut Papineau off as ordered.

'Dobrev!' Cobb shouted at the engineer. When he got

his attention, he urgently jabbed one forefinger at the northern tree line. The old man nodded and scuttled to the controls.

As the engine throttled up, Cobb helped Jasmine drag the limp, groaning Borovsky inside.

'*Spasiba*,' he said breathlessly.

Cobb offered him his own protective helmet.

The colonel declined with a grateful wave of his hand.

'Jasmine, tell Dobrev to get as close to the tree line as possible,' Cobb said. 'Garcia, how many?'

'Two dozen, more coming,' came the answer. 'Now three . . . four! More coming!'

Cobb silently swore. 'Everybody, retreat prep.'

'No!' McNutt shouted.

'Dammit, I said *prep*, not execute!'

'Roger,' said Garcia and Sarah almost at the same time.

And then Sarah hissed, 'Get with the freakin' program, McNutt.'

50

As the train began to pick up speed, Cobb slid to the southern side of the cab. He hazarded a look at the field just in time to see the nearest Black Robe kill a horse and rider with his AK-47. A second after that, the Black Robe cartwheeled off the ATV, his head erupting into a wet, red plume of mist.

'In range,' McNutt reported gleefully.

'We'll be too, in a few seconds,' Garcia said, comparing his map to the specs of the weaponry carried by the Black Robes.

Cobb heard another dull crack and saw a flying Black Robe.

McNutt cackled with delight. 'They gotta get through the killing field first. Let's see how many volunteer.'

He was right: the lead drivers who were trying to reach the train veered away to the east, moving out of range and rendering themselves ineffective. The Black Robes would have to wait and attack the passing train from the rear.

That bought Cobb's team some time.

Chalk one up to McNutt, Cobb thought, picturing the gunman using an Accuracy International AX338 long-range sniper's rifle, the one with the five-shot magazine.

Cobb's eyes moved northward. He saw fifty or more

Black Robes spread across the field ahead. Some were still riding, but most were parked and hunkered down behind their vehicles, firing at will. The local horsemen, too, had gathered behind the train, firing when they could, but mostly using the locomotive as a shield and waiting for orders.

Cobb turned back to see Borovsky propped up against the lavatory door, looking haunted.

'Ask him if he's ready for that *tuica*,' he told Jasmine without taking his eyes off their guest.

She did. Cobb watched as Borovsky's face changed. He said something in a slow, unconcerned voice.

'He says, "If you're buying."'

Cobb grinned. 'With pleasure. Tell him we're going to need his men to get us out of here.'

'Abandon the train?' Garcia gasped.

'Shut up, Hector, and listen. You've got work to do. I don't want them to be able to crack our computers even if they brought a Russian Garcia with them.'

'You want me to fry them?'

Cobb nodded. 'Anything you can't carry, kill. Understood?'

'Roger that,' Garcia said, his fingers already flying, his brain figuring out how many laptops to take with him and what kind.

'Sarah, you got what you need?'

'In my skull and at the end of my arms, Jack,' she replied.

Cobb looked back at Jasmine, pleased to see that Borovsky was leaning half out of the cab, already telling his men what to do.

'Anything I need to know?' Cobb asked Jasmine.

Just then, Borovsky turned and spoke.

'He says that the men are ready,' Jasmine said. She listened to the Russian for a few seconds more, then added, 'He says to jump on the back of a horse and hold on tight.'

'Hold – onto what?' Garcia gulped.

Borovsky was still talking.

'He says that the horses are amazingly well trained,' Jasmine assured everyone. 'They have been trained to ignore loud noise, sudden motion, and added weight. They won't flinch.'

'Not even if I puke?' Garcia said.

'Not even if you continue to cry like a two-year-old,' Sarah said. 'Jeez.'

'Okay everybody,' Cobb ordered, 'grab whatever you need that won't slow us down and double-time it up here.'

Garcia was the first to arrive, pockets bulging with flash drives and battery packs, arms full of bags of tablets, eyes darting for errant bullets. An additional shoulder bag contained two laptops and one wireless charger.

'Where are the others?' Cobb demanded.

Other than the occasional cough of McNutt's sniper rifle, there was only silence from the back of the train.

'McNutt? Sarah?'

'He won't leave, Jack,' they heard Sarah say.

'McNutt!' Cobb yelled.

'Covering the retreat,' McNutt said. 'It's in the prep drill, remember.'

Cobb felt like killing someone who wasn't a Black Robe. He hated having his own instructions flung back at him.

Sarah came through the door just then, and Cobb put her in charge of the evacuation.

Borovsky was already on a horse, behind the rider McNutt had netted. Five more riders milled around the northern side opening of the cab. The rest were spread out amongst the other cars, keeping the Black Robes from circling wide and coming at them from the east. Several additional horsemen were congregated at the front and rear of the train, helping McNutt keep any ATV from charging the train as it crept closer and closer to the protective embrace of the northern tree line. The mob of swirling dust made precise shooting difficult. It was basically a matter of shooting at the center of a tawny cloud and hoping you hit something.

Before Cobb looked back at his team, he took final inventory of the battleground. He had counted four horsemen and thirteen Robes down. The decrease was proportionate, but it was not the kind of loss his side could afford. They needed to regroup.

Cobb cupped his hand over his ear. 'Retreat, McNutt.'

They all heard the reply. 'Bit busy here, Jack.'

'That was an order, McNutt.'

Jasmine and the others were amazed that Cobb's voice was so calm.

Sarah was certain McNutt was going to say something massively stupid, like, 'We're not in the army now, Jack,' or 'You're not the boss of me.' Then again, she didn't understand the transformation that overcame men in battle. It was a sense of purpose, responsibility, and duty that caused every other trait to fade to insignificance.

Surprisingly, McNutt's response was calm, collected, without even a hint of attitude. He simply said, 'I can do this, Jack.'

Sarah felt a lump in her throat. It was the first time she had seen the true McNutt – a man capable of unflinching sacrifice, not a smartass playing Army.

'Sarah, get them off the train!' Cobb shouted.

The words snapped Sarah from her momentary daze. Cobb stared at her, waiting for an acknowledgement. Once she nodded, he started racing back through the cars.

Cobb was in the armory and rushing up to McNutt before the gunman even knew he was there. Cobb spoke the language he knew McNutt would hear, would understand: he picked up an M1 that was lying beside him as a weapon of last resort, brought it to his shoulder, and fired a round at an ATV. It was barely within range but, expertly leading the target, he managed to nick its left front tire. The vehicle lurched and threw its rider.

McNutt jerked around. 'Nice!'

'You keep firing, soldier!' Cobb barked. 'Do not take your eye from the target!'

McNutt grinned as he put his eye to his sniper rifle's scope. A moment later he eliminated the driver of yet another ATV who was trying to swing around to the northern side of the train.

'We can take them, Jack,' he said through gritted teeth. 'They keep rolling into range, we can take them all out.'

Cobb knelt and spoke quietly but directly into McNutt's ear. 'Priorities, McNutt, priorities. You should know by now that I have a bigger map up here.'

Cobb touched his own head for emphasis.

'I'm a marksman,' McNutt replied. 'I only see what's in front of me.'

'That's why I'm the boss,' Cobb said. 'Thing is, if you die here, you're taking me with you. End of mission. Waste of both of us.'

McNutt fired again, then threw the bolt of the rifle back and forth. The hot shell of the cartridge flew back and hit Cobb's cheek. McNutt heard the sizzle of it burning his skin, but Cobb didn't react.

McNutt fired again, then immediately threw the rifle down, slammed the slot closed, swung a Steyr Aug assault rifle onto his back, and grabbed a duffel bag full of high-caliber goodies.

'Well, what are we waiting for?' he teased. 'Let's go!'

51

Anna Rusinko was as tense as the rest of the villagers as she monitored the action from afar, although she couldn't be sure it was for the same reason.

They had all stood motionless – save for an occasional flinch after a volley of gunfire – as they watched the battle from the cover of the northern tree line. Anna felt both solace and concern when she saw Borovsky hop from the train cab onto the back of a horse ridden by village elder Alexandru Decebal – the latest in a long line of Decebals who led the militia of the village honor guard.

Alexandru meant 'defender of mankind' in Romanian, and Decebal meant 'strong as ten'. Anna was relieved to see that he more than lived up to his name, especially as the Black Robes tightened the circle around the mounted men for every meter the honor guard retreated.

Anna shifted her gaze to the train, which was still creeping up the hill toward them at a snail's pace. She looked from the train to the riders to the villagers, her eyes settling on a pocket of young girls. Images of her daughter flashed through her mind. *Will I ever see Alma again?*

Don't be defeatist, she warned herself. *You have organizational experience. These people have the will. Rally them, arm them with whatever they have at hand.*

Anna was sure that Borovsky would have a Russian proverb to match that sentiment, but she could think of none. For her, only one thing came to her mind. She directed her question to one of the Romanian elders, using hand gestures to make her point.

'Where are your pitchforks?'

The man, who had been conversing urgently with a small group of older men and women, was pointing left, then right. He turned and shook his head.

'No,' he said, then he started off with the others.

Frustrated and confused, Anna followed.

* * *

Before leaving the train, Cobb thought Garcia and McNutt would give him the most trouble, with Dobrev a close third. Now that he had McNutt under control, he was pleased to see that Garcia was downright eager to leave the train.

Jasmine had followed Borovsky out of the cabin, and Sarah had gone next to take the hand-off of Garcia's gear. His rider had just pulled alongside the crawling train when Cobb and McNutt entered the cabin.

'Protect your jewels,' Cobb advised.

'How?' Garcia asked, genuinely concerned.

McNutt stared at him. 'If you have to ask, you don't deserve to have nuts.'

Cobb rolled his eyes. 'Hector, just go! Now!'

Garcia flung himself forward like he was jumping into a pool. He planted his hands on the rider's broad shoulders, threw open his legs, and landed perfectly on the back of the horse as if he had been doing it all his life. At least until his computer-filled shoulder bag nearly pulled him over the back of the horse's bobbing rump. Taking Sarah's earlier advice, he quickly wrapped his arms around the rider's waist in a bear hug.

McNutt watched in awe as the double-mounted riders galloped out of the way of the single riders. It took a while, but eventually his steed arrived next to the train. McNutt carried the heaviest load by far, and Borovsky had reserved the biggest, hardiest horse for him. McNutt made a perfect jump, but there was still a moment when everyone worried that the horse, the riders, and the duffel bag would all topple down the slight incline that led to the trackbed.

But the horse and his rider proved deserving of Borovsky's faith. The big, beige Lippizaner with the black 'freckles' bent his legs as he absorbed the impact, shifted a step, then returned to full balance. McNutt immediately twisted around so he could call to Jasmine.

'Tell them, no, *ask them*, if I can please bring up the rear.'

Jasmine relayed McNutt's request, which was granted.

Before he would relent to Cobb's insistence, Dobrev took a moment to say goodbye to his old friend, Ludmilla. He knew he had to go, but he wished to God he could stay with her. It was a profound emotional parting, a psychological wrench. Dobrev was saying goodbye to more than just a beloved, vintage engine; he was abandoning an old friend. He laid a weathered hand on the cold iron of the engine's inner wall – a final 'thank you' for all she meant to him.

He did so with tears in his eyes.

Then, without hesitation, Dobrev jumped heavily and nearly slid off the back of his horse. But the rider threw his arms back to prevent it, spreading them like the wings of an eagle and turning his palms out and back to grab Dobrev's reaching arms.

The old man beamed gratefully.

Cobb saw Sarah gesturing forcefully toward the back of the train. He heard the *pop-pop-pop* of McNutt's weapon.

'There are too many!' she yelled. 'They're getting onboard!'

Cobb wasn't surprised. Even though Dobrev had locked the throttle in place, the incline had increased and the engine was slowing. Cobb's rider moved into position, and he jumped. He hadn't even shifted properly on the horse's croup when Decebal, Borovsky, and Jasmine trotted up beside him. The Russian cop was already speaking.

'They said we should not make a stand,' Jasmine translated.

'What do they recommend?'

Borovsky was already explaining.

'He says that we should concentrate on getting away,' Jasmine said.

'He wants us to run?' Sarah snarled from the far side of the group.

'The word he used was *"retreat"*' she said. 'A tactical retreat.'

'The word I use is *pussies*,' McNutt grumbled in their ears.

Cobb considered the odds, the potential losses, and the

fact that they were on Decebal's home turf, which meant he would know the best hiding places and most defensible positions. But Cobb also remembered Jasmine's story about the Argonauts. It was probably Decebal's job to make sure the treasure stayed where it was, even if it meant that he, his riders, and the would-be thieves all perished. On the other hand, Borovsky and the riders had agreed to a temporary truce before the Black Robes had attacked. Furthermore, they had just saved Borovsky's life.

'Let's do as he says,' Cobb announced.

The flock of villagers turned slightly, as one, toward a densely wooded spot atop a small rise. Cobb glanced back and was sickened by the sight. To Dobrev, the train had been a thing of love and beauty. To the Black Robes, it was a husk to inhabit with some vile purpose.

And that purpose was yet to be revealed.

Cobb's thoughts were interrupted by buzzing engines and gunfire from the rear of the group. The ATVs on the front line roared to newly invigorated life, and their big-treaded tires tore up the ground like a buffalo stampede. A thick fog of dust obscured the waves of Black Robes who charged after them, their AK-47s raised.

Cobb held on tight to the man in front of him as he turned sharply to watch. The weighed-down horses were losing ground to the motorized enemy, and Cobb realized that they might need to rethink their strategy. He didn't relish the idea of a Custer-like stand, even with the trees affording some protection, but he liked the thought of

McNutt and their rear guard being mowed down in 'tactical retreat' even less.

He could see that Borovsky was weighing that option as well.

From his half-turned vantage point, Cobb had a clear view of what happened next. Like an experienced trick rider, McNutt spun around, locked himself on top of the horse with just his legs, and brought up a Saiga 20K shotgun.

Cobb felt a flush of realization. When he wasn't acting the fool, this man was a lethal professional. The Russian-made Saiga was only twenty-four inches long and could carry more rounds than any other semi-automatic shotgun – twelve, to be exact. Twelve hot, hurtling rounds that would spread amongst their pursuers like flying piranha. And, carefully employed, it could provide a bonus: the ATVs of fallen riders would then veer off into the rest of the pack.

McNutt went to work, covering their rear, leaving behind something that looked like a scene from a video game. Riders jerked, blood sprayed, ATVs careened, and wheels flipped skyward. In the wake of the chaos lay the victims of McNutt's assault – all dead, or dying.

The remaining ATV leaders tried to get their rifles targeted, but their own jostling machines threw off their aim. Cobb heard the final two booms of McNutt's gun just before his own rider shouted something in Romanian that contained the urgency of 'Hold on!'

Cobb's next breath was sucked in as the riders jerked to the left and headed right for the trees. Cobb looked ahead, over the rider's shoulder, to see the shadows of the forest drawing closer. His instincts told him that something wasn't right. He didn't like not knowing what it was. Then they were up in the air, surging forward in a mighty leap as the horses vaulted over fallen trunks, bushes, and vines just as AK-47 bullets began biting chunks out of bark and branches all around them.

Cobb held tightly onto the rider as they landed, then hazarded a look back. Despite the danger they were still in, it was an incredible sight. One after another, the horses leaped inside the forest, avoiding tree limbs in a dazzling display of skill and strength. Then Cobb saw something move behind them. Many somethings, in fact: all massing to form a solid line of defense.

The horsemen halted so abruptly that the American and Russian passengers were nearly spun off to one side or the other. The riders pivoted to face the enemy as the last villagers revealed themselves near the culvert.

* * *

The people sprang forth like time-lapse flowers with thorns. Anna Rusinko, in the center, followed their lead. There were dozens of them, stretched for about fifty meters along the base of the tree line. In their callused hands, they held a net that was used to trap trout and salmon in the streams that fed the Mures River.

Anna and Cobb happened to grin at about the same time: wolves' grins of violent certainty. They both felt the growing intensity as the remaining Black Robe ATVs sped forth into the trap.

The villagers heaved as one, Anna among them. Half of them hunkered down on each end of the net, their combined weight anchoring the thick-woven lattice against the trees through which the riders would soon funnel. As the modern ATVs collided with the ancient net, those riders who were not cut down from their seats were ensnared in the mesh. Weapons fell to the ground as the first wave of drivers gasped for air or desperately clawed for freedom. Those that followed steered hard to avoid their comrades, but there was nowhere to go. ATVs collided and careened out of control, toppling riders and upending vehicles. Heads and bodies smashed into the rocks and exposed tree roots amidst the helpless gunning of engines. The sound was followed by the drone of spinning tires and the blood-gurgling groans of the fallen.

In an instant, the villagers pounced upon their defenseless prey. The elder women shielded the young boys and girls from the onslaught perpetrated by their mothers and grand-fathers; there was no need to burden them with the grue-some reality of what was about to happen. These were people of hearty stock, and they would defend their fam-ilies by any means necessary. With axes, shovels, rakes, and even sturdy logs, they set about bludgeoning the stunned Black Robes, ensuring their own survival. Once all of the invaders had been silenced, a murmur of excitement spread throughout the villagers. That murmur quickly grew into a cheer.

Anna was among them. Smiling, she looked up to see a

grinning Viktor Borovsky coming toward her. He had dismounted and was offering his hand.

She smiled and clasped his hand with both of hers.

In his eyes was gratitude and pride.

In hers was astonishment for what had happened.

52

The group remounted and rode up a breathtaking hill. They went through an awe-inspiring forest to a small village that even the most expert explorer might have missed. It wasn't exactly camouflaged, but the way the structures were set among the boulders and even the barren trees, it would have been mistaken for terrain unless you were right upon it.

Jasmine marveled at the Russian-helmet-shaped thatched huts carefully positioned around a community well and circular stone fireplace. The entire village seemed to be grown within a natural coliseum of protective trees. It was clearly unchanged since the time it was built.

At first, the riders and the triumphant villagers went to their own huts to tether, feed, water, wash, and brush their horses. Then they all began to congregate around the central fireplace – each bringing pots, knives, sacks, and other implements. Together they began to make a communal meal.

Jasmine sidled up to Borovsky. 'How long have they lived like this?'

'About a hundred years,' he said.

Cobb approached. Jasmine told him what the colonel had said.

'I'm guessing it's exactly ninety-five years,' he said.

The colonel nodded in agreement after Jasmine translated.

'Did you know about the Black Robes?' Cobb asked.

'Of their existence? Of course,' Borovsky said. 'Of their presence here today? No.'

McNutt nodded and glanced at Cobb. 'What do we do about the guys we left on the train? They're gonna come looking for us.'

'I know,' Cobb said solemnly. He ended that statement with a meaningful look at Garcia, who had just finished unloading his equipment. Garcia took that as his cue to start setting up a communications link using the gear from his shoulder bag. He sat on the ground near an open space in the trees and set the laptop on a tree stump.

'Why are you here, Colonel?' Cobb asked the old cop.

The Russian pressed his lips together hard. His eyes teared up as they took in the village and its people. 'Sergeant – would you mind?' he asked Anna.

'Not at all,' Anna answered through Jasmine. On their long journey here Borovsky had explained everything to her. 'You want to know what is here and how it arrived.'

Cobb nodded once.

'The colonel's great-grandfather, Dimitry Borovsky, was Prince Felix Yusupov's most loyal aide. His Excellency entrusted Dimitry to keep the Romanian treasure safe from mercenaries, tomb raiders, corrupt politicians, and treasure hunters until the time is right for the Romanovs' return.'

'The Russians hiding the Romanian —' McNutt mused. 'Neat trick.'

'Speaking of which,' said Sarah, 'that was a neat trick you pulled on the back of that horse. You a rider, too?'

'Rodeo clown,' McNutt said. 'And my sister always said it was a useless hobby.'

Cobb half listened while he thought about Anna's last words. 'When will you know the time is right?' He addressed his question to Borovsky.

The colonel considered the question carefully, then finally shrugged philosophically. 'Who knows?' He quoted another Russian proverb. '"The future belongs to the one who knows how to wait."' He motioned for his guests to relax. 'We can talk about that later. For now, sit, eat, rest. I daresay we all need it.'

He wandered away, Anna at his side, as the area filled with delicious smells. But before he got too far for Jasmine to translate, Garcia turned to him.

'Colonel, I'm having a little trouble getting a signal. Where precisely are we?'

'The village of the honor guard,' he replied.

'Yes, but that's not on any of my maps,' Garcia said.

As Jasmine continued to translate, Anna frowned, worried about revealing their location. But Borovsky just tilted his head.

'We are on the Transylvanian Plateau,' he told them. With that, he playfully bared his teeth, curled his fingers into hooked claws, and hissed loudly like a vampire.

'See, I told you!' McNutt said. 'Even he knows Dracula is out there somewhere.'

Borovsky smiled, his spirits buoyed by the levity, if only for a moment.

* * *

Cobb did not have to worry about the Black Robes. At least, not yet. Scouts had been sent into the field to watch for them. For the time being, he knew the wisest thing to do was to sit, eat, and collect his thoughts.

The meal was delicious. They started with *sarmale*, but instead of the usual mincemeat, the vine leaves were filled with minced apricots, plums, and cherries. The appetizer was followed by a hearty vegetable soup, which they sopped up with *mamaliga*, better known as 'the bread of the peasants'. The main course was broiled fish in garlic sauce.

'All from our own gardens, streams, lakes, and ovens,' Decebal said proudly.

Cobb only left the circle of villagers when Garcia had finally established the connection to Papineau. After Cobb brought him up to speed, he waited silently.

The usually loquacious Frenchman was speechless.

'Damn,' Papineau finally said.

'That doesn't tell me anything,' Cobb complained.

'Hear me out,' Papineau said. 'The Black Robes are a group of zealots who worship Rasputin. They follow his example of sinning, then repenting. Through that, the mad monk gained great political power, just as these men have in their own time. They approached me when we arrived—'

'How did they know who we were?' Cobb asked.

'I'm not sure,' Papineau lied, covering for the colleague he had given the Brighton Beach letter to. 'They have eyes and ears everywhere. They offered to help set up this operation using their influence in key portions of the Transportation and Migration Ministries.'

'Because?'

'I don't know,' he lied again.

'And you just accepted that?' Cobb asked incredulously. 'It never occurred to you that some sort of quid pro quo might be involved? No, don't answer that. I already know. Of course you did. You just didn't think it was necessary to tell us. You figured we'd muck through somehow, and if we didn't there was always some other sucker-team you could bribe with five million bucks.'

'Jack,' the Frenchman said. 'I know I've lost your trust—'

Cobb made a scoffing sound. 'You never had that. The best you can hope for is trying to regain some sliver of *credibility* at this point. Let's just leave it at that, okay? We'll find your treasure because we accepted the contract, and you figure out some reason, any reason, why I shouldn't take your head as a souvenir when we've delivered it.'

Papineau started to respond, but Cobb made the throat-slashing motion at Garcia. Once Garcia broke the connection, Cobb looked at him steadily.

'What do you think the Black Robes want?' Garcia asked anxiously. 'Some sort of revenge on Prince Felix?'

'It's possible,' Cobb agreed. 'And I think Borovsky might know the answer.' He dipped his forehead at the laptop. 'So the more immediate question is about Papineau. I asked you to find out about him. What've you got?'

The techie looked honestly at his superior. 'As far as

I can tell,' Garcia confessed, 'Papineau is who he says he is.'

'I'm aggressively uninterested in what he says, Garcia,' Cobb replied. 'I'm interested in what he's *not* saying. After you've eaten, dig more.'

Cobb turned around and nearly walked into McNutt.

'Hey,' the gunman said. 'You okay?'

'Yeah, McNutt, thanks.' Cobb thought that would be it, but McNutt just remained standing there. 'You?' Cobb finally asked him.

'Yeah. Listen, I just wanted to . . . you know . . . back in the armory?' McNutt looked down for a moment. 'Thanks, okay? Just . . . thanks.'

'Not a problem,' Cobb assured him. 'Maybe someday you'll return the favor.'

'I hope so,' McNutt said.

'*You hope so?*' Cobb teased. 'What do you mean by that?'

McNutt quickly realized his mistake. The only way he could save Cobb's life was if Cobb was in grave danger to begin with. That wasn't the type of thing he should be wishing on his team leader. 'Wait! That came out wrong! I mean, um—'

Cobb laughed. 'Don't worry. I know what you meant.'

McNutt breathed a sigh of relief.

Cobb continued. 'But just so you know, that's why soldiers don't try to put those things into words. A simple thanks is good enough.'

'How about thanks and a drink?'

'Even better.'

They both returned to the circular campfire and the villagers for some homemade cheese and that long-awaited *tuica*. When they were finished, Cobb, McNutt, and Sarah stretched out to look at the setting sun. They knew it was the calm before the storm.

'Okay,' Sarah said briskly. 'What now, Jack?'

Before he could answer, Borovsky appeared, accompanied by Jasmine. The two had been talking with Anna and Dobrev throughout the meal.

'I have thought about this moment for many years,' the Russian said through their interpreter. 'All my life, in fact. And the lives of my father, grandfather, and great-grandfather as well. And now that the time has come, I only can think of one proverb to say: "When you meet a man, you judge him by his clothes. When you leave, you judge him by his heart."'

One by one, Borovsky looked at the people he had come to respect. When he reached Cobb, he spoke in slow, heavily accented English. 'Would you come with me, please? There is something I would like to show you.'

53

As the group – minus Garcia, who stayed in the village to tend to his gear – made its way across the gentle foothills that led to a mini-plateau, Borovsky pointed out a narrow-gauge railway that cut through the sparse forest. Up ahead was a small mining train. It was covered by tattered tarpaulins and a blanket of carefully meshed twigs and branches.

Fueled by joy, Dobrev rushed over uneven stone and high grass to reach it. He excitedly pulled off the tarps and twigs, and stared at the train underneath. It consisted of a small, open trolley car; a slightly larger, open freight car; a four-seat passenger car with no glass in its few windows; and a diminutive engine that seemed little more than a lawn mower. In the train industry, it was known as an 'omnivore' because it could run on coal or firewood.

Chasing after Dobrev, Jasmine suddenly saw the little boy in the old man. His somber face erupted in a smile the likes of which she had never seen on him – or anyone else.

To her, the trains and track looked like an overgrown toy set.

To him, it seemed like the Romanian treasure itself.

As he talked, he ran his hands over everything: from the roofs above to the mini-tracks below. 'Our train rests on thousand-millimeter track. This rail is not even six hundred.'

Decebal, who was the only villager with the group, nodded in agreement. He waited until everyone had reached the train before he started to speak in broken Russian laced with Romanian. With Borovsky's help, Jasmine translated the information for her team.

'They laid down the tracks around 1912. Before that, everything was donkeys and carts. After that, they started exporting lumber, barely enough to keep the village going, but enough. Eventually they laid heavier gauge tracks further down, that's what we came up on, but then . . .' She paused. 'Well, that's weird. He said business just stopped.'

Jasmine confirmed her understanding with Decebal and Borovsky, then passed on the information. 'Business didn't decline,' she explained. 'It just stopped. Completely.'

'Meaning,' said Cobb, 'that when the prince rolled in he bought the town and didn't want any exports coming from this direction.'

'So they went back to carts,' McNutt said. 'After the fall of the Romanovs, that's all they could afford.'

'Imagine being the guardians of an immense treasure and being poor as dirt,' Sarah said.

'They didn't think of it that way,' Jasmine assured them. 'It was more like being the palace eunuch. They were honored to serve the queen or lady.'

McNutt snorted. 'Now there's a trade I'm not down with.'

'Yeah,' Sarah said. 'Without the boys, you'd have to change your name to "McNada".'

The other team members groaned. Except for Cobb, who

was studying the small, narrow tracks. They reminded him of the kind of tracks used for ore cars inside coalmines.

The group continued forward, following Borovsky over the flat but scrubby terrain. Since the colonel was left-handed, Anna remained on his right side the entire time. That way, if he ever had to draw his gun or knife, she would be out of his way.

'There's a reason I prefer cities,' Sarah said.

'Asphalt, right?' McNutt said.

'Nope, stores,' she said as she struggled with her footing. 'I could've stopped and bought the right damn hiking shoes.'

'Point taken,' McNutt said. 'That's reason number eleven in my onging list of ass-kicks I'm gonna give Papi when we get back.' He frowned. 'Hey, you *did* cut him out of the ear-loop, didn't you, chief?'

Cobb nodded.

'Good,' McNutt said as his grip tightened on the duffel bag full of weapons. 'I want it to be a surprise. After he gives me my money.'

As they continued their hike, the ground crunched like dry corn flakes. The underbrush was merciless and at least a foot deep. It hungrily snagged at their feet as they pressed forward.

'There hasn't been a wildfire here in at least a half-century,' Cobb observed.

'Is that significant?' Jasmine asked, after translating for Borovsky.

'The two major causes of big fires are lightning and cigarettes,' Cobb said. 'I've seen a couple of old, charred tree trunks here and there, meaning the region does get big storms. But I get the sense that this area is protected like a sanctuary.'

'Meaning?' McNutt asked.

'We might not see it, but there is security.'

Borovsky laughed when Jasmine had finished translating. 'Yes, there is,' Borovsky assured them.

McNutt paused in mid-stride. He glanced around nervously. 'What kind of security? Landmines? Bear traps? Dwarves?'

The group ignored him.

'The trees have always provided layers of concealment, offered food in the form of wildlife, and prevented erosion with their strong roots,' Borovsky said. 'When the train was built, it would have been difficult and counter-productive for the builders to cut the trees down. So the people who anchored the tracks went off in many directions, creating paths wherever they could. The effect is an impression of a train to nowhere.'

'Like one of those sightseeing railroads in parks and on mountains,' Garcia contributed.

Jasmine translated for Borovsky.

'Exactly so,' the colonel said. 'Complete with bear and deer in the woods to make the occasional appearance.'

'Bears! I knew it,' McNutt said. 'Ask them if they can shoot cannons.'

Jasmine rolled her eyes. She wouldn't be translating *that*.

'There was a side benefit to the multiplicity of paths,' Jasmine continued for Borovsky. 'Anyone following the train would be paying attention to the tracks – not to the sentries in the trees, who would be waiting with pistols or a noose.'

Garcia looked up anxiously.

'If you can see them,' the Russian said, 'then they've failed.'

'Right,' Sarah said. 'And those guys wouldn't be smoking up there. The lit butts would give them away.'

'Bad for your health in more ways than one,' McNutt laughed.

54

They continued walking toward what seemed to be another grove of trees. Borovsky told them to wait before he went into a bordering thicket, stepping around a batch of trees whose branches seemed weighted down as though bearing heavy snows. The limbs formed a wall through which nothing was visible. It took Borovsky nearly a minute of ducking and maneuvering to make his way to the other side. Suddenly, there was a *whoosh*, and the branches snapped back as if the curtain had never existed.

From the team's perspective, there didn't appear to be anything ahead – not even the Russian colonel. There was only a solid, sunless black that seemed to go on forever.

Decebal flashed them his gap-toothed smile and followed, stepping into the entrance and vanishing as if a carnival magician had made him disappear. The Americans looked at each other with raised eyebrows and appreciative grins, then followed Anna into the darkness.

'Some kind of spring release?' McNutt asked, looking around in vain for a pedal or switch.

'A prayer lock,' Sarah said. 'Four large branches on the bottom were twined together. That causes the smaller limbs and twigs to come together like hands folded in prayer. Cut the cord and the limbs snap back. The beauty of it is that it doesn't cause the trees themselves to bend and give the site away, and it doesn't cause any part of the adjoining trees to knit permanently.'

'And it's easy to reset,' McNutt said admiringly, glancing behind to make sure that one of those 'sentries' wasn't doing just that to keep them all inside.

They collected in a dark gray grotto. Sarah instantly produced a powerful, pen-sized flashlight, which she shined around them in a quick arc. Rock walls swelled up to a dome like a natural amphitheater. They stood on a stone pathway that was made of flat but unevenly edged slate obviously hacked from the walls. They could still see the scars, though some kind of crystalline film had collected over them.

'No stalactities,' Sarah said. 'That's a good sign.'

'How so?' Jasmine wondered.

'There's not enough water to drag down major mineral deposits. That means this is a very, very dry cave.'

Jasmine nodded in understanding. 'And a dry cave is a great place to store a treasure.'

'I didn't know you had a geology degree,' McNutt said.

'I don't,' Sarah explained, 'but I've been spelunking many times. It's a good way to keep in shape.'

'Over here,' Anna said in Russian. Sarah pointed her powerful penlight in the direction Jasmine indicated, illuminating Decebal. He was standing beside what looked like two large cauldrons on their sides with three iron bowling balls between them – all attached by wires.

'Electric generators,' Cobb recognized.

'Have to be at least sixty years old,' McNutt estimated.

As they watched, the Romanian leader churned a crank on the front of the sideways pot farthest to their left, as if he were trying to start an old Model-T car. On the fourth turn, the engine caught and coughed to life. The group looked around as recessed lamps lining the middle of the rock ceiling began to flicker.

They found themselves in a breathtaking cavern of reddish granite and greenish coral, with cobblestones off to their far left and right. And stretched out deep into the cave, seemingly part of the walls, were eight blue and gold train cars and a small engine. On the side of each car was the Romanov seal: a double-headed eagle with a golden scepter in one claw and a cross-bearing orb in the other, while on its chest a red escutcheon depicted St George on his horse about to slay the dragon.

On the back of the last car was the most imposing mark of all: the coat of arms of the Russian Empire. It contained the helmet of Alexander Nevsky, fifteen shields representing the Russian Empire territories, the archangels Gabriel and Michael, and the Order of St Andrew – all residing on an oak and laurel wreath amid a golden ermine mantle, crowned by a golden cap, and liberally decorated by black, double-headed eagles. They flew around the inscription, which Jasmine translated as: 'God is with us.'

'He sure as shit is,' McNutt said with a laugh. He wanted to say more – hell, he wanted to sing, and dance, and drink, and punch someone in the face for no reason at all – but Cobb had warned them about celebrating in front of

Borovsky or any of the villagers, especially on a day when so many of them had died. He felt that would be in bad taste.

But they took a moment to celebrate internally.

The discovery of the train led to visions of their own personal paradises, made possible by the millions they were that much closer to collecting. They all understood that finding the train was only the first step. They knew they still had to get the treasure past Borovsky and the villagers before they could deliver it to Papineau. But that didn't stop Sarah from imagining a well-funded climb of Mt Everest. Or Garcia from thinking about building a supercomputer that would make Microsoft jealous. McNutt's fantasy was simple: he wanted to buy his own tank. Then he wanted to drive it across America, only stopping for beer and whores. Unlike the others, Jasmine tried to focus on the historic value of the discovery, but her mind slowly drifted to owning her own museum.

The looks on their faces said it all.

They were a happy group.

Amid the daydreams, Cobb allowed himself a moment to admire the contents of the cave before he began to assess the condition of the train. The engine was in solid shape and the cars looked sturdy enough. They clearly housed royal compartments, though the filigree on the exteriors was cracked, chipped, or broken. Obviously, the train had gone through storms and trials to arrive before being seized by what appeared to be the craggy, gripping fingers of the cave. Some of those fingers were gloved and mossy, some were skeletal and crystalline, and some looked as if hard, fleshy sponge had grown over them.

'When I was a boy,' Decebal explained through Borovsky and Jasmine, 'my great-grandfather told me that when the train first arrived, they simply drove the cars inside and left them. They are safe in here. It is dry.'

Borovsky added, 'They are kept in good repair but have not moved a millimeter since then. The prince took only what he absolutely needed and departed.'

'Where are the rest of them?' Sarah demanded.

Her sense of awe had passed like a total eclipse. She was now the thief, cataloguing inventory. She stood defiantly with her fists on her hips and looked to Jasmine for an explanation. 'There were supposed to be twenty cars, right? Where are the others?'

Cobb smiled apologetically at Borovsky. 'The prince was exiled by the tsarina, but he still had to be guarded on this dangerous trip.'

'So?' Sarah demanded.

'If *you* were one of those guards, would you have done it for free?'

She groaned in understanding. 'Jesus,' she said. 'Twelve cars?!'

'No, not twelve,' Borovsky informed her through Jasmine. 'The Romanian treasure had already been looted by greedy politicians. That was one of the main reasons the prince wanted to take it away from Moscow. They were – they *are* – corrupt as the Devil. The prince personally selected the most important Romanian art, artifacts, and archives, then consolidated them in as few crates as he could.'

'But what about the gold?' Sarah demanded.

Borovsky seemed unhappy with her tone and opened his mouth to speak, but Cobb jumped in before the situation deteriorated.

'Cool it, Sarah.'

She looked indignantly at Cobb, then another realization seemed to splash over her. *They don't know we're here for the treasure.* Her jaw shut with an audible click.

Cobb looked to Jasmine, who nodded with understanding in her eyes. Thankfully she had not been translating.

'She is upset that the historical valuables have been lost,' Jasmine told a dubious Borovsky and equally distrustful Anna. She glanced apologetically at their Romanian host, who was behind them, and then looked to see where Dobrev was. He had gone over to the train, where he was muttering words of comfort to the poor, old girl.

'Viktor, Alexandru,' Cobb said through Jasmine. 'What did the prince do then?'

'He left,' Borovsky answered.

'How?' Cobb wanted to know. They looked at him in confusion. Cobb put his arm out toward the first car – the one farthest into the cave. 'You said they drove them in. Did he drive any out?'

Decebal spoke from behind them, cautiously watching everyone.

'He says his great-grandfather told him that the prince simply left,' Jasmine reported. 'He didn't say how.'

Cobb looked to the train cars with a growing sense of curiosity. He motioned again at them. 'May we?'

Jasmine passed on the request, adding her own declarations of respect, responsibility, and honor. Borovsky looked to Decebal, who nodded once. Borovsky turned back to Cobb and seconded the nod, adding, 'We will examine it together, then we are leaving.'

Cobb smiled tightly. Both men clearly knew that was not going to happen. At least, not without a disagreement.

'All right,' Cobb said, turning to the eight railroad cars. 'Calmly, respectfully, professionally. Let's see what we have here.'

Cobb heard what sounded like someone cracking his knuckles behind him. He didn't have to look back. He knew the sound of a gun hammer locking when he heard one.

55

None of the group looked back.

'That's Decebal, and a revolver,' McNutt said through clenched teeth.

Cobb saw McNutt's pinkie tap the handle of the duffel bag, just once. It was almost unnoticeable, but it was in no way an accidental twitch. He said, 'It was just a warning to behave. Otherwise we'd all be face down. Let's go.'

Decebal had positioned himself between the treasure train and the cave's exit. He didn't understand English enough to bother joining the others inside the cars. Even if he was right beside them, they could easily talk amongst themselves in secrecy. Frankly, he didn't care. All that mattered to him was ensuring that no one made it past him with any of the treasure.

'Please,' Borovsky said, 'come with me.'

He led the group toward the first car. The lights in the cave gave them enough eerie illumination to make out shadows, and they used their flashlights for clarification. Cobb suspected the only reason they didn't stop him was because there was still a veneer of entente in place. And Cobb knew there were two major reasons for that: arresting or killing them might bring others to the area, in even greater numbers; and they still had the Black Robes to worry about.

Against either foe, Borovsky would surely need reinforcements.

'We're up,' Garcia said in their ears. 'I can see everything you see.'

Without asking aloud, Jasmine, Sarah, and McNutt turned to Cobb for answers as to what Garcia meant. Without drawing attention, Cobb purposefully tapped his thumb against his flashlight, letting the others know that they doubled as high-definition video cameras. Even from almost a mile away, Garcia had isolated the signals being transmitted by the flashlights.

McNutt glanced down at the flashlight in his hand.

'Damn, that's slick,' he murmured under his breath.

* * *

Seven thousand miles to the east, Jean-Marc Papineau watched on his laptop in his compartment on the decoy train that he had taken to Vladivostok. Garcia had looped Papineau into the broadcast with Cobb's express permission – the images captured by the video cameras were being relayed through a satellite uplink. Cobb wanted the Frenchman to know that despite his treachery, Cobb's personal code dictated that once he accepted a job, he finished it.

'You're getting the audio and video feeds?' Garcia asked in the shrunken video chat window in the corner of Papineau's screen.

'Perfectly,' Papineau replied. 'Who am I watching?'

'This is Jasmine's cam,' Garcia informed him. 'She'll be the first one inside.'

'And what of your image recognition software?'

'We're about to find out if it works,' Garcia answered.

The program Garcia had designed would use computer-generated silhouettes to match any objects they encountered with known objects in the database. He had already uploaded images of countless artifacts into the system. If any of the Romanov treasures were here, they would know soon enough.

Papineau watched anxiously as Jasmine approached the train. From the video, he could see they were dealing with a sad necropolis of semi-gutted cars. It appeared as if the prince and his men had torn the interior asunder to make room for additional cargo. Their primary obstacles were apparently the passenger benches, most of which had been removed, mainly by means of brute force or being chopped into bits.

Why the hasty renovations? he thought. *What were they trying to hide?*

Then he had his answers . . . if only for an instant.

As Borovsky helped her into the first car, the image from Jasmine's flashlight held steady long enough to reveal a literal pile of treasure. Heaps upon stacks of crates, filling the space. Unfortunately for Papineau, Jasmine momentarily reverted to a six-year-old on Christmas morning, overcome with joy and unsure where to start.

'Queen Maria's jewelry!' he heard her say, but the images blurred as she spun around, trying to take it all in. 'The lost artwork! The historical archives! It's all here!'

'Tell her to focus!' Papineau yelled at Garcia, who relayed

the message. As Jasmine gained control over her emotions, Garcia's program finally had a chance to make its comparisons. Papineau watched his screen as thin, red outlines began to encircle various objects. When a possible match was found, the system briefly flashed an image of the artifact before adding it to a list of results. Like a massive, multi-player online game, the program kept a running tally of the discoveries.

Papineau watched with fascination as the program continued to outline, display, and compile with increasing speed, until his screen looked like an explosion of digital fireworks.

*   *   *

Borovsky smiled at the sight of Jasmine and the others combing through the artifacts. It was the fact that she seemed genuinely interested in the historical value of the pieces, rather than the price they would fetch, that pleased him the most. He hoped the others understood the heritage of these items, and the lengths to which he would go to protect them.

He was beginning to like these newcomers.

He sincerely hoped that he wouldn't have to shoot them.

'Before the prince fled,' Borovsky explained, 'decisions were made as to which pieces were to accompany him. Time was not on his side, and he left the treasure nearly exactly as you see it today. With no way to accurately determine which pieces are related, those sworn to protect it simply left it as the prince had left it.'

'This is amazing,' Jasmine blurted.

Again Borovsky smiled. 'It makes me happy to hear you say that. There are six more cars, all similar in content and disarray. But the eighth car is *different* . . . Come, there is something you must see.'

After helping everyone from the first car, Borovsky silently led them to the rear of the train. The suspense was working its own particular brand of magic on each of them. Jasmine couldn't wait to inventory the historical artifacts of the other six cars. Now that they had found it, Sarah and McNutt were wondering if they had to *deliver* the train before Papineau would hand them their money. Anna wondered how long her superior had been guarding his secret.

Meanwhile, two questions burdened Cobb: what treasure among treasures was in the eighth car, and what price would they have to pay for seeing it?

Cobb cautiously entered the eighth car and started to examine the last compartment. The front half was filled with crates, paintings, sculptures, and files – nothing note-worthy as far as he was concerned. Then Borovsky pointed toward the far corner. When he saw it, Cobb felt a rolling chill as a wave of goose pimples covered his arms.

It was a coffin.

As Cobb approached it, he studied the exterior of the box. Made of thick, heavy wood, it was spiked down in sixteen places along its edge. Strangely, it was also latched on either side with heavy iron locks that required a large key to open.

They all followed Cobb toward the coffin. Everyone

except for Jasmine, who literally froze for a moment in the doorway as if she'd gazed at the face of the Gorgon.

'Someone didn't want us to get into that box,' McNutt said.

'Garcia? You got anything?' Cobb quietly asked.

'Searching, boss, but I'm not optimistic,' he said.

It didn't matter. Borovsky was about to show them what was inside.

Borovsky removed a chain from around his neck and used the attached key to unlock the ancient locks. Picking up a small pry bar from a nearby crate, he thrust the sharpened end under the lid. Struggling to simply remove one of the sixteen nails, he motioned for Cobb to pick up the second pry bar and start on the opposite side. Working together, it still took them nearly five minutes to move their way around the coffin. As Borovsky pried loose the final anchor, Cobb and McNutt gently pulled back the wooden curtain while bracing themselves for the expected and inevitable stench of death.

There was none. Much to everyone's surprise, there were also no spiders, cockroaches, ants, maggots, flies, mice, or rats. There was only a slight aroma.

'What is that smell?' McNutt said. 'It's like . . . fruit.'

'Shellac,' Jasmine said, transfixed by the object within. 'Used as a preservative – made from lac, a deposit found on trees across this continent.'

'Oh,' he said. 'I thought it might be prune.'

McNutt was only partly kidding because the object inside the coffin looked like a human-sized, human-shaped prune.

Time seemed to have sealed its limbs against, and slightly into, its desiccated yet lumpy body, which consisted of what seemed to be eroding clothing combined with mummified flesh.

Whatever hair was left on its wrinkle-skinned skull now looked like stringy mold. There were only vague suggestions of ears, eyes, nose, or mouth. Over the years, its shape had shifted severely. Now it looked like a Halloween mask.

The only thing seemingly untouched by time was a ring that clung to what used to be its finger. The wide, gold band of the ring was encrusted with sparkling diamonds. The girdle held a magnificent, blood-red ruby. The face of the ring was oblong, with bands of onyx standing out against the polished jewel.

The emblem was clear.

It was the three-barred cross of the Russian Orthodox Church.

The ring was sanctimonious, yet righteous; decadent, yet humble. It somehow reflected lust and virtue at the same time. As if the designer recognized the sin of creating such a lavish bauble before asking for God's forgiveness by adorning the piece with the holy sign of his faith.

'We've found the ultimate treasure,' Jasmine said.

'We have?' Cobb asked. 'I mean – is this what I think it is?'

She looked back at the others with a palpable sense of dread.

'Yes,' she said. 'It's Rasputin.'

56

The reactions to the announcement were muted. The shock of the find was tempered by Borovsky's explanation that this body was what had drawn the attention of the Black Robes and why they were so fanatically determined to remain.

Cobb was not startled or unnerved by Rasputin's corpse. It was just one more dead body on a day full of them. Instead, he focused on the rest of the train car, searching for more surprises.

Sarah walked over casually to the coffin. She froze when she saw the ring on his finger.

'Get me a good image,' Garcia said.

McNutt brought the flashlight closer.

'How do you know it's him?' McNutt asked Jasmine.

Jasmine pointed to the ring. 'That's a gift from the tsarina.'

'Couldn't it have been looted from one of the palaces and left here with the rest of the treasure?' he asked.

'Hidden on a dead body?' Sarah said.

'In a coffin,' McNutt replied. 'Who'd look there with all the rest of this lying around?'

'Me,' Sarah said, looking over the perimeter of the pine box. 'The way that thing was sealed tight, they might as well have built a neon sign that said "Important!"'

Jasmine corrected her. 'Actually, the spikes and padlock weren't to keep people out.'

'What are you talking about?' Sarah asked.

Jasmine didn't answer. It took a moment for her meaning to penetrate.

'Oh,' McNutt gasped. 'It was to keep Dracula in.'

'It's Rasputin all right,' Garcia said. 'Facial recognition is a match. So much for the rumor that his body was immolated.'

There was no response.

For a moment, the train car was, fittingly, as quiet as a tomb.

McNutt broke the silence. He pointed at the ring and glanced at Sarah. 'Gonna go for that?'

Sarah looked down at the jewelry. The corpse still had a disquieting power about it. 'Too tough to fence.' She cocked her head slightly to one side, then knelt on one knee beside the coffin to get a better look at the infamous mystic.

'Praying to your master?' McNutt asked.

'Yeah, right.'

'Please tell me you aren't a Black Robe. I'd hate to shoot you before I get to bang you.'

Cobb glanced at Sarah and quickly studied her face. McNutt's idea wasn't likely, but it wasn't impossible. Papineau had strong-armed Garcia into spying for him; maybe he'd hired a second mole. Or maybe the Black Robes had bribed her. He took a second – literally, no more – to study her posture, her eyes, her hands. Her head was tilted to one side, not bowed. Her eyes were moving;

they were not down, not shut. Her fingers were relaxed and nowhere near a weapon. She did not have what the guys at Guantanamo Bay called 'snapback' – the look of a captive, or infiltrator, or sleeper, who was shedding a guise and reverting to their true self.

'Sarah,' Cobb said, 'you with us?'

'Yeah,' she assured him. 'Just looking.'

Cobb nodded. 'All right then. Let's go.'

No one asked where. The others in the group were still in the thrall of a man who had been dead nearly a century – a man whose mesmeric powers, at least, transcended death.

Cobb led his team members back toward the entrance of the cave when the hair on his arms began to prickle. The others would soon feel the same sensation, but Cobb's sharply-honed senses alerted him first. He froze, his head slowly panning from side to side.

'I feel it, too,' McNutt agreed.

'Feel what?' Sarah asked.

'The air's moving in here,' McNutt explained.

'That doesn't make any sense,' Jasmine argued. 'That would mean—'

'There's a second opening somewhere,' Sarah said. 'He's right.'

They looked back toward the front of the train. No one could honestly say that they knew that's where the cave opened, but it was the logical choice.

Sarah grinned and looked meaningfully at Cobb.

'You up for it?' he asked her.

'It's what I do, Jack.'

'Go to it then,' he ordered.

'I don't get it!' Garcia cried. 'What's going on now?'

'Garcia, I'm with you,' McNutt said. 'Except I'm here, and I'm lost.'

But Sarah was already sneaking past the front of the first car, going deeper into the cave. Cobb turned in the other direction and headed back toward Decebal, with a distracted McNutt and a confused Jasmine close behind.

'Did you know about this too, Papi?' Cobb asked as they walked.

'I'm not even sure what you're talking about,' the Frenchman said in his ear.

He sounded genuinely puzzled.

'Jack,' Jasmine said, frustration in her voice, 'what are we doing?'

'You saw the track we were on earlier, outside,' Cobb explained. 'It ended. Decisively. No hidden rails that would've let us push farther. Isn't that right, Garcia?'

'There was no iron anywhere up ahead,' he agreed.

'But this train got in here,' Sarah stressed in their ears, 'so there had to be more track at some point.'

'And after they drove this train inside, that track was pulled up and removed, probably melted,' Cobb said. 'Getting the treasure out again would take a small, properly equipped army to replace a missing kilometer of rail – all the while being picked off by the members of the honor guard.'

'Wait,' Jasmine said. 'Are you saying there's another way

384

out?' That the Romanovs never had any intention of going back, but they gave themselves the option of going forward?'

'I'll let you know soon enough,' Sarah offered.

Cobb checked his watch. 'Garcia, is that Papi-cam dried out yet?'

A moment later Garcia replied. 'Nope. Still not online.'

Cobb heard a snort from Papineau. Cobb felt a pinch of anger – not at the Frenchman's reaction but about his secrecy. If he had told Cobb that there was a camera in the command centre, Cobb wouldn't have short-circuited it and they could be getting valuable intelligence on the Black Robes right now. That was Papineau's error, not his.

Cobb motioned for Jasmine to follow as he went to confer with Borovsky.

*   *   *

Grigori Sidorov, the leader of the Black Robes, was not happy.

'I told you not to shoot at them!' he shouted, banging the flat of his hand on the table in the command center of the train.

Vladimir Losovich held the Heckler & Koch 91 sniper rifle he had taken from the freight car. He cradled it as if it were his child. 'We weren't shooting at them,' he grunted. 'We were shooting at the horsemen.'

The Black Robes were crawling all over the train, looking for whatever they could use, examine, or loot. After they had piled up their dead and removed the net to make sure it wouldn't get underfoot, a group of six went into the woods and tried to follow the trail. There was distant gunfire in the woods, but no indication of whose it was or what the result might have been. The majority of the Black Robes went back to the train.

Sidorov twisted his head toward the big, metal bracket holding the array of computer screens, where three Black Robes toiled. 'Any progress breaking their security?'

The one on the right, watching the actions of the one hunched in the middle as if he were playing a video game, shrugged noncommittally.

Sidorov sat down heavily where Papineau and Cobb once sat. He dismissed Losovich with a wave of a hand. He let the hackers continue to click away as he surveyed the situation.

They were close. The body he had sought all his life was out there, just beyond his reach. But not for long. The biggest danger, if not the biggest impediment, was his own desperation.

He finally admitted it to himself. He wanted it so badly that he had been reckless in his attack. Over-eager. Part of that, too, was that he felt alone. He drew strength from the knowledge that Rasputin must have felt the same way. *But I am just an aspirant, a pilgrim, a* strannik.

Sidorov missed Kazan: not just the city but the people. He missed his palace. He had been feeling the withdrawal from sin more and more, the same way an addict felt the absence of drugs. He needed a fix soon, and the shooting of a few villagers and horses had not sufficed.

A slaughter, he thought distractedly. *That would do. Finding these horsemen, their women, their children. Where were the six men he had sent out? Why had they not called, or sent a messenger, or returned? Could this golden opportunity be slipping away?*

Sidorov pulled his phone from his coat pocket and pressed the button that immediately linked him with his offices. 'Where are my reinforcements?'

'They'll be there soon, *starets*. We'll double your numbers before dawn.'

Sidorov smiled. Although they were based in Kazan, the Black Robes were a powerful organization with recruiting posts in Belarus, Ukraine, Moldova, and Romania. As luck should have it, one of their largest armories was located less than two hundred miles away.

'And the vehicles I requested?'

'We got you everything you asked for – and more.'

57

Cobb and Jasmine approached the Russian colonel, the woman police officer, the village elder, and the train engineer – who had joined them at the entrance of the cave.

'Я сожалею,' Cobb said in Russian. 'I'm sorry.'

Jasmine was openly surprised at the preciseness of his accent. She would not have been surprised to learn that wherever Cobb went he filled his head with the basic vocabulary of the place, but speaking with the effortless tongue of a native was a different matter.

Borovsky sighed, his chin sinking to his chest. Decebal turned away and stared through the close-knit branches of the protecting trees, as if seeing the past, present, and future of his village. Only Dobrev and Anna didn't understand the full import of what Cobb was saying.

'Why?' Anna asked through Jasmine. 'What's the matter? What have you done?'

'I've brought an end to their obligations,' he answered as Jasmine translated. He nodded toward the old men. 'They feared it when they decided to talk with us rather than fight us. They knew it when the Black Robes appeared.'

'It's the war we've always prepared for, but one we've feared,' Decebal said.

'But can't you just go?' Anna pleaded with Cobb. 'You

are honorable people, are you not? Can't you just lure the Black Robes away and let these people be?'

Borovsky shook his head. 'He could lure them to the other end of the earth, but it would not be enough.' He turned to Decebal and put a heavy hand on his shoulder. 'It is time, my friend.'

Decebal hesitated.

Borovsky continued. 'The treasure is no longer safe here.'

Decebal looked away from all of them, his face in his hand.

Borovsky turned to Cobb. 'We will deal with the treasure later. But first we must protect these people, yes?'

Cobb nodded. 'Yes. But first, a few questions. The train and the locomotive are still here. How did the prince and his entourage get out of here? Out of this region?'

Jasmine translated as Borovsky revealed, 'The loyalists took the prince and four personal bodyguards by horse cart to a waiting boat, where they went to Bacàu, Odessa, and finally Yalta.'

'Why Odessa?' Jasmine asked. 'That was one of the hearts of the Revolution, the mutiny on the battleship *Potemkin*—'

'It was chaotic, occupied by no fewer than five competing armies,' Borovsky agreed. 'They were too busy fighting each other to worry about another small, nondescript group of refugees making their way through the city.'

Jasmine paused, no longer translating. Her eyes were wide with wonder. 'This is amazing, truly amazing historical information.'

'Second question, Jasmine,' Cobb said firmly. She closed her open mouth and nodded. 'Those cauldrons back in the village, the ones they used to make our dinner. Pretty big. Where did the metal come from?'

Borovsky grinned. 'The melted iron of train tracks. You have a good eye. Would you care to work for the Moscow police department?'

'Maybe someday,' Cobb said, smiling. 'I'm guessing the village was here before the prince arrived. They weren't agrarian, since the ground is pretty dead, and they weren't fishermen, since the catch isn't significant. Here, in the mountains, I'm guessing a mine or quarry. The track used to go through this cave. I'm guessing it also knocked on the back door of the village. Is it still there, by chance?'

Borovsky's grin broadened. 'There is a trunk line about half a kilometer behind where your train stopped. It takes you right into the village.'

'But you buried it,' Cobb said, 'so that anyone who came this far wouldn't try to develop the village and its resources.'

Borovsky nodded. 'That culvert we crossed was dug by the villagers. They used that earth to build the berm that runs from the main line to the village.'

'We crossed that ridge,' Cobb said. 'Didn't suspect a thing.'

'Years of compacting, growth,' Borovsky said.

'Which brings me to question number four,' Cobb said. 'Money. The honor guard is well equipped, the village well fed. There's not a gaunt face among them. My guess is that the prince set up a trust fund to support their mission, and that he did it in the name of the Borovsky family, his devoted servants.'

'Impressive . . . and correct,' Borovsky said. 'All of the town's basic needs are financed by a portion of the wealth the Romanovs distributed among institutions throughout Europe.'

Jasmine's mouth and eyes were again open wide.

Suddenly, Sarah's voice whispered into Cobb's ear. 'I've got it, Jack.'

'Good,' he answered. 'Be right there.'

Cobb told Jasmine to tell the others that he would not permit the villagers to be harmed and assured them that he would be back momentarily. Instructing Jasmine and Dobrev to stay put, Cobb motioned for McNutt to join him. Then the duo headed deeper into the cave at a slow jog.

They followed the barely discernible path beyond the railroad cars to where Sarah's powerful penlight was flickering. She was crouched by what looked like a few mounds of loosely packed dirt, but as the men got closer they could see slat-like wooden cases.

'I'm surprised they didn't take it with them,' Sarah said.

McNutt peered as close as he could, whistled as he saw the outlines of howitzer shells, large cigar-shaped cylinders of black powder, and several big corkscrew-shaped implements used for boring holes. 'Looks like Prince Felix absconded with more than treasure.'

'He needed enough munitions to turn any tunnel, natural or unnatural, into a cave,' Cobb said. He turned his flashlight on the walls. 'You can see the darker blast markings, the parts where harder rocks scooped out chunks of softer ones.'

McNutt followed the light. Parts of the wall looked like the surface of the moon. 'So this section of the cave was an add-on?'

'No,' Cobb said. 'It wasn't a cave. It was a tunnel. They sealed it.'

McNutt's face uncreased in a big 'ohhhh' of understanding. 'He closed the door. But it was still letting a little bit of a draft through.'

'There are tracks buried under here,' Sarah confirmed.

'That lead to where?' McNutt asked.

It was Garcia who responded through their earpieces. 'To a whole set of tracks with a generous selection of destinations. Sorry I didn't notice it before. I didn't know where to look.'

As the group took that in, McNutt borrowed Sarah's light and ambled over to the wall in front of them. 'Brilliant. All of it.'

'What?' Sarah asked.

'The guys who made this wall knew what they were doing,' McNutt said.

'Why do you say that?'

'They used high explosives to take down the top of the walls and part of the tunnel ceiling. They wanted to pulverize the rock.'

'To keep from damaging the rails?' Sarah asked.

'No,' McNutt said. 'They knew they weren't going to

hurt the tracks.' He grabbed a handful of black soil. 'This used to be bark. They covered the tracks with logs to protect them from the impact of falling rock. Then they simply left the logs to rot. But they pulverized the rock to make sure that a subsequent explosion – *our* explosion, as luck should have it – would reduce it to itty-bitty pieces that a train with a cowcatcher like Ludmilla's could push right through.'

'How does the explosion play out?' Sarah asked. 'You can't just blow up the rock wall without blowing up the track.'

'You're right,' McNutt said, calling upon his background in demolition. 'We use the boring tool and the explosives they left behind. Set the TNT up and down the walls. The blowback from the walls and ceilings will be focused right on this spot, on the blockade. The small rocks become smaller rocks. The smaller rocks turn to dust. We drive right through. That's why I said all of it was brilliant. This was not something the prince and his team just improvised.'

Sarah walked over and took back her penlight. She shined it over the wall that she would have to climb to set the unstable, ancient explosives.

'Can you rig it?' Cobb asked.

'Sure.'

'How long?'

'Three days if McNutt helps. Before dawn if he leaves me alone.'

McNutt grimaced. Not at her comment, but at the steep walls of the cave. 'Don't you need a grappling hook?'

Sarah made an 'are-you-kidding-me?' face.

'What about the fuse?' Cobb asked.

'I found a detonator,' she assured him as she shooed them away.

Cobb left and McNutt followed. They met Jasmine and Dobrev at the mouth of the cave.

'Borovsky, Anna, and Decebal went back to the village to prepare the people for a showdown,' Jasmine said. 'What did you find?'

'The way out,' Cobb said. 'But first, we need to get our train back.'

McNutt looked as if dark clouds had parted and a shaft of heavenly light had shined directly on him. He cracked his knuckles in anticipation.

'How do you know they haven't started driving it back to Russia by now?' Jasmine asked.

Cobb smiled at Jasmine. 'For one thing, they think they'll need it to haul out Rasputin and the rest of the treasure,' he said before pointing at Dobrev. 'For another . . .'

The engineer looked like a cat that had just eaten a canary.

He held up the ignition key.

58

McNutt stared at the key. 'It's really that simple?'

'It's that simple,' Cobb replied. 'We needed something that wouldn't destroy the engine or take too long to rectify, so no sugar in the gas tank. He also blocked the air intake, but that's neither here nor there.'

'Can't they just bypass it?' he asked.

Cobb looked over to Jasmine, who passed the question to Dobrev.

When the engineer finished his derisively tinged words, Jasmine said, 'It generally translates to—' She stuck her tongue between her lips and made a slobbering sound.

'Russian raspberry,' McNutt laughed. 'I like it.'

'Nobody knows that engine better than Dobrev,' Cobb said. 'I had Jasmine ask him for a favor when we started out. He tied the cylinders into a central "starter" unit. Easy to do, given the way the fuel feeds into the engine. If you don't know how to untie and reconnect everything, the train won't run.' Cobb smiled appreciatively at the old engineer. 'You might not have been able to cripple the whole thing with one key before he got his hands on it, but you can now.'

'I'm still confused,' Garcia said. 'I thought there was nowhere for the train to go?'

'If nothing else, they could have gone in reverse and stranded us,' Cobb said. 'That would have bought the Black Robes time to call in reinforcements.'

'They're nothing if not well connected,' Jasmine said.

Cobb glanced at Dobrev. 'You sure he won't sit this one out?'

Jasmine shook her head. 'He's adamant. He says you need him. And more importantly, Ludmilla needs him!'

Cobb sighed. God save him from people who did things for love instead of money. There was no talking them into or out of anything.

Carrying a lantern that Cobb had appropriated from the train – amazingly, it still had oil inside and the wick still took a flame – they began walking the mile toward the village. As they traversed the dark woods, Cobb quietly discussed the plan of attack with McNutt. When they reached the edge of the settlement, not far from the site where the Black Robes had gone down, Cobb and McNutt checked the remaining ordnance in McNutt's duffel bag.

'Let me get this straight,' Garcia said as he met them outside the village. 'The train is crawling with Black Robes, all of whom now have access to everything remaining in the freight car armory, right?'

'Right,' Cobb said.

'And you're going to take the train back from them.'

'Correct.'

'There's something back there we need,' McNutt said. 'Jack's toy.'

'No more a toy than anything you use,' Cobb said. There was bite in his response. He enjoyed his work and his tools, but he never confused war for recreation, and he never took pleasure from it unless it was used for a purpose. 'We're going to teach the Black Robes the difference between someone who knows how to do this and someone who just thinks they do.'

'Even so,' Garcia pressed. 'You're severely outnumbered. What are you going to do, just hike over and take the train?'

McNutt grinned. 'More or less.'

* * *

Borovsky saw the lantern and came over with Decebal. They weren't sure what to expect, whether the team would be trying to make off with treasure. If they noticed that Sarah wasn't with them, they did not mention it.

They looked like they were going to throw a fit about the flaming lantern, but Cobb, through Jasmine, cut them off with a description of his intentions. That shut them up and ensured their cooperation. Both men said they wanted to go after the train. But Cobb impressed upon them the importance of concealment and surprise – not to mention that this was not a scorched-earth mission. At least not yet. This was retake and extract.

Besides, the leader of the honor guard already had plenty to do.

'If for some reason the Black Robes decide to come after the village,' Cobb said, 'you'll have to lead the defense.'

After Jasmine translated for Borovsky who then translated for Decebal, the men agreed. With a look that was a cross between disbelief and admiration, the two men left the team to go about their business. Cobb sent Jasmine and Garcia with them. He knew they would be safer with Borovsky and Decebal than they would be with him.

* * *

It was the middle of the night when Cobb, McNutt, and Dobrev walked quietly down the incline they had ridden up just hours ago.

Dobrev was dressed in dark clothes that Decebal had supplied from the villagers when they first arrived, along with soft calfskin boots that allowed him to walk without making a sound. Cobb and McNutt wore only the long-sleeve T-shirts and matching pants, with combat boots.

None of the three wore camouflaging make-up.

McNutt kept a Russian Val assault rifle in his hands. He found it to be one of the most effective sound-suppressed guns he'd ever used. It could also hold twenty rounds and a night vision scope, which greatly improved its already impressive efficiency.

In his holster at his waist was a Heckler & Koch USP Tactical nine-millimeter automatic, complete with a specifically designed sound suppressor. He had thrown these into his duffel bag because, as he explained to Cobb, 'I wasn't sure if we'd have to sneak away quietly from the village in the middle of the night.'

Cobb would make do with the leftovers – the only other weapons that McNutt had stuffed in the duffel that included silencers. Those were the Ruger Mark III with built-in suppressor that McNutt had carried while hunting the first Black Robe under the train back in Moscow and an Uzi-Pro – an improved version of the Micro-Uzi, made by the Israeli military to be even smaller, lighter, and more effective than its older big brothers.

If it had come to a firefight with the honor guard in the middle of the village, the villagers wouldn't have stood a chance. But Cobb was grateful it hadn't come to that. These people were good, and honorable. Just because they were on a different side of a situation didn't seem like a good reason to slaughter them. Taking their treasure, however, was an unfortunate necessity. Hopefully, it could be done without hurting anything more than their civic pride.

As for the Black Robes, they would receive no such consideration. They were the ones who had invited death to play at the table. It was too late to fold.

Cobb and McNutt would make sure of that.

59

Four Black Robes armed with AK-47s were spread between the front of the engine and the northern tree line. They were supposed to be vigilant. Luckily, they were not.

It corroborated what Cobb had been thinking. *The zealots were all passionate but they were not all trained fighters.*

The first guard was standing beside the engine, looking off at the countryside – glorious even in the darkness. The stars twinkled, the treetops rustled in the cool breeze, and the flowered grassland shifted like an animated work of art. The second guard leaned on the other side of the engine, admiring the Bren Mark I he had stolen from the armory. The third was actually stretched out in the grass between the two others, apparently napping.

Cobb motioned for the others to stay put. Thankfully, they didn't have to wait long. The fourth guard, who was leaning on the front of the engine, smoking – a glowing bull's-eye to mark the location of his head – pushed himself up and wandered into the woods. This was apparently his definition of a 'patrol'.

He roamed far enough away from his associates that no one but Dobrev noticed two shadows converging on the Black Robe's back from either side. The engineer was amazed at how quick and quiet the men were.

Dobrev saw the two shadows seemingly blend into the man's back, but he was surprised when they hesitated. Then he realized why. McNutt was waiting until he had clear access to the man's head, after which he snapped a garrote around the man's throat – blackened so it didn't glint in the moonlight. No sooner had he done so, even before the man could gag, Cobb slammed his palm into the man's nose using the cigarette as a guide. McNutt yanked the man back, holding him upright, as Cobb punched the Black Robe in the gut like a jackhammer.

Dobrev listened carefully. The man had barely made a sound; the attackers had made none at all. Since McNutt was now holding the man slightly off the ground, all there was to hear was the fluttering cloth of his robe. The dead man made more noise being lowered to the ground than the living man had made when they killed him.

Cobb and McNutt stripped the dead guard of his jacket, pants, and tunic in seconds – the garroting shadow slipping the outfit on in the same amount of time.

Leaving his rifle and automatic with Cobb, McNutt took the Ruger Mark III and held it low to his side so it blended in with his new pants. He calmly and silently walked out of the woods in the direction that the patrolling Black Robe had come, and sauntered purposefully toward the Black Robe who was resting on the ground.

Without attempting conversation, he simply sat next to the napping guard. The moment that the guard's body blocked the other guards' view, McNutt snaked the Ruger over so the suppressor's end was a millimeter away from the man's upper ear. McNutt coughed and pulled the trigger at the same time.

The dead guard turned his head, seemingly by himself – the small, .22 caliber round remaining within his skull. McNutt had fired at an angle that sent the spray of blood and tissue up and away from the man's tunic. They needed three more robes, and it wouldn't do to have bloodstains on their outfits, even if black robes covered it well.

'Be healthy,' said the guard nearest McNutt.

Dobrev knew it was the customary Russian reaction to a sneeze: the equivalent to 'gesundheit'. McNutt didn't know that, but he didn't need to. He just quietly mimicked the cough of the firearm as he got up and approached the well-wisher.

The third guard smiled and muttered something in Russian, apparently suggesting McNutt might be better off with a cigarette than with fresh air. McNutt passed, head down, and leaned on the side of the engine beside him with one arm, chuckling. A little laugh was a good response to just about anything that was said in a lighthearted voice. As soon as the third guard called over to the 'resting' guard to get up, McNutt placed the Ruger beside the man's temple. His head snapped hard to the opposite side and then back – a muscle reflex – as McNutt jumped aside to avoid the blood.

The moment the third guard went down, the fourth guard's head opened like a blossoming flower on the other side of the engine, courtesy of the Val that was now in Cobb's hand. As soon as they had three unstained outfits, it didn't matter how bloody the fourth one was – and it was soaked, as the nine-millimeter subsonic bullet drilled right through the man's brain and emerged from the other side, taking half his skull with it.

The final sound was the gentle clatter of a rifle hitting the ground as the fourth guard fell. Only the moon, stars, trees, and grass saw two more human shapes emerge from the wood and start dressing in the clothes taken from the fallen guards.

*   *   *

Holding a Val assault rifle in one hand and wearing his new disguise, McNutt moved silently alongside the length of the train and pulled himself up into the cab of the engine. He didn't expect it to be empty, and it wasn't. There was another Black Robe, peacefully sleeping against the wall. He put the end of the Ruger a hair from the bottom of the sleeping man's skull and pulled the trigger.

'Sweet dreams,' he mouthed silently.

McNutt moved the body to the back of the cab, out of their way, as Cobb helped Dobrev inside. If Dobrev was bothered by the presence of the dead man, he did not show it.

Heading for the back of the sleeping compartment car, McNutt heard talking. With the train engine off there were no compartment lights available, and the remaining guards were obviously conserving whatever battery power they had.

In fact, based on the cursing he heard and the gestures he saw when he peeked through the window between the cars, it looked as though their hacker even had to cut his work short when his PC battery ran low. Without their own satellite, there was no cell phone communication. No one had thought to build towers this deep in the middle of nowhere. Only their leader had a direct connection to his headquarters: a radio using non-digital technology.

Cobb stopped behind McNutt. They slowed as they neared the rear of the train, wary of any sentry. There was one, sitting on the lip of the door, his legs dangling above the track. He was casually holding an AK-47, looking out on the southern tree line. He seemed noncommittal, as if he wasn't guarding anything or watching for anyone – just resting while thinking of home.

From the safety of the empty adjoining car, McNutt conveyed his thoughts on the situation. 'Everyone's just sitting around. Like they're waiting for Rasputin.'

'They probably are,' Jasmine whispered in their ears.

With that, McNutt took three silent steps across the junction that linked the two cars, aimed his rifle at the base of the Black Robe's head, and squeezed the trigger. *Pffft*. The body slumped forward, but McNutt caught it before it fell from the train. He quietly laid the torso on the floor and then relieved the body of the AK. He didn't bother looking to see if anyone else was there before racing back the way he had come.

'Go,' McNutt said quietly as he leaped onto the ladder on the side of the freight car.

Cobb heard him in the doorway between the engine and the command center. He turned and saw Dobrev waiting tensely in the doorway of the cab, a dead body on the floor behind him.

Cobb gave Dobrev the thumbs-up. Dobrev turned, stepped over the corpse, gripped the end of the ignition key, and twisted it.

Ludmilla roared to life.

60

The entire, shuddering train seemed to come alive as the turnover of the engine began to power the generator, causing all the lights to flicker.

From his position on top of the train, McNutt saw silhouettes stirring in the freight car, and Cobb could hear activity in the command center from his station in the cab.

'We've got about one minute to button things up,' Cobb said, knowing that Dobrev would need time for the engine to warm up.

Black Robes poured from the freight car across the flatbed. McNutt let the first man almost reach the far door of the command center before he pumped a round into the back of his head.

The five other Black Robes barely had time to assess the situation when McNutt began picking them off one by one, going from front to back, shifting his Val by just centimeters, his steel grip unfazed by the vibration of the train.

The last of the six to emerge was the only Black Robe who had time to spin around to see McNutt standing on the roof of the freight car. It was the last thing he ever saw. McNutt took him down with a subsonic round between the eyes, then quickly surveyed the area. From this vantage point, he could not only cover the armory and the flatbed car but also see the terrain around the train. He was ready to mow down any that tried to get outside.

Similarly, back in the engine compartment, Cobb let the Black Robes from the command center nearly make it to the door of the engine before bringing them down with one or two shots from the silenced Uzi. Its coughs were completely swallowed by Ludmilla's moans as her wheels spun for traction on the cold rails.

The first Black Robe who tried to come into the engine compartment went down. The one behind him nearly tripped over the body before joining his comrade, a nine-millimeter round cracking open his skull like a hammered coconut.

Cobb heard the scrambling of a third man heading for the opposite side of the command center car, then the thud of his body hitting the flatbed floor as McNutt took him down.

The entire train jerked convulsively as Ludmilla began to move. Cobb was in motion. It was time to sweep the train for loose ends. For that, McNutt would make his way across the roof to the end of the sleeper car. Cobb would move through the command car and flatbed, and they would meet in the freight car.

Cobb moved low and fast, checking both sides of the command center entrance. The lights were still on, as were Garcia's video screens. That meant that back in the village Garcia could see what the train's security cams picked up. That was good. It was always nice to have fresh eyes.

'Chief,' McNutt whispered in his earpiece.

Cobb's heart raced slightly. It might as well have been the voice of doom. They both knew that talking before a mission was complete meant only one thing: complications.

'Go,' he said softly, remaining slightly hunched in the middle of the command center.

'The sleeping car,' McNutt reported. 'It's uncoupled.'

Cobb looked questioningly at the video screens to his left. One screen showed the sleeping compartment car at the end of the train sitting on the track as Ludmilla slowly pulled away from it. Cobb was dumbfounded.

'Did you do it?' he asked. He had to ask. McNutt had disobeyed a direct order less than a day before, and Cobb couldn't afford to assume he wouldn't warp his orders again.

'Of course not,' McNutt snapped with irritation in his whisper.

'Finish the sweep,' Cobb said tightly, his brain whirling. He moved quickly, but not recklessly, forward. He checked the flatbed, picking his way through and around the bodies McNutt had dropped there.

The bodies were not the problem. The two AK-47s and three nine-millimeter Russian Gyurza automatics lying beside them were.

The enemy had emerged from the armory car carrying the same weapons they had used earlier – low-end firearms. Now that Cobb thought of it, the Black Robe bodies in the command center car had been equipped the same way. *Why weren't they using the better guns that his team had brought?* Cobb didn't have to look in the armory to know the truth, but he did anyway. He stepped in from the north door as McNutt entered the south – as the sleeping compartment car got smaller and smaller on the track behind him.

The lights in the armory car refracted the silver ceiling, steel-gray walls, and deep blue gun racks. Except for a few heavy containers littering the floor, the place had been picked clean. And it certainly wasn't by anyone left on the train.

If Cobb were the kind of man whose face fell, heart skipped, or stomach dropped, they would be doing all three. But somehow he kept his composure.

'Team,' he announced, his mind racing, 'we've been had.'

* * *

Alexandru Decebal pulled back the reins of his horse so he could look back at the village nestled in the woods like fallen leaves. Decebal looked for a lingering moment, then he turned his horse away. He rode further southwest, sadness stabbing him. He was unsure if he would ever return.

The village had been here all his life; it seemed to him, from the stories told and the events that had transpired, as if it had been here forever. The truth was, before the coming of the prince there had been no real village – just another section of mountain railway with a few structures to house transient loggers and the people who serviced the rails. Water-bearers for the engine. Mechanics for simple repairs. Then there was the blasting of the tunnel through a relatively small hill. Some of the workers who had made the tunnel elected to remain here rather than return to the larger cities. Even before 1917, the first tremors of war were being felt in the economy: in the scarcity of food, in refugees coming and going, and in stealing to survive.

The creation of that tunnel was easy, compared with the danger and death experienced by the engineers and the workers who constructed the rest of that obscure section of rail. In fact, if it hadn't been for the tsar's desire for a variety of emergency escape routes, the rail lines would never have come this far into the wilderness of a bordering nation. When it was completed, other emergencies had taken precedence, so this portion of track was all but forgotten. No one remembered it, except for Dimitry Borovsky, who had brought Prince Felix here and introduced him to his most trusted friend in Romania: Marku Decebal, Alexandru's great-grandfather.

Marku was named appropriately. It means 'one who defends'. And in collaboration with Dimitry, that's exactly what they had done. Taking his wife and child, they had moved to the bluff top and started their honor guard work – each man inviting his most loyal friends and trusted associates to join them, many being unaware of the treasure just outside their camp.

Soon they had taken wives and raised families. Funded by the prince, their work became more about protecting their way of life than safeguarding the train. For Alexandru, born into it years later, this was not just a village. It was a living memorial – to people and to their future. He had buried his wife there. His children had remained here, eschewing the fortune and mysteries of distant lands to hold onto the old ways, the best ways.

And now Viktor Borovsky had told him it was over.

The strangers had come and the secret was out. Borovsky said that their work here was through. Romanovs would not return to claim the treasure. The old Russia was dead. The Romanians who had collected the treasure were gone. It was time to do what they had always said they would do if this day came: bury the gold and jewels, the art and gems.

Seal it in its tomb for all time.

But Borovsky was an old man now. Not as physically old as Decebal, yet Alexandru could see how tired he was – how the weight of Moscow had worn him down. He was so rarely here. For him, it was easy to give up the dream.

Not so for Decebal. The wilderness had always been home, and the wilderness was more than just one bluff with an aging train. It was an idea. He would start a new life elsewhere for himself, for the villagers, rather than stay here in a village that no longer had a purpose. And to do that required more money than the prince had left for them, funds stored in accounts that had been eaten away by a century.

Decebal quietly led his horse away, down into the grove in the shadow of the bluff. As soon as he entered the grove, he knew something was wrong. Before he even saw them, he knew that invaders were here.

His horse shied, then stilled beneath his powerful thighs. Decebal looked ahead and he saw them. Dark shapes stretched in a line all the way across the grove and into the valley beyond. He saw at least ten long, low shapes, with taller shapes moving amongst them. And amongst those taller shapes were even taller spikes with rounded ends.

His horse snorted and reared, whinnying. The taller shapes all seemed to snap around toward him. He saw slashes of moonlight reflected off lenses, scopes, and eyes.

'Kill him!' he heard a voice hiss in Russian.

Decebal was already galloping back the way he had come, as fast as his horse could take him. Behind him, it sounded like dragons. He hazarded a glance and saw several of the low, monstrous beasts clawing the earth at the lip of the grove.

As always, Decebal looked ahead, peering through the darkness. He could see the first suggestion of light outlining the horizon. He could see steam rising from the southwest. It had to be the explorers' train, retracing the prince's path. He could also see the sparks of the nocturnal village fires ahead and considerably above him.

Too far, he thought. He would have a better chance of reaching the train on the sloping ground than trying to climb up the vertical bluff back to the village. On the far side, where the train tracks were hidden, the ascent was a long, steady curve. On this side, it was a treacherous incline where he and his horse would soon be overtaken.

Decebal charged southeast to meet the rising sun, and the train, before it was too late. Behind him the growls got louder.

If anyone on the bluff had been looking down, they might have seen the galloping horse and its rider racing diagonally across the grassland. Puffs of dawn-lit dirt rose from the horse's hooves as two dark objects, as long as they were wide, seemed to sizzle across the field after him. From the grove, it was impossible to see they were gaining on the rider.

Grigori Sidorov stepped out from the waiting line of IMZ-Ural sidecar motorcycles, which were made by the military for the most extreme and hostile off-road conditions. The leader of the Black Robes held the Accuracy International AX338 long-range sniper's rifle – the one McNutt had used to kill his hired help – like a royal scepter.

'Idiots,' he muttered. 'They can't even kill an old man on an old horse.'

Sidorov waved for one of his men to join him. The man was part of his inner circle, not one of those newer, incompetent recruits he had left on the train, the men who joined for the sin but not for the labor. The man arrived quickly and stood in front of Sidorov. He was shorter than the leader by more than a head: the perfect size for his new assignment.

Sidorov set the barrel of the rifle on the man's shoulder and placed his eye behind the sniper's night vision scope. The Romanian rider appeared in the circle like a bobbing puppet on a string. Sidorov smiled, settled, waited just a moment, and pulled the trigger.

The twenty-millimeter-long, nine-millimeter-wide, copper-colored .338 Lapua Magnum spear entered Decebal's body traveling nine hundred and three meters per second. It was designed to penetrate five layers of military-grade body armor at a thousand yards, so going through the old man's torso, as hearty and healthy as it was, posed no problem.

It entered between his shoulder blades and, because of his galloping posture, exited through his sternum's manubrium, ravaging portions of both his heart and lungs while ripping muscle and shattering bone.

The projectile continued forward. Had the horse's head been on the upswing of the gallop, it would have killed the animal, too. As it was, the bullet only cut some hairs off the very top of the horse's mane before it buried itself in the turf ahead.

Sidorov's smile widened as he watched Decebal's body jerk, sag, then begin to topple.

'Kneel,' he ordered the man in front of him.

The Black Robe instantly knelt, allowing Sidorov to watch his victim fall.

Decebal landed heavily on his back. He bounced once, then slid, and finally settled. His eyes were blinking as he realized that, of all the responsibilities he had been given, or given himself, it was only this last one that he had failed. It was with some bitterness that he accepted it was also the most important responsibility.

But you did all right, he told himself as thoughts swirled in his head. *It has been an honorable life. A loving life. All in all, a very good one.*

He smiled his gap-toothed smile one last time – seeing his friends, his family, and his life all at once – then died under the stars he had loved so much.

61

McNutt saw a frightened Lipizzaner in the distance. The speckled stallion bolted along the tree line before it disappeared from view. 'That's Decebal's horse!'

Because of Ludmilla's monstrous roar, he had to shout even though he was right beside Cobb in the engine cab. Dobrev pushed her as fast as she could go without hurling them off the old, partially recessed rails. The train had taken an agonizing left at the tree line and swept up the slope on the far side, clawing toward a ragged swath of land between their position and the village. Using a map, Cobb had already showed Dobrev where the berm was that they'd have to plow through. The engineer had grunted, accepting the inevitability of the attempt, if not necessarily the success. Both men knew they had to hit it fast if they were going to get through nearly a century of compacted growth and debris.

Using hand gestures and the map, Cobb had made it clear to Dobrev that they had to get to the village as fast as possible. Although the treasure was being taken care of, they had to protect the villagers from the impending raid. Despite the urgency of the mission, they could only go so fast up the incline. Both men, by their intensity and silence, were clearly hoping they would be able to gain sufficient speed.

Cobb addressed the entire team through his earpiece. 'Everybody: if you haven't already, get your tactical vests and helmets on,' he instructed them. 'The Black Robes that we killed on the train were sacrifices. The rest of them are waiting in the darkness.'

'Where in the darkness?' Sarah hissed in his ear, as she hung onto a small ridge at the very top of the cave, her toes wedged in two rock fissures.

'Somewhere between us and you,' Cobb surmised. 'They're stalking the train. That was their plan all along.'

'Then why attack us here?' Garcia demanded. Back in the village, he was desperately trying to keep his eyes on all the train's security camera images – all crammed onto one laptop screen.

'To cover their flank or to take hostages,' Cobb said. 'They know the cave's around here somewhere.'

'God . . . damn . . . it!' Sarah cursed, realizing she was a sitting – make that *hanging* – target. McNutt had explained exactly what had to be done, but he had made things seem a lot simpler than she was finding them. Still, it was easier for her to learn how to set a charge than it would have been for her to teach him how to climb a cave. 'How much time do we have?'

'Not much,' Cobb stated. 'Jasmine, what's happening in the village?'

'Decebal left orders to organize then went to scout ahead,' she said. 'They're doing the best they can.' The young woman was ducked behind one of the iron cauldrons, watching as villagers were running all around her, some carrying rifles, others in a panic. 'Viktor and Anna are trying to organize them, but until they get orders from Decebal . . .'

'Decebal is dead,' Cobb guessed, the image of the galloping horse still fresh in his mind.

'That gunfire we just heard?'

'Yes,' Cobb said. 'The Black Robes killed him.' He refrained from adding 'probably with one of our own guns'.

McNutt, however, did not hold back. 'They stripped the armory of our weapons before leaving the train as a diversion.'

'Not now, McNutt,' Cobb said. 'Jasmine, tell Borovsky and Anna we're coming to get them and the villagers. We should get in okay because the Black Robes don't know there's track out there. But I have a feeling we're going to have to fight our way out.'

'Got it,' Jasmine said.

'What's with uncoupling the sleeper car?' Garcia asked.

'The Black Robes uncoupled it. They knew if we moved the train, it would stay as a roadblock,' McNutt explained.

'The armory was stripped? How stripped?' Sarah demanded.

Cobb and McNutt exchanged worried glances.

'Very stripped,' McNutt admitted. 'They got every gun we didn't take with us, including a Russian RPG-29 rocket-propelled grenade launcher.'

Cobb looked disbelievingly at McNutt.

'You said prepare for anything,' the gunman complained. 'I didn't bring it before we got here, but when Papi said I could have whatever I wanted . . .'

'Sarah, be ready to blow open that tunnel,' Cobb said. 'When you do, run for it.'

'She's going alone?' Garcia asked incredulously.

'For the moment,' Cobb said.

'What does that mean?' Sarah asked.

'The track that goes to the village doesn't end in the village,' Cobb said.

'How do you know that?' Garcia asked. 'There's no—'

'The village was a load-on terminal for timber,' Cobb explained. 'Which means the flatbeds would have to be pulled even with the stacks. Otherwise, you'd have to move the wood down the rail, which doesn't make a lot of sense.'

'The track is a circle!' Jasmine said. 'Of course!'

'Exactly,' Cobb said. 'The trains would loop through to load up the timber, then head back down the line. They never reversed. Too inefficient.'

Jasmine nodded in understanding. 'The prince tore it up on one end, but the treasure train still could have come out and joined the main trunk through the village. That is, if you could find a way past the blockade.'

'And,' Cobb added, 'if everything goes well, that's how we're going to do this.'

'Dobrev must have known that or at least guessed it,' Jasmine said. 'He kept talking about how Ludmilla could go both ways.'

'Wow,' McNutt said. 'Normally that statement would turn me on.'

Garcia ignored him. 'But what about the cave? And all

of that stuff clinging to the prince's train cars? And any debris that falls on the tracks?'

'He says Ludmilla will take care of that,' Jasmine reported.

McNutt saw the engineer mutter something encouraging to his cab and pat its wall. 'He can promise whatever he wants. First we have to get through the molehill these people built.'

'Get ready,' Cobb told them all. 'This promises to be interesting. Oh, and pass the word not to shoot us.'

'Why would they?' Sarah asked.

Cobb replied, 'We're dressed as Black Robes.'

'Maybe that'll make them hesitate as well,' Jasmine said.

'Exactly,' Cobb said.

The train was running hot and hard. In the glare of the single headlight, Dobrev could see a log fence where the track supposedly ended. He throttled up and tore through the barricade, then hit the end of the two-foot-high berm. Sparks spit from the wheels and lit the ground that was still dark beneath the dawning sky. The metal shrieked and the three occupants were jerked forward as the train slowed – but it did not stop. Like a snowplow it pushed through the sunbaked soil, which blew apart in clods. They heard the dirt crunch under the wheels, saw it fly like thousands of gnats in both directions. The screeching was terrible. Cobb hoped that the Black Robes were close enough to be deafened and pelted by BB-fast grains of dirt. It might not penetrate those robes, but it sure as hell would slow them down.

'Don't derail, don't derail, don't derail,' was McNutt's

mantra for the seeming eternity it took to cover what was, in fact, less than a half-mile. The longer they moved, the leveler the ground and the easier it was to push through the mound.

And then the village came into view.

62

Garcia saw the Black Robes before anyone else did.

The attack started as distant black dots on a postage-stamp-sized section of his crowded computer screen. They emerged from the grove line bathed in the dull red, orange, and yellow glow of coming sunrise. The tech looked above his computer to the lip of the bluff itself.

'They're coming from the grove, three o'clock east!' Garcia yelled, pointing.

Cobb ran through the engine to the command center and found the screen showing the northeast view. It was getting lighter outside every minute, and the train was picking up speed.

'They either want to follow us or escort us in,' Cobb decided. 'Either way—'

'They ain't,' McNutt seethed, charging past him toward the freight car.

'What are you going to do?' Cobb demanded.

'Welcome them with open arms, and I do mean *arms!*' McNutt shouted back without pausing, shaking the Val assault rifle in the air.

Cobb ran back to the cab. He and Dobrev exchanged intent glances, then both watched as the village came closer through a line of trees – one that would just allow the train to squeeze through. They also saw the honor guard horsemen waiting with their rifles.

'Other side!' Cobb yelled at Jasmine. 'Have them ride along the far side. Let the train take the brunt of the attack!'

'Viktor is way ahead of you,' he heard Jasmine say in his ear.

Cobb smiled grimly, gripped Dobrev's shoulder reassuringly, then ran to the gap between the engine and the command center. He balanced there, staring carefully off to the east. He saw the Black Robes coming around the sloping bend in the distance.

They were on IMZ-Ural 'Cossack' motorcycles, each with a sidecar. They were made in Russia, based on the superior BMW sidecar cycles of World War II. They were designed to battle storm troopers and Panzer tanks in the brutal terrain and climate of the Eastern Front. They could easily take this landscape and this ancient train.

Cobb recognized some of the weapons in the riders' hands: machine guns, fifteen-round automatics, even the shotgun he had declined all those hours ago. He looked at the Uzi, essentially ineffective at this range.

The horsemen who were unlucky enough to be within range fell under a peppering of fire.

As Cobb watched, McNutt shot the motorcycle driver closest to the back of the train. The man's head erupted like a popcorn kernel and the cycle veered off, the sidecar passenger shrieking.

The shooting had the proper effect. Now that they knew

they were in range of McNutt's weapons, the cyclists slowed down and fell back.

Cobb raced back to the cab. Through the windshield he could see the village up ahead as if it were a diorama model. He could actually pick out Jasmine and Garcia at the front of a long line of rifle-toting villagers. He saw Borovsky astride a horse, pointing and barking out orders to the riders. He saw all the people start to surge forward as the train entered the trees.

He motioned for Dobrev to slow to allow people to get onboard. The Russian understood. They would be safer hunkered in the command center or armory than they would anywhere else. Those who could grabbed the train and climbed on. Those who couldn't tried to keep up for protection. The rest sought cover wherever they could find it. It had been explained to them that the train would be coming back this way shortly.

At least they hoped.

Cobb knew where everybody was except for one person.

'Sarah!' he shouted. 'What's your status?'

There was no answer. Cobb stared slack-jawed at the cave entrance just a few hundred yards away.

'Jasmine, Garcia, where's Sarah?'

'We don't know!' they yelled back.

Cobb felt a familiar, unpleasant burning in his gut.

Meanwhile, some younger, stronger villagers had hopped onto the slowing train to help their elders aboard. They started filling the command center, the freight car, and the flatbed as McNutt kept up a steady stream of defensive fire behind them. More men joined him with their old carbines.

Cobb ignored it all. He just stared straight ahead as they passed through the village. There was enough light now for him to make out the geography ahead. He saw, about a mile in the distance, the back end of the tunnel. He grabbed the binoculars and looked ahead, focused. The wall was still intact. If Sarah had fallen, or if the unstable explosive had knocked her out or even killed her, this was going to be a very short trip.

Borovsky rode alongside, his head bobbing in the cab's east window.

'Go back!' Cobb shouted, pointing hard. 'Protect the rear of the train!' The colonel nodded and set off to do just that. Now, Cobb knew, if the train crashed, at least they would be in a better position to mount a last stand.

Cobb felt a hand on his arm. He turned to see what Dobrev wanted. Cobb saw something he wasn't expecting: the engineer staring straight ahead in amazement. Cobb followed his gaze and saw her.

Sarah was fifty yards away, running from the stone wall, wearing only the long-sleeved T-shirt and matching leggings. Having removed her shoes for the climb, her feet were bare and her toes were bleeding. Her face was smeared with dirt. Her blond hair was wet with sweat, hanging down in ringlets around her burning eyes.

'I couldn't blow it from the inside!' she panted through his earpiece. 'That much dynamite . . . my ears . . .'

'Right, of course,' Cobb grinned. 'So how . . .?'

'The rocks were loose on top,' she said. 'I pushed one out and climbed down. Sorry I didn't answer.'

'It's okay,' he said. 'So how about—'

'Blowing this sucker?' she said. 'I'd rather not get buried. Give me another few seconds.'

Cobb motioned for Dobrev to slow the train. He did a quick calculation and took Ludmilla to half-speed, about thirty-five miles an hour – still fast enough to keep cutting through the dirt embankment. It was falling apart easily now that the terrain was level.

Sarah was still running. Her right hand was up, the red button on the end of a detonator stick just beneath her raised thumb. The expression on her face was one of exhausted madness.

Her lips moved as she ran.

'Sure hope this works, Jack,' Cobb heard in his ear. 'In three . . . two . . . one . . .'

And then her thumb went down.

Twenty yards away, Sarah disappeared in a billowing cloud of white as the hill behind her exploded up and outward, as if it had been shot from the center of the earth.

63

Cobb recklessly stuck his head out and stared up, as a wave of dirt and rock swung overhead on either side of the train. Those BB-shots of dirt that he'd wished on the Black Robes hit his own scalp and exposed neck as he turned to watch the mass of debris crest over the flatbed and come crashing down between the tracks and the oncoming Black Robes.

The motorcycles veered off, swerving to avoid being buried, swept, or knocked away. Cobb was sorry there hadn't been time to warn his own people. The horsemen reined their horses hard and scattered in all directions, and the villagers fell wherever they were.

When Cobb ducked back in, Dobrev had not budged nor had the train deviated. It continued to groan slowly toward the billowing dust cloud where Sarah had once stood.

'Sarah? You copy?' Cobb asked.

There was only silence.

'*Look!*' Dobrev said in Russian.

Cobb knew exactly what he meant. Incredibly, where once there was a cave, there was now an open gap through the hillside – with only powdered residue of the wall coating the tracks.

Jasmine arrived in the engine. Her face was covered with dust.

'You were watching too?' Cobb said.

'Wouldn't have missed it for anything,' she replied.

'How many villagers we got on the ground?'

'About twenty,' she said.

'Garcia?'

'Yo!'

'Get them into the freight car. The armored walls will protect them better than the other cars. McNutt?'

'I know,' he said. 'Nobody's gettin' near them,' he promised as the *crack-crack-crack* of the Val rang out.

The train slowed just outside the mouth of the tunnel. As it did, Dobrev turned and shouted something to Jasmine, who quickly relayed the information to Cobb.

'We have to stop,' she reported as Dobrev grabbed a heavy iron mallet from the locker.

'Why? What's he doing?' Cobb demanded.

'He said the cowcatcher has to come off now,' she told him.

'Crap. I'm going with him,' Cobb said as Dobrev hopped from the cab.

Cobb told McNutt what he was doing. He told him to concentrate on not letting anyone get to the front. And most importantly, he told him to keep an eye out for Sarah.

There was a crack and a whirring skid of tires. 'Copy that,' McNutt said as a Black Robe went tumbling through the dirt.

Dobrev began swinging in hard, strong arcs at the old bolts that held the iron cowcatcher to the front of Ludmilla while Cobb drew his handgun and protected the train. Not a single Black Robe made it past the combination wall-of-gunfire and sniper-shots McNutt was unleashing. It seemed to Cobb like the man had at least three hands. Occasionally, as he paced the rocky terrain, Cobb looked around to see if he could spot Sarah.

'Give me a hand,' Dobrev groaned, in Russian.

Cobb didn't need a translator. He knew what that meant. As Dobrev handed the mallet back to Jasmine in the cabin, Cobb put his shoulder to the side of the heavy iron grate. Dobrev joined him, and together they pushed it toward the side of the tracks that sloped outward. It tumbled over with a dull clank, then skidded to a rest in a gully.

The men boarded quickly, and Cobb turned back to the other pressing matter.

'Sarah,' he called urgently. 'Where are you? I do not have a visual!'

Jasmine looked at Cobb with concern, but all thought of Sarah left her when she glanced back at Dobrev.

'Oh Jesus,' she whispered.

Cobb followed her glance. Dobrev looked ashen – his facial muscles tight, his forehead showing a telltale sheen of cold sweat.

Jasmine touched his cheek. He shrugged her off.

'I'm all right,' he said through clenched teeth. 'Only I can do this. I must do this.'

'No, tell me how—'

'*Nyet!*' he barked, and that was that.

Jasmine choked up as she and Cobb looked through the windshield.

433

'Don't think about it,' Cobb told her. 'Let him be.'

'But he's . . . he needs to rest.'

'You make him stop now, that will kill him,' Cobb said.

Dobrev was talking. 'This is the most important moment,' he said as if the words had to be forced out between his teeth. 'To couple the trains, I must push with the exact amount of pressure or the wheels will leave the rails . . .'

The engine covered the distance between the tunnel mouth and the prince's train in seconds. They were about thirty feet inside. Then the grated nose of the 2TE116 pressed against the coupling joint of the treasure train's engine. Everyone on board was jolted, but it was not enough to throw off McNutt's aim. He shot another Black Robe, who had been struggling to pull his motorcycle out of a mound of debris that the train had thrown to one side. Before the sidecar man could get to the Browning automatic rifle that he had stolen from the armory, a horseman planted a Nagant rifle round in his chest.

'Come on, Ludmilla,' Dobrev gasped. 'You can do it, girl . . .' He put the big train into reverse.

Cobb steadied himself as the clawing fingers of the tunnel began to crack and shatter from around the royal roofs and side walls. With a pop that sounded like a massive water balloon, the eight blue and gold cars jerked forward, pulled by Ludmilla. The stubborn, clinging walls of the tunnel began to break and pebbles of granite were raining down around them.

Cobb hazarded a look back out the window as he heard other cycles racing toward the entrance to the tunnel. But every time one tried to reach the forward cars, either McNutt, a Russian police officer, or a horseman would gun them down.

'McNutt,' he said, pulling his head in, 'status?'

'Holding them off,' McNutt grunted. 'But not for long. I'm running out of ammo and the horsemen's weapons take too long between shots.' The Nagant's bolt needed to be pulled back and shoved forward for each round. The guns the Black Robes had taken from their armory did not. 'And I'm worried about that grenade launcher.'

'Don't,' Cobb suggested. 'They want this train. They won't risk blowing it up.'

As they spoke, the train reversed out of the tunnel.

'Sarah,' Cobb said. 'Elvis is leaving the building. Care to join us?'

Still no answer.

'Damn it,' Cobb spat.

Suddenly light flooded into the cab as they emerged from the tunnel. Cobb could see Jasmine hovering protectively over Dobrev, who was leaning forward with one hand on the control, one palm pressed against the front of the cabin. He was breathing heavily, his clothes soaked with perspiration.

But the train was moving and picking up speed.

As it did, the Black Robes were beginning to regroup.

'Garcia, make sure everyone stays down,' Cobb said.

As if on cue, bullets began to splatter on the outside engine walls.

'Down!' Cobb ordered, as he and Jasmine went to one knee. Both looked as Dobrev remained rigidly standing.

'Andrei!' yelled Jasmine in Russian. 'Get down!'

But he didn't respond.

The train began to pick up even more speed. Now clouds were being reflected in the windshield glass, and tree branches were whizzing by the windows, flipping off their newly acquired dust as the train passed, still going backwards.

Jasmine saw none of it. She was watching Dobrev.

Cobb shouted at her, his hand out, knowing that Jasmine was going to do what she did anyway. She jumped up and grabbed Dobrev under his arms as he was about to drop.

'Andrei . . .' she shrieked.

Before she could say another word, Dobrev fell back like a stone slab. She went with him and just managed to keep his head from smashing into the cab's steel floor. His teeth were clattering, his eyes unfocused, and his right hand was spasmodically gripping his left arm. Jasmine looked over at Cobb in alarm.

'It's a heart attack,' she said. 'What can we do?'

'Here's what you're going to do,' Cobb said. 'You're going to drive this train.'

She hesitated as Dobrev's right hand clawed at her arm.

'You do it,' Cobb said sternly, 'or he will have suffered this for nothing. He and everyone else who died here.'

She tried to move – and then Dobrev yanked her head close to his, her eyes facing his mouth. Dobrev whispered something to her while placing his most treasured heirloom – the gold, twenty lei coin – in her grasp before he squeezed her hand closed.

Jasmine didn't translate right away.

She needed a moment to fight her emotions.

Eventually, she looked up at Cobb with tragic resolve in her eyes. She wiped away a tear while revealing Dobrev's final words.

'Andrei said, "Drive the train, and kill those sons of bitches."'

64

Despite what had just happened and all that was happening around them, Jasmine was surprised by what Cobb did next. He reached through the cab window, grabbed onto a rung there, and started pulling himself onto the roof of the engine.

Jasmine's mouth opened as her brain filled with questions, but the train lurched before she could ask anything. She instinctively leaped up, grabbed the controls of the train, and started to drive the eleven cars with all the skill she had picked up from Dobrev.

Cobb stood on top of the train, quickly surveying the scene. There was a mass of gathering Cossack cycles on the left, a few stragglers on the back right, and horsemen pounding through the woods after them. The tree cover was still pretty extensive, with branches all around him. The downward incline was slight at the moment, but as soon as they broke into the open, it would dip sharply.

He wasn't going to ask anyone to cover him. Whoever he'd ask would have his hands full as it was, and hopefully he could accomplish what he needed to do without undue attention. Thankfully, no one had yet noticed that he had climbed up there.

Cobb took a quick look down and said a fast prayer for

Andrei Dobrev. He had connected Ludmilla to the prince's cars perfectly. Although the securing spike was not pushed through the corresponding holes in each coupler, the trains were 'holding hands', the fingers and thumb-like joints intertwined. This had allowed Ludmilla to pull the treasure train free.

Cobb looked up to gauge the distance from the engine tip to the back of the prince's cars. He silently thanked the gods of Russian train construction that Ludmilla's roofing was relatively flat and free of projections. He turned and took a quick look along the track to make sure there were no sudden turns coming up for the backwards-running train. Then he ran and jumped.

Jasmine gasped as she saw his body hurdle above the windshield and land on the top of the prince's first car. He dropped, rolled, and came up on his feet in a well-balanced crouch. Barely stopping, he sprinted and leaped from one car to the next until he made it to the last car in the prince's train. He made sure there were no Black Robes coming, then he grabbed the lip of the door, and swung inside.

'Jack, what are you doing?' Jasmine demanded.

'I'm borrowing something from Rasputin,' he replied in her ear. 'Just keep the train as steady as possible, and be aware of the attackers' positions. If any happen to get by McNutt—'

'I know,' she said.

Jasmine kept low. She was cognizant of her peripheral vision, but her main focus of concentration was keeping the train moving steadily and safe. She watched Cobb as he climbed back onto the roof of the prince's last car and started sprinting across the roofs toward her.

'Watch it, Jack! We're coming into low branches,' Jasmine warned. She saw him hold onto the lip of the car roof and hazard a glance forward. Then he looked between the car and the engine snout.

'Black Robe trying to climb the engine,' he said, calm and to the point.

'Sorry,' McNutt said. 'They're starting to swarm.'

'Apology unnecessary,' Cobb remarked.

Jasmine's head snapped left. A stranger's face was rising in the window.

The .38 Special was in her hand with her arm outstretched before she was completely aware of it. She squeezed the trigger just as McNutt had shown her. The weapon discharged, and the rubber grip bucked in her hand. The face disappeared from the window.

The window frame was speckled in red.

Cobb saw the resulting mess. The Black Robe's head jerked back, and then his body followed. His ruined face swung down, the top of his skull banging against the train's wheel truck, and his legs slammed across his motorcycle sidecar.

The Black Robe smashed to the ground, and the cycle veered off into a tree, sending the driver ten feet through the air. In that amount of time, the train had already gone too far for Cobb to see him land.

'Good shot,' he said, then stood up again on the roof of the prince's car.

By the time Jasmine realized she had killed a man, Cobb had jumped back onto the top of Ludmilla's engine car and raced to the gap between it and the command car. He dropped down into the doorway with ease. The command center had seen better days. Bullets had broken glass, torn up the furniture, and shattered computer screens.

'McNutt, status,' Cobb said.

'The Val is out of ammo,' he grunted. 'Down to my last clip on the Steyr Aug, and making every round count.' That meant he only had about thirty bullets left. 'Could sure use the Sig that Sarah took.'

At that moment holes started ripping into the wall at about waist level along the entire length of the command center. Cobb kept low, judging that a Black Robe was racing alongside, having fun with the Mac 11 he had stolen from them. The nine-millimeter rounds wreaked havoc on Cobb's eardrums as the Black Robe emptied all thirty-two slugs into the command center – as if mocking McNutt's dwindling ammo supply. The echo of the shots combined with the wreckage it caused nearly drowned out the voice he had been waiting to hear.

Sarah shouted, 'Can anyone hear me? I repeat, can anyone hear me?'

'Finally,' Cobb replied. 'What's your status?'

'I'm alive and moving into position for phase two.'

Cobb nodded. 'Good. I'll try to distract them the best I can.'

Garcia, who was hunched over his tablet in the freight car amidst several frightened villagers, butted into their conversation. 'What's phase two?'

'None of your business,' Cobb said curtly. There were some things he refused to discuss over the air. 'Worry about your job. Not Sarah's.'

'Sorry, chief,' Garcia said. 'Won't happen again.'

Jasmine heard none of this in the cab. The rumbling and screeching were too pervasive. All of her senses were focused on keeping the unwieldy train on the tracks. Dobrev had rhapsodized about balance, and now she fully appreciated that they were guiding a snake with two heads. She had to be hyper-aware of both the weight they were pulling and the weight they were pushing, or everything would tear off the tracks.

Meanwhile, Cobb kept hustling through the train.

Garcia thought he had heard Cobb in his earpiece, but soon realized that he heard him in his other ear as well. He craned his neck to see Cobb rushing by. 'Jack?'

'Don't mind me,' Cobb said as he grabbed a fifteen-foot by three-foot container and dragged all two hundred pounds of it back toward the flatbed car.

'Let me help,' McNutt said, turning from the slat in the wall.

'No. You're needed here,' Cobb said without stopping.

'Bullshit,' McNutt retorted, suddenly pushing the container from the other side. 'I can pick off these bastards just as well from the flatbed. Better, in fact.'

'Giving them a better target at the same time,' Cobb reminded him.

'Like you have to tell me that?' McNutt blurted. 'Shut up and pull, chief!' He added the title to give his remark a veneer of respect rather than defiance.

They emerged onto the flatbed car, crouched to stay beneath the five-foot fence lip that encircled the space. Tree branches cracked and snapped overhead as the train muscled through, while the crack and snap of the Black Robes' bullets blended with the sneering roar of their cycles.

Garcia appeared in the doorway of the freight car just as Cobb swung open the container lid.

'Ohmigod,' Garcia exclaimed. 'Is that a GEN H-4?'

But Garcia knew it was. Designed by miniaturization mastermind Gennai Yanagisawa in the 1980s, it was upgraded, improved upon, and enhanced until it was the most portable, most versatile, cockpit-less, one-man helicopter in the world.

Cobb didn't have to answer. He just started to haul the two thirteen-foot rotors out of the carrying case.

Garcia raced over to where Cobb knelt in the center of the flatbed and helped remove the aluminum pipe framework, the bicycle-handlebar-style controls, the magnesium crankcase, and, most lovingly, the big bowl that contained the four miniature, two-stroke, two-cylinder, air-cooled engines.

'Ohmigod, ohmigod.' Garcia nearly hyperventilated. 'Why'd you hide this in the control center?'

'For safekeeping,' Cobb replied.

'What are you going to do with it?'

'I'm going to lure those bastards away from the train,' Cobb grunted as he started to assemble the framework.

'No, no,' Garcia snapped back, reaching toward him. 'You're doing it wrong.'

Cobb locked on the techie's eyes. 'How fast can you do it?'

'Faster than you!' Garcia insisted.

'Prove it,' said Cobb, his Colt .45 already in his hand as he moved to join McNutt at the rail.

The view from there was both dream-like and nightmarish. It was as if they had traveled back in time to both 1945 and 1845 in a parallel universe that was both the end of World War II and the Wild West. They were on an Iron Horse wagon train surrounded by galloping, bloodthirsty tribes. Only now, the flesh-and-blood horses were being chased by motorcycles, and the vintage rifles were being overpowered by automatic weapons.

The horsemen were incredible, but the Black Robes had superior numbers and firepower. What was worse was that the horses, although obviously well trained, were frightened by the Cossack cycles and unwillingly threw off their riders' aim. In some extreme cases, they threw the riders themselves.

McNutt, meanwhile, would pop up like a whack-a-mole, target a Black Robe, and snap off a shot before ducking from an angry swarm of bullets slapping the metal wall of the flatbed fence in return. McNutt had to keep sliding from place to place along the wall so they couldn't get a bead on him.

Cobb ran to get the Uzi. After checking for the horsemen's positions, he simply pushed the gun up over the flatbed lip from a crouch, and sprayed bullets at anything in range.

445

'Give me that,' McNutt hissed, sliding his empty Steyr across the metal floor. He sounded like a father who was disappointed that his toddler had gotten his hands on some matches. He grabbed the Uzi from Cobb, who gave it up willingly. 'Let me show you how it's done.'

Cobb grinned despite the situation and said quietly, 'You picked a good team, Papi. A very good team.' His head snapped back around when he heard Garcia howl.

He saw the techie on his knees, holding the big engine bowl like Oliver Twist asking for more food. On either side of him were the 'X' shaped rotors and what looked like the skeleton of a barber's chair. It was a simple slat of a seat, with a fuel tank as a backrest, positioned upon three wide-set, metal legs ending in tiny chair wheels. Attached to the front leg was a horizontal footrest bar.

'I'm trying to get the motors and rotors attached,' Garcia whined, 'but every time I stand up, they shoot at me!'

Cobb looked back at the flatbed fence to see McNutt looking at him from a crouch. 'The Uzi's running out of ammo, too,' he reported. 'And the horsemen are getting routed. A couple more minutes and we'll be the only ones left.'

Cobb's mind raced. Every scenario he played out in his brain ended badly. He and Garcia could try to finish erecting the H-4, but the odds they would complete it in one piece were negligible. Cobb could try his plan without the H-4, but that would only have the Black Robes swamping the train with reinvigorated mania.

And just when he thought it couldn't get any worse . . .

'Jack!' Jasmine cried. 'The uncoupled compartment car is up ahead!'

Cobb didn't have to look, and Jasmine didn't have to explain the danger. If they hit the stationary car at this speed, the crash would likely derail them. But if they slowed now, they'd be easy pickings for the Black Robes.

Cobb could see no alternative. White flags meant nothing to these lunatics. The explorers and villagers would have to fight to their last man, and their last breaths. Cobb shook his head.

'Jasmine, we're going to need to—' he started to say, but McNutt interrupted.

'Cobb—'

'I wasn't talking to you, McNutt—'

'No, Jack, look!'

McNutt stood at the rail, pointing northeast. Cobb blinked in bewilderment. McNutt was standing up straight, and no one was shooting at him. Cobb sprang to his feet and stared off to where his sniper was pointing. And then he saw it.

Roaring out of the tree line on a sidecar motorcycle were Sergeant Anna Rusinko and Colonel Viktor Borovsky.

And both were armed with assault rifles.

65

McNutt cheered as he watched Anna steer the bike while Borovsky held the AK-47 against his shoulder in the sidecar, targeting and hitting Black Robe drivers as though they were wolves.

The two had dragged the abandoned bike from a ditch near the village after hauling Black Robe corpses from it. Now they had the remaining Black Robes scattering for cover. Not a one of them charged the new arrivals.

'White, Red, and now Yellow Russians!' McNutt taunted.

The others weren't paying him – or the new arrivals – much attention. Cobb told Jasmine to slow to a crawl to buy time between themselves and the rogue car. He was busy on the flatbed, helping Garcia with the last steps of building the H-4. The only assembly still required for the seven-foot-tall vehicle was the rotor and engine attachments. The footrest had been attached to the two forward legs, the seat at their top, and the spine above, where the rotors were going to be attached. There was no cabin, no tail section. The controls sat on the bicycle-like handlebars that were suspended from the rotor base at the bottom of a periscope-like extension. The whole contraption looked like a skeleton – if a skeleton consisted of a skull, backbone, sternum, two hipbones, a pelvis, and a really long coccyx.

Cobb left the techie standing on the bucket seat to secure the engine atop the structure while he and McNutt stood on the packing case, lifted the rotors, and settled them into the aluminum tube on top. Jasmine had slowed the train and the side-to-side sway was minimal. With the *phut-phut-phut* of Borovsky's weapon echoing along the western side of the train, McNutt lent both hands as Cobb fitted the blades into place.

'So, is this a true helicopter?' McNutt asked. 'Not one of those – what do you call them?'

'Gyrocopters,' Garcia said as he tightened the screws.

'Right,' McNutt said. 'Saw a guy fly by in one during survival training in Death Valley. We survived. He didn't.'

'Nice,' Garcia said.

It was the casual chatter of weekend hobbyists, not men fighting for their lives. Cobb jumped from the wooden box and put a quick end to it.

'Finish, Garcia!' he barked as he ran over.

'Done, done,' Garcia told him, as he made sure the rotors were secure. That consisted of pushing them one way, then another, and watching for any vertical wiggle around the central axis. The blades themselves were designed to have significant up-and-down flexibility.

While he did that, Cobb straddled the seat of the H-4. It was plastic to keep the weight down, without padding of any kind.

'Chief, uh . . . what's the plan?' McNutt asked.

Cobb didn't answer. His silence was intended as a

conversation-ender. A seatbelt was attached to the metal spine of the mini-helicopter. Cobb strapped himself in. 'Jasmine, after I leave, keep the train slow and kiss that compartment car.'

'Can you spare any eyes on the back of the train?' she said.

'Garcia?'

'We have an undercarriage cam,' he said. 'I'll talk you through it.'

'Okay, back away, you two,' Cobb advised Garcia and McNutt.

Crouching low, the IT man hurried to a corner of the flatbed where he was exposed to gunfire but wouldn't be beheaded by the spinning blades.

'Which way you going?' McNutt asked, walking backwards more slowly.

'Where the action is,' Cobb replied, pointing west.

McNutt turned in that direction and knelt down on one knee, his arms firmly planted on the lip of the car, his hands steady, his fingers wrapped tightly around his last remaining weapon, which was his own sidearm – a Glock 17 Gen4 nine-millimeter automatic.

Cobb held a license for single-engine rotorcraft, training he had found useful on a number of missions – not so much for getting into places but for getting out of them. Though he had never flown this particular aircraft, he had selected it because, at least on paper, it didn't present any unusual challenges. There were only four controls: a starter switch, a switch to engage the rotors, a throttle, and a yaw switch; and one instrument, a tachometer. There were also more redundancies built into this baby than in any grownup aircraft: she had four 10 hp, 125 cc, two-stroke engines. They were connected to the transmission via a single clutch; if one shut down, the others automatically shared the burden to keep the rotors spinning. In theory, the H-4 could fly on a single engine – long enough to set down, anyway.

The engines revved, sounding like four lawnmowers. The two blades spun in opposite directions to provide counterbalance, rotating for all they were worth.

McNutt watched as the horsemen rallied to protect the villagers and the train. Borovsky's fire had given them that opportunity by driving the Cossack cycles back up the rise to where the hill met the grove. Anna and Borovsky's bike was racing down between the combatants, taking out Black Robes whenever they could.

As the rotors raced to full power, Cobb's survey of the battlefield was suddenly rendered meaningless when he saw a new monster cresting the hill in the middle of the remaining motorcycles. It was a stripped-down Boyevaya Razvedyvatelnaya Dozomaya Mashina combat reconnaissance patrol vehicle, otherwise known as the BRDM. Russia, the Ukraine, and Poland had been crawling with them since the 1960s, and there were rumors that many of them had been confiscated by local authorities and sold to militias to fight the Soviets.

Of the four-hundred-odd units that had left Russia, fewer than half had been found.

Like this one, for instance.

Obviously, the Black Robes had been building their own mechanized brigade in this province, knowing that Rasputin's body had to be somewhere in the area.

As Cobb watched the armored, four-wheel toad of a vehicle, the roof hatch opened and Grigori Sidorov emerged. He was holding their Accuracy International AX-50 sniper rifle. Cobb and McNutt both watched helplessly as the man aimed the gun at Anna and Borovsky's motorcycle. With the H-4 buzzing like a million bees, there was no way to warn them.

In Cobb's mind, that left only one option.

It was up to him to distract Sidorov.

In a flash, the H-4 rose into the air as if pulled by a string. Cobb gritted his teeth until he got the hang of the controls. Then he turned and faced the armored vehicle.

Unfortunately, it was not an ideal day for a flight. The wind howled, and strong gusts kept Cobb from getting the height he wanted. He only got up about thirty feet, but it would do. His sudden appearance above the flat car distracted Sidorov enough that the bullet meant for Borovsky's skull smashed into the front of the motorcycle instead.

McNutt groaned when the cycle's front tire exploded. Anna flew over the handlebars and rolled across the hillside, while the sidecar toppled over sideways – smashing, twisting, and bouncing. At some point, Borovsky was viciously tossed aside like a broken marionette.

Cobb saw it all from his elevated position, and with just

a push on the handlebars, he sent the H-4 swooping toward the BRDM.

At first, the combatants were too shocked by the appearance of the strange, skeletal helicopter to shoot it down, and Cobb took full advantage of the surprise. He sped in and hovered over the Black Robes, directly in front of the BRDM. Cobb remained stationary for only a moment – just long enough to threaten the destruction of Rasputin's grave – before he accelerated over them and headed toward an imaginary spot in the forest.

Sidorov gestured broadly, looking left and right as he pointed at the train before disappearing into the BRDM. A moment later the big vehicle stopped and pivoted on its central axis until it was facing in the direction Cobb had flown.

Then it set off in pursuit.

Of the remaining Black Robes, a dozen headed toward the slowing train and a half-dozen joined the BRDM to track down Cobb before he could harm their master.

* * *

Garcia stared at the camera footage on his video screen. 'You're nearly there, Jasmine. About ten feet . . . eight . . . five . . .'

She braked, hoping that the last expenditure of momentum would do the trick.

It did. There was a squeal, a thump, and then a clang as the couplings hooked.

'Beautiful!' Garcia yelled. 'Way to go!'

Half a flatbed away, McNutt swore. A dozen Cossack

cycles were tearing back toward the train, and he was the main line of defense. McNutt slammed his palm on the flatbed fence in frustration. He vaulted over the side of the flatbed car.

'Josh!' Garcia cried, seeing him land and sprint toward the nearest Black Robe.

McNutt fired two rounds at the ground, each one closer to the front tire than the one before. He was out of range, but hopefully the rider wouldn't know that. The Black Robe with the empty sidecar swerved a little too quickly and nearly tipped over. He skidded toward McNutt just enough. The gunman was already running at him, right arm stretched ahead, left hand supporting it at the wrist. The Glock spat twice, though the second 'insurance' shot wasn't necessary. The first had made a raw, red hole in the rider's forehead.

McNutt ducked and hurried over to snatch the AK-47.

He kicked off the dead driver and hopped on.

'Okay, you bastards,' he said. 'If it's killing you want . . .'

He gunned the engine and tore off across the field at the oncoming Black Robes.

The remaining eleven Black Robes bore down on him. McNutt grinned in ferocious anticipation at the sight of the arrogant driver who pulled away from the group, the occupant of his sidecar sneering as he carefully aimed his own AK-47.

McNutt watched the man's shoulder. Just as it rose, McNutt pulled back the throttle and quickly decelerated.

He felt the bullet go by his right ear an instant before he heard the sound of its firing.

Stupid headhunter, he thought. *You should have gone for the chest.*

With leisurely grace, McNutt placed a nine-millimeter slug into the man's heart. The Cossack driver reacted in surprise as the sidecar occupant's head snapped back, his chest opening like a broken window. McNutt punctuated the driver's surprise by putting a Glock round in his ear as he passed.

The driver flew off the bike as if in slow motion, and the cycle just kept going. So did McNutt – ignoring the driver as he crashed into the ground in an ugly heap.

There are more where he came from.

McNutt swung wide and passed to the right of the group, doing what he used to do in the rodeo: he ducked low and far to the side, giving the Black Robes nothing to shoot at but the bike. They were surprised to see him vanish and held their fire just long enough for him to speed into a protective thicket. When they recovered and turned to pursue, McNutt was upright again. He swung the motorcycle to its side, aimed through an opening, and took down a pair of Black Robes.

* * *

Sidorov had heard the gunfire coming closer – not toward the train, where it was supposed to be going. He looked back through the slotted window of the BRDM and saw the enemy, who was obviously an experienced warrior and sharpshooter, pick off three more cyclists.

Sidorov sensed it was time to make a stand. Cursing the incompetence of his men, Sidorov stared angrily at his two Black Robe assistants – one behind the wheel and one beside the driver. He knew what lay ahead. He knew what had to be done.

'The grenade launcher,' Sidorov said. 'Give it to me.'

66

McNutt pulled up to where Anna was cradling Borovsky's body. McNutt only had a few rounds left in the automatic. He would have to get a weapon from the Russians.

Anna looked at him with certainty, her face unmarked by tears.

'There's no blood on his teeth,' she said in Russian. 'I don't think he has any major internal injuries.'

McNutt shrugged helplessly. 'I'm sorry. I don't speak Russian.'

'He . . .' Anna said in halting, heavily accented English. 'No dead.'

McNutt could see that Borovsky was breathing, albeit raggedly. The gunman looked back to where the train had stopped in front of their old compartment car and where the villagers were swarming over the crashed and toppled Black Robe motorcycles he had dealt with. The horsemen had dismounted and had effectively circled their wagons using abandoned bikes. McNutt turned back to Anna and started talking rapidly.

She looked confused, but then a hand touched her cheek. She looked down to see Borovsky gazing up at her.

'The forest does not grieve for the loss of a single tree,' he said.

'Quiet,' she laughed in relief. 'You're not going to die. Not yet.'

McNutt did a somewhat elaborate mime to convey what he wanted to tell her.

'Leave him,' he said, pressing both palms toward the ground. Then he pointed at the train, made a cradling gesture. 'The villagers will take care of him.' He pointed at himself and Anna. 'We have to take out that bastard.' He indicated the armored car, crashed his fists together, then threw open his fingers, trying to convey that the vehicle must be destroyed.

'He makes a good point,' the colonel grinned, grimacing. 'Go. I will be fine.'

Her face cleared, and she nodded at McNutt. She laid Borovsky's head down tenderly, then grabbed an AK-47 and approached McNutt's motorcycle.

'Let us go,' she said in English.

He nodded, unholstered the only specialized weapon he still possessed, and took the AK-47 from her.

'You drive,' McNutt said.

* * *

Cobb laughed. Not at the Black Robes. The Black Robes were deadly, dedicated, and unafraid. But as soon as he crossed the grove, he had them at a very distinct disadvantage. In order to give chase, the Black Robes would have to follow a winding trail through the dense forest or trample through the thick underbrush. The gaps in the trees would give them only brief opportunities to take clear shots.

That is, if Cobb could navigate the H-4 through those same narrow gaps.

If the rotors clipped the nearby branches, the Black Robes would be the least of his worries.

Shots popped. Even over the hum of the engines, Cobb heard them whiz by. The air was buzzing with projectiles. And up here, an accidental hit would kill him as surely as a purposeful one. Any loss of control would surely send him careening into the trees. He rose above the canopy, but the fierce wind made it virtually impossible to control the light H-4 at that altitude. Cobb wasn't susceptible to vertigo or motion sickness, but the rush of air against his face made him wish he had goggles.

Dumb oversight, he told himself.

He dropped back into the forest, the Black Robes still in pursuit.

The first casualty was the lead motorcycle. Determined to be the ones responsible for taking out the aircraft, the driver took the motorcycle off of the beaten path and plowed through the forest in a beeline toward Cobb. Gnarled roots and exposed rocks nearly bounced the rider from the sidecar as low branches and saplings sliced into the driver's cheeks and forehead.

As the gunman took aim, the front wheel of the IMZ-Ural found an unseen tree stump, causing the motorcycle to jerk erratically. The jolt tossed the gunman violently toward the outside of the car, spinning his body wildly at the driver. In a split-second of panic, the gunman accidentally squeezed the trigger on his Uzi submachine gun, decapitating the driver with several close-range shots to his face.

Like the Headless Horseman, the driver's body refused to release the accelerator. Unfortunately for the gunman in the sidecar, the effect turned the motorcycle into an unguided missile. Overwhelmed with shock, the gunman simply watched in horror as the corpse rammed the sidecar into an oncoming tree at full speed. The impact crushed the sidecar and its occupant as the bike ripped in two.

Cobb watched the action from above and was dumbstruck by the sight of a headless Black Robe careening through the wilderness on what was left of his IMZ-Ural.

That leaves two more bikes, he thought.

Cobb spun the H-4 back around and charged forward. Suddenly, the ground dropped out from beneath him, and he found himself hovering nearly one hundred feet above a wide creek. The ravine had caught him by surprise, and he hoped it would do the same to the Black Robes. Cobb kept the H-4 over the edge of the chasm just long enough to make a show for the second motorcycle.

Sensing that they had closed the gap between themselves and their target, the second driver eagerly sped down the straightaway toward Cobb. As the second gunman took aim, Cobb fought the whirling updrafts and down-currents that raged over the stream.

It only bought him a few seconds, but it was all he needed.

Only yards from the cliff, the Black Robe driver realized his mistake. He slammed the brakes while cranking the

462

wheel as hard as he could. The sidecar rose as the bike tilted on two wheels. As it dropped to the ground only inches from the edge, the engine stalled. Both the driver and the sidecar gunman breathed a quick sigh of relief.

But their reprieve wouldn't last long.

They turned at the sound of the H-4, which Cobb was now advancing toward them as fast as the craft could carry him. His gun drawn, Cobb fired two shots, yet neither of the Black Robes was hit. It took them a moment to realize why, and by then it was too late.

Cobb hadn't aimed at them; he had fired at the third motorcycle behind them. As the Black Robes on the stalled bike turned back, they saw the third driver slumped over the handlebars. And the gunman's head was lolled back, a gaping hole where his throat should have been.

Meanwhile, the bike was heading right at them.

Before they could start the motorcycle again or even jump clear of the path, the last Black Robes were pushed over the cliff by the third IMZ-Ural. Cobb watched as four bodies – two dead, two screaming – tumbled down the rocky embankment.

The eventual explosion was music to his ears.

*   *   *

As the BRDM rounded the last bend before the straight-away, Sidorov opened the hatch. The heavy metal door clanked back, and Sidorov rose to his feet in the vehicle's roof opening. Ahead of him was the American in his skeletal flying machine. The man held a pitiful firearm in his hand – something from the American West, which suited this mad cowboy.

The American would pay for his transgression.

Sidorov brought up the six-foot-long tube to his shoulder, using the optical sight to home in on Cobb. His target was making a lazy curve in the sky, coming lower to align with his team. No matter. The TGB-29V's three-foot-long, thermobaric, anti-personnel warhead would blow him out of the sky even if it only detonated *near* him. The Russian pulled the shoulder brace tight against his body. He wrapped his hand around the pistol grip trigger mechanism.

The rocket engine would start, and the missile would leave the barrel at almost a thousand feet per second. The eight fins on the rear of the projectile would deploy, stabilizing the warhead. It would reach its effective range of sixteen hundred feet without delay or obstruction. The sixty-five-millimeter explosive would detonate, killing any living thing in its vicinity.

Sidorov had Cobb dead to rights in his optical sight.

He smiled and gripped the trigger.

67

With Anna driving, McNutt reached into the sidecar seat, pulled up his last remaining weapon, and shot it point blank at the leader of the Black Robes. There was a pop and a whooshing sound as Sidorov was enveloped in a net.

McNutt's timing couldn't have been better. Sidorov was knocked back against the edge of the hatch. On impact, he instinctively pulled the trigger even though the launcher was pointed aimlessly to the right. A moment later, the rocket engine of the missile ignited.

From his elevated perspective, Cobb saw it all. The warhead, designed to penetrate the armored hulls of tanks, flashed out in what looked like a thick line of yellowish smoke, then it smashed into the edge of the hill. The ground erupted in a billowing circle of red, gray, and brown debris that knocked the massive BRDM on its side. Rock and dirt cascaded onto it – some of it actually molten from the heat of the grenade. Then, as quickly as it had begun, it was over – save for the loud echo, which rolled through the distant hills like a roar of the gods.

When the dust settled, the BRDM was left dangling precariously from the edge of the hillside. The slightest shift in its center of gravity, and the entire thing would tumble to the bottom of the ravine, hundreds of feet below.

Cobb swung down above the armored vehicle. He edged toward the hatch where Sidorov lay half inside the truck and half outside, covered with net and earth and blood and wriggling like an earthworm. The leader of the Black Robes looked up. A curious expression came over his face as he realized he had been bested. He knew he would die today.

Cobb moved the handlebar controls and descended. He landed, unbuckled himself, and hurried over to the armored vehicle. The ground was brittle. He didn't have much time.

'Do you speak English?' Cobb asked as he squatted beside Sidorov.

The Russian coughed, then smiled with bloodstained teeth.

'I'll make a deal with you,' Cobb said. 'A trade before you meet your maker. I'll tell you what you want to know, and you do the same for me. Sound good?'

Sidorov laughed. 'What . . . do . . . I . . . want . . . to . . . know?' His English was heavily accented, and his breathing was increasingly labored.

Cobb reached into his pocket. He grasped the tiny object between his thumb and forefinger and stretched out his arm, giving Sidorov a closer view. 'This.'

Sidorov's eyes brightened at the sight of Rasputin's ring. He closed his eyes and smiled, content in the knowledge that his master's body had been found after all these years.

'Hey!' Cobb yelled. 'Don't you die on me! Not yet!'

Cobb, who had borrowed the ring while the train was moving, returned it to his pocket, then quickly pulled out his cell phone. Using the touchscreen, he scrolled through his photos. Finding the one he wanted, he held the screen toward Sidorov so he could see it. 'Is this the man you dealt with? The man in charge of this mission?'

Sidorov laughed at the question, blood spewing from his mouth. '*Him?* . . . In charge?' He laughed at the notion. 'He is *not* the boss.'

Cobb pulled the phone back and studied the picture of Papineau he had taken in Fort Lauderdale. He had long since known that Papineau had associates, men and women who helped him do his bidding, but now he had confirmation that there was someone higher up the ladder: a puppet-master, pulling Papineau's strings.

Cobb rose. He thought about shooting the Russian in the head for all the carnage he had caused but decided that Sidorov deserved a long, lingering death.

Cobb went back to the H-4 as Sidorov lay dying on the roadway, his body still lodged in the window of the heavy BRDM. As Cobb took off, the ground trembled, bringing the inevitable fall of the vehicle that much closer. Cobb floated above the BRDM and watched as Sidorov pulled a single-shot pistol from somewhere under his robe. Cobb could not distinguish the model, but he knew the weapon's singular purpose: it was designed to take one's own life.

Sidorov pressed the barrel into the middle of his brow.

He closed his eyes and pulled the trigger.

A bullet in the brain – just like Rasputin.

As Sidorov's limbs slumped to the earth, the ground underneath the BRDM finally gave way. Cobb watched as the massive vehicle slipped over the steep embankment and tumbled into the ravine. As a final insult, the BRDM burst into flames, sending a magnificent plume of smoke in Cobb's direction – a fire that would burn Sidorov's corpse beyond recognition.

Satisfied, Cobb turned the H-4 toward the village and the rest of his team, but deep inside, he wondered if anyone would ever go looking for the body of *that* lunatic.

* * *

Having returned to the train after the BRDM was immobilized by the rocket blast, McNutt kept an eye on things until Cobb's arrival. Garcia was there, too, standing beside Anna, who was tending to an injured Borovsky. He was lying on a stretcher made from branches and leaves that the old women had assembled in what seemed like seconds.

Everyone watched as the H-4 hovered inches off the ground before it touched down like a dainty ballerina. The two counter-rotating blades slowed, then stopped abruptly. Cobb unclipped his seatbelt and slipped out of the aircraft.

'What's our status?' he asked.

'Chief,' McNutt blurted, 'you're not going to believe this, but Jasmine and the treasure train are *gone*. Ludmilla is still here, but the old train is—'

'Gone,' Cobb said, not the least bit panicked. 'Don't worry. I'll explain later.'

Garcia exhaled. 'Good, because I'm totally confused.'

'Welcome to my world,' McNutt grumbled.

Cobb glanced around. 'What's the situation here?'

McNutt frowned and refocused. 'The villagers gathered all of the dropped weapons, and they went after the remaining Black Robes,' he reported, admiring the industry of the people, who were, even then, helping each other as much as they could. 'I don't envy any Black Robes who are unable to get away.'

Cobb looked over at the handful of surviving Black Robes. They looked simply numb – tired from their massive effort in a mission that they probably had never fully understood.

'If they haven't been killed yet, they won't be,' Cobb said. 'At least not at the hands of the villagers.'

'Trial or deprogramming?' McNutt asked. 'What do they do here?'

'Russian gunmen in Romania?' Cobb said. 'They'll have their brains rewired by the Serviciul de Informaţii Externe, the Foreign Intelligence Service. Then they'll be sent back to Moscow to spy.'

'Better than a bullet in the back of the neck,' McNutt opined. 'Speaking of bullets, you okay?'

'Dandy,' Cobb replied.

'We haven't found anyone that we consider, shall we say, "leadership material" amongst the Black Robes,' Garcia prodded. 'We were thinking maybe you knew something about that?'

'I do,' Cobb answered. 'And he's been neutralized.'

'Neutralized? Neutralized how?'

'Shot. Crushed. Incinerated.' Cobb answered. 'That good enough?'

'It wasn't the first time around!' McNutt joked. 'They did all that and more to good ol' Raspy, and he's still sitting in the damn train – wherever that is.'

Cobb nodded, smiled, and exhaled with honest relief. It was the first time in a while that he allowed himself to enjoy McNutt's humor. Then he visibly brightened and slapped McNutt on the back. 'Nice shooting out there.'

'Anna kept her steady when all get-out was . . . well, getting out,' he said.

Cobb stepped forward to where Anna was hovering protectively over Borovsky and saluted her. With a smile, she saluted back. Then he put his hand out, and she took it.

'*Spasiba*,' he said.

'You . . . are . . . velcome,' she replied.

Cobb knelt beside Borovsky, whose right arm was in a sling. He slipped a hand under the Colonel's shoulder, raised him slightly, pointed to the front of the train. On the track, in front of the locomotive, were three large, burlap sacks bulging to near bursting.

'Gold,' Cobb said. 'For the village. They can start over, anywhere.'

Borovsky nodded in understanding. It would have been an exaggeration to call him happy, but he seemed content-edly resigned.

He said something in Russian before Cobb laid him back.

Jasmine's voice was in his ear. 'He said, "If I had to lose the treasure to a thief, at least it was an honorable one."'

Cobb wanted to point out that the man was protecting stolen treasure. For that matter, the gold itself was probably bought with awful taxes levied on the Romanian people.

Instead, he simply nodded and walked away.

68

Choban, Romania
(63 miles east of village)

It was mid-afternoon when a virtually unrecognizable Sarah and Jasmine – dirty and sweaty from the blast and the battle – stepped off the treasure train on the edge of the sun-dappled town of Choban. Waiting for them was Jean-Marc Papineau, who had hired a crew of armed guards to protect the treasure on its journey to its final destination.

'Well done, ladies,' the Frenchman said.

'That was quite a ride,' Sarah said, running her hand through her soot-permeated hair. She took off her sunglasses and shook them. Black ash from the engine and white powder from the explosion drifted down, but her blue eyes gleamed.

Papineau's eyes settled on Jasmine. 'You learned quickly. I'm very proud.'

'I had a master class,' Jasmine said.

'Under fire,' Sarah added.

The moment Jasmine had finished the coupling maneuver with the rogue car, Sarah suddenly appeared in Ludmilla's cab. She had explained that there was a new plan – one that only she and Cobb had known about. If the engine of the treasure train was operational, they were to uncouple the ancient cars and leave immediately. While everyone else was busy with the Black Robes, they would ensure that the treasure was safe.

Jasmine hadn't wanted to leave Dobrev, but Sarah convinced her that they needed to put distance between the train and the Black Robes in case the fanatics triumphed; and that the conductor would be happier to lie in state with his lady.

Jasmine couldn't dispute either point. When the old engine didn't make an argument – it started immediately due to years of continual maintenance – she agreed to drive. As Ludmilla made her way back toward the main line they had traveled earlier, Sarah, Jasmine, and the treasure train took off in the opposite direction, down the other side of the mountain.

Under the watchful eyes of the armed guards, Papineau did a quick inventory of the treasure. He didn't stop smiling until he reached the final car.

'Is it all there?' he asked with a cocked eyebrow.

'We had to use some of it,' Sarah said.

'We?'

She cleared her throat. 'Chief, care to explain?'

Cobb answered in their ears. 'I told her to leave three bags of gold for the village. They need to start anew. They've suffered. They saved our lives. They earned it. If you've got a problem with that, you can send some of your armed guards to collect it.'

Papineau wanted to argue but decided against it. The treasure, or at least part of it, was in his hands. That was enough for now. He removed his earpiece and walked toward his waiting limousine for a drink.

69

Bundled in a warm jacket, Sarah stared out the window at the tundra. For the last hour, her view hadn't changed. 'And I thought we were in the middle of nowhere in Romania.'

Compared to the wilds of the Chukchi Peninsula, the Transylvanian Plateau was downtown Las Vegas. Stretching two hundred and eighty-five thousand square miles across the northeastern tip of Russia, this place was home to only fifty thousand hearty souls.

'It's the only part of Russia that partially rests in the Western Hemisphere,' Jasmine said.

'Very interesting,' Sarah admitted. 'Useless, but interesting.'

They soldiered on, using equipment Papineau had secured for them to cross the miles of undeveloped, unforgiving, and nearly uninhabitable wasteland. The air was heavy with frozen mist, created by the waves that continually crashed against the rocky shores of the Bering Strait.

'Who on earth would think a tunnel could be built out here?' Sarah wondered.

'The Russian railway, that's who,' Jasmine said. 'Andrei told me that Trans-Siberian rail links had been discussed for more than a century, and the Bering Strait tunnel had been planned ever since the nineteenth century. They had built all the way to Vladivostok before they figured out you were right: it's crazy to build out here.'

They were inside a converted Toyota Hilux off-road truck, specially made for Arctic regions. Complete with forty-four-inch tires, the dependable, comfortable Hilux would hardly look out of place even on tropical roads. Here it was their versatile, reliable home away from home. It was even outfitted with sleeping berths in the back and a satellite dish for cell phone communication.

'There were boats. Then there were airplanes. Why a tunnel?' Sarah continued.

'Why anything?' Jasmine asked. 'Simple. People are builders.'

'People are crazy,' Sarah said. 'I once went whaling up here. It's only—'

'You went whaling?' Jasmine looked at her disapprovingly. 'But that's—'

'Illegal?' Sarah blurted. 'Is that what you were going to say, Little Miss Shot-a-bad-guy-in-the-face?'

'I told you, he was trying to attack me.'

'Because you were stealing gold! And a body!' Sarah laughed.

'Tell me again,' Jasmine teased, 'why are you here?'

'Do you really think after all we've been through that I was going to miss this? Besides, you need me. I can smell a hiding place for miles.' She looked out the windshield. 'At least it doesn't snow much here.'

'Not much,' Jasmine agreed. 'Not in the coastal regions.'

In the rear driver's side seat, Garcia fumbled with one of the numerous electronic gadgets he had crammed into the vehicle. Even with the limited space available, Garcia had still insisted on two tablet computers, two military-grade GPS units, and two satellite-linked communications systems. On the opposite side of the second row, McNutt inspected *his* personal items: an FN Herstal P90 submachine gun and a Kahr PM9 pistol. Both were considered 'smaller' firearms, but each packed more than enough firepower for McNutt's satisfaction.

Each man had his own understanding of redundancy.

'Can you get a ballgame on that thing?' McNutt asked. 'Anything. I don't care if it's a bobsled race. I just can't listen to them anymore.'

Garcia chuckled as he shifted images around the screen of his iPad. 'Sorry.'

'Seriously, I think I liked it better when they didn't like each other.' McNutt closed his eyes and leaned back in his seat. 'At least I don't think they liked each other. Who knows? I give up.'

'Not exactly what one wants to hear from their fearless leader,' Garcia said. 'If Papineau knew you were in charge . . .'

McNutt opened his eyes and looked across the vehicle. 'Hey, I never asked Cobb to put me in charge of anything. If he thinks I should make the final call on things because of my military training, then that's his problem. As far as

I'm concerned, you guys can do whatever you want.' He closed his eyes again and pulled his hat down low over his brow. 'Just let me know when you need me to step in and settle things.' With that, he raised the P90 that was strapped to his shoulder, signifying the method with which he would handle any arguments.

Garcia just shook his head and laughed. 'Speaking of Cobb, what could possibly take him away from all this?'

'All this?' McNutt asked. 'You mean frostbite and constant bickering?'

'I mean the possibility of frozen assets,' Garcia replied, smiling at his pun.

'Oh . . . all of *that*. Yeah, that's the sixty-four-thousand-dollar question, isn't it?'

'I'd say it's a little more than that.'

*   *   *

Cobb had decided against joining the rest of the team who were en route to Alaska. The prospect of freezing temperatures didn't bother him; rather, he sensed an opportunity to get some answers. As the others traveled east by rail, Cobb drove west in his rented car – he'd had more than enough of trains. He sped through Hungary and Slovenia, across the northern edge of Italy and a quick stretch of highway in France, finally arriving at his destination after nearly twenty straight hours behind the wheel.

The Hotel Beau-Rivage.

Geneva, Switzerland.

*   *   *

Jasmine pointed out the windshield. 'Right there!'

They had locked their GPS onto one of Papineau's satellites and punched in the coordinates that they had established from what Andrei had told Jasmine. They had learned that while Prince Felix's Romanov military escort fled via Yalta, the officers loyal to the crown had gone in the opposite direction – settling in a place the Bolsheviks and Mensheviks would never find them or what they carried.

Now all four could see what little remained of the pole that marked the start of the last attempted excavation of the Bering Strait Tunnel between Russia and America. Sarah drove around it as Jasmine craned her neck over her shoulder to face the back seat.

'Hector, you're up,' she said.

The undercarriage of the Hilux had been fitted with ground-penetrating radar, and Garcia now studied the images it produced on his tablet. 'The buried rail line will have some sort of unique metal signature,' he said. 'Something that should make it stand out against the rock and ice. All we have to do is follow it.'

The women stared through the windshield, surveying the area for anyone or anything. There was coal, natural gas, tin, and tungsten being mined near the peninsula's few cities, but here the sparsely pocketed indigenous people, the Chukchi, who were descended from Paleo-Siberians, survived by fishing, whale hunting, and even reindeer herding.

Thankfully there was no sign of any of that. From what they could gather, the Chukchi and Siberian Yupiks considered this area 'spoiled' by the early twentieth-century incursion.

Sarah turned her head and impatiently addressed Garcia. 'Well, what do you see?'

Garcia sighed in frustration. He pulled a cable from his backpack and plugged it into the side of his tablet. He tossed the other end of the cable over Jasmine's shoulder.

'Plug it in. See for yourselves,' he said.

Jasmine plugged her end of the cable into the auxiliary port on the vehicle's in-dash display, which mirrored what Garcia saw on his screen. Sarah and Jasmine huddled closer to the monitor in the front seat while McNutt leaned toward Garcia to see for himself.

As the image panned forward, a distinct, bright line appeared on the screen.

'Is that a crack in the ice?' Sarah asked.

'Cracks are jagged,' Garcia replied. 'That's straight. That's—'

'Bent track!' Sarah screamed.

With that, she opened the overhead moonroof to get a better look.

Following Sarah's lead, Jasmine also stood up in the cab.

The view was magnificent: as if a furry, white rug stretched out to a sparkling green sea, with a ceiling of the bluest skies any of them had ever seen. It was cold. It was windy. But it was worth it.

After only a minute, the biting weather forced them back inside. Their noses were red and their cheeks were chapped, but their smiles were warm and bright.

Jasmine couldn't hide her excitement. 'Let's go see what's down there!'

*   *   *

When Cobb's team viewed the contents of the treasure train for the first time, Papineau had given Garcia not one, but two IP addresses that were to receive the feed of the broadcast.

The first IP address – a unique, numerical identifier that allowed computers to find each other across the Internet – belonged to Papineau's computer, which Garcia traced to Papi's train outside of Vladivostok. But the second IP address led somewhere strange: to a computer at Quai du Mont-Blanc 13, 1201 Geneva, Switzerland.

The site of the Beau-Rivage hotel.

Garcia's research had told them that the Beau-Rivage was one of the finest hotels in the world, a five-star, ninety-room, eighteen-suite enclave for those wishing to experience the height of luxury. It was also the international headquarters of Sotheby's auction house. Cobb wondered if the person on the other end of the video feed had been making arrangements to sell the Romanov treasure to the highest bidder – either through a legitimate auction that would have given the Romanian government a chance to reclaim their treasure, or through off-the-books transactions that would see the treasure sold, piece by piece, to the world's elite collectors.

Either way, Cobb figured he had little time to waste.

As he took his parking stub from the valet, Cobb felt confident he had come to the right place. He knew that whoever had financed their operation – and it wasn't Papineau – had more than enough money to burn, and this place reeked of old-world opulence. The building appeared to be constructed of polished stone blocks, with twenty-foot-high, arched windows spaced evenly around the main floor. Everything about the building was warm and inviting. The dusky glow behind the hotel and the recessed lighting under the eaves of the roof gave the hotel an ethereal, heavenly look, which only added to the moment.

Cobb had come for a name.

He wouldn't leave until he had one.

70

Sarah used the small plow extension of the Hilux to dig away the frosty surface and reveal a small, metal plate in the ground.

'They used a dromos,' Jasmine said enthusiastically. 'It's a marked entrance that leads to a passageway. The Egyptians used them to mark the entrances to their tombs.' She beamed at Sarah. 'In many countries they're virtually invisible amid the hillsides—'

'Jasmine,' Sarah said, putting her hand on her shoulder. 'Give it a rest for just a minute, okay? I need to focus.'

'Sure,' Jasmine said, wounded. 'Focus.'

Meanwhile, McNutt pulled a heavy chain from the storage in the bed of the truck. He anchored one end of the chain to the tow rings at the front of the Hilux while Sarah looped the hooked end of the chain behind the metal plate. When she was finished, she used a hand gesture to let McNutt know that things were secure on her end. McNutt nodded and slapped the hood of the truck. Garcia shifted the truck into reverse and floored the accelerator. The metal plate, locked in by decades of frost, held for a breathless moment, then gave in to progress.

It popped off, revealing a small rectangular opening in the tundra.

All four hurriedly grabbed their supplies from the truck and prepared to enter the unknown. Guided by flashlights and glow sticks, they squeezed through the gap they had created and entered a gently sloping hall. Pressing forward, they quickly discovered that the passage widened into a great cavern that sloped down and stopped just a hundred feet ahead.

Against the north wall were three blue and gold Romanov train cars.

The group ran toward them, barely able to contain their excitement. Jasmine jumped up into the first car as the rest of the group raced past her to investigate the others.

'It's a passenger car,' Jasmine announced. 'Nothing but seats.'

'Same here!' Sarah yelled.

'Seats and crates,' McNutt shouted. 'Broken, empty crates.'

'Garcia?' Sarah screamed, hoping for good news.

'Nothing but wood,' he said as he glanced through several wooden crates that had been discarded near the train cars. 'They're empty.'

'Shit!' Sarah cursed as she kicked a seat. 'Shit! Shit! SHIT!'

After a few minutes of searching, the four explorers regrouped beside the train. They sat in the snow, deflated and depressed, trying to come to grips with the fruitless end of their adventure. The light from the glow sticks that had once seemed warm and welcoming now cast an eerie radiance on the train as it lay there, taunting them.

Eventually, McNutt got fed up.

'Fuck this,' he growled.

Before anyone could stop him, McNutt opened fire, unloading the entire fifty-round magazine of the submachine gun into the cabin of the nearest car.

When the temporary fog caused by the hot muzzle flare finally melted away, they could see the aftermath of McNutt's assault: numerous holes had been torn into the side of the car.

Holes that revealed the faintest glint of metal.

Jasmine hustled forward to inspect the damage McNutt had caused – and the metal he had revealed. To the best of her knowledge, seats from Prince Felix's era were made of wood, covered in soft padding and leather to cushion the ride. But the gunfire had proven that these seats had been shaped from something shiny.

Something that twinkled in the soft light of the cavern.

'Guys, what would you do if you were a Russian soldier who wanted to keep his treasure safe until the revolution was suppressed?' Jasmine didn't wait for the others to answer. 'You would hide it in plain sight!'

Sarah stepped forward and brought out a switchblade. She quickly cut across the top of the seat nearest them. She pointed her flashlight down and gold reflected back.

'Holy shit!' she shrieked in sudden realization.

Then she looked for someone to hug.

She grabbed Jasmine excitedly. The two of them were quickly wrapped up by McNutt in a massive bear hug, a split second before Garcia joined the party. Then the four of them jumped up and down in unison, long before they had a chance to do the math.

Each seat concealed a layer of gold bars – bars that they estimated weighed twenty pounds each. Each layer consisted of three rows of twelve across. That meant thirty-six bars in each seat, with ten seats in each row, and two rows in each of the three cars.

Two thousand, one hundred, and sixty bars of solid, untraceable gold.

Gold that had never been reclaimed because the revolution succeeded. Gold that simply sat there because the handful of men who had hidden it had died in the bloodbath that followed the tsar's abdication.

Jasmine turned to the group. 'What now?'

Three smiles beamed back at her.

'The US is that way,' McNutt said, 'with a long, unguarded coastline. Chekov, plot us a course for home.'

'With pleasure,' Garcia replied.

Sarah wrapped her arms around the men's shoulders. 'And it just so happens I know this whaler in Port Spencer who owes me a favor . . .'

* * *

Cobb's expectations deflated the moment he pushed through the double doors into the lobby. The place was literally in ruins. Scaffolding stood next to every wall, where hundreds of spackled holes dotted the paneling all the way to the ceiling. The marble floor was pockmarked with tiny cracks and fissures. A stretch of plywood, hastily covered with a roll of plush, maroon carpet, led guests to the inner halls, a branch spurring off toward the registration desk.

Peering deeper inside, Cobb saw a large, marble fountain

in the middle of a towering atrium. The water no longer flowed from the top spout, and Cobb could see where bullets had damaged the walls of the pool.

Determined to hear the story behind whatever he had missed, he stopped the first member of the hotel staff that crossed his path.

'Hey, what the hell happened here?' Cobb asked.

The preoccupied concierge did a double take before he could manage a response. 'Oh, Mr Cobb,' he finally offered. 'Please, right this way. We've been expecting you.' With that, he returned to the front desk, motioning for Cobb to follow.

The young employee stood behind the desk, staring at his computer screen and clicking his mouse repeatedly. 'I'm terribly sorry about the renovations,' he said as he typed. 'Things around here have been very *interesting* lately. Who knew an air conditioner explosion could cause so much damage? Thank God that no one was hurt.'

That's bullshit, Cobb thought. He had seen enough firefights to know the damage caused by bullets and flying shrapnel. There might have been an explosion, but it definitely wasn't an air conditioner. More like an anti-personnel mine or a grenade.

But it wasn't the lie that bothered him.

'Did you say you've been expecting me?' he asked.

'Of course,' the concierge replied. 'We've got you . . . ah! Right here.' The concierge looked up at Cobb and offered him an envelope. His name had been neatly printed on the front, and a copy of his driver's license photo had been paper-clipped to the corner. 'We've got you in the Imperial

Suite. It has a great view of the lake. I hope that will be satisfactory.'

'You've been expecting me?' Cobb asked again. 'For how long?'

The concierge glanced back down to his monitor. 'The reservation was made on . . .' His face scrunched into a curious frown. 'Well that's odd. The date is missing, and so is the name of the patron who made the reservation. But your suite is definitely in the system.' He looked up at Cobb. 'Perhaps it's explained in the letter?' He nodded toward the envelope that Cobb still had not taken from the counter.

Cobb picked up the envelope and stepped aside. He ripped it open as he tried to piece things together. Inside, he found a room key and a single, typewritten page.

Mr Cobb,
Welcome to Switzerland. Please stay as long as you'd like.
Bill all of your local expenses to the hotel.
All my best.

PS – Try to enjoy yourself. You've earned it.

Epilogue

Same Day
Palace of the Parliament
Bucharest, Romania

Maurice Copeland was led to a lavishly appointed sitting room buried deep in the bowels of the Romanian government's central headquarters. One of more than 1,100 rooms spread over nearly eighty-five acres, the space included several suede couches and chairs, as well as heavy, polished oak tables. The marble-topped bar in the corner and the accompanying racks displayed only the finest wines and spirits. A magnificent crystal chandelier hung from the ceiling, and the walls were adorned with portraits of the Romanian ruling families – not only those that came after the country's independence, but dating as far back as the fourteenth century.

Copeland, a South African who had made his fortune in America, sensed that this was not a room frequented by outsiders. This was a place reserved for the back-room conversations of Romania's highest authorities. A place where they could feel safe and converse in private about matters with which the general public would not – *should not* – concern itself. He smiled. Given his purpose in being there, it was the perfect setting.

'Nicolai will be with you shortly,' the aide related before closing the door behind him as he left the room.

There was neither small talk nor an invitation for Copeland to make himself at home. This wasn't a social call. It was business. Nevertheless, Copeland chose a sofa and sat down. He spread his arms wide and rested his hands on the farthest ends of the overstuffed cushions supporting his back. He knew he would not be alone for long.

Impeccably dressed in a custom-made suit, Copeland thought of his subordinate, Jean-Marc Papineau. The Frenchman had once again proven his worth on this mission. After a decade of faithful service, Copeland had few doubts about Papineau's abilities to handle the day-to-day details of a complex operation. It was this faith that allowed Copeland to avoid the spotlight until victory was at hand. Unlike most men of extraordinary wealth, Copeland preferred to work in the shadows, protected behind a curtain of anonymity like the great and powerful Oz.

The only time that Copeland surfaced was to claim his bounty.

And this was one of those times.

Copeland remained seated when Nicolai Emilian entered the room. While most people would immediately bounce to attention out of respect for the Romanian diplomat, Copeland did not feel intimidated by or inferior to this man in any way. They were trading partners, each using the other as a means to an end.

'Nicky,' Copeland began, 'I was hoping *El Presidente* would be joining me.'

Emilian forced a smile. 'Maurice, you know that every precaution must be taken in matters such as this. He must be . . . *insulated* from any direct knowledge of your activities.'

'But he does know what we've been up to?' Copeland asked, prying.

'He knows everything he needs to know,' Emilian answered cryptically. He walked across the room to the bar and poured two glasses of Glenfiddich 1937, one of the world's rarest bottles of Scotch. He handed one to Copeland, who nodded his appreciation.

Emilian raised his glass. 'To a job *almost* done.'

Copeland smirked and nodded in understanding. 'I trust you're satisfied with the delivery of everything thus far?'

It had been seventeen days since Papineau, acting on Copeland's behalf, had supervised the return of the items they had found in the Carpathian Mountains back into the hands of the Romanian government. With the help of a modern train engine, Papineau's crew of armed guards had taken the treasure from the town of Choban to the capital of Romania.

'Where's the rest?' Emilian demanded.

Copeland's smile belied the efforts he knew lay ahead. It would take him a few weeks to transport the treasure from the Bering Strait tunnel to Alaska, across Canada to Newfoundland, and finally to Eastern Europe. There it would be transferred to a nondescript, though heavily guarded storage facility on the far side of Bucharest – all under the watchful eye of the *Brigada Anti-Tero a SRI*, the Romanian Special Forces.

'I assure you,' Copeland said, 'everything is underway. I would not have called this meeting without confirmation from my team that they had found the remaining gold.'

'To be delivered when?'

Copeland chuckled. 'Nicky, you must have faith. These things take time. An eighteen-carat-gold bracelet can be smuggled in a variety of ways. But eighteen *tons* of gold bars are a little more difficult to conceal.'

'To be honest,' Emilian replied, 'I thought it would be slightly more.'

'Slightly more than a billion dollars?' Copeland chuckled. 'Perhaps you didn't account for operating expenses? No one works for free.'

'What's a hundred million between friends? Is *that* what you're saying?'

'I suppose it is,' Copeland replied. 'If that's what we're calling ourselves.'

Emilian grimaced. He set down his drink and placed his briefcase on the coffee table in front of Copeland. 'Always an eye on business. That is what I like about you.' He spun the briefcase so that the latches faced Copeland. 'Please,' he offered, extending his hand as an invitation to Copeland to open the briefcase.

Copeland moved to the edge of his seat. His hands were nearly trembling as he unlocked the clasps and raised the lid. As he lifted the soft cloth covering the object inside, his poker face slowly melted into a wide grin.

The first of the legendary Pieces of Eight!

If Emilian could have read the rest of Copeland's thoughts, he would have understood that $1,000,000,000 was a bargain trade for the item he had been casually storing in his old briefcase for the last week. Yes, Copeland first had to secure the remaining seven artifacts, but the mere existence of this first piece gave credence to the legend. Once the collection was complete, Copeland would have everything he needed to pursue the ultimate prize: a treasure of immeasurable value and incalculable worth.

Beaming, Copeland calmly shut the case and reengaged the locks.

Emilian stood. 'I believe this concludes today's exchange. I trust you can find your way out.'

Copeland stood and extended his hand. 'Certainly.'

Emilian shook Copeland's hand. As he did, Emilian noticed the ring on Copeland's finger. It was Rasputin's ring, the gift the Mad Monk had been given by the tsarina, the one he had worn in his coffin for the last century.

'You *did* find him!' For the first time, Emilian's eyes were bright with excitement.

'I did indeed,' Copeland assured him, his smile fading into a stern expression. 'I assume you're interested in his safe return. Isn't that right, *starets*?'

Copeland had known of Emilian's association with the Black Robes from the start. He never entered into an arrangement without first conducting an exhaustive investigation into his consorts and confederates.

Emilian's face tightened in anger, but his eyes betrayed his true emotions.

'Name your price.'

Copeland grinned. He had just the thing in mind.

* * *

Confused, exhausted, and in desperate need of a shower, Cobb accepted the free room, even if he didn't know who had extended the invitation.

Simply put, it was the most impressive hotel room he had ever seen. King-sized bed. Seventy-inch widescreen television. A steam room, bigger than most New York City apartments And the concierge had undersold him on the view. It wasn't great. It was breathtaking. For a man accustomed to cramped barracks and seventh-floor walk-ups, it was Eden. Give him a cold beer and a rare steak, and he might never leave.

The phone on the bedside table rang at a quarter of eight. Cobb had just closed his eyes and was contemplating how much the hotel had spent on the linens. He knew little of thread counts or Egyptian cotton, but he did know they were the softest sheets he had ever felt. On the second ring, his training overrode his natural desire for rest, and he reached for the phone.

'Hello?' he asked.

'Good evening, Mr Cobb.' It was the concierge he had met earlier. 'I trust you find the room to your liking?'

'It's okay, I guess.'

'Excellent,' the concierge replied, picking up on Cobb's sarcasm. 'I am calling to remind you of your dinner reservation. Le Chat-Botté. Eight o'clock. Table for two.'

'Le Chat-Bo-*what*?' Cobb asked.

'Le Chat-Botté,' the concierge repeated. 'It's our restaurant, right here in the hotel. Five-star, I assure you. Simply exquisite cuisine.'

'I'm sure it is,' Cobb agreed. He sat up in bed and rolled his neck, knowing that his nap would have to wait. 'Listen, I assume I'm going to need a jacket, so I'm going to need a jacket.'

'One has already been arranged,' the concierge confirmed.

Of course it has, Cobb thought.

'A lovely, charcoal two-button from Yves Saint-Laurent. I shall have it sent to your room immediately.'

'As long as it looks good with jeans,' Cobb joked.

*   *   *

At five minutes after eight, Cobb entered Le Chat-Botté and was directed to a table in the far corner of the restaurant. His dinner companion had already arrived.

Cobb was carrying a pistol at both his ankle and his waist.

He was prepared for anything.

However, the only weapon the man at the table looked like he knew how to wield was a fork. He was a round man, with a thick, brown beard that covered his multiple chins. He was impeccably dressed, with a silk handkerchief tucked into his collar to keep the oysters he was slurping from dripping onto his tailored suit. A $1,500 bottle of Domaine de la Romanée-Conti 1997 sat uncorked on the table. The first glass he had poured was now almost empty.

Still, Cobb approached the table with caution.

The round man put down his wine and stood to greet him.

'Mr Cobb, I presume?'

Cobb was momentarily stunned.

Wait a second. He doesn't know who I am.

How can that be?

But Cobb kept his composure. 'And you are?'

'Petr Ulster, at your service,' the man replied. 'Please, sit.'

As they took their seats across the table from one another, Cobb tried to make head or tail of the situation.

'Petr Ulster,' Cobb repeated. 'Is that supposed to mean something to me?'

The portly man grimaced with confusion. 'Of the Ulster Archives . . .?'

'Keep going,' Cobb pressed.

Ulster sat back in his chair and smiled. 'I am Petr Ulster, director of the Ulster Archives. It is the finest private collection of documents and antiquities in the world. Second to none.'

'Director, eh?' Cobb repeated. 'I guess I have you to thank for the room.'

'I'm afraid not,' Ulster answered. 'Though we do owe someone a huge debt of thanks. I have stayed here many a night over the years, and I know how much the rooms and meals cost – especially when *I'm* eating. I will happily let someone else cover the expense this time.'

Cobb's mind raced with possibilities. Although he was reluctant to admit his confusion, Cobb sensed the best way to get answers from Ulster was to ask him direct questions. 'If you're not paying for our rooms, *who* is? And what are we here to do?'

'As for who is ultimately responsible for our meeting, I, like you, have not been told.' Ulster's chins jiggled as he smiled. 'But I *can* help you with the rest.'

Ulster leaned forward and poured his new friend a glass of wine.

'Mr Cobb, we're here to discuss your next mission.'

Author's Note

People always ask me where I get my story ideas. Normally, I'm not sure how to answer because my *real* answer – my ideas develop over time during several months of tedious research and stress-induced nausea – isn't very glamorous. But in the case of *The Hunters*, I can narrow it down to one specific moment.

Although I never met the man – he died six years before my birth – my great-grandfather (Jidah) grew up in a small village like the one described in this book. Not only was it nestled in the rugged terrain of the Carpathian Mountains, but it was located in the ethno-geographic blob along the Ukrainian/Romanian border that still confounds mapmakers, historians and, most importantly, *me* to this very day. (Not to mention Hector Garcia and his GPS.)

As a child, I was always told that my great-grandfather was Ruthenian. Not Romanian, but *Ruthenian*. The problem is, by the time I was born, Ruthenia no longer existed. The entire region had been swallowed whole by the Soviet Union, which had taken a red pencil and a pinko eraser and had reconfigured Eastern Europe to their liking. It didn't matter how many times I asked my family where Jidah had come from, they could never pinpoint a specific location because Ruthenia was no longer on any maps. The best they could do was narrow it down to the giant blob I referenced above.

Over time, their story seemed to change. Not a lot, but just enough for me to doubt how much they really knew about his birthplace. Keep in mind, these were the same people who had convinced me that Santa Claus and the Easter Bunny were real, so I knew my family was capable of some pretty devious shit. (Of course, that is *not* an insult coming from me because I make up stuff for a living.)

How did their story change? Let me give you an example.

As a teenager, I developed a bad case of insomnia, and my mother told me it was only natural because our ancestors were from Transylvania. Not Ruthenia, but Transylvania. Think about that for a moment. My mom tried to calm my fears by insinuating that I might be a vampire. How twisted is that? To the *Twilight* generation, that probably sounds like the coolest thing in the world. But to me and my overactive imagination, it meant angry villagers were going to hunt me down and stab me with sharp sticks.

Thanks, mom. I can sleep *much* better after that pep talk.

Anyway, after many sleepless years, I decided to get to the bottom of things in 2005. My extended family had gathered for Thanksgiving, and I realized it was the perfect time to uncover as many details about my ancestors as possible. I went directly to the oldest source in the house (my grandmother) and recorded everything that she said – whether real or imagined. Then I went online and tried to sort the facts from the fiction.

Discovery #1: My great-grandfather *was* Ruthenian, but that term wasn't used to describe people from a specific country. Instead, it applied to just about everyone who lived in the Carpathian region, whether they were Ukrainian, Hungarian, Czech, Belarusian, Rusyn, or Romanian.

Discovery #2: My great-grandfather's village was less than fifty miles from Uzhhorod, a border city in western Ukraine that is within walking distance of Poland, Slovakia, Hungary, and Romania. Of course, those borders didn't exist at the time of his birth, so I still have no idea what ethnicity Jidah was. Instead, the entire region was part of the Austro-Hungarian Empire, which stretched across a third of Europe and didn't collapse until my great-grandfather had boarded a ship for America.

Discovery #3: His departure undoubtedly led to Russian aggression, and – I'm just guessing here – probably triggered the start of World War I.

Discovery #4: I am *not* a vampire.

So, you're probably wondering, what does any of this stuff have to do with *The Hunters*? Well, it was during my investigation on that fateful day that I came across a document that described, in detail, the crates of gold and relics that were shipped from Romania to Moscow for protection. Strangely, I could find nothing about the treasure's return. Sensing a story, I quickly abandoned my ancestral research and focused on the treasure's fate – and what a fate it was.

One day it was there, the next it was gone.

Kind of like Ruthenia.

Since both of these events occurred at roughly the same time, I merged the two concepts in my mind and created a single book. To honor my ancestors, I set much of the action in a Carpathian village, named one of the Russian characters after my great-grandmother, and sprinkled in tidbits about my family tree throughout.

For additional flavor, I relied on the pages of notes that I took during the interview with my grandmother in 2005. I would have preferred to ask her specific questions about her parents and their upbringing in the old country; unfortunately, my grandmother got sick and passed away while I was writing this book.

In my heart, I know she would have loved the story.

I also know the story wouldn't have existed without her.

Read on for an exclusive extract of Chris Kuzneski's
exhilarating new Payne & Jones thriller:

THE EINSTEIN PURSUIT

I

Present Day
Monday, 22 July
Stockholm, Sweden

The lab was packed with many of the brightest minds in their field, all focused on a secret project that would change mankind for ever.

In a matter of seconds, they would all be dead.

Of course, none of them knew why they had been called to the facility in the middle of the night. Most had assumed a major breakthrough had occurred, and they had been brought in for an historic announcement that simply could not wait until morning.

Instead, they had been summoned to their slaughter.

The assault had started hours earlier, long before the researchers were misled. Guards had been killed. Locks had been breached. Specimens had been located and stolen. All had been done with a surgical precision the scientists might have appreciated under different circumstances – circumstances that wouldn't lead to their deaths.

Dr Stephanie Albright was the last to arrive at the sprawling warehouse. Not because she was running late, but because she had the furthest to drive and was on the verge of exhaustion. Over the past few months she had averaged less than four hours' sleep per day, a figure that included the naps she took when she was on the verge of passing out in the lab. But she never complained. Neither did the others. They knew how important their project was, and they were willing to forgo food and sleep if it meant reaching their goal a little sooner.

Tonight, they would give up more than that.

They would sacrifice their lives.

Albright rushed into the lobby and took the elevator to the third floor. She was so lost in her thoughts, she failed to notice the vacant guard station. And the blank security monitors. And all the other things that weren't quite right. Most importantly, she overlooked the man in the boat who had watched her every move from the calm waters of Riddarfjärden Bay.

He had waited nearly twenty minutes for her arrival.

It was time to finish the job.

His detonator included a state-of-the-art transmitter. It was capable of igniting multiple devices from up to a thousand meters away. Explosives had been placed throughout the warehouse near load-bearing walls and columns. His goal was to collapse the floors, one after another, with no time for escape. A smoldering coffin of steel and concrete for those trapped inside.

The assassin smiled at the thought.

He had killed many times before, but never so many at once.

This would be his masterpiece.

With the touch of a button, the charges erupted with so much force, he felt it in the bay. Chunks of stone and shards of glass filled the air before crashing to the earth like hail. Columns cracked and walls crumbled as the warehouse screamed in pain. Amplified by the water, the deafening roar forced him to cover his ears, but he refused to cover his eyes.

The show was just getting started.

Acetone is commonly used in laboratories around the world to clean scientific instruments. Most of the time it is stored in polyethylene plastic containers, but this particular lab was equipped with a customized delivery system that would pump the acetone throughout the building to a multitude of cleaning stations. This set-up required large drums of acetone to be housed in the upper floors of the building.

The assassin knew this and used it to his advantage.

To cover his tracks and to prevent survivors, he had rigged the barrels of acetone to rupture from the initial force of the blast. The flammable liquid rained down on the destruction below. Within seconds, the fumes ignited and a flash fire occurred. Flames swept through the warehouse like a blistering flood, killing everyone in its wake. The heat from the blaze was so intense that bodies and evidence literally melted.

Like a crime-scene crematorium.

On most jobs, he preferred to work alone. But that wasn't the case tonight. This project was far too complex for a single cleaner, even someone with his experience. To pull it off, he needed the help of a local team – men to do the lifting, and the drilling, and the grunt work.

Men to do the things he didn't have time to do.

Men who were expendable.

He had thanked them for their service with gunfire.

Then he had left them to burn with everyone else.

2

Nick Dial was miserable. Absolutely miserable.

He hated his office. And his desk. And the stacks of paper-work on his desk. He hated going to sleep after midnight and waking up before dawn. He hated the brown gruel the locals called coffee and the miniature mugs they served it in. Worst of all, he hated wasting his days in meetings instead of doing what he did best: finding clues and catching killers.

He was a cop at heart, not an executive.

Unfortunately, his business cards disagreed.

Dial was the director of the homicide division at Interpol, the largest international crime-fighting organization in the world. His job was to coordinate the flow of information between police departments any time a murder investigation crossed national boundaries. All told he was in charge of 190 member countries, filled with billions of people and hundreds of languages.

One of the biggest misconceptions about Interpol was their role in stopping crime. They seldom sent agents across borders to investigate a case. Instead they used local offices called National Central Bureaus in the member countries. The NCBs monitored their own territory and reported pertinent facts to

Interpol's headquarters in Lyon. From there, information was entered into a central database that could be accessed by agencies around the globe.

Interpol's motto: *Connecting Police for a Safer World.*

Dial was fully committed to a 'safer world', and he was more than willing to do his part. That was why he had left his position at the FBI to work for the Europe-based organization. At the time, the decision to accept the job was a no-brainer. Not only was he the first American to be named as a department head at Interpol, but he had been asked to run the new homicide division.

How could he possibly turn that down?

Initially, Dial was thrilled with his position. He wrote the rules. He set the budget. He hand-picked the personnel in his department. On a few occasions, he even went into the field to work on high-profile cases. Not because he had to, but because he wanted to. It was his way of staying sharp while he transitioned from a field agent to an administrator.

Plus, he loved doing it.

Being a cop was in his blood.

Over the years, Dial had never seen the harm in working on an occasional case – especially if he followed the local laws and customs. However, the new secretary general disagreed. He felt the personal involvement of a division head in an open investigation could lead to bad press or, even worse, an international incident. Dial had protested fiercely but was told in explicit terms that his participation in an active case would lead to his suspension and/or termination.

That was four months ago.

Since then, Dial had written and rewritten his resignation several times.

The wording still wasn't right, but it would be soon.

After all, there are only so many ways to say *shove it*.

Dial had just entered Interpol headquarters, an impressive fortress overlooking the Rhône, when he spotted a familiar face sneaking outside. Unlike most of the analysts who roamed the hallways in pressed shirts and polished shoes, Henri Toulon stood out from the crowd.

And not in a good way.

Known for his gray ponytail and his horrible disposition, the hard-drinking Frenchman had been cited for so many work violations over the years he should have been fired long ago. Sleeping during important meetings. Coming and going as he pleased. Using the nearest restroom, regardless of its intended gender. All were worthy of discipline, but Dial had overlooked his bad habits and promoted him to assistant director because he realized something that few people did: Toulon was a brilliant son-of-a-bitch.

And that wasn't just an expression.

Dial had met Toulon's mother on three occasions, and there was little doubt she was the meanest person on the planet. Like Darth Vader in a dress. In fact, her looming presence explained nearly everything about Toulon — from his bad attitude to his drinking problem.

The only thing it didn't explain was his greasy ponytail.

There was *no* excuse for that.

Dial glanced at his watch and realized it was awfully early to be taking a break, even for a misfit like Toulon. He immediately assumed something tragic had happened in the world, something so bad that the son of the Antichrist had to sneak outside for a breath of fresh air.

That is, if it was possible to get fresh air while smoking.

Dial followed him to find out.

By the time he caught up to Toulon, the Frenchman was sitting on a bench with a half-burned cigarette in his mouth. How he had smoked it so quickly was a mystery. His body was slouched, his head hung low. His eyes were closed, and he was humming a song to himself. As he did, ashes landed on his shirt like dirty snow.

Dial stared at him for several seconds, but Toulon didn't notice. He didn't think Toulon was reckless enough to drink at work, but he still had to ask. 'Are you drunk?'

'Not yet,' Toulon answered without raising his head. The cigarette bobbed in his mouth as he spoke, threatening to fall from his lips at any moment. 'I'm saving that for later.'

'Troubles at home?' Dial wondered.

Toulon straightened his back and cracked his neck. He took a long, final drag from his cigarette, then stamped out the ember with his tennis shoe. 'No. At work.'

'But you just got here.'

'No,' he said sharply, 'I've been here all night.'

'Really? Why's that?'

Toulon squinted at him quizzically, wondering whether Dial was feigning his confusion. Eventually he realized that he wasn't. 'Because *you* scheduled me for the late shift.'

Dial laughed. He had completely forgotten about that week's schedule. Toulon was being punished for a disgusting incident involving a co-worker's lunch. 'Well, you deserved it.'

Toulon cracked a mischievous smile. '*Oui*. You're right, I did.'

'If you agree with me, why are you pouting?'

'I'm not pouting; I'm relaxing. I foresee a long day.'

'Why? What happened?'

Toulon reached into his pocket and found his pack of cigarettes. He lit up a second time and inhaled the smoke deeply. 'Large explosion in Stockholm. The fire is still burning. We don't have many details – at least not yet – but it appears to be intentional.'

'When did this happen?'

'While *you* were sleeping.'

Dial knew if the homicide division had been notified, someone must have been killed. He only hoped casualties would be limited at that late hour. 'How many dead?'

'It's too soon to say,' Toulon said in between drags. 'But if my hunch is correct, the morgue will be full of Swedes.'

Dial groaned at the thought. Not only for the loss of life, but also because of the paperwork. 'Let me see that pack of cigarettes.'

Toulon did as he was told. 'Careful, they're a bit stronger than what you Americans prefer. And why do I not know that you smoke? What else have you been hiding from me?'

Dial took the cigarettes and tucked them inside his jacket. 'I don't smoke. And neither do you until we have some more answers.' With that, he turned and walked back toward the entrance. 'I'll see you upstairs in five minutes.'

Back inside the building, Dial took a deep breath and headed upstairs to start his day. He sensed it would be a rough one. In his office, he hung his suit coat on the wooden rack in the corner, then made his way to his desk. In the front center of the workspace, where most people would have put an engraved nameplate, Dial kept a plastic milk crate filled with hanging green folders. It had served as his inbox for years.

He stared at it, wondering what horrors it held today.

Important cases were loaded into the back end of the crate

and slowly made their way toward him as he worked through the never-ending stream of information supplied by police forces from around the world. Reports were collected by his division, organized by his secretary and funneled into this murderer's row for his analysis.

He wondered if the Stockholm blast was lurking in the lineup.

He shook his head, realizing that it didn't matter.

Right now, he needed to focus his full attention on the first file.

In his mind, it was the least he could do.

After all, someone had been murdered.

3

Dial had just finished reviewing his second file of the day when Toulon barged into his office without knocking. He slammed the door behind him.

'Nick,' Toulon said – which sounded like 'Neek' when the Frenchman tried to say it. 'The early reports were true.'

'Stockholm?' Dial asked, making sure they were on the same page.

'*Oui*. It appears the entire staff was in the building at the time of the explosion. The parking lot was filled with cars.'

'How many dead?' Dial asked.

'At least twenty, probably more. We won't have a solid figure until they have had a chance to sort through the rubble.'

'Any survivors?'

Toulon shook his head. 'Not likely. From what I've heard, nothing could have survived. The place was an inferno. It's still smoldering now.'

Dial nodded in understanding. Fire scenes were the worst. 'Let's get the list of names they put together from the cars. Check the nationalities of everyone involved.'

'*Oui*.'

'And get me a list of our top agents in Sweden. I want to know who we have in Stockholm who can answer our questions.'

'Of course. Anything else?'

'No. That's it for now.'

Toulon nodded, but he didn't leave the room. Instead, he just stood there, staring at Dial as if it would be rude to talk without his permission.

'What is it?' Dial snapped.

'I have yet to determine how this incident hit our radar so quickly. If this happened overnight and they haven't identified a single victim, why were we notified?'

Dial shrugged. It was a good question, one he hadn't considered until that very moment. Based on preliminary reports, he had assumed the case had been brought to his attention because it had met the basic criteria for Interpol's involvement, meaning it was an international incident of some kind. But Toulon was correct: if the explosion had occurred in Stockholm and no borders had been crossed in the commission of the crime, then Dial had no authority in the case.

This was a matter for the Swedish police, not Interpol.

'Start there,' Dial said. He opened the top drawer of his desk and grabbed Toulon's cigarettes. He tossed them back to Henri as if they were a reward for his insight. 'But first, go home and get some sleep. You look like shit.'

Toulon placed the Stockholm file at the back of Dial's inbox and headed for the door. When he opened it, he inadvertently collided with a young man who was attempting to enter. As they stepped back from one another, Toulon bowed and tipped an imaginary cap. 'So good to see you, *mademoiselle*.' Then he pushed by the visitor and continued forward without waiting for a response.

Dial knew Toulon well enough to detect his sarcastic tone. Then again, Toulon did little to hide the way he felt.

For his part, the young man looked equally disgusted by the encounter. He set his jaw and crumpled his nose, as if his unplanned interaction with Toulon was both the most insulting and the most repugnant thing he could envision.

'Sebastian,' Dial said drily. 'Why are you in my office?'

Sebastian James was the special assistant to the Interpol secretary general. He was the product of some of the world's finest educational institutions, and he had worked his way up through the ranks of Interpol by means of successful politicking, rather than years of field service. Few people could place his nationality, as he spoke several languages without the hint of an accent. He would regularly demean those he considered beneath him in a tongue they couldn't understand – and he considered nearly everyone to be beneath him.

To reinforce his 'holier than thou' demeanor, he was always impeccably dressed. From his Hermès ties to his Bruno Magli shoes, he made every attempt to exude importance. He was angling for Interpol's top post – at least for starters – and everyone knew it.

In short, he was the type of guy that Dial despised.

'You're going to Stockholm,' James announced.

'On whose orders?' Dial demanded.

He knew James didn't have the authority to send him out for coffee, much less a trip to Sweden, and he wanted James to admit it.

'The secretary general,' James clarified. 'He's sending you there . . . *today*. Pack your bags. Your plane leaves in less than two hours.'

Dial leaned back in his chair. 'I think I'll wait to hear from him . . . if it's all the same to you.'

'He sent me to tell you, and my word is the same as his.'

'Is that so? Does *he* know you feel this way?'

James's face turned bright red. He was about to clarify his

remark, but Dial cut him off before he had a chance. 'What's so important in Stockholm?'

'There was an explosion,' James informed him. 'At least twenty dead. Maybe more. It's all over the morning news.'

'I'm familiar with the incident,' Dial said, thankful that Toulon had brought it to his attention. The last thing he needed was to be briefed by James. He didn't have the time or patience to wade through the asshole's long-winded explanation. 'I'm waiting for the NCB report. I'll have it by the end of the day.'

'You're not getting it,' James countered. 'The secretary wants *your* report by the end of the day. We're not leaving this to the NCB. There's too much at stake.'

Dial didn't flinch. There was nothing about his body language that suggested he had any intention of going. 'Once again I ask: what's so important in Stockholm?'

James realized Dial wasn't going to jump to attention without a full explanation, so he pulled up a chair and sat down. 'It would appear the victims of last night's tragedy represent a multitude of nations from around the world. And I'm not referring to tourists. It seems that several highly respected scientists somehow found their way to the same laboratory in Sweden. We've been fielding calls all morning. Delegates want to know why their countrymen were targeted, and by whom.'

The General Assembly, the controlling body that governed Interpol, was comprised of delegates from every member country, and was responsible for most aspects of Interpol's operation: finances, staffing, agenda, and so on. Its power in the organization was virtually absolute.

Dial nodded in understanding. 'Everyone feels they've lost

their best and brightest. That they've been robbed of the next super-genius. Is that it?'

James grinned, relishing his sense of superiority. He might have been younger than Dial, but right now he knew something that Dial didn't. 'It's almost *nothing* like that. These men and women weren't the fresh-faced new generation of scientific prodigies. They were the old guard. Relics of a bygone era whose research, while once cutting edge, had seemingly reached its inevitable conclusions.'

'Relics, and yet the secretary's phone has been ringing off the hook?'

James nodded. 'They've all had their moment in the sun. They've all furthered the understanding of their respective disciplines. It's simply that nature has run its course, thrusting their once proud achievements into the realm of obscurity, if not complete obsolescence.' He paused, if only to set up his final remark on the subject. 'An ancient vase may be cracked and serve no useful purpose, but it still has some value in a museum.'

Although the last comment bothered him, Dial ignored it. His goal was to get to the heart of the investigation as quickly as possible, if for no other reason than to get James out of his office. 'You said respective discipline*s*, plural. Which scientific fields are in play?'

'A mix of studies – botany, zoology, anthropology, genetics, and so on. You can educate yourself on the plane. You now have . . .' he checked his watch, 'ninety minutes.'

'Tell the secretary I'll be ready in three hours,' Dial countered. He guessed the difference wouldn't upset the secretary general in the slightest, but he knew that delivering the news of a scheduling change would more than ruffle James's finely groomed feathers.

James glared at him. 'I suggest you take that imbecile Toulon with you. You're the only one who tolerates his nonsense. Heaven only knows what havoc he would wreak in your absence.'

Whatever disregard James felt for Dial paled in comparison to the utter contempt he felt for Toulon. He simply could not stand to be near the Frenchman – and interacting with him was entirely out of the question. Ultimately, if Dial took Toulon on the trip, it would be nothing less than a personal favor to James.

'I'll inform the secretary about your adjustment to his schedule,' James said as he stood.

'You do that,' Dial said. 'But before you do, close my door behind you.'

Dial waited for privacy before he stared at the inbox again. At the back of the row was the file Toulon had left for him.

Botanists, zoologists, and many other fields?

What the hell was going on in this lab?

He picked up the phone and dialed a familiar extension. After one ring, he was connected to Toulon's office voicemail.

'Henri, it's Nick. Things just got a lot more interesting. The director wants me in Stockholm to handle the case. While I'm gone, I'm putting you in charge.' He stared at the empty chair across from him and smiled. 'I need you to update Sebastian James on a daily basis.'

Then he grinned wickedly. 'No, scratch that. I'll need you to meet with him *hourly*.'